Praise for the novels of Kaki Warner

"A truly original new voice in historical fiction."
—*New York Times* bestselling author Jodi Thomas

"[An] emotionally compelling, subtly nuanced tale of revenge, redemption, and romance. . . . This flawlessly written book is worth every tear." —*Chicago Tribune*

"Romance, passion, and thrilling adventure fill the pages."
—*New York Times* bestselling author Rosemary Rogers

"A romance you won't soon forget."
—International bestselling author Sara Donati

"Draws readers into the romance and often unvarnished reality of life in nineteenth-century America." —*Library Journal*

"Kaki Warner's warm, witty, and lovable characters shine."
—*USA Today*

"Halfway between Penelope Williamson's and Jodi Thomas's gritty, powerful novels and LaVyrle Spencer's small-town stories lie Warner's realistic, atmospheric romances."
—RT Book Reviews

Titles by Kaki Warner

Blood Rose Trilogy

PIECES OF SKY
OPEN COUNTRY
CHASING THE SUN

Runaway Brides Novels

HEARTBREAK CREEK
COLORADO DAWN
BRIDE OF THE HIGH COUNTRY

Heroes of Heartbreak Creek

BEHIND HIS BLUE EYES
WHERE THE HORSES RUN
HOME BY MORNING

TEXAS TALL

Rough Creek Novels

ROUGH CREEK

Rough Creek

Kaki Warner

JOVE
New York

A JOVE BOOK
Published by Berkley
An imprint of Penguin Random House LLC
penguinrandomhouse.com

ISBN: 9781984806192

First Edition: July 2020

Printed in the United States of America
1 3 5 7 9 10 8 6 4 2

Cover art by Rebecca Knowles / Trevillion Images
Cover design by Judith Lagerman
Book design by Gaelyn Galbreath

To the amazing, versatile quarter horse
and those skilled men and women who train them.

And to Adeline,
whose courage and persistence helped bring
a neglected horse back into
the winners' circle of the show ring.
I'm so proud of both of you.

ACKNOWLEDGMENTS

My heartfelt thanks to the R. L. Boyce family, young and not so young, who have so patiently answered my endless questions. Hopefully I got most of it right.

To the dedicated readers who have followed my slight detour from Western historical romance to Western contemporary romance. I deeply appreciate your loyalty and patience and hope this book is as much fun to read as it was to write.

And of course to Joe, who had little impact on the writing of this book, other than to offer unconditional support, a few choice Texas expressions, many delectable home-cooked meals, and a barn.

Rough Creek

PROLOGUE

At five thirty A.M., Dalton Cardwell walked through his cell door at the Walls Unit for the last time and began the lengthy process of being discharged from the state prison at Huntsville, Texas.

He showered and ate, then went to the dispensary, where he was issued dress-outs—a set of clothing only marginally better than his prison garb and a size too small for his six-foot-four, two-hundred-thirty-pound frame. He was allowed to keep his shoes, which he intended to exchange for boots as soon as he was able. He wanted no reminders of this place.

He was then taken to the infirmary, where he waited to be fingerprinted and have blood drawn for the HIV test. At the business office, he sat for over an hour while his prison account was scanned and a check was processed for the remaining seven dollars and thirty-one cents. After another half-hour wait, he was handed a packet containing a state-issued check for one hundred dollars, a voucher for a bus ticket anywhere within the state of Texas, and the certifi-

cate of discharge ending his eighteen-month-long association with the Texas Department of Criminal Justice.

The clock was edging toward eleven o'clock—the time
inmates were normally released—when he was ushered out
the front door, told one of the taxis outside would take him
to the army-navy store near the bus depot, where he could
cash his state check, and was warned not to come back
because they always went harder on return offenders.

Then the door slammed shut behind him, cutting off the
noise, the stink of despair, and the endless clang of locks
and doors in a place that never slept.

The silence was deafening.

For a moment, Dalton stood motionless on the top step,
trapped between immense relief, euphoria to have nothing
but open sky above him, and a heart-pounding fear that the
door behind him would fly open, a hand would jerk him
back inside, and a laughing voice would say, *Just kidding.*

When nothing happened, he took a deep breath and
walked briskly toward one of the taxis waiting at the curb.

An hour later, he had five twenty-dollar bills and change
in his pocket, a hot cup of coffee in his hand, and a window
seat on an air-conditioned Greyhound bus headed up Highway 75 to Dallas, where he would change buses and continue
on to Rough Creek.

Twelve fifteen P.M. Tuesday, March 21, 2017. Five hundred and fifty-five days of being caged like an animal for a
crime he confessed to but didn't commit.

Done. Over. And heading home.

Finally.

CHAPTER 1

With grim determination, Coralee Lennox Whitcomb sat at her dressing table and set to work transforming a sixty-year-old grandmother into a confident woman in her prime. Her later prime.

In truth, she was tired. Tired of trying so hard. Tired of pretending sixty was the new thirty-nine. Tired of being tired. It was that empty, unsettled kind of weariness that came to those fortunate enough to have once lived full, useful lives, but who now had nothing to do. She didn't like the feeling.

She tried to convince herself that the face staring back at her wasn't truly old, but even she could see it lacked the vitality it once had. The top lip was a little longer and the smile lines sagged a little more. Her hair was still thick and shiny, but there was more gray than brown now, and the hair coloring never seemed to cover it all. But if she looked hard enough into the slightly faded blue eyes, she could still see the dynamic, energetic young woman she had once been. There was still time to make a change and hopefully find that woman again. But what change?

"What are you frowning about?" a voice asked.

Coralee turned to see her second daughter, Raney, come up behind her. "Do I look older to you?"

"Older than what?"

"Don't equivocate. I'm serious." Coralee turned back to the mirror. "I think I look old."

"Some days I do, too."

"You're not yet thirty, dear."

"Near enough." A pause, then: "Is this about your birthday?"

"My sixtieth birthday," Coralee reminded her. "That's over half a century."

"But not yet two-thirds of one. I hear that's when the real aging starts."

"You're not helping."

"Then stop fishing for compliments. You know you're beautiful." Raney stood at Coralee's shoulder and studied her in the mirror. "I thought you'd be happy, Mama, with all your chicks flocking back home to toast yet another year in your amazingly long life. Plus, you still have all your teeth."

Coralee smiled into eyes the same bright, electric blue hers once were. "Still not helping."

Despite her tendency toward sarcasm and a disinterest in anything not having to do with the ranch, Raney was the daughter most like her. She got things done. And with as little fuss or drama as possible.

Coralee had always considered herself the driving force behind the ranch—and her husband, if truth be told—but Raney was its heart and soul. She was the one who had stepped into her father's boots after his death, and in the nine years since, had given up everything—college, marriage, a family of her own—to keep Charlie's legacy going. Other than one ghastly near-marriage, Raney had never even made an attempt to build a life apart from the ranch. Perhaps she was as stuck as Coralee was.

"I am happy," Coralee insisted now. "But I think I might need a change." And with those words, an idea formed. Why shouldn't she try something new?

Dating was out of the question. Not in a town as small as Rough Creek. Pickings were too slim and gossip too rampant. She'd learned that after her "date" with Walter Esterbrook, a man she'd known for two decades and who faithfully attended her church every Sunday. At least, she'd thought she knew him.

She could start a business, or manage something. If Rough Creek had a zoo or museum or even a hospital, she could do volunteer work, other than her weekly afternoon at the food bank. But the only thing around worth managing was the ranch, and Raney already did an excellent job of that.

Despite her sometimes-frivolous facade, Coralee considered herself an astute manager. She always had been, whether it was finding ways to double the size of the Lennox family farm or helping guide her husband through the backwaters of Texas politics toward a lucrative career in the oil and gas industry, or ensuring that she and her daughters were well protected and financially independent after his death. If she was relentless, she'd had to be. And it had paid off. By the time of Charlie's passing, the Lennox farm had doubled yet again, been renamed the Whitcomb Four Star Ranch in honor of their four lovely daughters, and was known for breeding prize-winning Angus cattle. But what had she done lately?

"You're scheming again, aren't you?" With a sigh, Raney sank down onto the edge of Coralee's bed. "What is it this time? A parade of acceptable marriage prospects for your unweddable daughter?"

"If you're unmarried, dear, it's by your own choice."

"Exactly. So, stay out of it. Please."

Ignoring that, Coralee picked up her tray of shadows and went to work on her eyes. Her slightly wrinkled, aging eyes. "I'm not scheming. I'm planning. With KD starting Officer Training School soon, it might be months—years, even—before the five of us can be at the ranch at the same time." She paused to dab a spot of turquoise to the outside corners of her upper lids to bring out the blue of her eyes. "I thought we might make a festive occasion of it."

"Such as?" Raney gave her a wary look.

"We could start with a nice chat to catch up on all the news, then dinner, followed by wine on the back veranda. What do you think?" She checked her eyes, thought they looked trashy, and wiped the color off.

"I think it'll be cold out there," Raney said.

"We can light a fire." Coralee tried basic, unimaginative taupe. Boring, but better. "And drop the shades if it's windy." Which it invariably was in spring in northwest Texas. And when they were all comfy and mellowed by wine, she would make her announcement. Hopefully, by then, she would know what that announcement would be. At this point, all that was certain was she needed to do something different. Refocus. Make herself her next project. If she explained whatever it was clearly and calmly, maybe they could avoid the drama that characterized most of their family gatherings.

"You said 'change.' What kind of change? Nothing involving me, I hope."

Where had her daughter gotten such a suspicious nature?

"I haven't decided." A faint ding from her watch saved Coralee from further explanation. "Mercy! KD's plane has landed and you haven't even left yet."

"That's what I came in to tell you." Raney rose from the bed. "Len and Joss are picking her up on their way from Dallas."

"Wonderful!" A last fluff of her hair and Coralee rose from the dressing table. "I'd best help Maria get the hors d'oeuvres ready." She paused to scan Raney's outfit—her usual baseball cap and ponytail, jeans, boots, and plaid shirt over a tank top. Why did she insist on downplaying her fine figure and beauty by dressing like a lumberjack? She would never attract a man dressed like that, unless he was as horse-crazy as she was. "You are planning to change your clothes, aren't you?"

"They're my sisters. What do they care?"

"I care. Please, dear. It's my birthday. And hurry along. They'll be here soon."

Later that afternoon, Dalton Cardwell stepped off the bus at the crossroads in Rough Creek. It was as if nothing had changed in his eighteen-month absence. Same dusty storefronts, same beat-up trucks in front of the Roughneck Bar, same galvanized water troughs and cattle feeders stacked outside the feed store. The only things different were the weather and the plants in the baskets hanging outside Mellie's Diner. It had been September when he'd left. Now it was early spring and Mellie's flowers were just starting to bud. That sense of sameness was both comforting and disturbing. He liked the constancy of things that had been part of his life for all of his thirty-two years. But he was surprised that nothing had changed in a year and a half. He certainly had.

His stomach rumbled, reminding him that other than a vending machine snack when he'd changed buses in Dallas, his last meal had been almost fourteen hours earlier. Since he hadn't told his parents when he would arrive and it didn't seem right to show up and expect to be fed right off, he crossed to the diner. He figured he'd earned a last unhurried meal before facing his old life and reassessing the burdens it represented. If he'd learned anything while he was in prison, it was that he was done taking orders and having every move dictated by the schedules of others. He'd been doing that for most of his life, from working beside his father on their small cattle ranch, to his stint in the army, to the regimented directives of his time in prison. He was ready for a change.

Other than a waitress refilling ketchup bottles, and a couple of Hispanic ranch hands at the counter talking to the cook through the serving window into the kitchen, the diner was empty. He recognized the waitress, not the workers. Crossing to a booth next to the back window, he slid into the bench against the wall when the waitress walked toward him armed with a coffeepot and mug.

"Dalton? That you?"

Warily, Dalton looked up, not sure what to expect.

Like most small towns, there were few secrets in Rough Creek. His arrest had been big news, and he wasn't sure how many friends he had left. He had known Suze Anderson for most of his life and had even taken her out a couple of times back in high school. But he was an ex-con now, and that had a way of killing friendships.

Her friendly smile said otherwise. "When'd you get out?" she asked.

"This morning."

"Well, welcome home, stranger." She set the mug down in front of him and filled it with coffee. There was an awkward silence, then she said, "I never thought you did it, you know."

He looked up at her.

She made an offhand movement with her free hand. "Yeah, I know. You confessed. But I always figured there was more to it than what the papers said." She leaned closer and dropped her voice. "Heard the commissioner's nephew had been drinking. If you hadn't waived a trial, that might have gotten you off."

He poured a packet of sugar into his cup. "Water under the bridge." To change the subject, he added, "You look good, Suze." And she did. Hair the color of ripe wheat, skin like clover honey, and eyes as brown as dark, rich coffee. *Hell.* He must be hungry if he looked at a pretty face and thought of food.

She grinned and patted her flat stomach. "Not bad for two kids. Buddy wants to try for two more. Girls, this time. But I don't know. That's a lot of kids."

Buddy was Suze's husband, and through school, had been Dalton's closest friend. A country boy in the best sense of the words, and a good match for Suze. Solid farm folks and hard workers, totally content to stay in Rough Creek forever. At one time, Dalton had thought that would be enough for him, too.

She gave him an assessing look, her gaze flicking from his scuffed prison shoes to his overlong dark brown hair and the too-tight shirt he'd been issued on discharge. "Gotten even bigger than when you got home from Iraq, I see. Bet nobody calls you Beanpole now."

"Not lately." Not after months of daily two-hour workouts. Another thing he'd learned in prison. If you don't want to fight, look like you can.

"I like it. Even with that god-awful haircut, you're still handsome enough to turn a girl's head." She winked. "Even one that's happily married."

He waved the comment aside, embarrassed, yet gratified that after being locked away with nothing but men for eighteen months, he still had enough polish left that a pretty woman would give him a second look. "Watch out, Suze. I don't want Buddy gunning for me."

The door opened and a couple came in. Tourists, by the look of them. Suze told them to sit anywhere they liked, then took Dalton's order—bacon cheeseburger with extra onions, fries, iced tea, and a piece of Mellie's lemon meringue pie for desert. She started toward the kitchen, hesitated, then turned back, a flush rising up her cheeks. "Look, I'm not sure if you heard, but Karla left. Moved to Fort Worth just after Christmas."

"I know. She wrote to me."

Suze looked relieved. "She talked about leaving Rough Creek all her life. The only reason she stayed so long was because of you."

Dalton had no response to that. He hadn't been surprised that Karla had cut and run after he was sent to Huntsville. Not many women as smart as she was would want to pin their futures on an ex-con. Still, he missed her. She'd been fun to hang with, even though he'd known from the beginning that she'd eventually move on.

His meal came in record time and was every bit as good as he remembered.

By the time he finished, the place was filling up with late diners, probably heading home after a local high school sports event. Spring football practice, or maybe soccer or baseball, judging by the uniforms. He recognized a few of the customers, but despite some curious looks pointed his way, no one approached him.

"How was it?" Suze asked when he went to the register to pay his tab.

"Best meal I've had in a long time. Especially that pie." Seeing how busy the place was, he didn't linger, told Suze to tell Buddy "hi," then stepped outside.

A sense of hope spread through him. Maybe this wouldn't be so bad. Maybe he really could put it all behind him and make a fresh start.

"Heard those idiots on the parole board let you out early," a familiar taunting voice said behind him.

Or maybe not.

Dalton turned to see Deputy Langers coming from the direction of the sheriff's office down the street. He and Toby Langers hadn't gotten along since high school, when Dalton, a fourteen-year-old freshman, had taken over the older, smaller boy's position on the football team. After Dalton's arrest and while he'd been in county lockup awaiting sentencing, the taunting had only gotten worse. Not surprising, since Toby was the county commissioner's local toady, and it was Commissioner Adkins's nephew that Dalton was supposed to have killed. He had hoped the animosity between him and Toby might have cooled during his absence, but Dalton could see it hadn't.

"Thought you'd have sense enough not to come back to Rough Creek," Langers said. "'Specially now that Karla's gone." At one time, Toby had had his eye on Karla, himself.

"It's my home, Toby."

"Maybe not for long. And it's Deputy Langers to you." Puffing out his chest, Langers hooked his thumbs in a duty belt that boasted more paraphernalia than Dalton had ever carried as a grunt in Sandland. "I'm guessing you haven't been out to the ranch yet," he went on, rocking back on his heels so he wouldn't have to tip his head back so far to smirk up at Dalton.

"Heading there now."

"How?" Langers made a show of looking around. "You got a car? Oh, that's right. You're not allowed to drive, are you?"

Not strictly true, since his suspension was for only a year. But Dalton didn't want to get into a discussion about it. "Thought I'd walk."

"Probably wise. Hard for ex-cons to get rides nowadays. Best start now, if you plan to get there before midnight."

Dalton turned and started walking, his jaw clamped on a rush of angry words best left unsaid.

"You be careful," Langers called after him. "Lot of bad things happen on that road. But then, you already know that, don't you? Be sure to give my best to your folks, in case I don't see them before they go."

Go where? But Dalton didn't prolong the conversation by asking.

Luckily, he didn't have to walk more than two miles

before he heard a truck rattling up behind him. Spinning a one-eighty, he walked backward, facing the oncoming vehicle, his thumb out.

The truck slowed, tailpipe popping out a barrage of backfire that jittered along Dalton's nerves and made him think of Iraq. He recognized the driver. Harve Henswick, an elderly man who lived two miles past his parents' place and just over the county line.

With a belch of black exhaust, the truck rolled to a stop. The driver sat for a moment, studying him through the dust-and-bug-smeared windshield, then nodded.

"Thanks." Dalton climbed in. Not sure if the old man remembered who he was, he stuck out his hand and was about to introduce himself when Henswick turned and gave him a hard stare.

"When'd you get out?" he asked.

Dalton let his hand drop to his thigh. "This morning."

"Thought you were in for two years."

"I got six months off for good behavior."

"Well, then." Henswick shifted into gear and gave the engine enough gas to make it shudder forward in fits and starts.

And that was the extent of their conversation for the next eighteen minutes.

Dalton watched ten miles of barbed wire fence roll by, broken by the occasional metal gate leading to wooden holding pens with loading chutes. In the middle distance, windmills slowly churned, their grit-scoured blades flashing orange in the lowering sun, while here and there, rusted pump jacks sat silent, their walking beams tilted down, heads to the ground like grazing horses.

The pickup began to slow. When it finally rolled to a stop, Dalton climbed out and shut the door. "Thanks for the ride," he said through the open window.

"Tell your pa I'm still waiting for that ratchet he borrowed. I'd prefer he didn't leave town with it." Without

waiting for a response, Henswick pulled out slow enough
that Dalton was only mildly peppered with pebbles and
black soot.

He stood listening to the rumble and pop of the truck's
exhaust until it faded and all that broke the silence was the
rustle of the gentle breeze through new grass, the distant
hum and whir of big irrigation sprinklers in nearby hay
fields, and the *skree* of a hawk floating past on rising ther-
mals. After a year and a half living in close quarters with
almost two thousand restless convicts and shouting guards,
the still openness was a balm to his battered senses. Even
the air felt better.

Dalton closed his eyes and breathed deep.

Gradually the stink of sweat, disinfectant, rancid cooking oils, and harsh cleaners gave way to the familiar smells
of alfalfa, cow and horse manure, and good old Texas dust,
all underlaid with the faint scent of petroleum rising out of
the abandoned wellheads.

It was good to be home.

He turned and walked up the drive toward the sagging
gate with the familiar plank sign that read CARDWELL in
faded gray letters. But as he drew closer, he slowed to a stop
and stared.

On the tilting post that anchored the gate was another
sign. Smaller. Not familiar. Made of cardboard and carrying a single word in bold back script.

SOLD.

CHAPTER 2

"You're leaving?" four high-pitched female voices cried in unison.

So much for minimizing drama, Coralee thought.

Dinner was over and they were on the veranda. Coralee had turned on the gas fireplace, as much for ambience as warmth. She'd already poured the first bottle of wine—another two were at the ready—and everyone was settled comfortably into the plush patio furniture overlooking the long, gently sloping lawn down to the rippling waters of Rough Creek. A lovely, relaxing scene.

Except for the astonished faces gaping at her. It was apparent Coralee's carefully worded announcement had not been accepted as calmly as she'd hoped.

"Just to travel a bit," she explained. "Walk the sands of Tahiti, as it were. Zip-line through a rain forest. Cruise past glaciers in Alaska. Whatever. Sixty isn't too old to do that, you know."

"Not alone, I hope." Thirty-three-year-old Lennox gave her a look of concern. Living an insulated, wealthy, country club life in Dallas with her surgeon husband and two busy school-age children, Len thought dining alone—much less traveling unaccompanied—smacked of lonely desperation.

"I've always wanted to go to Tahiti," Josslyn of the wandering feet said, surprising no one. Free-spirited Joss would go anywhere with anyone, as long it furthered her dream of becoming a country music star.

"Tahiti's a fifteen-hour flight," practical KD informed them. "With stops. Hawaii would be closer. They have nice beaches, and you wouldn't have to take as many shots as you would if you went to a rain forest."

Coralee battled a sense of loss. She still couldn't believe her baby, Katherine Dianne—or KD, as she had renamed herself in high school—was now Second Lieutenant Whitcomb, recent West Point graduate, soon off to Lord knows where for who knew how long. Coralee might not see her for months. Years, even. It was too upsetting to consider.

"I think she should go," Raney said. "Take as long a trip as she wants."

"Naturally, you'd say that," Joss muttered. "Then you'd have this big house all to yourself."

Raney grinned and nodded.

"Oh, God!" Lennox bolted upright, eyes brimming. "It's cancer, isn't it? You have cancer and you're trying not to tell us!"

"Cancer? You have cancer?"

"Cancer of what?"

"Hush! All of you!" From drama to hysteria. And Coralee thought the evening had been going so well. "Of course I don't have cancer! I don't have anything but a need for change. Good Lord!"

"Oh my God!" Joss clapped her hands in delight. "It's a man! You've met someone, haven't you?"

"Why is it always about men with you, Joss?" KD muttered.

"Who is it?" Len demanded. "Do we know him? Is he safe?"

"Lord have mercy." With a weary sigh, Coralee rose. "Anybody else want a refill?" Amid a chorus of yeses, she uncorked another bottle of pinot noir, split it between four goblets—Joss still abstained, making Coralee wonder if she was planning a quick escape later—all the while assuring them that she wasn't suffering Alzheimer's, cancer, MS, ALS, or any other terrible disease, and had not turned into the town pump at the ripe old age of sixty—not in those words, of course. "I just want to have some fun," she said, sinking back into her chair. "Try something different. Is that so hard to understand?"

"But what about the ranch?" Raney asked.

And there it was. The question Coralee had been dreading. She fervently hoped they would be reasonable and listen to what she had to say before they started overreacting. "That depends on what you decide." Seeing their confusion, she explained their options. "We could sell it and put the proceeds into the family trust, rent it out, or keep it and let your sister continue to run it as she has for the last nine years." She smiled at Raney, hoping to ease her anxious expression. "And doing an excellent job of it, I might add."

Len frowned in thought. "Since I'm married, if we did sell and split the proceeds, would my share become community property?"

Coralee gave her eldest a sharp look. She knew that like most marriages, Len and Ryan's had its ups and downs, but they'd always muddled through. That her daughter was voicing concerns about community property made Coralee wonder if she was contemplating divorce. "We wouldn't pocket the proceeds," Coralee explained. "Since the family trust owns the ranch, as well as the various accounts and funds that your father set up, the money would go back into the trust. And the only names on the trust are mine and you girls'. So, no, it wouldn't become community property. All of us are paid a monthly allowance from the trust. Raney, you're paid an additional salary as manager of the ranch."

"In other words," Raney said, frowning, "we couldn't sell the ranch without breaking the trust?"

"I'm not sure. If you're worried about it, Raney, check with the accountants and lawyers next time you meet with them. I'm as confused as you are."

"But I don't want to sell it," Raney argued. "None of us needs the money, so why sell and risk having it broken up or subdivided? And what would we do with the horses?" How like Raney to worry most about her beloved horses.

"The ranch might not sell that easily, anyway," KD argued. "Not on a cashout. Unless a big corporation bought it for development."

"I'd hate that," Raney said.

Lennox nodded. "Me, too. I may not ever want to live here permanently, but I like knowing it's here, in case we need it."

"For what?" KD asked.

"Financial security. Emotional security. It's our child-hood home, KD. Mama was born and raised here. We were raised here. Ryan and I got married out there on the back lawn. Losing it would be like losing part of our lives."

Coralee watched them talk it over, hearing her own argument in their voices. She didn't want to sell, either, and selfishly hoped they wouldn't. But she couldn't deny them that option if they chose to move on, too, so she remained silent.

After a half hour of what-ifs and if-onlys, Raney turned to her with tears in deep-set eyes so like her own. "Is that what you want, Mama? To sell?"

Coralee twirled the stem of the wine goblet in her fingers and watched the dark liquid swirl up the sides. "No. I don't want to sell. I love the ranch, too. I love having it in our family. But I don't want the responsibility of it any-more. Seems I've been tied to this piece of land forever, and I'm ready to try something different while I still can."

Solemn faces stared back at her.

Coralee wondered what they saw. An aging mother suf-fering an identity crisis? Or an energetic woman not ready to give up?

"You could date," Len suggested. "Maybe you're just bored and looking for something to do. Why not start going out again?"

"I bet old Westbrook would give you another go," Joss said.

Coralee almost shuddered. "Esterbrook. And I wouldn't go with that man across an icy street in the middle of a hailstorm!"

"Why not? He seemed nice enough."

"He's strange."

"Strange how? Like he cries at Hallmark movies?"

"Oh, I love Hallmark movies," Joss said.

"Or strange like he keeps a shed full of doll heads and a shrine to his mother?" Raney had the most peculiar sense of humor.

"Why would he have doll heads? That's creepy."

"Laugh if you want," Coralee scolded. "But the man has issues."

"Like what?" KD asked.

"He's too . . . touchy-feely."

Joss nodded in understanding. "I get that a lot, too."

"It's been nine years," Len reminded her. "Maybe you're just out of practice."

Coralee sighed. "I thought that, too. And I tried. I truly did. But it was awful."

Joss reached over and patted Coralee's hand. "Maybe you need drugs. Or props. I read that—"

"Stop!" Raney shouted. "I'm calling an audible. Let's get back to the matter at hand. Joss, do you want to sell?"

"No. I love the ranch. I loved growing up here and it's a great place to raise babies. It's been an island of tranquility in my turbulent life."

"Good God," KD muttered under her breath.

Lennox laughed. "Sounds like a line in one of her songs, doesn't it, KD?"

Joss's brown eyes lit up. "I know! I just thought it up. Do you like it?"

"Can we please get this settled?" Raney cut in before they wandered too far again. "Do we sell the ranch, or not?"

Lennox raised her goblet high. "I say we keep it, have Raney run it, and give Mama the best send-off ever!"

Joss seconded that. "Yay, Mama!"

KD held up her glass. "I'm in. Assuming Raney wants to keep running it."

"I'll have to think about it," Raney said hesitantly. At their looks of surprise, she burst into giggles. "Of course I'll run it! I'd love to run it!"

"Then it's settled."

"But . . ." Raney held up a hand. "Before we make it final, there are some changes I'd like to make. If y'all agree."

"Such as?"

"Fewer cattle." She explained that beef futures were unpredictable and hard to forecast, especially with all the Canadian beef coming in. Plus, the trend was toward organic, which meant lower weight and higher losses to disease. "I'd like to trim the herds and concentrate on a breeding program. AI is the only way to go, and prize-winning, proven bulls are money in the bank."

Joss looked confused. "Artificial intelligence?"

Raney rolled her eyes. "Artificial insemination."

"The gift that keeps giving," KD said with a snicker.

"Turkey-baster ranching. It sounds so . . . festive."

More giggles.

Coralee decided not to open another bottle.

Raising her voice over the laughter of her sisters, Raney

continued, "And I also want to focus more on horses. Cutting horses."

"No surprise there," KD said.

Raney lost patience. "Do you know what a champion stud can earn? Maybe a million dollars. One horse. Think of what a stableful would bring."

That sobered them up.

"We'd have to invest in young stock with strong bloodlines. And good trainers. But the sale of the cattle would cover most of that. What do you say?"

They liked it. While they discussed appropriate names for these champion stallions and mares Raney would breed, Coralee sipped from her glass. A mother's pride added to the warm tingle in her throat as she watched her daughters laugh and tease and make plans for a future that seemed to stretch forever. She had done well. They were all good, strong women. Charlie would have been proud.

Her gaze swept over their lovely faces, each different from the other, and each beautiful in her own way. Lennox, so smart and chic and forgiving—she'd had to be with a husband like Ryan. Raney, the son they'd never had, capable and efficient and so beautiful she still had men trailing after her like lost puppies. Little KD, destined for a life Coralee could only imagine. And Joss, the family wild child, chaser of rainbows and butterflies, heading into the greatest adventure of all.

How she loved them.

As if sensing her mother's gaze, Joss turned and looked at her. "What?" When Coralee just smiled, Joss's puzzlement gave way to a grin. "You know."

Raney looked from one to the other. "Knows what?"

"Why Joss wasn't drinking tonight," Len answered.

"Joss wasn't drinking?"

"How did you know?" Joss asked Coralee.

"She always knows," Len said. "She knew about both of mine before I did."

Raney gaped at her little sister. "You're pregnant?"

"Almost four and a half months! I'm surprised you couldn't tell!"

"I thought you were a little curvier," KD said. "Not surprising, considering the amount of food you put away at dinner."

"I'm eating for two," Joss said defensively.

"And doing a damn good job of it."

Questions flew across the room—"Who's the father?" "Are you getting married?" "What about your music?"

"It doesn't matter who the father is, it's my baby. So no, I'm not getting married. And I can work on my music here while I wait for the baby to arrive."

"Here?" Raney almost choked on the word.

"Yes! It'll be fun! Just like when we were growing up!"

Coralee understood Raney's panic. No doubt she was remembering all the broken rules, missed curfews, forgotten promises, and general chaos that followed her little sister like a trail of dust.

"And after?" Raney asked Joss. "If you go back to touring with Crystal, do you plan on leaving the baby here?"

"Of course not! I know it won't be easy, but I won't leave my baby behind. And I don't want to go through this alone. Mama, promise me you'll come back."

"Yes, promise!" Raney insisted with a steely-eyed look.

Coralee smiled. "I promise I'll try."

"Wonderful! Mark it down, everyone! We'll all meet here in September to welcome the new baby and hear all about Mama's grand adventure! It'll be such fun!"

His mother came out onto the porch as Dalton came up the weed-choked gravel walk. "Sonny," she said.

"Hi, Mom." Dalton climbed the stairs and gave her a hug. She felt so small and fragile in his arms he was afraid if he squeezed too hard he might break something. "It's good to see you."

Always uncomfortable with displays of affection, even with her own family, his mother pulled back first. "Sorry we didn't come get you."

"That's okay. It's a long drive. Where's Dad?"

"Inside."

Something in her face alerted him. "Is he sick?"

She shook her head, sending wisps of gray hair fanning her wrinkled cheeks. "Tired, mostly. And ashamed."

She looked tired, too, Dalton thought. And a lot older than when he left. Was his absence allowing him to see changes that had been coming a long time? Or had something happened while he was gone?

"Ashamed, why?" he asked. Surely not about what happened a year and a half ago? Dalton thought they'd gotten past all that.

"For selling the place. And for not talking to you before he did."

"Why didn't he?" Dalton tried to keep an edge from his voice.

She shrugged her thin shoulders. Looked past him into the distance. "He had no choice, sonny. Selling was the right thing to do."

Dalton thought of the smirk on Langers's face when he said this might not be his home for long. "You weren't being pressured, were you?" He hoped the county commissioner's fury at him hadn't spilled over onto his parents.

"Commissioner Adkins has been a bother, but that's not the main reason for selling. Dad will explain it all." There was a pause, then she said, "You heard Karla moved to Fort Worth?"

"I know." Surely that wasn't the biggest news in his absence. "She wrote me."

"Never figured she'd stay in Rough Creek."

"I didn't, either." And he was tired of talking about it.

"All right, then." She motioned toward the sagging structure behind the house. "Timmy's in the barn, unloading bales off the harrow bed. Give him your hellos while I fix some iced tea. Then you and Dad can talk."

His parents had been in their late thirties when Dalton was born. Mom had given up on having children and often called him her miracle baby. Then eleven years later, Timmy had come along. Another miracle, since it was a difficult birth with complications for both her and the baby. Timmy had a long recovery and seemed slow to flourish. By the time he was four and barely beginning to talk or walk, they knew he would remain childlike forever. The doctor said that sometimes happened with difficult, late-in-life pregnancies. Mom didn't care. Even if Timmy's intellect never rose above the early-elementary-school level, Mom still saw him as another miracle baby.

Dalton didn't care, either. Timmy was easy to love, and the most joyful, playful, kindhearted person he had ever known. But his brother was over twenty now, and almost as big as Dalton at six-two and close to two hundred pounds. He might be too much for his aging parents to handle.

"Dalton!" Timmy shouted when he saw his big brother coming down the center aisle of the barn. "You came back!"

"I did."

After a vigorous reunion that involved a lot of hugging, laughing, arm-punching, and more hugging, Dalton was able to hold his brother at bay long enough to take a full breath. "I missed you too, buddy. But no more hitting. Even between us. Remember, we talked about that."

"Yeah. Okay. No more hitting. I remember. No hitting."

"Good man." Dalton gave his brother's shoulder a gentle squeeze. "I see Dad's letting you run the harrow bed." He eyed the crooked alfalfa bales leaning at an angle against the log support posts that were intended to keep the stack from tipping over.

"But not on the road," Timmy stated with firm emphasis as he shook his head. "Dad says not to go on the road. I have to stay in the pasture or the field. Not on the road."

"He's right. You listen to Dad."

"Yeah. Okay."

Dalton reminded himself to check the tractor later to make sure the fuel and hydraulic levels were where they should be. "You like working the harrow bed?"

"Yeah." More nodding. "Dad says I do good, maybe I can run the tractor again. But not on the road. I can't go on the road."

They talked for a few minutes longer, then Timmy said, "I have to go now, Dalton. I have work to do. Important work, Dad says. Maybe now you came home, you can work with me. Okay?"

"We'll see."

His parents were waiting for him in the front room they called the parlor, which served as both the den and living room in their small, century-old, wood-sided farmhouse. At Mom's insistence, Dad had added on a laundry room and second bathroom a decade earlier, but when she pushed for a den and porch across the back, he said he had neither the time nor money to invest in "beautification projects" and that put an end to it. Now it didn't matter anymore. The new owners would likely bulldoze the house and build something bigger and more modern. Rich city folks, probably. Looking to play at cattle ranching while earning a fat tax write-off on a fancy weekend home. Poor people couldn't afford to work a place smaller than a half section anymore. The only way his folks had lasted so long was because they owned the land and everything on it free and clear.

"I see you made it through," his father said from his recliner when Dalton settled into the chair next to Mom's usual spot on the couch.

"I did."

"Gained some weight."

"Easy to do on prison food."

"I'll make up a big pot of chili tomorrow," his mother promised.

"That'd be great."

Silence.

His folks had never been talkers, but Dalton could see his father had something on his mind, and the best way to get Harold Cardwell talking was to sit tight and wait him out.

"I guess you saw we sold the place," his father said after a while.

Dalton nodded.

"We had no choice," Mom put in with a sidewise glance at Dad.

"How come?" Dalton asked.

"It's Timmy." His father sighed and shook his head. "The boy needs schooling. We won't be around to take care of him forever."

That feeling of alarm returned. Was his father sick? Was there something they weren't telling him?

"We found a place for him," his mother assured Dalton, misreading his alarm. "A group home in Plainview, close by a little house we're thinking to buy. A place where he can learn to be more self-sufficient."

The idea was so alien to Dalton he couldn't respond.

Years ago, his folks had talked about finding a school for Timmy. But the closest was eighty miles away and required he live there. They wouldn't do that.

"Timmy is family," Dad had said. "And we take care of our own. He'll be happier here with us, and Mom can teach him. She's already talked to the social services folks and they're sending out books to help." And that put an end to it.

Now they were talking about putting Timmy in a home and moving over a hundred miles away? Was he to lose his family as well as the ranch?

"Truth is, the boy's getting too much for us," his father went on. "He's restless. Wants to do things we can't teach him."

"I could have helped out."

His mother shook her head. "You got to make your own way, sonny. Besides, Timmy needs similar folks around him. Friends who understand him and don't look at him funny. I've taught him all I can. But there are teachers at this home who can show him how to care for himself. Maybe teach him a trade. Selling the ranch will pay for that. And we'll be close by if he needs us." She looked at Dad for confirmation. He nodded.

Another long silence while Dalton tried to digest all these plans that had been formed and set in motion without him. Good, reasonable plans, maybe. But they were coming so fast he could hardly keep up.

His father said, "You're probably thinking we should have talked all this over with you first."

Dalton was thinking exactly that. But he doubted talking it over would have changed anything. The cattle market being as erratic as it usually was, it was getting harder and harder to keep a small ranch going. Dad did look worn out. Mom, too. They deserved some ease, and Timmy did need specialized training.

Dalton understood all that. Still, the idea of giving up the ranch that had been home to the Cardwells for three generations left an empty place inside. And the thought of putting Timmy in a home made it feel even emptier.

And yet . . .

As Dalton pondered the loss of the home place and the breakup of his family, a sense of release gradually spread where that emptiness had been. It would be good to get out from under the burdens the ranch brought. If they sold, he could plot his own path, rather than following in the footsteps of his father and grandfather. And if Timmy could be happily situated in a safe place where he could learn to be independent, that would be good, too, and might allow Dalton to do something different. Something he'd had on the back burner for a long time.

"Well," his father said. "The final papers haven't been

signed yet. I suppose if it's important to you, we could take some time to talk it over."

Dalton shook his head. "The ranch belongs to you and Mom. You need to do what's right for yourselves and Timmy. If selling is the right thing, then I'll back you all the way."

Saying the words aloud brought a finality that wasn't as troubling as Dalton thought it'd be. A place of his own. A job more to his liking. A new start. That feeling of hope built again as possibilities raced through his mind.

Dad let go a long, deep breath. He glanced over at his wife of nearly sixty years, whose eyes were shimmering with unshed tears. Yet they both looked relieved. And maybe a little happy, despite the changes to come.

Mom smoothed her apron and stiffened her back. "All right, then. Now that that's decided, alls we have left to figure out is what you're going to do, sonny."

Dad nodded. "After everything's taken care of and we get Timmy settled, we might be able to help out if you wanted to start up something on your own."

"Thanks, but I'll be okay. All I need is a strong back, an even temperament, a lot of time, and a little luck." Seeing his parents' quizzical look, Dalton gave a big smile. "Who knows? Maybe I'll hook up with a rich heiress or win the lottery. Or if that doesn't pan out, I know I'd make a hell of a horse trainer."

CHAPTER 3

After the sale of the ranch was finalized and the papers signed, the hard work of disposing of a hundred years of accumulated crap began. But first, in case Deputy Langers decided to make an issue of it, Dalton renewed his driver's license and checked in with the parole board. He also got a haircut and threw out his prison shoes and all his too-small clothes and got some shirts and jeans that fit.

Then he set to work.

He spent the next few weeks helping his parents prepare for their move to Plainview, packing up his and Timmy's stuff and dealing with ranch issues. They donated the older horses and extra tack to the local 4-H, found deserving homes for the working horses, and auctioned off the cattle to the local slaughterhouse. After dumping the usable ranch equipment at fire-sale prices, they called in the scrap metal dealer to cart off what was left.

Timmy took the sale of the tractor harder than the loss of his home, but after Dalton let him drive it around the north pasture for what seemed like half a day, he climbed off, gave the oversized rear tire a pat, whispered a tearful good-bye, and waved it out the gate.

Luckily, his parents had already started packing up their personal and household belongings, so Dalton focused on the tools and equipment. After a month of culling and sorting, they were down to items they would keep, those they would sell, and a dozen trips to the dump. Dalton was amazed at the stuff a family could accumulate and resolved to keep his own life unburdened by things he didn't use or need.

On a bright Thursday morning in late April, he polished his boots, put on a set of new clothes, knocked the dust off his summer Stetson, then drove through the gate in search of a job. Since there were several fine quarter horse breeding and training outfits nearby, he decided to try locally first. With that in mind, he drove east out of Rough Creek toward the top ranch in the county, Whitcomb Four Star. If he couldn't sign on there, he'd head on toward Fort Worth, or if necessary, up into Oklahoma.

The Whitcomb place wasn't the largest ranch in the area, but it had a reputation for breeding fine stock that made decent showings on the Texas and Oklahoma reining and roping circuit. Since he'd returned, Dalton had heard they were expanding to include cutting horses. If so, they might be looking for trainers.

He had ridden in a couple of shows several years ago and had great admiration for the cutting horse. But his real talent lay in understanding the animal and knowing how to bring out the best the horse had to offer. He didn't follow a set training formula, but relied more on feel and instinct, working each animal according to its temperament, ability, and trainability. He'd been told he had the touch. He wasn't sure what that was, but he had a fair understanding of how the minds of horses worked, and they always seemed to respond well to him.

He'd never been to Whitcomb Four Star, and as he drove

down the long drive, he was impressed by what he saw. He knew that in addition to being a rancher and lawyer, Charlie Whitcomb had been on the board of Texas Gulf Explorations and had strong ties to the TRC—Texas Railroad Commission—the agency that oversaw the oil and gas industry throughout the state. Lots of money there, and before his death a few years back, Whitcomb had apparently made a bundle of it, judging by the investments he'd made in the ranch. It was as fine a place as Dalton had ever seen, even though it was only a medium-sized outfit.

The drive split, the right fork leading to a rambling two-story stone house backing up to Rough Creek, the left continuing on to a series of farm structures.

The first was a long stone horse barn, with a large, covered arena out back, a round training pen attached to one side and paddocks jutting out on the other. All the fencing was white-painted, welded metal rails. A hundred yards farther up the drive, rose an open-sided hay barn next to a two-story building with windows above, more stalls below, and loading chutes out back that led to several stout metal-fenced paddocks holding blocky Angus bulls. And in the distance, behind another white fence, stood a rambling house that looked to be housing for the ranch workers.

Dalton drove past the round pen and pulled in by the stone barn. As he climbed out of the truck, a lanky middle-aged man in a flannel shirt, jeans, and dusty Stetson came to meet him. Dalton recognized him from the few quarter horse shows he'd entered: Glenn Hicks, foreman of Four Star. A good man, but not much of a talker.

"Morning, Mr. Hicks." Dalton held out his hand. "Doubt you remember—"

"Dalton Cardwell. Yeah, I remember." He didn't smile, but then, Dalton had rarely seen him do so.

He shook Dalton's hand, let it go, and stepped back. "When'd you get out?"

Dalton wondered how many more times he'd have to answer that question. "Last month."

"Looking for work, I suppose."

"Yes, sir."

"Doing what?"

"Horse trainer. Heard you were expanding."

Hicks thought about that. "Got any experience with cutting horses?"

Dalton listed the shows he'd been in, whom he'd ridden for, and how he'd finished. Which was decent, considering the horses he'd been riding.

"Alls we got now are two- and three-year-olds," Hicks told him. "You any good with ground work?"

"Yes, sir. Gives me a chance to know the horse before starting the hard training."

Hicks thought that over, too. Finally, he nodded. "Go on up to the house, then. Back door. Ask for Mrs. Coralee. You get her okay, then you'll need to get past her daughter Raney. And good luck with that." The foreman almost smiled when he said those last words. It wasn't an encouraging expression.

After thanking him, Dalton walked back up the drive he'd just driven down. As he passed the round training pen, he noticed a woman on a chestnut gelding working a half-dozen cows.

Competent, but stiff in the back. It kept her a quarter beat behind the movement of the horse. Not that noticeable, but enough to count against her in a show. The calves were bored and sluggish. The horse worked harder than it needed to and didn't keep its head down like it should. Nice confirmation, though. The rider, too.

At first glance, Mrs. Coralee Whitcomb looked like the typical rich rancher's wife—expensive haircut, expensive jeans, expensive boots, and a silky blouse that showed off a well-kept figure. But if you looked closer—which Dalton did—and noted the shrewd intelligence in her bright blue eyes and the hint of a smile lurking at the corners of her wide mouth, you saw a handsome, capable lady, and not one to be taken lightly.

Before Dalton could introduce himself and explain why he had come, she gave him a friendly but puzzled smile and asked if they'd met.

"No, ma'am," he answered. He would have remembered a woman like her.

"You're sure? You look familiar."

Dalton decided to be forthright. "Maybe you saw my picture in the paper. I was convicted a year and a half ago of vehicular manslaughter."

Her smile faded. "You're Clovis Cardwell's boy."

"Yes, ma'am. Dalton Cardwell."

"The commissioner's nephew died. You waived a trial and were sent to Huntsville."

It wasn't a question, but Dalton nodded anyway. "I got out last month. Time off for good behavior," he added, hoping that would help.

She studied him for a moment, then called to the woman who'd let him in the back door. A cook, maybe. "Maria, could you please bring iced tea to the veranda?"

Motioning Dalton to follow, Mrs. Whitcomb led him down a short hallway pass-through onto a covered porch. She took a seat in one of the several cushioned chairs grouped around a huge footstool in front of a big gas fireplace. "Have a seat, Mr. Cardwell, and tell me how your mother is doing with the move."

She must have seen Dalton's surprise. "I've known Clovis for years, ever since we worked together on the auxiliary committee to fix up that eyesore of a town square. She and your father are well, I hope?"

"Yes, ma'am," he said as he sat down. "A little tired from all the packing."

"After being part of Rough Creek for so long, it must be hard for her to leave."

Dalton was saved from more small talk by the arrival of Maria. After setting a tray bearing two frosted glasses, a pitcher of iced tea, and a plate of chocolate chip cookies on the oversized footstool, she accepted Mrs. Whitcomb's thanks, nodded to Dalton, and left.

Mrs. Whitcomb poured the tea, offered Dalton the plate of cookies, which he declined although they were his favorite, then she sat back and eyed him over her glass of iced tea. "Tell me about the wreck."

Startled by the abruptness of the question, Dalton was slow to respond. Aware of that sharp gaze, he opted for the simple version. "It was late. I was tired and not paying attention. When I started across the road, a car ran into the side of my tractor. The driver died instantly."

"Jim Bob Adkins."

"Yes, ma'am."

Silence. Those eyes seemed to drill into him like two sharpened pieces of ice.

"I heard he'd been drinking," she finally said. "And was speeding."

"Maybe. I don't know."

"Yet you took full blame."

"I was at fault. I pulled onto the road without looking."

"A shared fault, I think. But I appreciate your honesty." She set her glass down on the tray then sat back again, ready for business. "While you were on your way to the house, Glenn called. He said you were looking for work as a horse trainer."

"Yes, ma'am."

"Have you any experience?"

"Some. After the army, I trained for a while with Roy Kilmer. Rode for him in a few local shows back in 2013."

"How'd you do?"

"'Bout as you'd expect on soured horses."

Her brows rose in that silent way women have of expressing disapproval without risking confrontation. "You're blaming the horses?"

"No, ma'am. Kilmer worked them too hard. I told him so and he fired me." Fearing that might not sit well, either, Dalton added, "I may not have a lot of show experience, Mrs. Whitcomb, but I'm good at ground work and I understand horses. How to get the best out of them. When to push and when to back off. If the talent's there, I can find it and make it shine."

Those eyes bored into him for a moment longer, then she pulled a cell phone from her pocket. She punched in several numbers, told whoever answered to bring the colts to Paddock Four, punched out, then rose from her chair. "Show me," she said, and without waiting to see if Dalton followed, went down the veranda steps and across the side yard.

A test, Dalton guessed, following her up the drive toward the horse barn. He understood and was even encouraged by it. Most would have discounted him right off, either for his lack of experience or his prison record. That she was giving him a chance despite those drawbacks raised her a notch in his regard.

When they walked past the training pen, the woman working the calves reined in and watched them. Mrs. Whitcomb didn't notice.

Dalton did.

He recognized the rider, even though he was two years older and had seen her only from a distance maybe a half-dozen times since high school, between the time he got out of the army, trained with Kilmer, and his two years at Texas Tech.

Raney Whitcomb. Homecoming queen and head cheerleader at Clinton High. A beauty, still. And she had her mother's intense blue eyes.

He couldn't remember if she'd ever married. She'd certainly had chances. Boys from every high school in Gunther County had been after her. She'd smiled at him once, but they'd never spoken. Different schools. Opposite sides of the county. She didn't attend the church his parents favored, and he never saw her at Harley's Roadhouse dance hall outside Rough Creek, or at any of the other hangouts.

Maybe she thought herself too good for the local boys. Or maybe she was shy. He never knew. Never heard any rumors about her, either, which was odd for a small community that thrived on gossip. Not like her younger sister—Joss, or Jess, or Juicy, as some of the wilder boys called her. He never knew firsthand about that, either. He wondered what it would be like working here with Raney Whitcomb hanging around. Probably wouldn't matter. She was way above his rank.

When they reached the paddocks on the other side of the barn, a Hispanic man was waving five young colts through the gate into a large, rectangular pasture bordered by more welded, white-painted tube metal fencing. Dalton figured there must be at least two miles of it just in paddocks and pens. He liked the look of it.

Mrs. Whitcomb stopped at the fence. "These are our two-and three-year-olds." Resting her forearms along the top rail, she watched the colts scatter as they came through the gate. Three immediately dropped their heads to graze, but two others kept going, racing past them along the rails, heads and tails high, hooves flinging up tufts of grass. Running just for the hell of it.

"What do you think?" Mrs. Whitcomb asked, still watching the horses.

"Nice colts."

"Any standouts?"

Dalton studied them, his gaze moving quickly over the grazers and fixing on the two runners. They were all fine horses—good confirmation, good bone, well muscled through the chest and butt like any top-bred quarter horse should be. But one drew his attention.

Dalton watched him near the far railing at a dead run, tuck and roll back without breaking stride, and knew that was the one he'd want to train. Strong, athletic, fast on his feet, running flat out and happy to leave the others in his dust. He had the potential and the heart. "The big buckskin," he finally said.

"The three-year-old. Rosco. He's my favorite, too." Mrs. Whitcomb sent him a wide, approving smile that told Dalton he'd passed the test.

"How far along is he?" Dalton asked, watching the colt put moves on the other horses, trying to get them to play.

"Far enough to know he's worth the extra training. He's been worked on a single cow, learning to mirror the cow's movements—stop, start, turn, so on. He got it right off. Now he's ready to start bringing a cow out of the herd, but the trainer who has been working him can no longer do it." She gave Dalton a long, appraising look. "Want to give him a try?"

A charge of excitement cut through Dalton. "You bet. Yes, ma'am."

She got out her cell phone again and punched in more numbers. "I'll have Alejandro, our head wrangler, saddle him and bring him to the arena out back."

It was a standard arena. Covered, about 120 feet across, enclosed by a five-foot, wire-and-mesquite picket fence. Unpainted, this time. Less distracting. A few minutes later, the same Hispanic guy who had turned the colts out into the pasture led in the saddled buckskin. Mrs. Whitcomb made the introductions, then she and Alejandro left the pen and stood watching at the fence.

Dalton took his time, keeping his movements slow and easy, letting the animal grow accustomed to his scent and voice and touch. Then he gathered the reins and eased into the saddle. He patted Rosco's neck and talked to him in a low, calm voice, then sat back and sent him into a walk.

Halfway around, he asked the colt to trot, then after a

lap, moved him into a lope. When it was time, he rolled him to the right toward the fence and on around in a half-turn spin, then loped him off, all in one continuous, unbroken movement. They made a lap, then repeated the turn to the left. Dalton asked him to do that two more times in each direction, then backed him until he dropped his butt, spun him into a tight right turn, then loped him off, stopped, and backed him onto his haunches again, spun him into a left turn, and rolled him out into a lope. Stop, back up, tuck, spin, and roll out. The horse got it all, smooth as silk, sensitive to the slightest signal. He'd been trained well.

At Mrs. Whitcomb's nod, Alejandro opened another gate and a cow trotted into the pen. Immediately, the colt tensed, eyes and ears focused on the cow. Dalton could sense the same excitement he felt in his own body running through the young horse. He was definitely ready.

He walked the colt toward the cow, gave him the go-ahead, then sat back and enjoyed the ride as Rosco followed the cow around the pen. He did everything he'd been trained to do, mirroring perfectly the cow's movements with little or no input from Dalton, staying on point and calm and totally focused on the task. This horse had the makings of a true champion, Dalton decided, and he was determined to be a part of that journey.

"So, what do you think?" Mrs. Whitcomb asked a few minutes later when Dalton handed off the colt to Alejandro.

"I think you should hire me, ma'am. And right away, if you want him ready for the Fort Worth Futurity next fall."

Mrs. Whitcomb laughed and held out her hand. "Done."

Raney was coming out of the barn after tending her horse, when she saw an unfamiliar dark blue pickup driving out the front gate. Curious, she walked over to where her mother was watching Alejandro and a helper drive the young colts in the paddock pasture back into their stalls.

Alejandro was a longtime and highly valued employee at Four Star. He was a hard worker, unquestionably trustworthy, and had the uncanny ability to notice things in horses that went below the surface. Like a slight shoulder weakness, or a mare being ready to foal, or a young colt favoring one leg.

He was short and stocky and very strong, with black hair and eyes, a broad smile, and a tattoo on his chest that said *Amada*, which meant "beloved" in Spanish. Raney suspected he'd told both of his ex-wives that he had gotten the tattoo to honor them. Quite the charmer. He had fathered a son by each of his wives and had named both boys Alejandro—numero Uno and numero Dos. He adored both boys and extended that same fatherly protectiveness toward Raney and her sisters. He was part of the family now and she couldn't have run the ranch without him.

"Who was that?" Raney asked, nodding toward the blue pickup as she joined her mother.

"Dalton Cardwell."

Raney looked at her in surprise. "Are you sure? The Dalton Cardwell I remember was a lot skinnier. They called him Beanpole."

Mama chuckled. "He's certainly no beanpole now. You might consider—"

"Don't start." The last thing Raney needed was her mother pimping her out. The man was a criminal, for heaven's sake.

Laughing, her mother turned and walked toward the house.

Raney fell in beside her. "You know he's the guy who killed Jim Bob."

"He told me all about it." Mama made a dismissive gesture. "It was an accident. And probably as much Jim Bob's fault as his. I heard the Adkins boy had been drinking and might have been speeding."

"Says who?"

"Marlene."

"The hairdresser? That's your source?"

"She's great with hair. You said so yourself."

"Good Lord."

Raney remembered how shocked she had been when she'd read about the wreck. Even though they went to different high schools, she'd heard Dalton Cardwell was a quiet guy, smarter than most, never causing trouble or drawing attention to himself, except on the football field. She had never talked to him, but she remembered a lot of girls thought he was cute. Which he'd been, in a skinny, awkward sort of way.

He was also a natural athlete and made a name for himself as a wide receiver, despite being such a "tall drink of water," as Daddy had called him after watching him play. Dalton might have earned a college football scholarship if he hadn't enlisted in the army. It was two years after 9/11 when he graduated, and like so many boys his age, he'd been gung ho to get the guys who had brought down the towers. She heard that after the army, he'd ridden in some of the nearby cutting shows before using his VA benefits to go to Texas Tech. Then just before his third year, he'd had the wreck that had killed Jim Bob and a month later had been sent to Huntsville state prison.

A sorry waste of two lives. She never would have thought quiet Dalton Cardwell would be so careless as to cause another person's death. But then, he had been in the army and had probably seen a lot of death in Iraq. Things like that could change a person. She'd seen it happen.

"What did he want?" Raney asked, following her mother up the veranda steps.

"A job."

"Doing what?"

"Trainer. Maria, is there any tea left?" Mama called as they sank down into two overstuffed chairs in front of the fireplace. Propping her booted feet next to Raney's on the ottoman, her mother lifted her shoulder-length hair off the back of her neck. "Lordy, if it's this hot already, summer will be scorching. I'll be glad to escape the heat."

Mama had already planned her escape. A June cruise up to Alaska, a tour of Denali, whale watching in Glacier Bay, watching grizzlies fishing for salmon at Brooks Falls, then down to Puget Sound for an extended visit with friends, followed by a horse-pack trip up and around Mount Rainier. Come September, after Joss's baby came, she'd be off to Hawaii, then Tahiti, then God knows where. It was a little shocking how eager Mama was to get away from her family. But considering that Joss would be moving back next month, Raney didn't blame her.

Maria brought tea and sliced avocados and the little cucumber sandwiches Mama loved. They ate in companionable silence. Once she'd cleared her plate and returned it to the tray, Mama sat back with a contented sigh. "I'll miss those sandwiches."

"They have cucumbers in Alaska."

"But nobody can make them into sandwiches the way Maria can. Thank you, Maria," she added when their cook came to clear the plates away. "Delicious, as always."

Mama always spoke English with their Hispanic employees. She felt it was to everyone's advantage if they all used the language of the country where they lived. Not very PC, but it made sense to Mama. And the workers didn't seem to mind.

"I wonder why he decided to come here," Raney said after Maria left with the tray.

"Who? Dalton?"

First names already. That wasn't good. "There must be other jobs available."

"He heard we were branching out into cutting horses. He seemed quite knowledgeable."

"About our plans to expand?"

"About cutting horses. I think he'll make a good trainer."

Raney felt the stirrings of alarm. Surely her mother hadn't hired him without talking to her? "You're serious."

"He knew right off that Rosco was the best of the colts. And he knew exactly what to do when he put the colt through his paces in the big pen."

"No. Oh, hell no." Raney's boots hit the slate floor with a resounding thud. "He's not training any of my horses."

"Why not?"

"He's a convict!"

"Ex-convict. And that doesn't make him a poor trainer. Have some grace, Raney. Everybody deserves a second chance."

"He killed a man!"

"Actually, it was Jim Bob who ran into Dalton's tractor, so in a way, Jim Bob killed himself."

"Are you kidding me? You're defending him?"

Her mother frowned at her. "It's not like you to overact this way. Is there something I don't know?"

Raney had the insane urge to leap over the ridiculous giant ottoman and strangle her mother.

Oblivious, Mama continued. "He seems like a nice young man. And he has a low opinion of Roy Kilmer, which says a lot about his character. Besides, I know his parents. The Cardwells are good, churchgoing people."

"I can't believe this. You would actually go off and leave me and Joss—your pregnant daughter, and a terrible judge of men, I might add—with an ex-con."

"Don't be silly. I've already spoken to Alejandro. He'll keep an eye on him. Just give him a chance, darling. That's all I'm asking."

"Why are you so taken with a guy you don't even know?"

"I'm not sure. He just seems right for the job. Maybe a little lost. And you know how I am about strays."

Raney did. The barn was overrun with cats because of it.

"And he loves horses as much as you do," Mama went on. "Talk to him when he starts Rosco tomorrow. You'll see."

Tomorrow? She'd already hired him?

"And if you're worried about experience," Mama added, ignoring Raney's astonished outrage, "we'll send him to Preston Amala for training. Press would be just the man to bring him up to snuff since he's the one who started Rosco's training."

God help me. A convict and a half-blind old man so crippled from his years rodeoing and breaking horses he could barely climb into the saddle. Just what Raney needed to make her dream of raising championship horses into a reality. "You've already hired him, haven't you? Without even talking to me. I thought I was supposed to be running the ranch." Raney could barely keep her voice steady.

Mama heard it and gave her that weary *let's be reasonable* smile. "You are, darling. But I'm the majority holder in the trust. Let's give him until the fall Futurity, then we'll reevaluate. If you're still opposed, you can fire him. How's that?"

Feeling the reins slipping from her grip, Raney tipped her head back and watched the ceiling fan spin lazy circles overhead. It was probably a good thing that Mama would be leaving soon.

CHAPTER 4

The next morning, Raney overslept. Not surprising, since she'd been awake most of the night trying to figure a way to get rid of Dalton Cardwell.

It wasn't personal. The man might have served his time, but he was still a convicted criminal. Not the kind of worker she wanted representing the ranch on the show circuit. Whitcomb Four Star was a top-run outfit with a reputation for integrity and unquestionable honesty. Hiring felons didn't fit with that image. And who knows what other dangerous types might show up once word got around that she was hiring ex-cons.

Forgoing a shower, she quickly tossed on the clothes she'd left on the chair the night before, finger-combed her hair and stuffed it under a ball cap, then raced downstairs.

The kitchen was empty. Mama never came down before ten. Maria had left Raney's usual breakfast on the counter— a chocolate protein drink, a granola bar, and a piece of fruit—this time, a plum. Raney chugged the drink and was starting on the granola bar when she looked out the kitchen window and saw a dark blue pickup parked by the barn.

Shit.

Tossing the half-eaten granola bar onto the counter beside the plum, she slammed out the back door and headed to the barn.

Raney felt bad about what Dalton Cardwell had been through—even if he deserved it—and wasn't looking forward to turning him out. But Mama had no right to hire him in the first place. She'd tell him sorry, they weren't hiring right now, and send him on his way. Hopefully he'd be long gone before Mama woke up. Cowardly, maybe. But confrontations with Mama always ended badly for Raney.

Following the sound of a horse whinnying, Raney tracked Dalton Cardwell and Alejandro to the arena behind the barn. They were leaning against the railing, watching Rosco trot around, snorting and whinnying at the other horses in nearby paddocks. Dalton had his head bent to hear what Alejandro was saying. Raney didn't remember him being so tall. Or so well built. He made Alejandro, who was a foot shorter, look like a kid beside him. She'd seen Dalton ride in a couple of cutting shows after he got out of the army. He'd filled out by then, but was now even bigger. Broader. A man now. Bold and assured. Mama was right: he was definitely not a beanpole. And no longer awkwardly shy, judging by the way he turned to watch her approach. Probably horny after almost two years in prison, Raney thought, growing uncomfortable with the way he continued to stare at her.

Dream on, cowboy.

"Good morning," she said as she stopped beside them. She gave Dalton a reserved smile. "We never officially met, but I'm—"

"Raney Whitcomb," he cut in. "I remember. Nice to meet you finally." He flashed a broad smile that crinkled the corners of his eyes.

Green eyes, with long, dark lashes. She'd never been close enough to him to notice that. Or his smile.

She forced her mind back on track. "I'm sorry you came all the way out here this morning, but I think there's been a mistake. We're not hiring right now."

His smile faded. "Your mother seemed pretty sure you were."

"She was wrong."

"I see." He turned to Alejandro. "Would now be a good time to tell her that her shirt is on inside out?"

Raney looked down and was shocked to see he was right. *Idiot.*

Alejandro's black brows came down in a hard, straight line.

"How do you suppose she got it on?" Dalton continued, ignoring Raney as if she weren't standing two feet away, listening to every word. "Seems she'd know it was inside out when she tried to button it. Unless it was still buttoned when she slipped it over her head. Maybe she was in such a hurry, she grabbed whatever was on hand so she could rush out here and send me packing before her mother found out."

Finally, he turned to Raney. Not smiling now. Green eyes no longer crinkling at the corners. Angular jaw so tight a muscle bunched in his cheek. "Is that how it happened, Raney? You wanted me gone before your friends found out you had an ex-con working for you?"

"It's not like that—"

"Cuidadoso, gringo," Alejandro warned Dalton. *"Ella es tu jefe."*

"Actually, Alejandro, she's not my boss," Cardwell said in a friendly tone, eyes still locked on Raney. "Unless she's the owner of this outfit, of course. Are you the owner of Whitcomb Four Star?" he asked her in a calm, low voice.

"I run it," she hedged, not wanting to get into all the details of the family trust.

"And doing a damn fine job of it, from what I can see. But it was the owner—your mother, I'm guessing—who hired me. She even had me sign a six-month contract to seal the deal. So, until she tells me otherwise, I'm staying. It would be rude to do otherwise, don't you think?" That smile again.

It made Raney so mad she didn't know who she wanted to kick first—this hulking asshat or her mother. Instead, she turned and stomped back to the house.

"What's her problem?" Dalton watched her go, regret already eroding his anger. It was a stupid move, antagonizing a woman he'd have to work with. But he was tired of the sidewise looks and muttered comments and wasn't about to take it from a woman who'd never ever bothered to speak to him before.

"*Culero,*" Alejandro muttered.

"I don't think she's an asshole," Dalton argued. "Just too accustomed to getting her own way."

"I was calling you the asshole, *pendejo.*"

"*Basta ya, amigo.* Enough of that, friend." Dalton grinned and clapped him on the back. "What say we put a bale of hay and some cows in the middle of the arena and see what the colt can do."

While Alejandro dragged the hay bale into the center of the arena, Dalton put Rosco through an extended warm-up. When he felt the colt was ready, he signaled Alejandro to let in the cows.

They immediately went for the hay and Rosco immediately went for the cows.

Dalton backed him off and sent the colt around several more times until he calmed down, then reined him toward a cow on the outside. Using more lower-leg pressure than rein, he had Rosco peel the cow off from the others and bring her a few yards away. Then to signal the end of the exercise, Dalton put his right hand on the colt's neck and reined him off into another lap while the young heifer returned to the hay. He did that several times, peeling off cows from both directions, being careful to keep the training session short—maybe thirty minutes—because he wanted to end it with Rosco wanting more, rather than feeling overwhelmed.

Finally, Dalton dismounted, scratched Rosco behind his ears, massaged the crest of his neck, gave him a pat, and turned him over to Chuey, the Hispanic worker waiting to take the colt back to his stall. Then Dalton walked over to where Alejandro stood watching, his arms resting along the top of the fence.

"How'd I do?" he asked, knowing Alejandro had stayed to watch so he could report Dalton's every move to his employer. Or employers. Despite what he'd said to Raney, Dalton still wasn't sure whom he answered to. Or for how long.

"Better than most, gringo. But not as good as me." Alejandro's grudging smile told Dalton he had passed another test.

"I won't argue that," Dalton said. "He's a fine colt. Smart. But easily bored. We should keep his training sessions short and varied."

If Alejandro objected to his use of "we" he didn't show it. Which Dalton took as a good sign. He didn't want to have to fight both Alejandro and Raney. He just wanted to do his job and bring out the best in a promising young horse.

"Who was his other trainer?" Dalton asked as they walked over to where another colt was saddled and waiting for his workout.

"Amala," Alejandro said. "Press Amala. He was once a big-time roper."

"I remember the name. Heard he has a bad hip from his roping and rodeoing days. Never saw him ride, but everyone says he has a hell of a touch with horses."

"He does." Alejandro looked over at him. "As do you."

Dalton was too pleased to respond.

They worked together through the morning, and Dalton's respect for Alejandro grew when he saw how well the horses responded to his gentle handling. He was able to point out the weaknesses and strengths of each animal and showed Dalton different approaches to problem areas. By noon, Alejandro had taught him more in just a few hours than Dalton had learned in months with Roy Kilmer.

At the sound of the lunch gong, Alejandro led Dalton to the ranch building beside the hay barn. It was two stories and bigger than Dalton had first thought. The ground floor held the ranch offices and breeding facilities for the bulls in the paddocks out back. The second floor housed the unmarried ranch hands, except for Foreman Hicks, who had his own little house near the main gate. In the upstairs was a kitchen with a long table down the middle, a bathroom with two stalls and showers, and a large dormitory room across the back, divided into four cubicles, each with a small window, bed, and locker. Nothing fancy, but nice enough. Definitely better than a prison cell or a dirt hut in Iraq.

Other than Alejandro, who slept somewhere else, there were two other men living in the bunkhouse who worked the cattle and helped where needed. Chuey and Harvey, an old, bald white guy sporting a bushy white mustache and a nose sharp enough to split kindling. The two married workers lived with their families in a duplex past the ranch buildings that was surrounded by a white-fenced yard full of toys and kids. A close-knit group, very friendly and hard-working.

Alejandro showed Dalton to the end cubicle in the dormitory, told him he could bunk there, then took him back to the kitchen, where they joined Chuey and Harvey, who were putting together sandwiches.

Breakfast was buffet-style, prepared by the two wives of

the married workers. *Las esposas*, Alejandro called them, a mark of respect, and to make it clear they were married and off-limits. Lunch was make-it-yourself from sandwich fixings or whatever was cooking on the back burner. Supper was sit-down at the kitchen table.

He and Alejandro ate their sandwiches in silence, then went back to the round pen and worked more colts.

It was a long but good day. Dalton was encouraged by the quality of the horses he'd be handling and the men he'd be working with. Being outside and doing something constructive was a pleasant change, and as the day wore on, some of the wary restlessness he'd battled in prison began to fade. By the time the supper bell sounded he was ravenous.

The kitchen table was already crowded when Dalton and Alejandro arrived, but two more chairs were scrounged and space was made. The food was tasty and plentiful, and Dalton had enough Spanish to get the gist of the conversation going on around him.

Mostly, it was speculation about him, his prison record, his spotty experience, and why he wasn't eating at the main house like most trainers did. Dalton didn't participate, but finished as fast as he could, thanked the cooks, and escaped to get his old army duffel from the truck.

A familiar sense of alienation crept over him. After living with dozens of soldiers in a hostile foreign country, and later, with over a thousand inmates behind windowless walls, and now in a houseful of people who spoke a different language—Harvey never spoke at all, so Dalton didn't know what language he spoke—he should have become accustomed to feeling isolated. Yet it still bothered him. He wondered if it would always be like that, or if someday he might be able to carve out a place for himself and feel that sense of belonging again.

"Evening," a voice called.

Dalton turned and saw Hicks walking toward him. He couldn't tell if the foreman was bringing bad news or not. The guy never seemed to change expression.

"Mrs. Coralee was wondering why you didn't come down to the house for supper."

"Didn't know I was supposed to."

"Trainers and foremen eat supper at the main house. Alejandro knows that. Probably funning you. Food's pretty much the same as what you'd get at the bunkhouse since the cooks are the same, but it makes the owners feel democratic to have a few workers at their table."

"I doubt her daughter wants me there."

That almost-smile. "Sounds like you met her already. Kind of protective about her horses, Raney is. Wants things done her way. Bear with her. If you're good for the ranch, she'll put up with you. Even if she hates you."

"Sounds fun," Dalton said. And in an odd way, it did.

"Why did you have to put him on contract?" Raney demanded the following afternoon—the first time she'd seen Mama since talking to Dalton Cardwell the previous day.

After leaving him and Alejandro by the paddocks, she had spent most of the rest of Friday in Gunther with their accountant and lawyer, finalizing the changes necessary now that she had officially taken over management of the ranch. She'd gotten home late to a cold supper, and this morning had overslept again. By the time she got up, her mother had already left for her Saturday beauty parlor and shopping trip. Mama could be slippery as an eel when she put her mind to it.

But now, Raney had finally cornered her at her dressing table in between wardrobe changes, and she was determined to get some answers before her mother could escape again to some meeting, or church do, or another hot evening with the menopause set. "Not even Hicks has a contract."

"Nor does Alejandro," Mama argued. "They're family. And I didn't have to, I chose to. I thought we were through arguing about this, Raney. Do you like the way Marlene feathered my bangs? They seem a bit long to me."

"Plus, you're giving him room and board? Is that really necessary?"

Mama put down her brush and swiveled on the stool to frown at Raney. "Of course it's necessary. Trainers are valued employees. The top ones get houses, trucks, a hefty salary plus expenses, and a cut of the winnings. Anyway, the Cardwells are moving to Plainview. Dalton has no place to stay."

Great. Another stray. "But he's not a top trainer," Raney pointed out. "He's won nothing. He hasn't even trained a single horse for us."

"But he will. I'm certain of it. And, Raney . . ." Her mother gave her a stern look. "I expect him to be at the supper table tonight. You, too. And from now on, he will take his evening meals and Sunday lunch here at the house, the same as Glenn and Alejandro. That's the way it's done at the top ranches and Whitcomb Four Star is no exception." She let that sink in for a moment, then in a gentler tone said, "Now, let me ask you a question. What is it about Dalton Cardwell that has you so upset? Has he done or said something I should be made aware of?"

"Other than causing another person's death?" Raney let out a deep breath and, along with it, most of her anger. She knew she was being hardheaded. But the guy made her uneasy. She wasn't sure why, but something about him put her on edge. "No," she finally answered, plopping down on the end of her mother's bed. "I'd never even spoken to him before yesterday."

"Then why are you so opposed to him? It's not like you

to be intolerant. In fact, you're more often too easy on people and only see the good."

Mama didn't say it, but they both knew she was referring to her botched engagement.

Raney crossed her arms and looked away. "And that's bad?"

"Of course not. In fact, it's one of the things I most admire about you. Which is why I'm so confused by this aversion to Dalton."

"It's not exactly an aversion. But the fact that he's spent time in jail concerns me. Prison hardens people. He might have picked up bad habits there that we don't know about."

"Good point." Mama rose and went into her closet. Raney heard her flipping through the hangers. A moment later, she came back out in a lightweight sack-looking thing that should have looked frumpy, but only enhanced her mother's slim, yet curvy figure.

"I'll admit I have concerns, too," Mama said, turning to check the fall of the dress in the full-length mirror on the inside of the closet door. "There's something about that accident that never seemed right. I think there's more to it than what we've been told."

"Like what?"

After fluffing her hair back into shape, her mother turned and faced Raney. "Jim Bob had been stopped more than once for drunkenness and speeding. Yet the commissioner always got him off, when what he should have done was take away that fancy sports car and put the boy in rehab. But I hear the commissioner's a drinker, too, so go figure." Mama shook her head at the utter idiocy of it. "I'm sure he's regretting that now. Which might be why he pushed so hard to have Dalton receive the maximum sentence. Guilt. Pure and simple."

Despite putting away her fair share of wine on occasion, Mama had a low tolerance for drunkenness. Daddy was the hard-liquor drinker. "Cowboys don't squat to pee and they don't drink wine," he'd said many a time. After he died, Mama had cleared out the liquor cabinet. But as a concession to cowboys and non-wine drinkers, she always kept a stock of Lone Star longnecks in a cabinet refrigerator on the veranda. She thought since neither beer nor wine had enough alcohol to be dangerous, there would be fewer tendencies to overimbibe.

Poor Mama. If she only knew.

"And from what I hear," her mother continued, voice rising in agitation, "it was just a matter of time before Jim Bob killed himself or someone else. Everybody says so. If Dalton hadn't foolishly waived a trial, he'd never have gone to prison."

"So why did he confess? Take a deal rather than go to trial."

Mama brushed that off, still a little worked up from her rant. "I asked him that. He said he'd pulled onto the road without looking, so it was his fault."

"Technically, I suppose that's true."

"I don't think so. I think there's more to it. In fact . . ." Her mother pursed her lips and narrowed her eyes in that speculative way that always put Raney on guard. "I think I'll ask Clovis about it at the good-bye dinner the auxiliary is hosting for her this evening. Maybe she can explain it."

Alarmed, Raney rose and put a hand on her mother's shoulder. "Mama, don't. The poor woman's been through enough. She's probably leaving town just to get away from all the talk." Mama could stir up trouble faster than a teased snake.

"Well . . ."

"It's done. Over. Let's just let it go."

"Really?" Mama gave her a bright smile. The kind of *gotcha* smile that told Raney she'd just fallen into her web. Again. "I totally agree with you, darling. Let's drop it and move on. For everybody's sakes."

Outmaneuvered again. Taking her hand from her mother's shoulder, she crossed toward the door. "You played me."

"Don't be silly." Picking up her purse, Mama smoothed her hair one more time, then followed Raney into the hall. "Remind Maria that I won't be here for supper tonight, but Dalton and Hicks and Alejandro will, so she'll still need three places, plus yours. Have fun and I'll see you later."

A waggle of her freshly manicured fingers and she was gone. Mother of the year. Champion of ex-convicts. Master manipulator.

Raney only wished she could be more like her.

CHAPTER 5

Raney took extra care with her appearance that evening—curling iron, makeup, blouse instead of a plaid shirt, even perfume—but she kept it casual with boots and jeans. Granted, the boots were custom handmade by R.L. Boyce and the jeans cost over a hundred on sale, but she felt like dressing up. Especially after some of the "lumberjack" comments her sisters had made at their little family reunion last month, and yesterday, when she'd dashed out of the house with her shirt on inside out. It was a matter of pride. Nothing more. She wasn't a slob.

Like a herd seeking safety in numbers, the men arrived at the kitchen door in a group. "Welcome," she said, motioning them inside. Since the bugs weren't busy yet, and because Mama wasn't there to overrule her, Raney had made the daring decision to have dinner on the veranda—which was no more than a covered porch, but sounded more elegant when called a veranda. Mama's decision, of course.

"I thought we could eat on the veranda."

Smiles of relief all around.

Several months ago, Mama had decided they would take Saturday dinner and Sunday luncheon in the dining room, complete with linen tablecloth, silver, bone china, and crystal goblets. Probably influenced by *Downton Abbey*, her favorite TV show of all time. Raney thought it was a bit pretentious and doubtless uncomfortable for the ranch hands who were obligated to join them. She guessed it was Mama's way of showing that the Whitcombs weren't complete rednecks, despite the boots and jeans and living on a ranch. Raney didn't care one way or the other. But then, she hadn't grown up on a hardscrabble farm like Mama had.

"I have wine," she told the men as they filed past. "Or if you prefer, there's beer in the reefer out back. Alejandro, show Dalton where."

Being manly cowboys, they preferred beer.

Raney saw that Alejandro had duded himself out in a starched shirt, pressed jeans, and a flashy silver belt buckle with mother-of-pearl inlays—a gift from the Whitcomb girls last Christmas. He obviously had plans for later. Hicks looked the same as he usually did—plaid shirt, jeans, boots.

But Dalton Cardwell had cleaned up, too. Both the shirt and jeans were new. She could tell because the shirt manufacturer's fold creases were still noticeable, and the jeans were stiff as cardboard. His boots were worn but free of dust, he'd recently shaved, and his hair was still wet from his shower. He had a lot of hair. And the way it kept sliding down his forehead might have made him look boyish if his hulking form hadn't dwarfed the doorway. Not that she noticed.

She was hopeful the meal would go well until she realized that without Mama there to keep the conversation going, there would be no conversation. Hicks rarely spoke anyway, so that was no loss. Alejandro had his mind elsewhere, and Dalton just kept his head down and ate as much as he could, as quickly as he could.

And she'd dressed up for this? She looked from one to the other and shook her head. It was like they were in a race to see who could eat the fastest and last the longest without speaking, and each was determined to win. A collection of mutes.

It was the longest and quietest meal she had ever suffered through.

Sunday morning. The ranch workers had the day off, the good churchgoers were off warming their pews, and the horses had eaten. Dalton was turning them out into the pasture and thinking about how pretty Raney had looked the previous night, when he was startled by a sudden eruption of gunfire.

For an instant, his mind flashed back to the desert. His heart lurched. Panic stole his breath. Then it penetrated his brain that he was in Texas, not Iraq, and the sound he'd heard wasn't the quick staccato burst of a rifle on full-auto, but the spaced-out report of a semiautomatic handgun. Nearby. In the brush along the creek, not far from the paddock fence line.

Furious that someone would shoot so close to the house and barn, he shoved his way through the spooked horses and vaulted the fence. Taking a roundabout route so he could come through trees that would offer cover, he sprinted toward the creek.

As he ran, he counted fifteen shots. Not the boom of a .45. More like the pop of a lighter round, like a .38 or a 9mm. A pause to reload, then more firing. He counted as he moved closer, saw a clearing through the trees ahead, and waited. At the sound of the fifteenth shot, he stepped out of the brush.

A woman stood less than twenty feet away, her back to him. A pistol was holstered at her hip and she was thumbing rounds into a magazine. She wore yellow-tinted safety glasses and noise-blocking headphones over a baseball cap.

He recognized the cap and the blond-streaked ponytail poking through the hole in the back of it.

Raney.

"Hey!" he shouted, and charged toward her.

She whirled, ponytail flying, her hand dropping to the gun. When she saw who it was, she pulled off the glasses and shoved the headphones back on her head. "What the hell are you doing?"

"I'm asking you the same thing." He waved a hand in the direction of the pasture. "You do know there are horses over there, don't you?"

"Of course I do. That's why I'm out here." She dropped the headphones and shooting glasses into an army surplus ammo can by her feet, then pulled out the gun and slapped in the magazine.

Dalton watched her, his nerves settling now that he knew there was no immediate danger. But he still didn't know why she would pull such a stupid stunt.

She slid the loaded gun—maybe a Glock 19, or HK VP9—back into the holster. "Why are you out here?" she asked.

"Curiosity. Now that I know it was you shooting, do you mind telling me why? It was spooking the horses."

"That was the point." Seeing his confusion, she laughed.

It rocked him back. She hadn't laughed often, especially around him, but it was worth the wait. Even with no makeup, a sunburned nose, and her beautiful hair hidden by a dusty ball cap, she was a knockout when she smiled.

"Not all our horses will make it into the show ring," she explained. "Most will end up as working horses. And working horses on a Texas ranch need to get accustomed to shooting."

Dalton knew that and felt foolish that he'd been so rattled by the gunfire he hadn't figured it out sooner. They'd put their own horses through a similar process. Hoping to cover his lapse, he shifted subjects. "That a Glock 19?" He motioned to the pistol on her hip.

"It is." She pulled it from the holster and held it out, butt first. "Want to try it?"

Dalton shook his head. "I fired all the guns I'll ever want to in Iraq."

With a shrug, she reholstered the pistol. Her gaze flicked over him. "I guess if you're built the way you are, you don't need a gun for protection."

"Do you?" It bothered him to think that she might. Just because he was done with guns, didn't mean he was against women arming themselves for protection. Or anyone else, for that matter. As long as they got training to go with it.

"Not yet." She bent down, closed the hinged lid on the ammo can, secured the latch, then straightened, the metal handle in her hand. "But if the occasion arises, I'll be ready."

Dalton didn't doubt it.

She started toward the creek.

He walked beside her, matching his pace to hers. It wasn't a hardship. Even though she was half a foot shorter than he was, she had long legs and stepped out with authority. So much authority, in fact, he knew better than to offer to carry the ammo can. It was never wise for a man to underestimate the sensitivities of an armed woman.

"Do you plan on working Rosco today?" she asked.

"I do." Dalton grinned down at her. "He's a hell of a horse. We bring him along right and keep him healthy, he might earn you a lot of money someday."

She smiled back, almost knocking him off his stride. "That's the plan."

And right then Dalton realized it was going to be a lot harder than he'd thought, working around this woman. He'd have to keep his distance or he'd forget why he was here.

* * *

They crossed the creek and were headed to the barn when Raney broached the idea of him being sent to work with Prescott Amala for a week or so.

"The old guy who started Rosco?" Dalton asked.

She nodded. "Mama thinks Press might bring you along faster as a trainer."

"Faster than what?"

"Than you muddling through on your own."

"You trying to get rid of me again?"

She looked up at him. Saw the laughter in his green eyes and had to smile. "Could I?"

"Not without your mama's say-so."

Still smiling, she looked away, feeling nervous but not sure why. "Then no, I'm not trying to get rid of you. Mama's convinced you're just what I need."

"Really?"

"As a trainer."

"Oh. As a trainer."

He was laughing at her again. It was there in his voice.

She couldn't blame him. It seemed every time she was around him, she acted like a complete idiot. Determined to avoid making a bigger fool of herself, she decided to keep her head down and speak only when she had to.

"I never met Press," he said. "Never saw him ride, either. But I heard he was a hell of a roper in his day. How old is he now? Seventy?"

"At least. But he's still got the know-how. He could teach you a lot, if you were willing."

"I'm sure he could. And I'd jump at the chance to learn from him if I wasn't already employed here."

"You'd still be working for Four Star. We'd send you to him for a few training sessions, is all. We'd pay for it, too, since the ranch would benefit." When he didn't answer right away, she shot him a smirk. "Do I have to seal the deal with another contract?" she asked, mimicking his words from the other day.

Abruptly he stopped and stuck out his hand. It was huge. Could probably span a dinner plate. "With you, Raney, a handshake is enough."

Not sure if he was joking, she hesitated before putting her hand in his. It felt tiny in his broad, callused grip. A quick squeeze then she let go. "It better be," she said, fighting a smile. "'Cause that's all you're going to get, cowboy."

"Ouch," he said, and laughed out loud.

It changed things—the teasing, the laughter, the touch of his hand. Now she was more aware of him than ever. And trusted him even less.

When they reached the barn, Raney saw cars coming down the drive. Sunday services were over. She watched her mother's Ford Expedition turn into the parking area behind the house, then an older-model SUV pull in beside it. Three people got out of the second car. A big guy and two smaller people, one wearing a dress.

Raney sighed. "Mama's back and she brought company. You know what that means." Dalton didn't respond, his attention focused on the people talking with her mother. "Sunday dinner with all the fixings. Brace yourself. And dress up." With a backward wave, she headed toward the house and left him still staring at the cars.

"Dress up?" he called after her. "What does that mean?"

Without slowing, she called over her shoulder, "White shirt, tucked in. Tie, clean jeans, and boots. No hat. If you don't have a tie, Alejandro can loan you a bolo. And don't be late." She never glanced back to check, but the itch between her shoulder blades told her he watched her the whole way.

She took a quick shower to get rid of the dust and smell of spent powder, then hunted for a dress that would be comfortable, flattering, and meet her mother's exacting, if illogical, requirements.

As part of her edict that they eat in the dining room, Mama had decreed that since her daughters rarely joined her for church services anymore, they should honor the Sabbath by wearing a proper dress at Sunday luncheon. No matter that her daughters were all grown women, fully capable of picking out their own clothes. Even Joss, the unmarried, pregnant one, had been dressing herself—and apparently, undressing herself—for years. But who dared argue with Mama, especially on a Sunday? Her house, her rules.

Raney finally settled on a simple blue, knee-length dress with a flared hem and draped neckline, one she'd been told was the exact color of her blue eyes. She put her hair up in a loose knot, smeared on enough makeup to tame the freckles and sunburn, added gloss, mascara, and a dab of perfume, and that was that.

The three guests were Dalton Caldwell's parents and his younger brother, Timmy, who had a learning disability. Since Mama rotated between churches to maintain her social contacts, Raney had met the elder Cardwells years ago, although she hadn't spoken to them often. They were at least a decade older than Mama, and looked it. Dalton's arrest and the last two years with him gone had probably been hard on them, and now with the move, they looked worn to a nub. Raney felt bad for them. Her family had weathered rough patches, too, but there were enough of them to hold each other up when times were tough.

Timmy was the same as always, only bigger. A big, friendly teddy bear. He was no longer a harmless little kid, but a fully grown, very strong young man. Mama had told her that part of the reason for the Cardwells' move to Plainview was to find a group home for Timmy, which sounded like a good idea. For Timmy and his parents.

Right on time, the three guys showed up. "Welcome," Raney said, waving them inside. "The others are in the den."

Alejandro looked like he'd had a rough night. Hicks looked

the same, except for trading in the plaid for a white shirt with snap pockets and adding a slightly frayed string tie. Dalton wore a clean, but faded, light beige shirt and one of Alejandro's bolo ties. She recognized the silver arrowhead tips and the garish four-inch-wide silver-and-turquoise sliding clasp. Another Christmas gift. He was partial to silver.

"I hope this is fancy enough," he murmured to her as he stepped inside. "It's as close as I have to a white shirt. I'll get a proper one next time I go to town." He looked down at the bolo tie. "And a better tie."

"You don't like that one?" Raney fought a smile as she walked with him to the den. "I was thinking to have Alejandro loan you his matching belt buckle, too."

He started to say something, but was interrupted by Timmy shouting, "Dalton! You came back!"

Seeing his brother charging toward him across the crowded den seemed to fluster Dalton, but he recovered quickly, accepting Timmy's boisterous bear hug with a tolerant smile. "Hey, buddy, what you been up to?"

As the other people in the room went back to chatting, Raney watched the brothers, impressed by Dalton's patience and his obvious love for Timmy. There was an element of protectiveness there, too. She recognized it, had felt it directed at her earlier, when he'd asked why she needed a gun. Maybe because of his size and military training, Dalton felt he had to watch out for everybody. Or maybe it was that protective instinct that sent him into the army in the first place. A complicated guy, Dalton Cardwell. And not nearly the hard-ass she'd thought him to be.

Timmy pulled out of the hug with a hurt look. "Why did you leave, Dalton? You said you would work with me."

"I know I did, buddy. I'm sorry. But I had to come here to work instead."

"Here?" Timmy looked around the opulent room, his eyes round with wonder. "You work here?"

"In the barn out back. I'm training horses."

"Horses." Timmy's face fell again. "Our horses went away. Dad says they won't ever come back."

Raney could see that Timmy was getting worked up, but his mother arrived in time to head him off. "Timmy, did you see the buffalo head mounted in the other room? Come, I'll show you."

"Yeah. Okay. Just the head? Where did the rest of it go?"

With an apologetic smile to Raney, Mrs. Cardwell led Timmy to Daddy's office—the one room in the house Mama hadn't redecorated at least twice.

Beside her, Dalton let out a deep breath and rubbed a hand over the back of his neck. "This might not be such a good idea."

"Bringing Timmy? He'll be fine."

"He might break something."

"It's just stuff, Dalton. Around here, stuff is like Doritos. We always get more."

As it happened, Timmy didn't break anything. In her usual efficient way, Mama replaced his china plate and crystal goblet with a plastic Superman set she kept on hand for visiting ranch children.

His parents were relieved. Timmy was thrilled and mentioned several times—five or six, at least—that Superman was his favorite. Raney was filled with pride, and mentally added Hostess Extraordinaire to Mama's list of remarkable traits.

This time, there was actual conversation as they ate. Mostly about weather, cattle prices, and how spring practice was going for the various college football teams, mostly Texas Tech. Hicks was even moved to nod once in answer to a direct question from Mr. Cardwell.

When the meal ended, since the day was mild and sunny, Mama sent an invitation to the workers' quarters inviting everyone, especially the children, for ice cream and cookies and games on the veranda and back lawn. She loved children, and her rowdy, impromptu gatherings were some of Raney's fondest childhood memories. As soon as Mama brought out her gigantic box of toys, the children crowded around, the younger ones pulling out trucks and dolls, the older ones challenging their parents to a soccer match. Timmy thought it was great fun and one time even connected with the ball, which took them fifteen minutes to track down by the creek.

By late afternoon, Hicks had awakened from his nap in one of the patio chairs and had made his escape with Alejandro. The parents began rounding up their kids and putting toys back in the box, while the elder Cardwells said their good-byes and herded Timmy toward their car with the new kitty Mama had insisted he take. One down, five to go.

Only Dalton stayed behind.

Raney offered him another beer. His second. She'd counted. Mama often warned her girls, *"You watch how a man drinks and you'll see the future ahead."* It looked like Dalton Cardwell wasn't destined to be a big drinker.

He accepted the beer, knocked back half of it in a single breath, then sighed and plopped down into the chair Hicks had kept warm for him. "That went better than I expected."

"It was fun." Raney topped off her wineglass and took the chair across from him. "Mama's gatherings always are."

"She's a hell of a lady."

"That she is. But please don't tell her. It'll only egg her on." She studied him as she sipped from her glass. "What had you worried? Timmy?"

When he didn't answer, she went on. "He's a sweet guy. And was very gentle with the children. They loved having him play with them."

"Kids instinctively know. They don't judge." He took another swig, then idly scraped at the label with his thumbnail. "But he's getting too big to play with little kids. He could hurt one and never know. It's best that he goes to the group home in Plainview and learns how to fit in with other people like him. People with learning disabilities. He'd be better off there."

He didn't sound convinced. Raney wondered whom he was trying to persuade. Then a piece of the puzzle that was Dalton Cardwell fell into place. "You feel like you're letting him down, don't you? That you should do something— keep him close so you can watch out for him."

He looked over at her but didn't say anything.

His silence made her want to fill it. "You shouldn't. I felt that way when Daddy died." It surprised her to hear the words spoken aloud. She'd never admitted those feelings to anyone. But once started, she couldn't seem to stop.

"I was in the truck when he had his heart attack. We were taking hay to the cattle in Pasture Three. I don't know what we were talking about. Nothing important. Just talking. Then, suddenly, he yanked the wheel to the side. I thought maybe an animal had jumped in front of us. Or a tire blew. I remember slamming into the door and the truck careening off the road and into the fence." She looked down at her wineglass. Deep red liquid. The color of blood where it met the sides.

"For a moment, the truck bucked against the barbed wire, the motor revving. The wheels dug up such a cloud of dust it filled the cab. Then the wire broke and we lurched forward and into a tree."

Hardly aware she was doing it, she touched the faint ridge of a scar hidden in the hair by her temple. "I hit my head against the window post. Next thing I knew, the airbag was hanging out of the dash and smeared with blood, and Daddy was hunched over, grabbing at his chest and making terrible groaning, gasping noises. Like a cow having a calf, only worse."

The words came faster. Her voice started to wobble. "At first, I thought his airbag had hurt him. I yelled at him and shook his shoulder. Panicky. Crying. Desperate to make him stop making those awful noises. But he didn't.

"Until he did. And everything went quiet."

Dalton's silence weighted the air.

She struggled to take a deep breath. She wanted to cry but couldn't. Hadn't since that day.

And the words kept coming. "I always felt I should have done something. God knows I wanted to. But I didn't know what. It was so quiet and still. Not real. So, I just sat there, watching blood soak into my jeans and hoping it would all go away."

More silence.

Embarrassed to have blurted out such a thing, Raney gave a shaky laugh. "How's that for a mood killer?"

When Dalton still didn't respond, she looked over to see him staring at her, unmoving, the beer warming in his hand.

"I didn't mean to burden you with all that," she told him. "I just wanted you to know I understand why you might feel like you might be letting Timmy down."

He set the beer aside and moved over to hunker beside her chair. The look in his eyes was as full of pain as the memories clutching at her throat.

"I'm sorry you went through that, Raney." He cupped her cheek, his palm warm against her cold skin, his fingers so long they reached into her hair at her temple. "I would change it if I could." Leaning in, he put his lips against hers. Gently. Briefly. Without passion. Like Daddy would do every night before he said good night and turned off the light.

It nearly broke her.

Then he drew back and looked so deeply into her eyes she felt stripped bare. "But I'm glad you told me."

Then he rose and walked away.

CHAPTER 6

I'm in trouble now, Dalton thought, heels coming down hard on the packed-gravel drive as he walked toward the bunkhouse. It was probably written somewhere—in an FBI memo, or an OSHA manual, or a Supreme Court ruling—that it was against the law to kiss your boss. *Workplace harassment,* they'd call it. *Rampant sexism. Toxic masculinity.*

It hardly even qualified as a kiss. A quick, passionless press of his lips to hers. As a kid, he'd kissed his dog's head the same way. Nothing to it. Almost fatherly. Meaningless, as far as kisses go. He could definitely do better.

But he wouldn't.

Couldn't even try.

Because she was his boss, and he didn't want to be that guy.

He played it through his mind. Every word, every move, that sad, lost look in her eyes, the way her mouth trembled against his. A man and a woman and an expression of sympathy. He refused to consider it might have been more than that. Just an innocent kiss, that's all.

With a woman who happened to be his boss.

Shit.

There was no way around it. Despite the power games she and her mother played, Raney was the boss of Whitcomb Four Star. It was Raney's signature on the checks. Her voice issuing the orders. Her guidance the workers sought when they had a question or a problem. In only a few days, he had seen it happen again and again. No matter whose name was listed first on the deed, Raney ran the show.

And he wouldn't be that guy. The one who overstepped, opened her to speculation and innuendo, diminished her in the eyes of the men who worked for her. He'd suffered that same kind of scrutiny since the day of his arrest. And he wouldn't be the guy who brought it down on her.

Shit.

Doing an about-face, he walked back to the main house and knocked on the kitchen door. When Maria opened it, he said, "I need to see Mrs. Whitcomb as soon as she's available."

Raney was sitting at Daddy's desk, calculating the projected irrigation costs versus the hay yield in Pasture Two when Mama walked in with a bemused expression on her face.

"I just had the oddest conversation with Dalton Cardwell."

"About what?" Surely not what happened on the veranda an hour ago.

"About working with Press Amala. Did you talk to him about it?"

"I may have mentioned it. Is that a problem?" Raney bent over the ledger again. She didn't want to talk about

Dalton Cardwell. Or even think about him kissing her an hour ago. What was that about?

"Well, he's all for it." Her mother walked over to straighten a picture of her and Daddy with some long-dead senator. "He even gave me a half-dozen reasons why he thought it was a good idea."

"Isn't that what you wanted?"

"I suppose. But he was so pushy about it. He even insisted I call Press this evening to see if he could start right away." She brushed dust off a bookshelf, then turned and frowned at Raney. "Did something happen between you two?"

"Happen?" Raney put down her pen and sat back. With the shift of weight, the worn leather gave a soft exhalation that carried a faint scent of the cigars Daddy would smoke at his desk when Mama wasn't home. "Like what?"

"Like you trying to fire him again."

"Who told you about that?"

"Glenn. He heard it from Alejandro. I know you were opposed to—"

"No, I didn't try to fire him again," Raney cut in. Hadn't even thought about it.

"Then why is he so intent on leaving? He's only been here a few days."

Probably embarrassed to face her after that emotional scene on the porch. Raney was embarrassed, too, but she wasn't going to hide because of it. "Maybe one of his prison buddies is in town."

"It's the Sabbath," her mother scolded. "At least try to be charitable."

Raney flipped to another page in the ledger. She had no idea which one. "What'd you tell him?"

"That we'll set it up. He seemed quite eager to get going."

Eager, my ass. One little kiss and he cuts and runs as if he expected to feel the barrel of a shotgun jammed into his back. Like that would ever happen. A Whitcomb and an ex-con? Mama would have a conniption.

Besides, it wasn't that great of a kiss. Pleasant, maybe, but no heart-stopper. Certainly not something a girl would put in her diary. Which Raney wouldn't have even if she'd ever owned a diary, which she hadn't, not with three sisters nosing around and an overprotective mother lurking at her shoulder. Still, it was disappointing. She had actually started to like the guy despite all the baggage that came with him.

Her mother cruised the room, then stopped by the desk. "What do you think?"

"About what?"

"Haven't you been listening? About sending him to Press."

"Send him, if that's what you want." Raney picked up her pen. "I'll have Alejandro work Rosco."

"Still . . ." Her mother dragged out the word, a sure sign she had more to say.

Raney didn't bite.

That didn't stop Mama. "It does seem odd that he would be so anxious to leave. Especially after the way he kept looking at you at dinner."

And there it was. The bait had been flung. In silence, Raney watched it drop with a thud, then smiled up at her mother. "I wouldn't go down that trail if I were you. I suspect he's gay. Probably something he picked up in prison."

"Gay? Really?" Mama thought about it and shook her head. "I think you're wrong about that. He would be staring at Alejandro, rather than you, I'd think."

"Whatever. You calling Amala, or should I?"

"You do it. I'm going to bed."

Raney made the call. Press wasn't there. His stable hand told her he was over in Arkansas, visiting with his married daughter and wouldn't be back for a week. Raney asked him to have Press call when he got back and left her cell number. Then she went to bed, too. First thing tomorrow she'd give Dalton Cardwell the bad news that he wouldn't be able to avoid her for at least a week.

* * *

Another restless night and she was wide awake Monday morning in time to see dawn lay a bright orange line along the eastern horizon. Not wanting to show up early and have Dalton Cardwell think she was anxious to see him, she took her time showering and getting dressed. But when she was finished, she realized she'd overdone it, and Cardwell might think she'd fixed up just for him.

She checked the mirror and shook out her hair. She did look hot, even if she said so herself. Certainly better than how he usually saw her, except for last night at dinner. And after. When he kissed her. Unwilling to let all this hotness go to waste, she picked up her cell phone and called Bertie.

"Breakfast or lunch?" she asked when Bertie answered.

"Brunch. Mellie's Diner."

"Ten." Raney hung up, dabbed on a spot of perfume, and headed to the barn.

Dalton Cardwell was gone, left the previous night, Glenn told her.

"He left?" Raney was caught off guard by the strength of her reaction. First, disappointment. She was actually beginning to enjoy their little confrontations. Then on the heels of that realization, came irritation. At him, for being such a coward. And at herself, for getting so upset about it.

"Left for where?" she asked Glenn. "Why?"

"His folks called last night. Needed his help, he said."

Irritation faded. "Nothing bad, I hope."

Glenn shook his head. "Their rental truck came through sooner than they expected. Said his folks need him to load it and drive it to their new place in Plainview. Didn't say when he'd be back." The foreman scratched his bristly chin. "Probably not long, the way those rental places charge. Maybe Wednesday. Want me to have Alejandro work Rosco? Or do you want to do it?"

"I have to go to town." She told him Alejandro should

work the colt for no more than half an hour, then take Rosco out to check on the cattle in the east pasture. "Do the colt good to get out of the pen for a while."

Forty minutes later, Raney pulled up to the diner. Bertie was already there, sitting in a booth by the window, scrolling through her phone.

Roberta Barton had been Raney's best friend ever since their first 4-H meeting in the second grade. Through the years they'd done barrel racing together, flag parades, team roping, and spent the better part of their teenage years hanging around local horse shows and rodeos, dreaming of the day they'd be in the big arena.

Those dreams came to an abrupt end for Bertie in her senior year when her horse stumbled and threw her head-first into the arena wall. She recovered okay, although she never regained her fearless enthusiasm for riding. Her love of horses remained the same, though, so while Raney stepped into Daddy's role at the ranch, Bertie went off to Texas A&M to earn a veterinary degree. After graduating, she left Rough Creek to work at a big clinic outside of Fort Worth. Now Raney saw her only once or twice a year, whenever Bertie came to town to visit her parents. It was still fun. But different.

Raney studied her friend through the diner window. How many more times would they get together before they slowly drifted apart? It was already happening, Bertie heading in one direction, building a new life in Fort Worth, while Raney stayed planted in the same place she'd been her whole life.

Bertie had a guy now. Marriage would be next, then kids. A few high school reunions, and those chatty, once-a-year newsletters inside a Christmas card, then even those would eventually stop. It was inevitable. Raney had seen it happen to Mama and to a lesser degree to her sisters— except for Joss, who collected and discarded people like shoe store coupons.

She could already feel it happening to her and Bertie.

But not today. Resolved, Raney grabbed her purse, opened the truck door, and hopped out. Today, she would enjoy her friend while she could. And maybe a piece of Mellie's coconut cream pie.

They picked up where they'd left off a week ago, when Bertie had first come into town to help her mother after her hip replacement. Mom was doing well, Bertie loved her job and her new apartment, Fort Worth was amazing, the clinic was awesome, and Phil was the perfect guy.

Pretty much the same things she'd said last week.

Raney mostly just listened. Her life hadn't changed much since Bertie's visit six months ago. And the visit before that. Except that now Mama was having a menopausal crisis and was about to run off to parts unknown, and Joss was pregnant and fixing to move back in to make Raney's life miserable, and they were selling off most of their cattle so they could focus on breeding championship quarter horses, and—oh, yeah, and they had an ex-con working for them who'd accidentally killed a guy. Nothing Raney really wanted to talk about, so she just sat there and nodded and smiled. Which was fine with her.

Until her cell phone chimed.

Unknown caller, the screen read. She was about to press DECLINE when she saw it was a local number. Probably spam. But maybe not. She accepted and immediately said, "If this is a solicitation—"

"Don't hang up, Raney. It's me." Dalton Cardwell.

Surprised, it took her a moment to respond. "How'd you get my cell number?" Not her friendliest greeting.

"Hicks. I hope that's okay. I wanted to tell you I'd be gone for a couple of days to help my folks move."

"Glenn already told me. I'm surprised you didn't mention it last night."

"My folks didn't reach me until after ten. Figured it was too late to call."

"Oh, well . . . thanks for telling me." Twelve hours late.

There was a pause. Raney was about to end the call when he said, "I also wanted to talk to you about last night. About what happened on the porch."

"I already apologized for that." She was starting to lose patience.

"What?"

"I shouldn't have dumped all that stuff about my father on you, Dalton. It was inappropriate. Old history, anyway."

"No, that's not what I meant. I'm glad you told me."

"Glad? Why?"

"It shows trust. That you were comfortable enough with me to talk about it. But that's not what I was talking about."

"Then what?"

"I wanted to apologize for what I did."

Realizing where this was headed, Raney decided to exact a little payback. For what, she wasn't sure. "Refresh my memory. What did you do?"

"You're going to make me say it, aren't you?" She could picture him smiling as he said it. She heard it in his voice.

It made her smile, too. "Say what?"

This time he chuckled. Low and intimate and totally masculine. "Okay. I'll say it. I shouldn't have kissed you. It wasn't a good idea."

Raney waited a beat to keep the laughter out of her own voice. "You kissed me? When?"

They both laughed then, and she stopped being mad at him.

"Can't blame you for forgetting. It wasn't that great of a first kiss."

"First? That implies there'll be more. Didn't you just say it wasn't a good idea?"

"I did. But that doesn't mean there won't be a repeat."

"You're dreaming again, cowboy."

"Am I? Maybe. Gotta go. Got a hundred years of crap to unload. See you Wednesday."

Still smiling, Raney ended the call, then looked up to see Bertie gaping at her. "What?"

"Oh my God! Raney Whitcomb, you were flirting!"

"No, I wasn't." Raney took her time putting her phone away, hoping the heat in her face would fade.

"I've never seen you flirt!"

"Not so loud. And I've flirted plenty of times."

"When?"

"Oh, please."

"You called him Dalton. Who—" Bertie's hazel eyes went even wider. "It was Beanpole, wasn't it? Dalton whatshisname—Cardwell!"

Raney looked around, grateful the place was empty except for the waitress, who was frowning in their direction. Suzanne—Suze—Anderson, a girl she remembered from her teen years, but from a different school. "You're shouting again."

Bertie leaned forward and dropped her voice to a stage whisper. "Isn't he the one who had that wreck that killed—"

"Jim Bob Adkins. The commissioner's nephew. It was an accident." Raney was getting tired of talking about Jim Bob, his drinking problems, the wreck, whose fault it was. And Dalton Cardwell.

Bertie wasn't. "If it was an accident, why did they send him to jail?"

"Because he confessed and waived a trial. If he hadn't, he probably would have gotten off." Seeing Suze heading over to take their orders, Raney opened her menu. "You know what you want yet?"

They ordered their usual. Chicken salad, light on the mayo, avocado on the side, and iced tea. Raney thought the subject of Dalton Cardwell had been dropped, but as soon as Suze left, Bertie leaned forward again. "What about Karla?"

"Who?" The name sounded familiar, but Raney didn't know from where. Then she remembered the redhead she'd

seen with Dalton a couple of times before he went to Huntsville. "Karla Jenkins? What about her?"

"She and Cardwell were dating before . . ." Bertie glanced
over to see Suze eyeing them again. "You know."

"They're not now. She moved to Dallas. Or maybe Fort
Worth. I don't remember."

"I think they were pretty serious."

Raney was saved from responding when Suze came
back with their iced tea.

She thunked the glasses on the table, propped her fists
on her hips, and said, "Karla Jenkins moved to Fort Worth
last Christmas. After she wrote Dalton a Dear John letter
in prison. A pretty low-class thing to do, in my opinion."
She turned to Raney. "And you're right. Dalton should have
gotten off. Everybody knows Jim Bob was drunk and
speeding. But Dalton took responsibility because that's the
kind of guy he is. Anything else you want to know? No? All
right, then. Your orders will be up in a minute."

Raney and Bertie blinked after her as she stomped off to
the kitchen. But they got the message, and for the rest of the
meal they limited the conversation to Phil, Bertie, her job,
her mother's new hip, and Phil, Fort Worth's most amazing vet.

"You'd like him," Bertie said later after they'd left the
diner and were standing outside, going through the motions
of a protracted good-bye. "Maybe next time I come visit my
folks, I'll bring him."

"I hope so. I'd like to meet him." In truth, Raney didn't
care if she ever met Amazing Phil. He sounded pretty full
of himself. Or maybe she was just upset because he was one
of the main reasons she and Bertie were drifting apart.

As she watched Bertie drive away, a sense of loss stole
over Raney. She wondered why she couldn't be more social,
like Mama. Apparently, even an ex-con had more friends
than she did.

But it had always been that way.

As a little kid, she'd hated being dressed up and paraded around—Mama and Daddy's little darlings. So precious. So pretty. Even at an early age, the weight of her parents' expectations and all that attention from people who didn't even know her felt false. Consequently, she avoided it whenever she could. Which only generated another, more hurtful kind of attention. One messy or off day, and she might be whispered about for weeks. Eventually, she learned to go along to get along, but it still felt false.

She'd never wanted to be in the rodeo court, or wear a homecoming crown, or kick up her heels as a cheerleader. Yet she did it to avoid the whispers, and because that was what was expected of the Whitcomb girls, who were pretty and rich and so special they even had a ranch named after them.

Over time, she gained a lot of admirers, but few friends. And because she hung back whenever she could, she never learned how to be sociable. If it didn't involve horses or the ranch, Raney didn't have much to say.

Except to Dalton Cardwell, it seemed.

The ex-con.

CHAPTER 7

"Where have you been?" Mama asked when Raney came up the veranda steps after her brunch with Bertie.

"In town."

"But you're so dressed up."

"I'm not dressed up." Raney wondered again if she'd turned into a complete slob without even knowing it.

Mama gave an indulgent smile. "Whatever the reason, you look very nice."

She was sitting in one of the overstuffed chairs, nibbling on her usual tiny triangular-shaped cucumber sandwiches. Raney wondered if she was trying to make herself allergic so if she found herself stranded on some non-cucumber-producing island somewhere, she wouldn't feel so deprived. Mama didn't handle deprivation well. Hence the Jimmy Choo sandals and designer capris with Swarovski crystals on the pockets.

Her mother waved a hand toward the plate on the ottoman. "Join me?"

"I had an early lunch with Bertie."

"Oh, that's why you're so dressed up."

"Yeah, that's it. I was trying to impress Bertie."

"Don't be sarcastic, dear. It's unbecoming."

"Then quit making it so easy."

Raney plopped into the chair facing her mother and crossed her ankles atop the ottoman. Even though it was barely midday, the sun was already baking everything it touched. If it was this hot in early May, by summer they'd be cooked.

"How's her mother?" Mama asked.

"Well enough for Bertie to leave in a day or two."

"That's nice."

Obviously, Mama had something on her mind. All these bland pleasantries came at a cost. But Raney didn't pry, content to enjoy the silence while she could.

After her mother finished her tiny sandwich, she brushed the crumbs off her lap and said, "I heard from Josslyn this morning. She'll be here by the end of the week. Or next week, at the latest."

"To stay?" Raney tried to keep the panic from her voice. She and Joss were so different it was hard for them to live in close quarters without going at each other's throats. Raney considered Joss irresponsible and undisciplined. Joss thought Raney was a rule-bound stick-in-the-mud. Right brain versus left brain. Life of the party versus fringe dweller. And now they would be adding a newborn to the mix.

Instant chaos.

"She wants to get everything ready for the baby," her mother said.

"So soon?"

"She's due in just a few months," Mama reminded her.

Maybe Joss would be late. She was late for everything else, why not a baby, too? Three or four months until the baby, then at least two more months before Joss would cut and run. Six months total, with Mama there only between trips to referee or run interference. Raney wondered how she'd get through it.

"I thought we could turn the guest room into a nursery," Mama suggested.

"Downstairs? Will she want the baby that far away? Why not use Len's or KD's room?" Seemed impractical to make a permanent kid room when it was doubtful Joss would stay very long.

Mama shook her head. "It's superstitious, I know, but as long as your sisters' bedrooms stay the same, I'm convinced they'll come back. I want them to know they'll always have a place here at the house."

"I think they already know that."

"It's not the same, Raney. When you have children, you'll understand."

And there it was. Another gentle reminder that Raney was still the odd one out, the unnatural daughter who was unmarried, childless, and happy about it.

"I forgot to mention she just found out it's a girl. Isn't that wonderful?"

And the family curse continues.

Tuesday afternoon, Raney was in the round training pen with Rosco. She'd worked him on spin turns and roll backs, pivots and quick breaks, and keeping his head down. The colt was moving along really well, but Raney wasn't sure how much more she should ask of him, so she walked him a few laps to cool him down, then dismounted by the gate. She had just pulled off the saddle when she looked over and saw Dalton, elbows on the top fence rail, watching them.

Her concentration faltered. Rosco sensed it, whipped his head back, grabbed the saddle blanket with his teeth, and sailed it across the pen.

Dalton laughed. Rosco snorted.

Raney ignored them both. Not wanting the colt to think he could get away with that, she set down the saddle, led him over to the saddle blanket, picked it up, and put it on his back again. This time when he tried to whip his head around, she said, "Quit!" and elbowed him in the jaw. The second time, she punched him in the eye, not hard enough to cause damage but definitely enough to get his attention. He got the message. After putting the blanket on again with no incident, she decided to stop while she was ahead.

Calling to Chuey in the barn, she handed off Rosco then walked over to where Dalton still leaned against the fence. "Thought you weren't coming back until Wednesday," she said, taking off her gloves and stuffing them into her back pocket.

"Counting the hours, were you?"

"I'd say you're the anxious one, rushing back a half day early."

"You could be right."

Not sure what that meant, she switched subjects. "Your folks get moved in okay? Timmy likes his new place?"

Dalton nodded and held open the gate for her. "He's taken the change better than I expected. I'll admit, I'm relieved." He secured the gate, then fell in beside her as she walked toward the house. "When did you start working with Rosco?"

"When his new trainer ran off."

"Alejandro couldn't take over for me?"

"He had to pick up his kid. One of his ex-wives wants to go back to Honduras. He's trying to convince her to leave his twelve-year-old son here in Texas. Alejandro numero Uno, I think."

"Who would take care of him while Alejandro works or goes with me to shows?"

"There's plenty of folks around here to look out for him if needed. Our people are like family. We all watch out for each other. Especially the kids."

When he didn't respond, Raney looked over at him.

He had a nice profile. High forehead, straight nose—not too long, not too short, with only a slight lump where his helmet had come off during the game against Gunther High—the newspaper made a big deal of it—and a jaw that could chisel stone. Like now, as he stared into the distance, dark brows drawn low over his beautiful green eyes. She couldn't tell if he was squinting or fretting.

"I don't like you working Rosco," he finally said.

Fretting. "Why not?" She tried to keep her voice neutral. She didn't like being questioned about how she worked her own horses. He might be the trainer, but she was the owner.

"He can be pushy. Rowdy, even. Plus, he's a stud. They can be unpredictable on their best days."

Raney was about to tell him she knew all about handling horses and didn't need him telling her which ones she couldn't or shouldn't work, when he said, "I don't want you to get hurt, that's all."

"Thanks for the concern, but I can take care of myself. And my horses."

He looked down at her. Not angry. More like worried.

"I know what I'm doing," she assured him.

"That was obvious when you didn't let him fool around during a training session. But what if it had been your shoulder he'd grabbed?"

"What if it had been yours?" she challenged back.

"I would have put him on the ground. Can you do that?"

Raney didn't answer.

"He's headstrong, Raney. And playful. He could hurt you without intending to. I worry, is all."

She forced a laugh, not sure if she should be insulted or not. Did he really think her that incompetent? "Worried about Rosco, or me?"

"Rosco, of course. If he hurts you, your mother will sell him, and I'll be out of a job." His crooked smile belied his words.

"You keep second-guessing me, you'll be out of a job anyway."

He had no response to that.

They walked in silence, then she said, "I've already got an overprotective mother, Dalton. I don't need another."

He chuckled. That same low rumbling sound she'd heard on the phone. It sent a tingle into her chest. "I'm definitely not thinking of you like a mother would. But I don't have to be your mother to want you to be safe."

Raney kept walking, thoughts bouncing through her head. No one ever worried about her—except Mama—but that was her job. That Dalton was worrying made her wonder again if he was truly concerned about her, or afraid she'd mess up Rosco's training. If so, he had a point. The colt's antics today proved he wasn't taking her seriously.

"You may be right," she admitted.

"I am?"

"I know. I find it as hard to believe as you do." She softened the barbed words with a smile. "But Rosco does respond better to you than me. It would probably be best if I stayed out of his training."

"It wasn't the horse I was worried about, sweetheart."

Unable to ignore that, she stopped and looked up at him. "Sweetheart?"

"Too much? I never know."

"Are you putting a move on me, Dalton Cardwell?"

"I think so."

She had to laugh. "You're not sure?"

"It's been a long time. I'm out of practice."

"You said it wasn't a good idea."

"It's not."

"So why are you doing it?"

"I'm an optimist." He tipped his head toward the back of the house. "I think you're being summoned. She looks upset."

Raney looked over to see her mother waving from the veranda steps. Definitely upset.

Raney quickened her pace, Dalton right behind her. "What's wrong?" she called as they crossed the yard.

"It's Joss."

Raney almost missed a step. "Is she okay? Is the baby all right?"

"I think so. She didn't say."

"Then what did she say?" They were all on the veranda now, crowded in a tight knot, not sure where to go or what to do. "Mama, tell me what happened."

"They dumped her, that's what happened. The poor thing." Raising her hands in exasperation, Mama turned to Dalton. "I guess we shouldn't be surprised. Those musicians she runs with are no better than traveling carny folk, after all."

"Who?" Dalton asked.

"Dumped her why?" Raney almost shook her mother to keep her on track.

"Lord knows. It seems there was some hoopla over I don't know what, and they kicked her off Crystal's bus. Right there in Waco, of all places. Can you imagine doing that to a pregnant woman?"

"What were they doing in Waco?"

Mama waved a hand in dismissal of such a silly question. "They weren't in Waco. They were driving through it on their way to Dallas. There's a big music festival up by Arlington. Joss was supposed to be one of the backup singers for Crystal, but something happened, she didn't say what, and now she's been abandoned in some Walmart parking lot with no money or clothes and no way to charge her cell phone."

"She's naked?" Even Joss wouldn't run around naked in a parking lot.

"Of course not, Raney! Good Lord! But she left all her

clean clothes on the bus, and she never carries any cash. Does Walmart take debit cards?"

Raney put a hand over her racing heart and let out a deep breath. "Only about a thousand of them. And they have food and clothes and an entire baby section, plus they're open twenty-four hours."

"I don't know if she's ever been to Walmart. The nearest one to the ranch is two hours away, and she mostly shops online."

"I'm sure she has. Millions of people shop at Walmart every day and live to tell the tale. She'll be fine."

"You'd better hurry, then. Take my car. It rides easier than your truck and won't jostle the baby as much." Mama turned toward the hallway.

"What? Wait!" Raney made a grab for her arm. "You expect me to make a six-hundred-mile round-trip just to pick up Joss and bring her home? What's wrong with her own car?"

"It's still in Houston."

"A bus, then."

"Don't be silly."

Raney slumped onto the ottoman. Of course Joss wouldn't take a bus. That would probably entail a dozen stops, a bus change, and a layover in Dallas, likely turning a nine-hour round-trip into a twelve-hour one-way trip. Besides, Whitcombs didn't ride buses, unless, of course, they belonged to nearly semifamous country-western singers. There was no train service, and Rough Creek didn't have a long enough runway for any plane bigger than a puddle jumper, which don't fly at night anyway.

She was so screwed.

"I'll be glad to go get her, ma'am," a deep voice said.

Dalton! She'd forgotten he was there and was so relieved she almost raced into the kitchen to get the keys to Mama's Expedition. Then she realized that wouldn't work, either. She doubted Joss would accept a ride from an ex-con, especially one she probably didn't remember and if she did, definitely wouldn't recognize now that he'd gotten so . . . big. Assuming Mama would ask him to make the trip.

Which she did by pretending not to. "Oh, I couldn't ask you to do that, Dalton."

But it's okay to ask your daughter? What the hell?

"It's after three, ma'am," Dalton said over Raney's head like she wasn't there. "Even if she left now, Raney wouldn't get back before one in the morning. That's a long, hard drive at night. At least let me go with her to keep her awake."

Raney gaped from one to the other. Did he really think Mama would allow a man convicted of vehicular manslaughter to play chauffer to her daughters, one of whom was pregnant and a dimwit, besides?

Apparently so. Mama pretended to give it some thought, then looked to her daughter—the unnatural, expendable one who had bailed out Joss a thousand times over the years and seemed destined to do it again. "What do you think, Raney?"

Raney thought it was a colossally stupid idea. The guy already had one notch on his steering wheel. Was Mama willing to risk two more?

"I promise I'll be careful," Dalton said, before Raney could answer. "And if it would make you feel any better, ma'am, I won't do any driving. I'll just ride along to make sure they're safe."

He was good. No doubt about it. He fairly reeked of sincerity.

But then, he did have that protective streak. So maybe he truly was sincere. She almost laughed at the notion.

"Dalton, you're a godsend." Mama all but gave him a hug. "I'll admit, I would feel better if you were there to watch over them."

I own a Glock, Raney started to remind her. *I don't need to be watched over.*

But Mama was already in planning mode. "I'll go put

together sandwiches and snacks for the road. Raney, you have time for a quick shower. I don't want my car smelling like horses. Dalton, if you're not driving, there's a longneck in the cabinet over there. Thirty minutes, Raney," she called back as she left the veranda.

Raney waited until Mama disappeared into the kitchen, then glared at Dalton. "You must be the dumbest man in Texas."

His wide grin hinted at mischief and improper thoughts. "You think so?"

"If you're hoping to make a move—"

"Raney, Raney." He gave a weary sigh and shook his head. "You've got to quit slamming the door in my face before I even get a chance to knock. It's kind of discouraging."

"I'm bringing my Glock."

"Whatever makes you happy, sweetheart."

Forty-two minutes later, they pulled out of the main gate, Raney, with no makeup and wet hair, and Dalton, still nursing his lukewarm beer.

"I never thought you'd be the one driving on our first date," Dalton said as they settled into a mile-eating pace.

"This isn't a date."

"Road trip, then."

She glanced over. He had racked the seat back as far as it would go and still had to spread his knees to keep from jamming them against the glove box. Maybe she should have driven her crew cab truck. It was roomier up front, had four doors, and a full backseat. But if she had, Joss would have insisted on sitting shotgun because of her tendency to car sickness, and Dalton would have had even less leg room in back than he did now. Would have served him right.

"This isn't a date or a road trip," she said, slowing for the turn outside of Gunther. "It's a rescue mission. That's all."

When she stopped at the light, he opened his door, poured the rest of his warm beer on the ground, then closed the door.

Raney watched him look around for a place to put the empty bottle. "You'll have to eat that. Mama doesn't allow trash in her car."

He looked at her like he might consider it. Or worse, toss it out.

"There are eight cup holders in this car," she told him. "Pick one."

He chose the one on the door by his foot.

When the light changed, she turned right and headed south on US 83, which put the lowering sun at Dalton's window. Then in front. Then back in his window as the road followed a winding wagon trail laid down a hundred years ago. Instant oven. She turned up the AC, set the cruise for seven miles over the speed limit, and settled back for the ninety-five-mile run to Abilene. "Tell me about Texas Tech."

"Why?"

"Because I'm bored. And because I thought about going there."

"Why didn't you?"

"I got busy and kept putting it off. Then Daddy died and I got really busy. What's it like?"

"Big, crowded, noisy. Lots of drinking and partying, like most Texas universities. But it did have a decent football team."

"I heard you went there for two years."

"Me and thirty thousand other shitkickers and goat ropers."

She shot him a quick smile. "Which were you?"

"I never roped a goat, but I've kicked plenty of shit."

"It's always important to be good at something, I suppose."

He turned his head toward her. The low sun slanted

across his face for a moment and made his eyes glow like green fire. His grin had the devil in it. "What are you good at, Raney? Or better yet, what are you not good at?"

She shifted in the seat, uncomfortable with the question. "Lots of stuff."

"Like what?"

"Dancing, for one. I'm a klutz. I only got through cheer-leading by endless practice. I can't cook, either. And I'd rather have a root canal than go to a jazz concert."

He chuckled. "I bet you put that on all the Internet dating sites, just to chase men off."

"Would it work? I'll have to try it next time a guy makes a pass."

"You get a lot of passes, do you?"

"Lately, I have."

There wasn't much traffic until they neared Abilene. The gas gauge showed under half a tank and they still had 180 miles to go, plus, she needed a pit stop. She found a relatively new convenience store with gas pumps just before the turn onto Interstate 20 and pulled in. While Dalton pumped the gas, she went in to pay, use the restroom, and grab a couple of cups of coffee.

Dalton was sitting in the car, munching on an energy bar when she came out. He must have made a pit stop, too.

"We spill, we die," she warned him when she handed him his cup.

"Then I'll make sure I spill it on myself."

"That'd be best."

As soon as she turned onto I-20 east, she reset the cruise to eighty-eight for the drive to the Highway 6 turnoff. Behind them in the west, the sun sank lower, perching like a giant, lit-up plastic pumpkin on the edge of the horizon. Within minutes it was gone, leaving behind a fading wash of oranges and reds and wispy purple clouds.

"Pretty, isn't it?" Dalton said, head bent to study the sky

behind them in the big sideview mirror. "I sure missed Texas sunsets in prison."

"They don't have sunsets in Huntsville?"

"Not where I could see them."

Raney debated for a minute then blurted out, "Can I ask you a question?"

His smile faded. His attention shifted to the road ahead. "As long as it's not about my tour in Iraq or my time in prison."

"It isn't." Not really. "Why did you waive a trial?"

He hesitated so long, she thought he wouldn't answer. Then in short, clipped tones, he said, "I did what I thought was right, Raney. I was at fault. Maybe Jim Bob was, too. I don't know. Considering the price he paid, I figure I got off easy."

"But—"

His head whipped toward her, green eyes flashing. "Do you know the maximum sentence for vehicular manslaughter? Twenty years. That's what the county commissioner wanted and he has a lot of influence in this county. So, I took a plea and paid the fine."

"But everybody knows Jim Bob was a drinker. You might have gotten off."

"Might have." He gave a bitter laugh. "And what would a trial have cost my family? No, they'd been through enough and I just wanted it over with. We all did. And now I'm done talking about it."

Chastened, Raney said no more and focused on the traffic around her.

A few minutes later, he said, "Now I'll ask you a question. Are you mad at Joss because she's pregnant or because she's Joss?"

"Who said I was mad at Joss?"

He gave her a look.

"Okay. Maybe both. She never takes anything seriously and refuses to follow even the simplest rules. I've had to cover for her over and over, but she still won't grow up and take responsibility. And now she's going to be a mother? How's that going to work?" Raney knew she was ranting, but it felt good to vent a little.

"Why would she take responsibility if you're always around to cover for her?"

"What are you, my shrink?" She'd heard that lecture from Len, and a couple of times from Mama. But what else could she do? Joss was her little sister and it was Raney's job to watch over her. When they were younger, it had mostly been fun. But once Joss hit puberty and discovered boys, it got a lot harder.

"Is she going to keep the baby?"

She glared over at him. "Of course she is! In fact, she's very excited about it—her. She was coming home next week to start fixing up the nursery."

"Sounds pretty responsible to me."

Raney refrained from backhanding him. Everyone always stuck up for Joss. Or made excuses for her. Or wondered why her party-pooper sister was constantly trying to rein her in. "I should have guessed you'd take her side." She tried not to sound too resentful.

"Why?"

"Because you're a guy. And guys drop like stones at Joss's feet."

"I didn't."

"You were too skinny."

He grinned and spread his hands as if to show off his broad, sturdy frame that was anything but skinny. "Well, I'm not anymore. Think she'll like me now?"

"Oh, I'm sure of it." And that was what concerned Raney most of all.

They didn't talk again until she turned off the interstate onto State Highway 6, a winding two-lane dotted with small towns already buttoned up for the night even though the sun had barely gone down.

"You've been driving for over two and a half hours," Dalton said. "If you want, I can take us on into Waco. I'm familiar with the route and promise I'll drive safe."

She saw he was serious and realized how hard it must be for someone as capable as he was to take a backseat and let others do for him. "Sure," she said, and hoped she was doing the right thing. "I'll look for a pullout. We can take a break and see about those sandwiches Mama packed in the cooler."

"Thanks."

"Best wait until you see what she made. She's partial to mashed cucumber."

"No, I meant thanks for trusting me to drive."

Raney nodded. But it wasn't really his driving she distrusted. It was everything else. Especially the way she was starting to enjoy being around him.

They found a pullout a mile up the road that had an overflowing garbage can and a picnic table under a stand of elms. No water, so hopefully no mosquitoes.

Dalton brought over the cooler while Raney scouted for snakes and dead things as best she could in the fading light. Finding neither, she sat across from him at the warped table and ate triangular ham sandwiches, chips, bottled tea, and Maria's homemade pecan pie. It was a lovely evening.

As she watched the first stars blink on in the eastern sky, Raney thought this was the best non–first date she had ever been on.

Until Dalton went to put their garbage in the trash can.

CHAPTER 8

The can hadn't been emptied in days. Even from twenty feet away, Raney could smell it. Decaying apricots, maybe. Apple cores. Something fruity. She didn't think wasps were normally that active at night in spring, but as soon as Dalton lifted the lid, hundreds of yellow jackets swarmed out.

And they were pissed.

"Shit!" He dropped the lid and their bag of trash and started running, arms waving madly as the yellow jackets dive-bombed him from every direction.

At first Raney thought it was funny the way the oversized cowboy hopped and flapped like a cartoon chicken. Then she realized he was actually getting stung.

Alarmed, she raced to the car and yanked open the back door. "Get in," she shouted, and jumped into the driver's seat.

He flung himself onto the seat behind her, cussing and waving to head off the wasps trying to follow him in. "Drive!" he shouted as he slammed the door. "Maybe the wind will suck them out."

She drove, flinching every time she heard him swat a wasp on the seat, the headrest, the ceiling, the window. She'd have to have the car detailed before Mama saw it. She hit the controls to open all the windows. After a few minutes, things got quieter behind her. She checked the rearview mirror and saw him flinging dead yellow jackets out the window.

"I think I got them all," he said. "You can slow down now."

She glanced at the speedometer and saw she was going over seventy on a fifty-five-mile-an-hour road. Easing off the gas, she looked for a place to pull over.

"You okay?" she asked.

"Damn bastards got me good."

Seeing a wide graveled spot where a ranch road joined the highway, Raney turned in, put the car in park, and swiveled to look in the backseat. She had been a Girl Scout. She knew yellow jackets could sting multiple times and the pain from their venom lasted a long time. And she also knew too much venom could send a person into shock. "How many times did they get you?"

"Not sure. A dozen or so."

"Are you allergic to bees?"

"They weren't bees."

"Are you allergic!" she repeated, trying not to panic.

"Not that I know of."

She dug through the console to see what might help. Nothing for insect bites, but several pairs of sunglasses, hairspray, Kleenex, a year's supply of antibacterial gel, and at the very bottom, a small bottle of Benadryl.

She popped the lid, shook out two pills, and passed them back. "Take these."

"I don't have any water." Even in the dim light, she could see the bumps rising on his neck.

"Do it anyway!" She jumped out of the car and started toward the rear door, then remembered they'd left the cooler and all their ice by the picnic table. *Damn!*

She got back in and checked the map on the GPS display. Eight miles to the next town. Hopefully, something would be open. "How do you feel now?"

"Same as before. Maybe a little dizzy. Why are you getting so worked up?"

"I'm not worked up." She opened her door again. "Get out."

"Seriously?"

"I need to see how many times you were stung and if the stingers are still in you. Just do it, Dalton. Please."

"Well, since you said 'please.' First time, I might add." He got out, moving slow, keeping a grip on the top of the doorframe for balance.

She stood beside him, cell phone in hand. "Take off your shirt."

He gave that sideways grin. "Now you're talking."

"Stop fooling around, Dalton! I need to see if you're all right!"

He took off his shirt.

Using the flashlight on her phone, she saw two red swollen spots on his forehead, five more on his neck and shoulders, and at least six on his arms and hands. Thirteen, minimum. Three of them had stingers in them, two of which still had venom sacs attached. She would have to get those off before they popped and released more venom. Reaching into the car, she found her wallet and pulled out a credit card. "I'll try to be gentle, but this may hurt."

"I thought that was my line."

"You're being an asshole and I don't appreciate it. Now stand still!"

He stood still.

She carefully scraped off the stingers with the edge of the card, checked the others again to make certain she hadn't missed any, then told him to put his shirt back on and get in the car.

"If I'll be good, can I sit up front? There's bug guts in back."

She ignored him, slid behind the wheel, and shifted into drive.

He climbed into the passenger seat, shirt on but unbuttoned. She thought his face looked pale, but it was hard to tell in the glare of the interior lights. He took a deep breath and let it out. It seemed labored, but she wasn't sure.

"You having any trouble breathing?" she asked.

"No, but my tongue feels fat."

"Buckle up." She hit the gas, fishtailing and flinging gravel as the tires dug in. As soon as the car reached pavement, she put her phone in the dash cradle, punched 911, and turned on her hazard lights.

The operator's voice blasted through the car speakers. "911, what is your emergency?"

"The guy with me was stung by at least thirteen yellow jacket wasps. I think he's going into shock."

"I'm not going into shock."

Raney shushed him and told the operator that he didn't know if he was allergic to bees but she had given him two Benadryl anyway. She added that his neck was a little swollen, he was slightly dizzy and said his tongue felt fat.

"What is your location?" the operator asked.

"Heading down Highway 6, a few miles south of the I-20 turnoff. We're in a 2016 dark blue Expedition—I don't remember the plate number—and I have the flashers on." She glanced at the display map. "Gorman is the next town. Are there any EMTs there? Or a clinic or doctor?"

The operator said she'd dispatch an ambulance to the Shell station on her approach into town and for Raney to please stay on the line.

"I'm not going into shock," Dalton said again. "I've been there and this isn't it."

"I hope not." Raney slowed for a turn, then stepped on

the gas again when the road straightened. The steering wheel bounced in her hands as the car shimmied and rocked over the uneven surface, the big motor roaring.

He laid his head back against the headrest and closed his eyes. "Hell of a first date."

"It's not a date."

"Road trip."

"It's a rescue mission. That's all."

"Hell of a rescue mission, then." The words were slow, almost mumbled.

Terrified, she shot him a glance. His mouth was open, slightly slack. "Are you going to sleep? Or passing out?"

He didn't open his eyes. "I'm fine. Watch the road." The places on his face and neck were now the size of marbles. The hand resting on his thigh looked swollen, the long fingers puffy.

Raney focused on her driving, eyes burning, fear clogging her throat. How could someone so strong die of a wasp sting? That familiar, stomach-churning sense of helplessness pressed against her chest. It was Daddy all over again.

"I've got you on my screen, ma'am," the 911 operator said. "How's he doing?"

"The swelling's worse. He's breathing okay, but he may be passing out."

"I'm not passing out. I'm just afraid to watch."

"You should be approaching the Shell station," the operator said. "There's an ambulance waiting."

"I see it." First, the Shell sign, high up on a tall pole, then below it, flashing red lights. "I'm coming up on it now."

"Then I'll be hanging up, ma'am. Good luck."

Raney moved her foot from the gas to the brake and pressed hard. In a swirl of dust, the Expedition came to a sliding stop ten feet short of the ambulance.

Thank you, God.

Her hand shook so much it was an effort to get the gear

lever into park and punch the ignition button on the dash. As soon as the motor died, two men in blue uniforms pushed a gurney loaded with medical cases toward the car. After hitting the power button to unlock the doors, she slumped back into the seat, so relieved she was almost light-headed. "Dalton, wake up. The EMTs are here."

"Not asleep." His head rolled toward her. His forehead was so distorted with swelling he looked like Quasimodo. He lifted his head off the headrest and studied her. "Are you crying?"

"I never cry."

"Sweetheart, it's okay. I'm fine."

Before she could tell him to stop calling her sweetheart, the door beside him opened, and the EMTs took over.

They didn't use the gurney, but let Dalton sit in the car while they pumped him full of epinephrine, checked his vitals, put him on oxygen as a precaution, and gave him something for pain and to reduce inflammation.

Within minutes, Dalton sank into a drug-induced doze.

While he slept, the EMT with TOM stenciled on his shirt checked all the places Dalton had been stung. Gouging, pressing, poking. Dalton never flinched.

The other EMT, Roger, came around to Raney's window to ask her questions while he filled out various forms. Probably trying to distract her from what Tom was doing.

She didn't know anything about Dalton's medical history, other than what he'd said about not being allergic to bees, so she mostly answered his questions about what had happened, where they were from, and where they were going. Then he answered her questions about how Dalton was doing and what she should do next.

"He's not anaphylactic," Roger assured her. "And he doesn't need to be transported to a hospital. But he'll be pretty uncomfortable for a while. It might have been worse if you hadn't given him the antihistamine."

At least she'd done something right this time.

Roger gave her a detailed list of things to do until Dalton could follow up with his primary care physician: Ice the worst stings, ten minutes on, ten off. Treat them with ammonia and alcohol or a paste made of water and baking soda. Since he had so many stings, an Epsom salt bath might provide relief. He could take ibuprofen for pain and inflammation, but no more than 3,200 mg a day until his doctor checked him out, and an antihistamine as per the directions on the bottle.

"He a vet?" Tom asked, drawing her attention to the other side of the car.

Dalton was still dozing. His oxygen mask was gone and Tom was sealing a hazardous waste bag filled with various wrappers and used medical paraphernalia. "I noticed what looks like a shrapnel scar by his waist."

"I don't know," Raney said. "He was in Iraq but he doesn't talk about it."

"Most vets don't." Tom tossed the hazardous waste bag onto the gurney and closed his medical case. "He's a big guy. This many stings on a kid would be problematic, but Dalton should be fine." He straightened and put the case on top of the unused gurney. "Slow down and drive safe," he called back as he pushed the gurney toward the open doors on the back of the ambulance.

"Keep an eye on him for the next twelve hours," Roger said, still bent by her window, hand resting on the top of the car. "If he shows any breathing problems or has a feeling of swelling in his tongue or throat, take him to emergency. Meanwhile, do what I told you and have him follow up with his doctor as soon as he gets home." He looked at Dalton one more time. "Don't be surprised if he sleeps all the way to Waco." He straightened, thumped the roof of the car, said, "Y'all be careful now," and walked away.

Raney watched them drive off, then went into the Shell

station bathroom. She was still shaky from the adrenaline rush but it was fading fast, leaving behind a knot of tension in her stomach. In the cracked mirror above the sink, her eyes looked swollen and red rimmed. Like she'd been crying. Which she hadn't done in nine years.

He's alive, she told herself. *He's okay. It's not like Daddy.*

After splashing her face with cold water, she took a few deep breaths, then went back to the car. Dalton was still dozing, mouth open, snoring softly. Not wanting to wake him, she grabbed her cell phone and went behind the car to call Joss and tell her to find a hotel because they would be staying overnight in Waco.

She expected a protest.

Instead, Joss told her Mama had already taken care of everything. "She tried to call you. She decided she didn't want us driving so late and got adjoining rooms at the Hilton, 213 and 214. I'll text you the address as soon as we hang up. She even had them send a shuttle for me, so I'm already settled in our room, munching on a Cobb salad she had room service bring. Who's the guy with you?"

How like Mama to leave that explanation to her. "A trainer who works at the ranch. Look, Joss, we still have a ways to go, so I better—"

"Do I know him?"

Raney closed her eyes. She wasn't ready for this. She was tired, had a grinding headache that was making her slightly nauseated, and didn't want to get into long explanations when she still had an hour-and-a-half drive ahead of her.

But she probably should prepare Joss so her sister didn't say something tacky.

"It's Dalton Cardwell."

"Beanpole? I remember him—wait! Isn't he the guy who killed Jim Bob Adkins and went to prison? Oh my God, you hired an ex-con?"

"Actually, Mama hired him. It's late, Joss, I—"

"What's he like? You know, after being in prison? That can really screw up a person, I hear. Is he dangerous?"

"No, he's not dangerous. He's not a beanpole anymore, either. In fact, he's big enough to get stung thirteen times by yellow jackets without going into shock."

"What?"

"I'll tell you all about it when I get there. Call Mama for me and tell her we're almost to Waco and to stop worrying."

"But—"

"My phone's going dead, Joss. See you soon." She ended the call and got back into the car.

Seconds later, Joss's text came in with the address of the hotel. Raney put it into the GPS system, started the car, and pulled back onto Highway 6, which would take them all the way to Interstate 35 in Waco.

Dalton continued to snore.

A nearly full moon rose out of the east, which meant deer would be all over the road. Remembering what the EMTs said, Raney drove slower and watched harder, which only added to her weariness. She combated it by making lists.

She was good at lists. She liked that sense of accomplishment when she scratched off each item. Lists were a necessary part of running a ranch as big as Four Star, and in this case, they kept her awake.

Fresh underwear. Something to sleep in. Tank top. Check.

She wondered if she should get anything for Dalton, then decided against it. He would probably see her buying him boxers and a shirt as a marriage proposal. She glanced over, wondering if he wore boxers. Or anything. Not something she wanted to dwell on, yet, oddly, she did. Which led to her wondering why he kept making passes at her and insisting on calling her sweetheart. Assuming they really were passes. It had been so long she wasn't sure.

Baking soda, alcohol, ammonia, Epsom salts. Check.
More Benadryl, ibuprofen, cotton pads. Check. What else?

She tried to remember what was in her purse. A brush
and gloss. That was it.

Foundation, blush, mascara. Check. Toothbrush and
toothpaste. Check. Whatever she forgot, Joss would have.
Her sister couldn't travel across a room without her makeup
case in hand. Unless she'd left it on the bus with her clothes.

At nine thirty, Raney turned onto Interstate 35 south of
Baylor University, and was backtracking north when the
GPS lady started in with directions to the hotel.

"What?" Dalton said, struggling to sit up.

"Sorry. It's the GPS. Didn't mean to wake you."

He looked around, his face not as swollen, but still
lumpy. She couldn't take him through the Hilton lobby
looking like that. They'd have to go through the garage or
an exit door around back.

"Where are we?" he mumbled.

"Waco. We're staying here tonight. Mama got us adjoining rooms at the Hilton. Joss is already there."

"We're staying here? In Waco?"

"Yes, Dalton." Had the venom reached his brain? "How
do you feel?"

"Like I just woke up." He poked at a lump on his arm
and winced. "And sore."

Raney saw a lit-up WALMART sign ahead on the right and
made a quick decision. "Do you mind if we make a short
stop before we go to the hotel? I'd like to get some things at
Walmart since I didn't pack anything."

"Can I stay in the car?"

"I insist on it."

Luckily, the off-ramp passed directly by the Walmart
parking lot. She turned in, found a place close to the non-
food entry, and parked.

"Can you get me something to eat?" he asked.

"At Walmart? This time of night?" She shuddered.

"We'll get something at the hotel. I won't be long." She opened her door, then hesitated. "You want me to get you anything? Other than food?"

"Like what?"

"Underwear? A shirt? Socks? A toothbrush?"

"Okay," he said around a yawn.

She waited. The yawn ended. His eyelids drooped.

"What size, Dalton?" she prodded in a loud voice.

He blinked at her.

"Underwear, shirt, socks?"

"Boxers, 36. Socks, big. T-shirt, 2XL. Blue."

"Blue T-shirt?"

"Toothbrush." He gave her a sleepy grin. "So we don't get ours mixed up."

The man was relentless.

"I'll be back in a minute," she said, and got out.

Actually, it took longer than she anticipated because she wanted to get the most garish, outrageous, tacky boxers she could find. She had to settle for orange-and-white plaid with a Texas Longhorns logo, and a Mickey Mouse toothbrush.

"Can you tell time?" Dalton groused after she loaded her bags in the backseat and climbed behind the wheel. "You said a minute. Not forty-seven of them."

She smiled sweetly. "The meds must be wearing off. Luckily I got more."

"And how do you start this thing? I about died of suffocation with all the windows closed."

She held up her index finger.

"If you're trying to flip me off, you're doing it wrong."

She poked the ignition button. The car rumbled to life. "That's how."

"I punched that thing at least ten times. It doesn't work."

"That's because I keep this in my purse, not the car." She held up the fob that activated the keyless ignition. She wondered what else he might have missed while he was in prison, other than a contentious election and a slump in cattle prices.

"Can we go now? Or do you need to get your hair done?"

"Yes, we can go now."

And they did.

CHAPTER 9

"Honey, we're home," Dalton sang out when Joss opened the door to Room 213.

"Asshat," Raney muttered, nudging him in the back with the Walmart bags. She hadn't let him carry any because of his swollen hands, bless her heart.

"Mercy sakes, you've changed," Joss exclaimed as he walked in. "And I'm not just talking about the yellow jacket lumps."

"Does that mean you like me better now?"

"Why, I think I do." Joss winked at him and twirled a lock of multicolored hair. Green, blue, and bright pink. And lots of curls. It looked like a clown wig.

"Don't get bigheaded," Raney muttered to him as she kicked the door shut and dumped the bags on the nearest queen bed. "She says that to all the guys." After separating her stuff from his, she picked up his bags and asked her sister for the key card to the adjoining room.

Joss handed her two. "I had an extra-large robe sent up."

She gave Dalton another once-over and a smile. "Hope it fits."

Before he could voice any of the half-dozen clever quips rattling through his head, Raney herded him into the adjoining room, kicked the door closed, and tossed his bag of clothes onto the single king bed. "Best lock it. She might not be able to help herself now that she likes you better."

"Good point."

Raney looked at him like she thought he was serious. When she saw he wasn't, she allowed a small smile. The woman hoarded her smiles like treasure. But when he finally did manage to get one, Dalton felt he'd been given something special.

Raney picked out all the medical stuff, carried it into the bathroom, and dumped it into the sink. Alcohol, ammonia, cotton balls, baking soda, a box of Epsom salts, bottles of ibuprofen and Benadryl, a small tube of toothpaste, and a Mickey Mouse toothbrush.

Dalton held up the toothbrush and met her smirk with a grin. "Just like the one I have at home. Timmy got it for me for Christmas."

Her smirk faded. "Really?"

"No."

With an unladylike snort, she bent over and started filling the tub. An inspiring view of a truly fine butt. Or it would have been if he'd felt any better. As the tub filled, she went back into the bedroom and returned with a white robe, which she hung on the hook by the tub. "If it doesn't fit, wear it backward. I wouldn't want her to jump you."

"I'll try, but sometimes I can't—"

"The boxers, T-shirt, and socks are on the bed." She opened the Epsom salt box, poured a goodly amount into the water, bent over again to slosh it around—to his delight—then turned the water off and straightened.

"Stay in as long as you can," she said, all business and

nursely concern. "After you're finished, dry off real well, then dab on the ammonia or alcohol. While that's drying, make a paste with water and baking soda. Dab that on, let it dry, then rinse it off, and dab on the ammonia again. Just before you go to bed, take two ibuprofen and another Benadryl. If you have any trouble breathing or swallowing, or if your throat feels thick, come get me. Good night."

"Could you repeat that?"

"No." She left, closing the door behind her. Both doors.

Dalton sat on the edge of the bed and pulled off his boots. He felt like hammered shit. Yet knowing Raney was nearby helped. They'd been together in the car for six straight hours and it felt odd to be apart. Which was odd in itself.

After his soak, he stood at the sink and dabbed every red place he could see. It stung, but not too bad. He only found eight spots, which meant there were several he couldn't see. He debated bothering Raney about it, then heard noises on the other side of the wall and figured she wasn't asleep yet. Either that, or she was moving furniture against the adjoining door.

He pulled on his new boxers—UT Longhorns—really?— then his jeans, left the robe, and padded barefoot out of the bathroom, ammonia and cotton ball in hand. After opening the first adjoining door, he listened at the one into their room, heard them talking, and knocked with his elbow.

Joss opened the door. Behind her, Raney disappeared into the bathroom. Both wore T-shirts and flannel shorts under robes like his. Raney's legs were amazing.

Joss stared at his chest, then her gaze did a quick drop to where his buckle would be if he'd had on a belt, then across his shoulders, and finally up to his face. It happened so fast he didn't have time to flex.

Then he saw Raney coming out of the bathroom, and all thoughts of trying to impress her sister fled. She looked exhausted. Drained. Like maybe she had been crying again.

That concerned him, but he knew better than to comment on it.

He held up the ammonia bottle. "I only found eight." Then before her sister could offer to help, he turned and walked back into his bathroom.

"I can't reach the ones on my shoulders in back," he said to the mirror when Raney walked in behind him, closing the door so they could move around in the small space.

"Turn around so I can check the others."

He faced her. She was so close he could smell the shampoo in her damp hair and the same soap he'd used in his bath. He watched her face as she gently brushed her palm over the bumps on his chest, then up to those on his neck and shoulder, and down to others on his right arm.

It was torture. Especially the way her eyes followed the sweep of her fingers over his skin. He understood now why dogs craved the stroke of the human hand. Although not in the way he was craving this.

"The bath seems to have helped," she said in an odd voice as she took her hand away. "Did you try the baking soda paste?"

He cleared his throat. "On those I could reach."

Her gaze flew up to his. Blue as a mountain lake. Or a hot summer sky. He watched a furrow build between those remarkable eyes and wanted to rub his thumb over it to make it go away.

"You sound hoarse," she said. "Is your throat okay? Are you breathing okay?"

Not now. "I'm fine." He thrust the bottle and cotton ball toward her.

"Did you get the back of your arms?" she asked.

"Those I found."

"Turn around."

He faced the mirror again. Not as much fun. He could barely see the top of her head above his shoulder. Her hair was lighter when it was dry, almost the color of light amber ale but with blond streaks where the sun bleached it. He doubted the color came from a bottle.

She dampened the cotton ball with ammonia and started dabbing. "They look a lot better than they did. Does it sting?"

He shrugged and tried to focus on the molding above the mirror, rather than the warm whisper of her breath against his back.

"Mama would put ammonia on any kind of bite. Especially itchy mosquito bites. It helped." She ran her left hand up the back of his neck to push hair out of her way and dabbed at his hairline.

It was just a hand. Barbers had touched his neck plenty of times. But none had ever made him feel like this.

She moved to the back of his other arm. He shifted so he could see her face in the mirror. The furrow on her brow was deeper and her lips were pursed in concentration as she dabbed away. Her eyes seemed slightly swollen and he thought again that she might have been crying. Over him?

The thought spread through him in a warm rush.

"I'm sorry I overreacted," she said. "The EMTs probably thought I was crazy."

"I doubt it." They were probably as hot for her as he was. "They said if you hadn't given me the antihistamine, it could have been a lot worse."

She shot him a glance. "You heard that? I thought you were asleep."

"I was resting up. In case I had to fight them off."

She made that snort again and resumed dabbing. "I doubt you were in any danger."

"I meant fight them off of you."

She didn't say anything, but he was rewarded with a slow flush of color across her cheeks. "Why were you so worried?" he asked on impulse. "You don't seem the type to overreact."

"I usually don't. Joss and Len are the hysterics. Mostly Joss."

"So why did you?"

"It's complicated. You can turn around now. I think I got them all."

He stepped back as she dropped the cotton ball in the trash. She looked like she might say more, so he waited. But when she finally spoke, her words surprised him.

"It was Daddy all over again." He watched her blink hard against tears. "I didn't want anyone else to die while I sat there and did nothing."

"Sweetheart."

"Don't call me sweetheart."

He put his arms around her and pulled her in until her forehead butted against this chest. "Sweetheart," he murmured again, gently stroking her back. "I'm okay. Because of you, I'm all right."

She nestled closer so that her cheek lay above his thundering heart. She wasn't wearing a bra under her T-shirt and the soft press of her breasts against his bare chest was a whole different kind of torture.

A moment later, she let go a deep breath and slid her arms around his waist. "I was so scared, Dalton."

"I know."

"I didn't want you to die, too."

He pulled back, not far enough to break her hold, but so he could see her face. "Look at me," he said.

She hesitated, then raised her head and looked at him.

She seemed so wounded. He wondered how such a strong woman could be brought so low, and was touched that she was allowing him to see it.

"What you went through with your dad was terrible, Raney. And I hate that you carry that memory in your head. But it wasn't your fault he died. Or his fault that he left you. Shit happens and you can only do your best to get past it."

He watched tears build. He could drown in those eyes. Lose himself forever without even putting up a fight. "Now brace yourself, sweetheart, because this is important."

"Don't call me—"

He dipped his head and kissed her.

She went stiff in his arms. But her lips were as soft as he remembered. Still trembly, a little salty from her tears, but not reluctant. Which made him bolder. He kept kissing her, trying not to rush her, but not wanting to stop, either. Then she brought her hands up, palms flat against his chest. He thought she was telling him to back off and started to do so, when her arms slid up and around his neck.

His thoughts scattered. It was the kind of kiss a man in prison dreamed of. Slow and sweet and perfect in every way because the woman in his arms was the only one he wanted there.

When she finally drew back, they were both out of breath. She ran her hands down to his elbows and back to his shoulders. He almost shivered at the contact. "You're so lumpy and swollen."

"Your fault." He tried to kiss her again, but she backed off even more.

Despite the amusement in her eyes, she gave him what he'd come to think of as The Raney Look of Disapproval. "I was talking about the yellow jacket lumps."

"Me, too," he lied, and was going in for another try when her sister's voice sounded on the other side of the bathroom door.

"Raney, you two better stop whatever you're doing in there. Mama's on the phone and I can't hold her off any longer."

The ride back to Rough Creek was long and uneventful. They left early to avoid commuter traffic and were out of Waco and heading north by eight o'clock. As expected, Joss took shotgun and Raney drove, while Dalton sprawled in the bucket seat behind Joss. Raney couldn't see him in the rearview mirror because of the angle. But she could feel him back there, like a watchful presence just out of sight and waiting to pounce. It made her nervous.

She didn't lack experience with men. She'd even been engaged once—for all of two weeks. But Dalton was a different kind of animal altogether.

For one thing, he was older than she was. Not by much, but between his tour in Iraq and his time in prison, his realm of experience was much broader and harsher than hers. That made him an unknown entity. He had seen violence and death. He had caused one death here, and probably more in Iraq, and that had to affect a person. Yet, he didn't want to talk about it, so how could she ever know him, or learn to trust him, if he kept that part of himself closed off?

She liked things neat and orderly. Especially emotion. But with Dalton, she could sense control slipping away. He infuriated her. Shocked her. Made her laugh and feel things she didn't understand. Dalton was chaos. That frightened her.

And yet . . .

She glanced up and was startled to find him looking back at her in the rearview mirror. He had shifted so that he had a clear line of sight, which meant she did, too.

He winked at her then waggled his dark eyebrows like a flirtatious used car salesman. It was so unexpected and absurd she almost burst out laughing.

Meanwhile, oblivious to the foolishness going on behind her, Joss went on a rant about having to leave so early they couldn't even order real room service but had to settle for muffins and yogurt, then moved seamlessly into a rambling monologue about her concerts, the songs she was writing, the dear friends who had abandoned her in the Walmart parking lot, and whether she should name her daughter Aria or Melody or Star.

"Actually, they didn't abandon me," she admitted in hour two. "I was tired of arguing with Grady, so I got off the bus."

"And they drove away?" Dalton asked from the backseat.

"I insisted. That much tension isn't good for the baby."

"But being stranded in a Walmart parking lot is?" Raney muttered.

"I wouldn't expect you to understand, Raney. You never get worked up about anything except your horses and the ranch."

"I've seen her worked up," Dalton said. "It was something I'll never forget."

Raney glared at him in the mirror.

He waggled his brows again.

"When?" Joss asked.

"Yesterday. When the yellow jackets were chasing me. At first, she laughed. But when she saw all the bites, she got so worried she cried. Bless her heart."

"Raney doesn't cry."

"That's what she said. But there you have it. Tears everywhere. I thought it was sweet."

Raney flexed her hands on the steering wheel, wishing it were Dalton's throat instead.

"Who's Grady?" Dalton asked in hour three after they'd stopped at a gas station outside of Abilene for gas and snacks and yet another potty break for Joss.

"Just a guy." Her sister flipped her hand in a dismissive motion. "A very bossy guy who thinks he knows best about everything."

"Like what?"

"I don't want to talk about it."

Raney gave Dalton a *please don't encourage her* look in the mirror.

"Why not?" he asked Joss.

"I'm tired of him telling me what to do, what not to do,

what to eat, what not to eat—the man acts like he's my mother, for heaven's sake."

"Maybe he's got the hots for you."

"Well, I don't have the hots for him. Are there any chips left?"

Dalton gave up talking to Joss and went back to staring at Raney in the mirror.

She ignored him as best she could.

They were almost to Gunther and had a little over thirty minutes to go when Joss brought up the subject Raney had hoped to avoid. "So, Dalton," her sister began with a sideways smirk at Raney. "What's between you and my big sister?"

"Nothing," Raney blurted out before Dalton could say anything.

Dalton gave a hearty laugh that sounded fake to Raney. "Your sister's just being modest. There's a lot between Raney and me. Especially yesterday."

Joss perked up. "Really? What happened?"

"For one thing, she saved my life. And then later—"

"Dalton," Raney cut in. "Let's not make a big deal out of something so trivial."

"Trivial? How can you say that, Raney? It was one of the most inspiring moments of my life. You seemed pretty moved, too." He was all but rocking in his seat with suppressed laughter.

"What'd she do?" Joss asked.

It took him a moment to get himself in hand. "Well, after the yellow jacket attack and she was through laughing at me and crying, she made me take two Benadryls. The EMTs said I might have gone into shock and died if she hadn't."

"That's awful."

"It was," Dalton agreed. "You know, in some cultures, Joss, if you save a person's life, you're responsible for them forever."

"I thought it was the other way around."

"Nobody's responsible for anybody," Raney snapped, needing to put a stop to this before it went too far. "And you weren't anywhere near dying, Dalton. Not then, at least. But there's still time."

Joss gave her a shocked look.

Dalton laughed silently.

Raney drove faster.

They turned through the front gate just before one o'clock. Joss had called ahead to Mama to make sure there would be something to eat, since "mean ole Raney was so desperate to get home she barely let us pee, much less get anything decent to eat."

As soon as they stopped, Raney handed out the Walmart bags she'd saved and told them to collect their trash or they'd have to answer to Mama. By the time they got everything gathered and were heading to the house, Mama was waiting with a full spread on the veranda table.

"I've been so worried," she said, not quite wringing her hands, but showing a goodly amount of motherly concern. Sadly, none of it was directed at her offspring. "Dalton, dear, how are you feeling?"

"Much better, ma'am. Your daughter, here, took good care of me."

Mama looked at Raney, brows raised. "She did?"

"Gave me two Benadryl and got me to the EMTs in record time."

"EMTs? I had no idea it was so serious."

"It wasn't," Raney cut in before Dalton could elaborate on his harrowing, near-death experience. "But you know what babies men can be. I had to do something to keep him calm. Can we eat now? I'm starving."

As soon as they settled at the table, Mama took charge of the food and the conversation, which hopefully would put a damper on Dalton's foolishness.

"How soon do you think you'll be able to work, Dalton?" Mama asked as she passed around a jar of blackberry preserves to complement the croque monsieur. Or, as unpretentious Americans called them, Monte Cristos. Or, as the even less pretentious called them, fried ham and cheese and turkey sandwiches. Raney wondered who Mama was trying to impress. And why.

"I'm ready now," Dalton answered. "These stings look a lot worse than they feel, thanks to all the medicines Raney put on them." He sent her a fond smile.

She ignored him.

"That's good news," Mama said. "Press Amala got back sooner than expected, and he's ready to take you whenever you're up to it. He suggested you bring Rosco so he can see how you do together."

"Good idea. I'm assuming Rosco's been trailered before."

"Many times. Amala's barn is this side of Gunther, so you should be able to commute unless he needs you to stay overnight."

"I can start tomorrow if that suits him."

Mama said she'd check with Press and let him know, then turned to the soon-to-be mama and lapsed into an elaborate and enthusiastic explanation of all the plans she'd already put in motion to fix up her new granddaughter's nursery. Poor Joss.

As soon as the meal ended, Dalton thanked Mama and said he needed to check on Rosco.

Raney almost went with him—only to see how the colt's session with Alejandro had gone—then saw the way Mama and Joss watched her, and went to Daddy's office instead.

When she sat behind the desk, motion caught her eye and she glanced out the big office window to see Dalton heading up to the barn. Even from this distance, she could see that sway in his shoulders with each authoritative stride, the hotel laundry bag containing his dirty clothes and the medicines swinging at his knee. His head was down as if in thought, and the sun brought out the reds and golds in his dark brown hair. Or maybe she was only remembering how he'd looked the night before, with the bathroom light shining down on his head and shoulders just before he'd kissed her.

That was a hell of a move he'd put on her. And a much better kiss than that first one on the veranda. It had kept her tossing half the night, thinking about it.

She watched him until he disappeared into the barn, then sat back, wondering what she was going to do about the quirky, outrageous, damaged ex-con who managed to steal a little more of her heart each day. It sure as hell couldn't go on like this much longer. Whatever was happening between them made her feel like she was riding an emotional roller coaster without a seat restraint. It was ruining her appetite and her sleep.

Yet, she wasn't altogether certain she was ready for the ride to end.

CHAPTER 10

Saturday afternoon, three days later, Raney was sitting at her desk in the office, working on revised feed orders now that they'd reduced the herd, and getting a supplies list ready for the esposas' bimonthly shopping trip, when she saw one of the ranch trucks drive by the office window.

No horse trailer. Not Dalton.

This was the third day he and Rosco had gone to Amala's. At supper the two previous nights, Dalton had reported that the training was going well, Rosco was learning fast, and Amala was a huge help explaining what they needed to do to impress the Futurity judges at the big fall event in Fort Worth. And each evening, as soon as the meal ended, he had excused himself and gone back to the barn with Glenn and Alejandro.

It made her wonder if he was avoiding her. She never got a chance to ask him, which was probably a good thing, since she wouldn't have known what to say anyway.

Hey, Dalton, been avoiding me? And by the way, why did you kiss me?

She was pathetic.

Even though they rarely spoke directly during the evening meals, she was still intensely aware of him sitting at the other end of the table with Glenn and Alejandro. Maybe he was aware of her, too. She caught him looking at her several of the many times she looked at him.

Last night at dinner, when Dalton had given Mama his daily Rosco report, he'd said he'd only be going to Amala for one more day. "Once the colt learns how to peel a cow out of the herd, then work it for a set length of time without letting it go back to the herd or letting the herd get around him, there might be more sessions. But for now, I'll just work him on that."

Mama had asked him how long he thought that would take.

"Depends on Rosco. He's still young. If we bring him along too fast we run the risk he'll get overwhelmed or burned out."

The two mutes sitting beside Dalton had nodded sagely and continued to eat.

Joss fought a yawn.

Raney refilled her wineglass. For two days they'd talked of nothing except Rosco—how well he was doing, how smart he was, how utterly amazing he was, and so on. Surely, they could find something else to talk about. Like, say . . . why he might be avoiding her.

"He's still progressing well?" Mama had asked, intent on keeping the redundant conversation going. "And you still think he'll be ready for the US Cutting Horse Association's fall Futurity?"

"No reason to think otherwise. He's got the talent. And he dearly loves working with cows. That's not to say he'll win the USCHA. But he's got a chance for a great start."

More nods from the mutes.

Raney studied Dalton as she chewed. He looked tired.

She wondered if the yellow jacket bites were bothering him. Or maybe he was regretting what she'd come to think of as the "bathroom kiss" as opposed to the "veranda kiss." Maybe he was sleeping as poorly as she was.

Over dessert last night, Mama had mentioned the possibility of taking Rosco to several of the summer horse shows in the area. "Not to participate," she had added, "since he can't enter or compete until his debut at the Futurity. But he needs to become accustomed to the other horses, the noise of the crowd, the loudspeaker, and so forth. These early shows can be a useful training opportunity."

Dalton said Press had already given him a list of shows he thought Rosco should attend. "You ladies would be welcome to come along for moral support," he'd said, looking around the table. "You, too," he added to the mutes.

His gaze might have lingered on Raney more than the others, but she wasn't sure. Neither of the mutes responded.

Joss pushed her plate aside. "Count me out. I'm not the horse-crazy one."

"Well, I'd certainly like to see how Rosco does," Mama put in.

So much for being able to talk to Dalton alone. Raney wasn't sure if she was relieved or upset about that.

"But I'll tell you where I will go," Joss said with a grin that always meant trouble. "Dancing! I heard Jerry and the Kickers are playing at Harley's Roadhouse next weekend. Anybody want to go with me?"

Raney glanced at Dalton, wondering if he remembered their conversation on the drive to Waco.

Apparently so. "How about it, Raney? No need to miss the fun just because you can't dance. Joss and I will teach you the two-step. It's easy."

"Can't dance?" Joss laughed. "Who told you that? Raney can dance. Not very well, maybe. But at least she tried back when she still had a social life."

"Now I've got a real job," Raney shot back. "You might try that sometime."

"It is going to be a long summer," Alejandro muttered.

Glenn nodded.

After telling Mama he'd check on local cutting shows and get back to her, Dalton and the mutes had excused themselves. As she'd watched them leave, Raney decided if Dalton was seriously trying to put a move on her, this had to be the slowest pass in history.

That was yesterday. But today, after he got back from Amala's, she would talk to him even if she had to follow him into the barn. Hopefully, by then she'd know what she wanted to say.

But an hour later, Dalton and Rosco still weren't back and she was starting to worry. So many things could go wrong when trailering horses, and Dalton didn't have the best driving record. Surely, he would call if there was a problem. Pushing that troublesome thought aside, she closed the ledgers and slipped them into the desk drawer, then went upstairs to get ready for supper.

After a quick shower, she changed and was sitting at her vanity, trying to do something with her hair, when her mother walked in with a big bag of baby stuff, Joss on her heels. Once they'd talked Mama into turning KD's room into the nursery since it was next door to Joss's, she had been on a decorating tear.

"Who are you getting so dressed up for?" Joss asked, eyeing the new blouse Raney had ordered online from Saks.

"Mama, of course. She doesn't like to smell horses while she eats."

"You sure it's not for Dalton?"

Mama waved the idea away. "Don't be silly. Dalton's gay. Look what I got for the nursery." She dug through paint samples, color charts, and cloth strips.

"Who told you he was gay?" Joss asked.

"Raney. I'm thinking pink, since she's a girl. But I know how you modern mothers hate gender typing, so we could use blue accents here and there. How's this?" She held up a bright pink swatch with blue butterflies.

Raney thought it was insulting to females of all ages.

Joss didn't even look at it. "You told Mama that Dalton is gay? If he is, then what were the two of you doing in the bathroom with the door closed?"

Raney stared at her reflection and wondered what it would feel like to step through the mirror into another dimension.

"What?" Mama whipped around. "You were in the bathroom with Dalton? Where? Doing what?"

"In Waco. Putting ammonia on yellow jacket bites he couldn't reach. And I only said Dalton was gay, Joss, so Mama would stop trying to foist me off on him."

"I never tried to foist you off on him."

"Only him and every other man past puberty."

"And I never believed he was gay, either. Not the way he keeps looking at you at the dinner table." Mama pulled out more swatches. "Yellow is gender neutral, isn't it?"

"Really?" Joss eyed Raney in speculation. "I'll have to watch for that at supper tonight. Desire over dessert," she mused. "I like that. I should use it in one of my songs."

Raney dropped her head into her hands. "Jesus, take me now."

"Hush that talk, Raney," Mama scolded. "He can hear you, you know. Now, what do you think of these fabrics for the nursery drapes?"

"I don't want drapes in the baby's room. I want blinds."

"It's a nursery, not a dentist's office," Mama argued.

"I'm with Joss," Raney cut in, hoping a show of loyalty would get her sister to back off. "Once she's crawling, the first thing the baby will go for is the drapes."

Mama raised a hand in surrender. "All right. But at least let's put up a valance. We can make a matching baby blanket to go with it."

"We who?" Raney muttered. "None of us sew."

"I'm sure we can figure it out," Joss said airily. "How hard can it be?"

Mama was packing her goodies back in her bag when Joss let out a squeal. "She kicked me!"

Before Raney knew what was happening, her sister grabbed her hand and pressed it to her rounded belly. "Can you feel it?"

Raney could. And it was freaky feeling something moving around inside another person's body. "It doesn't hurt?"

"Not unless she kicks a kidney. Isn't it wonderful!"

"It's weird."

"If you ever get pregnant, you won't think so." Blinking against tears, Joss patted her rotund midsection. "It's amazing, isn't it, Mama?"

"It is." Mama smiled from Raney to her new favorite daughter. "And I think every woman should experience it."

Two against one. Great. Raney admired how her mother could smile so sweetly and look pitying at the same time.

Her cell phone buzzed. Raney saw it was Dalton and was debating whether to answer it with her mother and sister in the room, when Joss snatched it off the vanity top where Raney had set it.

"Miss Raney Whitcomb's office," she said in a lilting secretarial voice. "I have you on speaker. How may I help you?"

"I need to talk to Raney. Now."

"Take it off speaker and give it to me," Raney ordered.

Instead, Mama grabbed it. "This is Raney's mother, Dalton. What's wrong?"

"Mama! Give me the phone!"

Mama shushed her and held it out so they could all hear.

"Toby Langers is pulling me over," Dalton said. "I don't

know why. But he'll probably trump up some bogus charge to take me in and I don't want to leave the truck and Rosco beside the road. Can you send somebody to get them?"

In the background Raney could hear the deputy asking for registration and proof of insurance.

"Put Deputy Langers on the phone, Dalton," Mama said in her kick-ass voice.

Rustling, muted conversation, then a man's voice said, "Good afternoon, Mrs. Whitcomb. Deputy Langers here. What can I do for you today?"

"You can tell me why you've pulled over my employee. Was he speeding?"

"No, ma'am."

"Drinking?"

"No."

"Smoking pot? Doing drugs? Asleep at the wheel?"

"Not that I can tell. But I—"

"Do you suspect him of any wrongdoing I should be made aware of?"

"No, ma'am, but—"

"Then why did you pull him over?"

"Routine check, ma'am, that's all."

"Routine check. I understand. But what I need for you to understand, Deputy, is that the horse Mr. Cardwell is trailering is very valuable and I'd hate to have anything happen to him while you were conducting a routine and unnecessary traffic stop."

"I'm entitled to make traffic stops whenever I see fit, Mrs. Whitcomb. Dalton Cardwell is a convicted felon. For all I know, he might have been stealing the horse."

"That's why you pulled him over? You thought he might be stealing a horse?"

"Well, I—"

"Do speak up, Deputy. I'm recording this."

Silence.

"Shall I have my lawyers meet you and Mr. Cardwell at

your office, Deputy Langers? Or would you prefer we handle this directly with your boss, Sheriff Ford? I'm certain either he or my lawyers can explain all about probable cause, illegal searches, and what the penalties are for police harassment."

Silence.

"Or you can simply apologize to Mr. Cardwell for this misunderstanding and send him on his way. He'll be late for supper as it is."

A long sigh. "Yes, ma'am. I'll do that. And you have a nice day." Mama returned the phone to Raney.

"I could have handled it," Raney snapped.

"Of course you could. But the deputy is less likely to take the reprimand personally if it comes from a grandmother, rather than from someone who wouldn't even dance with him at the Grange Christmas party last year." Mama's smile would have made a preacher sweat. "But as it happens, I did dance with Sheriff Ford, and I can assure you the man hasn't forgotten it. Vinegar or honey, my dears. Men always choose honey. Now can we get back to the swatches?"

Supper was delayed while they waited for Dalton to return, put Rosco away, and change clothes, since it was Saturday and they would be eating in the dining room. When Raney opened the door a while later, his hair was wet and he was slightly out of breath, but grinning. "Sorry I'm late."

Mercy, the things that grin could do to an empty stomach. "No problem," she managed to say.

As soon as they took their places at the table, the interrogation began. To bring the mutes up to date, Dalton spent the next half hour going into a detailed rendering of every "he said," "I said," and "Mrs. Whitcomb said" during his run-in with Langers. At least it was different from the usual Rosco report.

Glenn was so transfixed by the account he stopped chewing for a moment.

"Es un culero," Alejandro muttered when Dalton finished.

"What was that, Alejandro?"

Alejandro met Dalton's grin with a shrug. "I said he is an asshole, Senora."

Mama's smile faltered momentarily then quickly recovered. "He certainly is. Would anyone care for more potatoes?" Ever gracious, Mama was.

Joss, not so much. "Why is Deputy Langers out to get you?" she asked Dalton.

"I took his spot on the high school football team."

"Seriously? He's still upset about something that happened twenty years ago?"

"Seventeen. Toby was two years older than me. He took it hard."

"And that's it? Some seventeen-year-old grudge? God, men can be so dumb."

Raney watched color rise up Dalton's neck. A very nice neck. Full of muscles and tendons and that angular Adam's apple that slid up and down whenever he swallowed. Like now.

"I also dated a girl he had his eye on."

"Karla Jenkins?" Joss guessed.

A darting glance at Raney. "Before that."

"Suze Anderson. No, wait! Mary Freed. Or was it Rachel Whatshername?"

"Yes."

"All of them? My, you've certainly been busy." Joss grinned at Raney. "He doesn't sound gay to me."

Five gazes swung toward Raney. Two showed amusement.

Dalton's didn't. "Who said I was gay?"

"It was just a silly joke," Mama said with a blindingly

bright smile. "Who wants dessert? Shall we take it on the veranda?"

Dalton followed Raney onto the porch. Herded her, actually. Knowing her moment of reckoning was coming, she decided to forgo the strawberry shortcake and concentrate on wine. She was more embarrassed than afraid of Dalton's anger. He didn't deserve to be the butt of her offhand remark and she was ashamed that she'd used him that way. But she couldn't come up with the right words to explain it. *Mama thinks she's my pimp* seemed a bit harsh.

The mutes were finished and heading down the veranda steps when Dalton turned to Raney and said, "Could I talk to you a minute?"

"Sure." Unwilling to have this conversation within hearing of her nosy mother and sister, Raney suggested they take a walk. By mutual unspoken agreement, they headed down the long sloping lawn toward the creek.

It was another beautiful evening, warm, but with enough breeze to keep the bugs away, and the western sky gearing up for another stunning Texas sunset. They didn't speak and were careful not to touch, not with her mother and sister watching from the veranda, so Raney spent the silence rehearsing what she might say in her own defense and wondering what Dalton was thinking.

Nothing good, judging by his concentrated expression.

The creek that had given the town its name was little more than a meandering brook that cascaded from one shallow, rock-lined pool to another as it followed the pitch of the gently rolling grasslands. It provided more music than water, but was so picturesque that photographs of it had appeared in several magazine articles aimed at bringing tourists to the area. On the other side of the county, a natural dam had created a clear swimming hole that had been a favorite teenage hangout for decades until the state took it over for a day-use-only state park.

Here, at the ranch, it was less picturesque and served the

more practical purpose of providing water for the stock and irrigation for the small vegetable garden tended by las esposas. Years ago, Daddy had hired workers to cut back the brush to make a small clearing along the bank under the shade of a wide-limbed oak tree where the four sisters often had picnics when they were younger. It was a quiet, peaceful place, and Raney hoped it would have a soothing effect on Dalton.

She had just reached the tree when Dalton put his hand on her shoulder, spun her around, and pulled her into his arms.

Startled, she froze.

He looked anything but soothed as he stared down at her, unsmiling, his gaze fixed on her mouth. "I came out here to give you hell. Now all I want to do is get you naked."

"Does that mean I'm off the hook for saying you're gay?"

"Not a chance," he said, and kissed her.

It wasn't a tentative kiss like that first one on the veranda. Or a tenderly sweet one like the more forceful bathroom kiss. It was the kiss of a man who had been without kisses as long as she had, and needed them as much as she did. Like he was sealing a promise. Branding his woman. Staking his claim. Every overblown cliché in Joss's songs swirled through Raney's mind, but now she finally understood what they meant. And she reveled in it.

When at last he lifted his head, she was glad he kept his arms around her because she wasn't sure her legs would hold her. She was also surprised to realize her arms were wrapped around his waist and holding on to him just a little too tightly.

Dropping his forehead against hers, he let out a deep breath that smelled of strawberries and ruffled her eyelashes. "Do you still think I'm gay?"

It was a moment before she could speak. "No. I never did."

He pulled back and looked at her. "Then why did you say I was?"

That tingly, weak-kneed feeling faded. She took her arms from around his waist and tried to put space between them but his big hands stayed on her ribs. "It was just a stupid remark, Dalton. I'm sorry I said it."

He waited, eyes locked on hers.

"I only did it to make Mama leave me alone." She tried to sound offhand, but the warmth of the hands almost spanning her rib cage was starting to make her sweat.

"What's your mother got to do with it?"

"She keeps trying to foist me off on you." There. She'd said it. Now he would know she was so pitiful her own mother was trying to pimp her out. Sort of.

He didn't respond.

When she got the nerve to look at him, she saw mischief in his eyes. His lips—soft, yet utterly masculine, and ringed by a slight stubble of dark whiskers—widened in a grin. "Smart lady."

Relief spread through her. Teasing she could handle. It was emotion that flustered her. "Don't take it personally," she told him. "She tries to pass me off on any man old enough to father children."

His grin faded. But he kept his hands where they were, still holding her captive and making her sweat. "Why? You're beautiful. Sexy. Smart—"

"Don't forget rich," she piped in, hoping her bitterness didn't show. After one disastrous near-marriage, she'd learned the hard truth: forget honey—what really drew men was money.

He didn't laugh with her. In fact, he almost looked angry.

This time, when she stepped back, he let her go. Unsettled by his intense scrutiny, she started walking again, following a faint game trail worn into the grass along the bank. He fell in beside her. "But I'm also almost thirty," she went on. "Still unmarried and childless."

"So? That's your business. Not hers."

Raney felt a swell of gratitude. No one ever took her side

against Mama. "Tell that to my mother. She thinks if she doesn't intervene, I'll end up alone with a ratty, fur-covered lap blanket and twenty cats for company."

"You're kidding."

"Sadly, no."

He laughed. "Then, sweetheart, you can tell your mother that her worries are over." He spread his big hands wide. "'Cause here I am. Every mama's dream."

CHAPTER 11

Naturally, Joss didn't give up on the idea of going to Harley's Roadhouse the following Saturday. And naturally, Mama was all for it. She even insisted they take either Dalton or Alejandro along for protection—which was code for "chaperone." Mama wasn't a big fan of women going unescorted to dance halls, taverns, or bars.

Alejandro was still negotiating with his Honduran Amada for custody of numero Uno, so he had an excuse not to go. Dalton didn't need one. He was all in. Raney realized she didn't want an excuse, either. She was actually getting excited about going out, catching up with old friends, and doing something other than ranch work for a change. Like dancing with Dalton.

On Friday night, a rumbling thunderstorm came through, dumped three inches of much-needed rain on the thirsty ground within an hour, caused a one-hour power outage, then moved on. Luckily, the barns and paddocks were on higher ground and when the creek flooded overnight, they weren't threatened.

When Raney got up on Saturday morning, it was as if nothing had happened, except for the water swirling around the trunks of the trees beside the creek. But by noon, the water started to recede, and by midafternoon, the cloudless sky was so clear and clean it was almost the same turquoise blue as the blouse Raney chose to wear to the dance hall that night.

A few minutes before supper, Joss came in to offer her critique of Raney's outfit. Did everybody in her family think she was incapable of dressing herself?

"You're wearing jeans? You'll roast. Do you think I look pregnant in this outfit?"

"You are pregnant."

"That doesn't mean I want to look pregnant." Joss twirled, her handkerchief-hemmed skirt swinging around her tall fringed boots. "What do you think?"

Raney thought she looked like something in a '60s hippie catalog. But knowing Joss wouldn't want to hear that, she gave her a thorough once-over. The full peasant blouse disguised the slight bulge of her belly, and the short suede vest with six-inch fringe provided additional camouflage. The layers of beads and bangles hanging around her neck would also draw the eye away from her thicker waistline, as would the multicolored hair and dangling earrings. And those boots would certainly keep the illusion going. Each individual garment was a testament to poor taste. But put together, and considering they were headed to a raucous Texas honky-tonk, the ensemble was inspired. "You look like a lady out for a fun evening," Raney announced.

Joss clapped her hands. "Perfect! Now let's work on you. You need a skirt."

"I don't have one that will go with this blouse."

"I might." Joss swept out and returned a few minutes later with a slinky floral skirt that came past the knee. "Try this."

Raney held it up and studied her reflection in the full-length mirror on the closet door. "Flowers? Really?"

"It's feminine, and they look more like paint splotches. You need to remind Dalton you're not just another cowboy."

"As if he cares," Raney said, trying to pretend Dalton Cardwell wasn't the main reason she was going out in the first place.

"Oh, he cares, all right." Joss's gaze met Raney's in the mirror. She wasn't laughing. In fact, her expression was serious. And troubled. "The question is, do you care whether he cares?"

Raney didn't answer.

"I know he's been to prison, Raney. He made a mistake and he suffered for it. But he's a good guy and he deserves a second chance. Can't you give him that?"

Raney turned and faced her. "I want to, Joss. I really do. But . . ."

"But nothing. He's handsome, built like a brick shithouse, and obviously has the hots for you. You don't have to marry the guy, but what's wrong with having a little fun?"

"Says my fun-loving, pregnant, unmarried sister." Raney said it as a joke.

But Joss didn't smile. "I fell in love with the wrong guy, but at least I was trying. How long are you going to hold that against me?"

Raney immediately reached out to her sister. "Oh, Joss, I didn't mean it like that. I admire the courageous way you're handling the baby and the changes she'll bring. Good changes. But scary, too." She brushed a blue curl off her sister's cheek. "I just worry about you, is all. Seems like I've spent most of my life worrying about my baby sister."

"You don't need to. You never really did, you know. I'm not as wild or crazy as my family thinks I am."

"No?" Raney slipped off her jeans and tried on the skirt. She checked it in the mirror and liked the way it moved when she spun to check the back. "That wasn't your bra hanging over the goalpost upright after homecoming?"

"Okay, maybe I was a little wild. But what choice did I have? That skirt looks better on you than me." She ducked into Raney's closet and came back out carrying a pair of boots with turquoise leather cutouts. "Here, try it with these."

"Cowboy boots?"

"It's a cowboy roadhouse. You'd prefer flats with support hose?"

Raney tried them on. They were perfect with the skirt. She should have Joss pick out her clothes more often.

Joss motioned to the vanity. "Now sit down and let's do something with your hair. And no, you're not wearing a ball cap or Stetson."

With a wary glance at her sister's mop of blue and green and hot pink streaks, Raney sat. "What do you mean, what choice did you have?"

Joss plugged in the hair straightener and began brushing out Raney's hair. "Len was the smart one. You were the hardworking one—and Daddy's favorite, I might add. And even as a kid, KD knew exactly what she wanted and worked to get it. The only role left was party girl and dream chaser."

Raney looked at her in confusion. "But I thought that's what you wanted to be."

"Like you wanted to give up college?" She must have seen Raney's shock. "Yeah, I know about that. And I saw how broken you were when Daddy died and how desperately you tried to fill his shoes. I wouldn't have minded helping, too, but you and Mama had everything under control. So, I just did my thing. I think you'd look better with curls. Where's your fat curling iron?"

While Joss transformed her nondescript hair into a mass of tousled curls, Raney stared into the mirror, her mind in turmoil. How had she not seen how Daddy's death might have affected her little sister? Joss had been sixteen during that terrible time—still a kid—and Daddy had been her father, too. "Joss, I'm so sorry. I had no idea you felt this way. Why didn't you say something?"

Joss laughed, breaking the tension between them. "And miss all the fun of being the wild one?" She gave that smirk Raney hated, although now she suspected her sister did it more in self-defense than an attempt to hurt. "I'd much rather be a party girl than a workhorse."

"A workhorse? That's how you see me?"

"No. Not really. In fact, I envy the way you take charge and everybody listens. I doubt Mama could have made it without you. But wouldn't it be great if we were both a little of each? There, how's that?"

Raney looked into the mirror. "It looks like I just got out of bed."

"Exactly. Now hurry up. I hear the guys downstairs and you know how restless they get if they don't eat on time."

Dalton couldn't take his eyes off Raney. He'd never seen anything so beautiful. Or sexy. Just looking at her got him worked up. Judging by the way Joss and her mother kept eyeing him, he knew he was making a spectacle of himself. But Raney looked too damn good to look away. He could hardly even concentrate on Mrs. Whitcomb's usual questions about Rosco and how the colts had handled the storm last night. And it wasn't until the meal was almost over that he realized he couldn't remember what he'd eaten.

It was a relief when Joss asked Alejandro about his custody battle. They talked about that for a while, which gave Dalton cover to study Raney. He was pleased to catch her studying him back. He gave her a wink, which made her blush. A female with a Glock who blushed at a wink. The woman was a bundle of contradictions.

What she'd said last night about her mother pushing her on men had shocked and infuriated him. Raney didn't deserve being treated like something was wrong with her just because she wasn't married and didn't have kids. He knew it wasn't because she had an aversion to men. Despite her efforts to keep her distance, he had felt her response when he'd kissed her. But now he knew why she held back. Like a crack opening in that armor she hid behind, when she'd said she was rich, he'd gotten a glimpse into her mind. Somewhere, somehow, she'd gotten the idea that her money was the most important thing she had to offer. Bullshit. It was no wonder she was so skittish if she thought every man who showed interest was only after her money. As far as he was concerned, that money was what he liked least about her, since it created a barrier he couldn't get past.

Mrs. Whitcomb's voice cut through his thoughts. "Dalton? Is something wrong? You seem upset."

He looked up, saw the faces staring at him, and struggled to put on a pleasant expression. "Just thinking about something Amala suggested yesterday." Not an outright lie. He had been thinking about what Press said. Just not right then.

"Care to share? Perhaps we can help."

Realizing he'd have to respond or arouse more suspicions, he said, "While I was there, I saw a mare you might be interested in. Not for showing. Press said she'd been overworked years ago and doubted she'd ever be showable again. But she has strong bloodlines, and since you're expanding your breeding program, I thought you might want to take a look at her."

"How old is she?" Raney asked.

"Ten." Dalton explained that she'd been bred before and had dropped two healthy foals. Neither had made it into the arena, but the sire wasn't anything special. "Breeding always tells, and he didn't have it."

"And you think this mare does?"

"I've seen her papers. She's top-notch." As he said the

words, it occurred to him how similar the mare's situation was to Raney's. Both were outstanding females that had been poorly used and overworked, and both were scarred because of it. It fit, but he doubted Raney would appreciate him making the comparison.

"And Press is willing to sell her?" Mrs. Whitcomb asked.

"He has no use for her. He's selling off most of his horses. Wants to go live near his daughter. He's said several times that if you were to breed her to Rosco in a few years, you'd have a real winner."

"What do you think, Raney?" Mama asked.

"I think we should take a look at her."

"Then I'll call him," Mama decided. "See what he's asking."

A few minutes later, Maria came in with dessert. Brandied fruit compote, Mrs. Whitcomb called it. Smelled more like booze than fruit, but was pretty tasty.

Beside Dalton, Glenn started fidgeting, which usually meant he was working himself up to say something. After a lot of throat clearing and hemming and hawing, the foreman voiced his concern that the short power outage during the storm the previous night might have caused an issue with the liquid nitrogen tanks where the straws of bull semen were stored. Obviously, a difficult subject for the shy man to bring up in the presence of the ladies, although Dalton suspected those same ladies had set up the artificial insemination program in the first place.

"Did you check the gauge this morning?" Raney asked him.

"It showed a slight rise in temperature, but didn't make it into yellow."

"It should be fine. The technician comes next week. I'll have him look at it."

Joss tossed her napkin beside her plate. "Mercy sakes. All this talk about breeding and semen reminds me we'd better get cracking or we'll never find a parking place at the Roadhouse."

"Lord's sake, Joss!" Mama scolded. "You'll mark the baby with such talk!"

Dalton hid a laugh behind his napkin.

Glenn almost toppled his chair in his rush to excuse himself, Alejandro right behind him.

"I can be the designated driver," Dalton offered. If he had to keep an eye on these two ladies, he'd have to keep his head clear. Plus, he didn't intend to waste his time drinking when he had Raney to dance with.

"You can drive us out there, but we'll let Joss drive home," Raney suggested. "She's off alcohol for now, and I don't want to drink alone. We can take my truck."

A few minutes later, they loaded up. As expected, Joss hopped into the passenger seat. Dalton opened the back door for Raney. "I never thought our first date would include your pregnant sister," he murmured as Raney hopped inside.

"This isn't a date."

"We'll see." The door slammed before Raney could think of anything to say.

It wasn't a long drive, but Raney was relieved they made it to the Roadhouse in one piece, since Dalton spent as much time watching her in the rearview mirror as he did watching the road. She knew this because every time he looked in the mirror, he caught her watching him. And winked.

It promised to be a long night.

Joss was right about the crowded parking. The closest spot they could find was at least thirty yards from the door. Because Dalton had the pockets, Joss and Raney gave him their vitals—money, credit cards, IDs—so they wouldn't need purses.

The night was clear and brightened by a gazillion stars

but the air felt warm and humid after the storm the previous night. Raney hoped there would be enough AC to keep from getting overheated, especially since Joss had talked her into wearing a short bolero jacket over her silk blouse.

They could feel the throb of the big bass speakers as they walked across the lot. Jerry and the Kickers were a popular semilocal band that had a pretty decent vocalist backed by a wildly enthusiastic drummer and nimble-fingered guitarist. Joss had sung with them a couple of times, mostly after she'd been drinking, and when they walked in and Jerry saw her, he announced her like visiting royalty.

Raney was embarrassed when a sea of faces turned their way, but she smiled gamely and waved to friends she knew. Dalton stood stoically by her side. As far as she knew, this was his first big social outing since his release from prison. She figured it must be difficult for him, seeing familiar faces and wondering how many of them he could still count as friends. Some—like Suze and Buddy Anderson—were welcoming. Others watched him warily—men sizing him up, women showing muted interest. And one was openly hostile—Deputy Langers, in full uniform, posted in a corner by the bar as a reminder that the law was on duty.

Joss immediately disappeared into the crowd. Squeals and shouts of welcome marked her progress across the cavernous room and luckily drew the press of people near the door away from Raney and Dalton.

"How about a beer?" he shouted over the noise, leaning closer to add, "You'll have to go with me to get it. I won't risk losing you in this mob until I get at least one dance." He straightened, and the look he gave her made her knees weak. If she was this flustered just standing beside him, how would she manage a dance without falling on her face?

A waitress came by with a loaded tray. Dalton tossed a ten on it and plucked off two longnecks, then steered Raney up onto the raised mezzanine that curled in a U shape around the gigantic dance floor—the only place where al-

cohol could be consumed on site. After weaving through a
tangle of crowded tables they found an empty one in back.

Dalton took off his Stetson and set it on the corner of the
table, then pulled out a chair for Raney next to his against
the wall. The sat side by side, not touching, but close
enough to talk if they shouted loud enough. Dalton sat at an
angle, his long legs outstretched and crossed at the ankles,
his muscular arm draped along the back of her chair. His
entire posture showed relaxed assurance. The arm resting
on her chair spoke of a connection between them, a claim
of possession apparent to anyone who walked by. Raney
thought it was amusing. And flattering.

Harley's Roadhouse was a dying breed—a family-
friendly, old-time, rural Texas dance hall that welcomed
patrons of all ages. In deference to underage guests, no alcohol was allowed on the dance floor, and minors weren't
allowed on the mezzanine. The dancers ranged in age from
shuffling octogenarians like the Polaskys—in their eight-
ies, at least—to teenagers wearing NO ALCOHOL wrist-
bands, and a few youngsters who hadn't even reached
puberty yet. The Roadhouse was considered a safe place by
Texas standards, best known for music and dancing and its
hard line against drunkenness or brawling, although occasional bouts of disorderly conduct were overlooked. It
helped that, although guns weren't allowed where alcohol
was served, there were plenty close at hand in the parking
lot. This was Texas, after all, and by God, Texans knew
how to have a good time and how to protect themselves
while doing it.

Raney slowly began to relax, relieved that Dalton wasn't
expecting her to be chatty and vivacious, and seemed content to sit quietly beside her and sip his beer. She'd never
been that great at small talk, and she was tired of talking
about Rosco and his training, so silence was best.

Then Joss rushed up, her smile wide, her hazel eyes dancing. "Jerry wants me to sing with them. Isn't that great? Best

stay here. It's really crowded up front. I'll find you after. Wish me luck!" Then she was off again, trailed by a couple of young women Raney vaguely remembered from Joss's high school years. She motioned Dalton closer. "Have you ever heard her sing?" she shouted over the music.

He dipped his head down next to hers. "Say again?"

Raney could smell his aftershave and feel the heat of him along her shoulder. His breath against her neck made the nerves beneath her skin tingle. "Have you ever heard Joss sing?" she repeated.

He shook his head, sending a wave of glossy dark brown hair over his forehead.

Raney fought the urge to brush it aside so she could test the softness of it and feel the warmth of his skin against her fingers. "Then you're in for a treat."

The family joke was that Joss had come out of the womb singing. All Raney remembered was how noisy she was. But as soon as her baby sister could string two sounds together, it was the beginning of her singing career. From church choir, to glee club, to every talent show for miles around, Joss was a star. And when she wasn't singing, she was writing songs. They had all expected her to be on concert tours, opening for big stars by now, but somehow, that chance had never come.

Crystal, the aging singer Joss had been with for the last couple of years, had never risen above the dance hall and casino circuit, which hadn't given Joss much exposure. And now that her sister was having a baby, Raney feared her big break might never materialize, which would be a shame. Joss definitely had the talent and charisma to be a star.

Being a local favorite, Joss had the crowd eating out of her hand before she'd sung more than a few words. They went crazy, stomping and clapping and singing along with her, and pride in her sister brought tears to Raney's eyes.

She glanced over at Dalton's surprised expression and laughed out loud. "I told you," she shouted, then stood up to give her little sister the piercing, two-fingered whistle Daddy had taught all his girls.

Joss finished to loud applause, then rushed back to plop into a chair by their table. "Was that amazing, or what? God, I've missed singing! Isn't it hot in here?"

"Why haven't you been singing?" Raney asked.

Joss's head swiveled as she checked out the people dancing past. "Crystal didn't want a pregnant woman singing backup, much less opening for her. Aren't y'all going to dance?"

"Then what have you been doing all this time?"

Joss bolted to her feet. "We'll talk later. Unlike you two, I'm here to dance!" And she was off again, calling and waving as she wove through the tables toward the dance floor.

"That's odd." Raney turned to Dalton. "Don't you think that's odd?"

"What I find odd is driving fifteen miles to a dance hall and not dancing. You ready yet?" He held out his hand, palm up. "Sweetheart?"

"You're relentless."

"I try."

Raney rose and took his hand. "Lead on. And don't whine about stomped toes."

After the first half-dozen missteps, Dalton learned to anticipate where she would stomp next and kept his feet moving. Luckily his boots had steel toes. He didn't really mind that she danced like a heifer in heels, or spent most of her time looking down between them at her feet, or kept apologizing every time she stumbled. But it seemed to bother her a lot, so he did the only thing he could do—pulled her tight against his body, locked his arm firmly around her slender rib cage, and told her to quit trying so hard and listen to the music.

"I've got you," he shouted into her sweet-smelling hair. "I promise I won't let you go. Just follow my lead."

It worked. To an extent. Raney wasn't a woman who easily relinquished control, even on a dance floor, but somehow, they managed. After a few laps, he could feel her body begin to relax against his, and that furrow of worry between her brows went away, and her smile of happy surprise made something clench deep in his chest. She looked so beautiful, her blue eyes sparkling and her cheeks rosy from exertion, and soft, shiny curls bouncing against her shoulders. He hadn't had so much fun in a long time.

But it also caused a problem for him, having her firm, slim body rubbing up against his. It interfered with his ability to think. Or remember that this wasn't a good idea. Or that he was fast becoming that guy he'd vowed not to be.

But he persevered. Because it was Raney in his arms. And she was worth it, and he didn't want whatever dance they had going on between them to ever end.

But a few minutes later, it did, when Jerry announced a short break and turned the music over to the in-house DJ, who immediately opened with a quieter, slower tempo to encourage dancers to fill up on beer while they could. Good marketing ploy, Dalton thought, as he steered Raney back to their table.

"Did I step on your toes a lot?" she asked, taking her seat.

"You're a great dancer," he said loyally, scooting his chair closer so he wouldn't have to shout. At least, that's what he hoped she'd think, rather than accusing him of putting a move on her. Which he was.

Raney gave him a look. "Liar. I'm terrible. But you made it fun, Dalton, and I thank you for that."

"I enjoyed it, too." He leaned closer and whispered into her ear, "Especially the way you felt rubbing up against me, your hips pressed—"

"Oh my God!"

He flinched and sat back as Joss flopped into the chair on the other side of her sister, flushed and breathless. And not happy, it seemed. "What's up, Buttercup?" he asked.

Ignoring him, Joss grabbed Raney's arm, her face tense, her words an angry hiss. "You'll never guess who's here!"

CHAPTER 12

"Hi, Raney," a deep voice said.

Dalton looked up, saw a tall guy, dressed like he'd be more comfortable in an accountant's office than a Texas dance hall, smiling down at the woman beside him. Smiling in a way that implied a past history between them.

"Hello, Trip," Raney said, the flush of exertion Dalton had so admired fading from her cheeks.

"Mind if I join you?" the interloper asked, smiling all around.

Actually, Dalton did. Joss, too. But he was asking Raney, not them. To give Raney time to make the right decision and send the guy packing, Dalton stood, stretching to his full six-four so the two-inch-shorter man would have to look up to him. He stuck out his hand. "Dalton Cardwell. And you are . . . ?"

"Trip Kaplan. I'm an old friend of Raney's." He studied Dalton's face as they shook hands. "Have we met? You look familiar."

"Are you a lawyer? Hang around jails a lot? Consider Commissioner Adkins a close personal friend?"

"No."

"Then we haven't met."

Knowing it wasn't his decision whether the guy stayed or left, Dalton said to Raney, "You want to dance, sweetheart? Or should I get us a beer?"

She got the message. He could tell by the softening of her mouth. "A beer would be nice, Dalton. Thank you."

"I'll go with you," Joss said, and shot to her feet. As soon as they were out of earshot, she said, "You called her sweetheart."

"Think he noticed?"

"Who cares. He's an asshole. I hate him."

Dalton didn't respond. If Raney wanted him to know about the guy, he'd wait for her to tell him. At least, that's what he thought in his head. What came out of his mouth was, "Why do you hate him?"

"I told you already. He's an asshole."

"Right. Got it."

"And he treated Raney bad."

"Does he know she owns a Glock?" he asked, trying to keep it light. Maybe she had it stashed in her truck. Not that he would ever look for it. Or need it.

"Raney's got a handgun?"

"Maybe."

They arrived at the bar. Thirsty people stood three deep waiting to order under the watchful eye of Deputy Langers, still standing in his corner, ready to defend the world against rowdy behavior and bawdy language. Another asshole.

"You want anything?" he asked Joss.

"Yeah. But I'm pregnant and can't have it."

Dalton took that as a *no*. Being taller than most, he could see over the heads of those around him, and when he spotted the waitress he had overtipped earlier, he held up two fingers and another ten.

"Trip worked in our accountant's office," Joss told him. "They were engaged a couple of years ago."

"Engaged? To that asshole?" Dalton was surprised how much that bothered him. "He looks like an accountant." Probably afraid of horses, too.

"I know, right? Not at all Raney's type."

"Raney has a type?" Dalton wondered which category he fit into.

"Yeah." Joss grinned up at him. "Guys like you."

He grinned back, mollified.

The waitress swung by with her loaded tray. Dalton handed her the ten, smiled his thanks, and relieved her of two longnecks. He and Joss left the bar area and went to stand by the mezzanine rail.

He glanced over. Raney and the asshole were still talking. It didn't look like they were having fun, so Dalton stayed out of it for now. "What happened?" he asked Joss.

"She caught him cheating."

Dalton snorted. "Only an idiot would two-time a woman like your sister."

Joss gave him a look that reminded him of some of the looks Raney had sent his way. Impatience with a hint of disgust. A look most females mastered by puberty. "Not that kind of cheating. He was going through the ranch books."

"That wasn't his job?"

"Exactly. That wasn't his job. Neither the ranch nor the Whitcomb Trust were on his client list. And once he saw how well the trust was doing, or rather, how well Daddy's investments were doing, he fell instantly in love. Asshole."

A trust, too? What else didn't he know? But it explained a lot. Especially why she might think every guy was after her money. Dalton sipped his beer, which was getting warm, while in his head, all the pieces that defined Raney began to fall into place. "How did she find out about it?"

"He let something slip just before their engagement party. When Raney confronted him, he didn't even try to deny it. He said with him running the operation and handling the investments, they'd be rich enough to move to Dallas and hobnob with all the other Highland Park millionaires." Joss laughed. "He actually thought she'd leave the ranch and turn everything over to him. Can you imagine that? Raney giving up the reins? No wonder she dumped him."

No, Dalton couldn't imagine it. Even in the short time he'd known her, he'd realized the ranch was as important to Raney as breathing. And woe be to any man who stepped between her and Whitcomb Four Star.

"How'd she take the breakup?" he asked.

Joss shrugged. "You know Raney. She took it in stride. I think I was more upset about it than she was."

Dalton shook his head. "I doubt it. Your sister feels a lot more than you give her credit for. She just locks it all inside."

Joss frowned up at him. "You think?"

"Talk to her. You might have her figured wrong." Raney and the asshole were still talking. Neither was smiling. Dalton finished his beer and set the empty on a passing tray. "I think they've chatted long enough," he decided. "Ready to head back?"

"Only if you promise to run him off."

"I'll do my best."

When they arrived at the table, the accountant was scowling and Raney didn't look any happier than when they'd left, which told Dalton their differences hadn't been patched up. Excellent. "Sorry it took so long, sweetheart." He handed Raney her warm beer.

"Thanks." But instead of keeping the longneck for herself, she passed it to the asshole. "You take it, Trip. I'd rather dance." And before Joss and Dalton could sit down, Raney rose and turned to her sister. "Joss, it's the Electric Slide. Or Tush Push. One of those line dances. Whatever. Want to show me and Dalton how to do it?"

"Sure," Joss said.

Taking Dalton's hand like it was the most natural thing in the world, she smiled down at the befuddled man sitting alone at the table with his lukewarm beer.

"Thanks for stopping by, Trip. My best to your folks." Then with a finger waggle that looked more like a brush-off or a poorly executed flip-off than a good-bye wave, she led Dalton after Joss toward the dance floor.

"I think I love you," Dalton said as they took their places in line.

"Of course you do. Everybody does. I'm a Whitcomb and I'm rich. Now be quiet so I can learn how to do this."

If Raney was a klutz at the two-step, she was a disaster at line dancing, despite her years as a cheerleader. It was like being caught up in a Three Stooges routine. She gave it a good try but after only a few minutes, they were both laughing so hard at all her missteps they left the dance floor before they injured any of the other dancers.

"They must practice for hours every day," Raney said as they stood at the rail, watching the dancers stomp by, hands in pockets, heels banging in unison on the floorboards.

"It keeps them off the streets, I guess."

Dalton looked around. The asshole was gone. But two guys eyeing him from a table nearby looked familiar. Late twenties, wearing faded Texas A&M ball caps. When one of them leaned over to say something to the other, Dalton saw the bright red hair poking out from beneath the cap at the back of his bullish neck and realized who they were.

Cousins of Jim Bob Adkins. He had seen them in the gallery at his arraignment, sitting with the commissioner, Jim Bob's uncle. They'd made no secret of their hostility then. It was no different now.

Trouble. Dalton recognized the signs. He'd seen it over and over during his short time in prison. The whispers. The looks. Then after they'd built up enough courage with talk, or drugs, or booze, they'd make their move.

He couldn't stop whatever was about to happen. But he could pick the place.

"Want another beer?" he asked Raney.

"No. I've got to hit the restroom as it is. Meet you back here."

Dalton waited until she was lost in the crowd, then rose and walked out the exit door to the parking lot, the two Aggies following close behind.

Showtime.

Raney was talking to Suze Anderson in the ladies' room when Joss burst in. "Two guys are heading outside to fight Dalton. He'll get hurt. We have to stop it!"

Shit. Trying not to panic, Raney reached for her cell phone, then realized both she and Joss had left them in the truck. "You have a phone?" she asked Suze.

Suze nodded and pulled it out of the back pocket of her jeans.

"Call 911. Report a fight at Harley's Roadhouse."

Suze punched in the numbers. As it rang through, she glanced at Raney in confusion. "Deputy Langers is here. Won't he stop it?"

"He'll probably egg them on, the jerk!"

The operator's voice sounded. "911. What is your emergency?"

Raney grabbed Suze's arm before she could answer. "Ask her to send the highway patrol. If she tries to route you to the sheriff's office, tell her Deputy Langers is part of it."

While Suze repeated that to the operator, Raney told Joss to find people who had cell phones with them. "Ask them to video the fight. All of it. Tell them I'll pay fifty dollars for a clean copy."

Joss barged out the door.

"Have Jerry announce it!" Raney yelled after her.

Suze ended the call. "The highway patrol is on the way." She followed Raney out of the restroom. "You sure Toby won't help?"

"He hates Dalton because of some girl Toby had the hots for."

"Karla Jenkins. She thought Toby was a perv. I better warn Buddy. He'll want to back up Dalton."

"No! Tell him not to interfere, Suze. No use getting your husband involved and turning this into a free-for-all. But you could video it and send it to Sheriff Ford."

After they left the bathroom, Suze went looking for her husband, while Raney hurried across the dance floor. As she neared the exit, Jerry made the announcement. As soon as he said "fifty dollars," the crowd surged toward the doors, carrying Raney along with them.

When she finally got outside, she saw Dalton and two other guys walking across the parking area, not far from where her truck was parked. Dalton led, the other two following close behind. One was jittering around. The other was a huge redhead, not as tall as Dalton, but a lot heavier.

And off in the shadows, Deputy Langers watched and did nothing. Damn him!

Heart pounding, Raney shoved through the crowd, desperate to get to the truck and her phone.

Dalton's prison experience had taught him a lot, and one of the most important lessons was how to fight like a street brawler. That meant relying less on fancy footwork and fists, and more on his knees, elbows, feet—as long as he had on boots—and his head. Literally. Headbutts could end a fight with one blow. Fists were too vulnerable, unless they were aimed at soft tissue, but that called for close work, which Dalton didn't want. The object of those lessons was to put his opponent down as soon as possible, while minimizing damage to himself.

These two guys didn't worry him, unless they were armed. But he hadn't seen any suspicious bulges in the pockets of their tight-fitting jeans, so he figured they hadn't come prepared to fight. They were both big and beefy, probably played football, maybe even at the college level. But that was at least seven or eight years ago, and most of that beef had since turned to fat.

Besides, in a street fight, size wasn't as important as speed and agility. And Dalton had both. In addition, he had very quick hands—sticky hands, the newspaper had called them, back when he'd been an all-state wide receiver three years in a row. That was more than a decade ago, but he could still move. And thanks to the hours of weight training in the prison yard and his few early run-ins with other inmates, he figured he could handle these two assholes. Probably.

He stopped in a clearing on the edge of the parking area. Solid ground. Dirt, rather than loose gravel. Well lit, but far enough from the parked vehicles to give them space. As he waited for them to make their moves, he rolled his neck and shook out his arms, then said, "You sure you want to do this, fellas?"

"You killed Jim Bob."

"And you spending time in a hospital bed with a tube up your nose will make you feel better about that?"

Behind the assholes, people spilled out of the Roadhouse. Most were holding up phones turned sideways. Videoing. That could complicate things. But it might also keep him from going back to prison for assault—a clear parole violation—as long as he let the assholes make the first move.

He could do that.

He studied his opponents, watching their hands, how they moved their feet, where their eyes were looking. They were younger than Dalton, but not by much, and they hadn't aged well.

The redhead was the calmer of the two. He had long arms and a thick body. A scar through one eyebrow and a lump on the bridge of his nose marked him as either a fighter or a defensive lineman. Able to take punishment. Able to dish it out. But he also had a beer gut that hung over his belt. Plus, he had to move a lot of weight. At least two-seventy. Maybe more. He'd be slow and tire easily. But if he got Dalton inside those orangutan arms, he could pin him against that beer gut and squeeze the air out of him.

The other guy was slightly smaller and skinnier. Wired. He couldn't keep his hands still. His feet kept shuffling side to side, and his eyes darted back and forth like he was watching a Ping-Pong match. Hopped up on something and raring to go. He'd come first, but he wouldn't last long. He was already rattled. A quick elbow to the side of his head and it would be lights-out.

Dalton just had to make sure he came at him first.

"Hey, crackhead," Dalton called to him. "You still giving blow jobs for smack?"

Childish, maybe, but it worked. With a shout, the guy charged.

Instead of backing off, Dalton stepped toward him, side-stepped into a half turn at the last second, swung around as the guy went by, and brought his elbow with all of his two hundred thirty pounds behind it against the side of the druggie's head. The guy's forward momentum kept him going several steps before his legs gave way and he face-planted into the dirt.

Down for the count.

The other guy was already moving. Not fast, but not slow, either. His fists looked as big as cantaloupes. He held them high, protecting his face, his right hand slightly behind the left, his left foot forward. A right-handed boxer's stance. He wouldn't go for the face and risk hitting bone and breaking his hand. He'd go for the gut. Dalton would have to go lower.

He watched the Aggie come closer and shifted his weight from one foot to the other, timing it in his head. As soon as the guy started his swing, Dalton would feint left and kick out his right foot, hook him behind the knee and pull him down.

But just as the guy's shoulders signaled his move, Dalton saw Raney running behind him toward her truck. He thought *gun*, and yelled, "Raney, no!" just as a sledgehammer fist slammed into his stomach.

He staggered back, head spinning, gasping for air.

Somehow, he stayed on his feet.

The redhead kept coming.

Dalton kept moving backward to give himself time to catch his breath.

The Aggie came closer. Fists lower. Eyes darting down. Moving in for a kick.

Right-handed usually meant right-footed. Dalton watched the guy's feet. When the Aggie planted his left foot and jerked his right foot back, Dalton took a hop-step forward and drove the heel of his boot into the redhead's left knee.

A howl of pain, and the Aggie went down.

The crowd jeered and clapped.

Dalton bent over, hands on knees, and struggled to fill his lungs, hardly aware of the movement around him.

Until a voice shouted, "Freeze, Cardwell!"

Shit. Langers. Dalton slowly straightened.

Deputy Langers stood in firing position, both hands on the pistol pointed at Dalton's chest.

"You're wrong, Toby," Dalton said, still breathing hard. "I didn't start this."

"Put your hands up!"

Dalton slowly raised his hands above his shoulders. Another lesson learned in prison: never argue with a man who has a badge and a gun.

"On your knees!"

Dalton dropped to his knees beside the two Aggies. One

wasn't moving, but Dalton was relieved to see he was still breathing. The other was cussing and holding his knee.

"Hands on your head," Toby ordered.

Dalton put his hands on his head.

Still holding the gun on him, the deputy came around behind him. A moment later, Dalton heard the click of the cuffs closing around his wrists. It was a sickening sound. One he remembered well. And for the first time since he'd walked out of the Huntsville state prison, he felt afraid.

The onlookers murmured, phones still up, not sure what was happening. Maybe videos would help. Maybe not. If Langers had his way, Dalton would be headed back to prison tomorrow.

The crackhead rolled over and vomited into the dirt. The redhead moaned.

"Stand up," Langers ordered.

Dalton stood. He looked out past the sea of faces and saw Raney staring back at him, eyes stricken, a hand clamped over her mouth. *I'm sorry, sweetheart.*

"Why are you arresting Cardwell?" a familiar voice shouted. "The other guys started it."

Dalton looked over, saw Buddy Anderson standing in front of the crowd, a belligerent scowl on his face. Suze stood beside him, phone up and recording.

"He's right," another man said. "I've got everything on video."

Other voices shouted they did, too.

Toby ignored them. "Step aside!" Gripping Dalton by the elbow, he shoved him through the crowd toward his cruiser parked next to the building.

Then suddenly Raney stepped forward and blocked their way. She no longer looked stricken. Now her blue eyes were snapping with fury. "Why didn't you do anything, Deputy?" she demanded. "Instead of just standing there and watching?"

"If you interfere, Miss Whitcomb, I'll have to arrest you, too."

"Then do it." Raney held out her arms, wrists up. "Cuff me and within half an hour a dozen videos will post on the Internet. They'll show that those other two guys started the fight while you watched and did nothing then arrested the wrong man because of some twenty-year-old grudge."

"Seventeen," Dalton reminded her.

Joss stepped up behind her sister, arms out. "Arrest me, too, Deputy Langers. You'll be an Internet star. I've already sent a video to your boss, Sheriff Ford."

Other people stepped forward, arms out, asking to be put in cuffs. Laughter, catcalls and whistles, voices chanting, "Arrest me, too!"

And in the distance, the wail of sirens. Several sirens.

But Dalton could only stare at the woman in front of him. Fierce, brave, beautiful Raney. God, how he loved her. He reminded himself to tell her that when this was over.

Waving people aside, Langers continued to push Dalton toward his patrol car.

Dalton looked over, saw the nervous sweat sliding down Toby's temples, the look of panic in his eyes, and decided this had gone on long enough. "Don't do this, Toby," he said in a calm voice. "You know I didn't start it."

"Shut up." They reached the car and Langers yanked open the door. "Get in."

Dalton tried one last time. "Don't ruin your career over something that happened when we were kids. Stop now before it's too late."

"Shut the fuck up and get in the damn car!" Toby shoved him into the backseat, then leaned down and glared through the open door, breathing hard, his breath foul and smelling of beer. "If neither one of those guys presses charges, I will. Count on it!" Then he slammed the door so hard it rocked the car, just as an ambulance drove up, lights flashing. Two

Texas Highway Patrol SUVs came in behind it in a swirl of dust, followed by another ambulance.

Someone had called out the troops, and Dalton could guess who. God love her.

It took two hours to sort it all out. Deputy Langers received a call from Sheriff Ford and left soon after. The ambulances carted off the Aggies, one with a concussion, the other with a damaged knee. After talking to witnesses and viewing more videos than he wanted to, the trooper in charge issued disorderly conduct citations to all the combatants, told Dalton when and where to show up if he chose to contest it—which he advised him to do—then he and the other state troopers left.

Excitement over, the onlookers went back inside, lured by Joss's and Raney's promise of a free beer for everyone old enough to drink. Within minutes the music started up again, life went on as usual, and only Dalton and Raney remained in the parking lot, arms crossed, leaning side by side against the front fender of her truck.

"You owe me at least three hundred dollars," Raney said.

"I'm good for it."

Off to the east a late moon poked over the horizon. Dalton could see a tiny reflection of it in Raney's eyes. "You have a lot of your mama in you," he said. "And I'm not just talking about the color of your eyes."

"Is that a good thing, or a bad thing?"

"It's a miraculous thing. You're both amazing women." Seeing she was about to argue with him, he added, "But you're a lot prettier."

"And younger."

"That, too."

With a deep sigh, she tipped her head over to rest against his shoulder. "You keep scaring me."

"I don't mean to."

"Then stop."

They didn't speak for a time. Dalton felt his energy level drop as the rush of adrenaline left his body. Aches and pains became noticeable—a throb in his elbow, a hitch in his rib cage whenever he took a deep breath. But he'd had worse. And it probably would have gone worse tonight, if not for Raney. Joss had told him about her sister's fifty-dollar offer for a clean video and how she had made sure the 911 call went to the state troopers, rather than the sheriff's office. Without her help, he might have been headed to the county lockup right now, instead of standing under the stars with her head on his shoulder. "Have I told you today that I love you?"

"Only the once. And as I recall you only thought you loved me."

"I'm pretty sure I do."

"Hmmm."

He looked down at her. "You don't believe me?"

She lifted her head and studied him with an expression he couldn't decipher. "You don't know me well enough to love me, Dalton. When—and if—you decide you do, tell me then."

"Will you say you love me back?"

"I don't know." She dropped her head to his shoulder again. "You stay out of trouble and keep saying nice things to me, maybe I will."

Dalton took that as a *yes*.

Miles overhead, a satellite blinked to life. He watched its wavering path across the night sky and wondered if its camera could see his grin.

CHAPTER 13

Spring slid through May into early June. The days grew longer, the temperature higher, and life went on as usual. Which was part of the problem. Despite changes all around her, Raney felt stuck in a slow-motion cycle that went nowhere. Dalton was spending more time with Rosco than with her, Joss was nesting like crazy as her pregnancy advanced, and Mama was a little too excited about abandoning them and heading off to God knows where.

Yet, what did Raney have going but more of the same?

Now on the eve of her mother's departure, she was helping her sort through and fold clothes into the suitcases—one big roller for the cruise out of Seattle, and another to be shipped directly to the outfitters for the pack trip around Mount Rainier—which only worsened Raney's mood. Maybe she should cut and run, too.

"Is something wrong?" Mama asked as she pulled more clothes out of the closet and tossed them on the bed. "You've seemed distracted lately."

Raney was distracted. And restless. But she didn't know why.

Things were going great. Other than a reprimand in Deputy Langer's file, there had been no blowback from the fight at the Roadhouse. Dalton had gotten out of his citation and was now working hard toward Rosco's grand debut at the USCHA fall Futurity. She and Joss were getting along better than they ever had, and Press Amala had given them a generous price on Sassy, the mare Dalton had recommended. Even the AI program was doing well—despite Glenn's resistance—and the horses they'd bought after selling the herd showed great promise. Everything was good. So why did she feel so off?

Maybe last week's letter from Bertie had something to do with it. *Guess what?* her friend had written. *Phil and I got married!*

Raney had been shocked. And a little hurt. She and Bertie had promised each other since grade school to be in each other's weddings.

I'm a little sad, Bertie's letter had gone on, *that we didn't have time for a traditional wedding with you beside me as my maid of honor. But Phil got this amazing offer from a clinic in Oklahoma and had to start right away, so we ran off to Las Vegas and tied the knot in the cutest little pink chapel just off the Strip. Isn't that romantic? We'll talk more when I come visit Mother after we settle in. Love you. Bertie.* A disappointment, Raney realized, but not a surprise. She had felt Bertie drifting away the last time they'd been together in the diner.

But she did feel a little lost. Everyone around her was making changes, moving on to newer and better things while she stayed where she'd always been. And now Dalton seemed to be drifting away, too. What was she doing wrong?

"Is it Dalton?" her freakishly perceptive—and nosy—mother asked. "Is that why you're feeling so down?"

"I'm not down," Raney lied.

"Did something happen between the two of you?"

"Why would you say that?" Had Mama noticed he was avoiding her?

"Because I see you pushing him away, darling. Like you do with any man who shows interest. Is it because of that fight at the Roadhouse? I never liked that place."

"I didn't push Trip way."

"Sadly, no. Not until he showed where his interests truly lay. And for the record"—Mama waved a silky cover-up for emphasis—"I never liked him, either."

"Then all that so-happy-to-have-you-in-the-family stuff was just for show?"

"I was supporting you. Not him. Have you seen my green capris?"

Raney dug them out of the pile and tossed them across the bed. "I'm not pushing Dalton away." She almost added that she'd let him kiss her. Repeatedly. But decided against it. Mama didn't need more ammo.

Yet, what if her mother was right? What if she was pushing Dalton away, rather than the other way around? More likely, he was so focused on making a name for himself through Rosco, he didn't have time for anything else.

And why shouldn't he? It was his future at stake as much as her hopes for a successful cutting horse program. He deserved to be successful. Even Alejandro admitted the colt responded better to Dalton than he did to anyone else. And when Raney had called Press Amala about the mare, the old man couldn't say enough about Dalton's gift with horses.

"Maybe not this year," Press had said, "but soon Rosco and Dalton will be top tier on the cutting circuit. Just stay out of their way. The boy and that colt have an understanding and you don't want to mess with it." With a recommendation like that, what could she do but turn over the prize colt she had raised to an unproven trainer who was also an ex-con?

Actually, Raney was proud of both of them. She was excited about Rosco's progress. And despite all the marks against him, Dalton's hard work and easygoing manner had earned the friendship and respect of the other workers. Mama and Joss already treated him like family and Maria always had a plate of his favorite cookies on hand. He never asked, but people happily gave. She didn't begrudge him all the positive attention he was getting. He'd earned it.

Yet, for the first time since she'd taken over management of Four Star, she felt a little left out. Or better said . . . left behind. She wasn't usually on the sidelines, observing. She liked being in the thick of things, making sure everything moved smoothly. As ranch manager, that was her job. A workhorse, like Joss said.

But of late, she'd begun to feel irrelevant. She didn't feel like she fit anymore.

She still managed Four Star, of course. But it could be stressful, keeping a grip on all the threads that held the ranch together, while at the same time, balancing the needs of the workers, the expectations of her family, and the edicts of the moneymen and accountants who oversaw the family trust. She loved taking care of the ranch. But horses were her passion. And ever since Dalton came, she'd had to sit back and watch someone else do what she had always done. And do it better.

No wonder she was a little discouraged.

Mama sat on the end of the bed and patted a cleared space beside her. "Sit down and talk to me, Raney. I hate to leave when you're so troubled."

Reluctantly, she sat. "I'm not troubled. I'm just tired." She hesitated, then added, "Bertie got married. Ran off to Las Vegas with her veterinarian."

"Without you?"

"No big deal. They're moving to Oklahoma."

"That's too bad." Her mother reached over and took Raney's hand. "But are you sure that's what has you upset?

I know you're not sleeping well. No, don't deny it. I'm your mother. I can tell when my girls are fretting. What's wrong?"

Raney shrugged, not wanting to put all her petty resentments and doubts into words. She felt ridiculous even having them. She was a grown woman, for heaven's sake, not some whiny teenager.

"I know Dalton cares for you, Raney," her mother went on. "And I think you might have feelings for him, too. What's holding you back? Is it the accident?"

"Maybe. A little. Not as much as before." Yet it was still there, a shadow in the shadows. Accident or not, Dalton had taken a life and gone to prison for it. A life-changing thing. Yet he seemed to have blocked it from his mind as easily as if it were a minor mishap.

Like he was blocking her now? God, she was pathetic.

"It may not be all it seems," her mother said.

Raney frowned. "The wreck? What do you mean?"

Mama looked away. "Nothing. Just wishful thinking, I guess."

They talked a few more minutes about ranch stuff and how Raney should bully the trust accountants into giving raises to the workers, then with a final pat, Mama let go of Raney's hand and rose. "We can talk while we finish up here. UPS is picking up the suitcase for the outfitters this afternoon."

Dalton wasn't sure what he'd done wrong. All he knew for certain was that something was pushing Raney away from him. The fight at the Roadhouse? Because he'd told her he loved her? Because the sun was shining?

He didn't understand women at all. But unwilling to give up, he cornered Joss the afternoon before Mrs. Whitcomb was to leave on her trip and asked her if Raney was mad at him.

"About what?" Joss asked.

Dalton struggled to hide his impatience. "If I knew, would I be asking?"

Apparently he hadn't hidden it well enough. "Don't get pissy with me, Mr. Fancy Pants," Joss snapped. "I'm pregnant."

"Right. I forgot." Which earned him another glare before she stomped off. Now he had two sisters mad at him. Which left him no choice but to go all in.

"Mrs. Whitcomb," he said, after dinner that night. The sisters were carrying empty plates back into the kitchen and only Raney's mother remained on the veranda. "Can I talk to you?"

"Certainly." She studied him with a knowing smile. "About Raney?"

The woman must be psychic. "Yes, ma'am."

"Will it keep another day?"

With reluctance, Dalton nodded.

"Then drive me to the Lubbock airport tomorrow."

Lubbock? He had hoped for a quick answer, not a two-hundred-mile round-trip. "Isn't there a shuttle from Gunther to Lubbock?"

"It leaves midafternoon. My flight to Seattle leaves in the morning."

"Raney's not driving you?"

"I'll tell her you're stopping in Plainview on the way back to visit your folks."

On the way back? Plainview was fifty miles in a different direction. "Amala's bringing the mare tomorrow afternoon."

"I'm sure your parents miss you terribly, Dalton. Cancel Press. He'll understand. Unless you don't really need to talk to me."

Blackmail. Dalton sighed. "Yes, ma'am. I'll be happy to drive you." What was another hour to Plainview if he got the answers he needed?

"We leave at seven thirty in the morning."

*   *   *

When he arrived at the parking area the next morning, he was surprised to see Raney leaning against her mother's Expedition, a cup of coffee in her hand. "I thought I was driving your mother to Lubbock."

"You are." She tipped her head toward the back door. "If you haven't eaten, Maria can whip up some eggs while you get Mama's luggage."

A few minutes later, he knocked on Mrs. Whitcomb's door. "Bellhop."

"We'll have to hurry," she said, waving him inside. "I forgot about TSA, although why they would be worried about a woman my age, I'll never know." She pointed to the big roller by the bed. "Take that one. I'll bring the carry-on." As he rolled the suitcase into the hall, she said, "Raney insisted on coming, too."

"I saw."

"I know you wanted to speak to me about whatever's going on between you two, but it's probably best if you speak directly to her."

It probably was. But how was he supposed to do that when she would barely talk to him?

"She just needs reassurance, Dalton. Have patience." She pointed down the stairs. "You go first. I don't want you falling on top of me."

"Reassurance about what?" he asked over his shoulder as he headed down.

"You. You don't share much of yourself, you know."

That again. Why did women insist on knowing every little detail about stuff that didn't concern them? "I won't discuss the accident," he said when they reached the first-floor landing.

"I know. I talked to your mother."

He stopped so abruptly, she almost ran into him. "My

mother spoke to you about the wreck?" They had promised each other to never talk about that night.

"In a roundabout way. Nothing specific. Keep moving. I'm late as it is."

Dalton was so shocked he could barely wolf down the scrambled eggs waiting on the kitchen counter while Mrs. Whitcomb gave out last-minute instructions to Maria. What had his mother said?

Since Raney was sitting in the backseat when he went out to load the luggage, Dalton assumed that meant he'd drive. By the time he'd stowed the big roller into the rear deck of the car, Mrs. Whitcomb was in the passenger seat, passing kisses through the open window to sleepy-eyed Joss and promising she'd be back well before the baby came.

When they drove through the main gate a few minutes later, Mrs. Whitcomb turned to Dalton and said, "Since we're running fifteen minutes late, you may speed, but only if you do it prudently. I don't want to die before my cruise."

He didn't question the weirdness of her comment, but happily pressed down on the gas pedal, making the hundred-mile drive in an hour and twenty minutes and pulling up to the terminal with time to spare.

More good-bye hugs, this time directed at him, then, leaving him to guard the car, Mrs. Whitcomb and Raney went inside to make sure her luggage was sent to Boeing Field, rather than Seattle-Tacoma International.

Fifteen minutes later, Raney came back out, a big smile on her face. Dalton didn't know the cause, but guessed it wasn't because she'd be alone with him on the drive back, but rather that she'd be motherless for several weeks.

"I thought she'd never leave," she said with a deep sigh as she climbed into the passenger seat. "Mama can drag out a good-bye for hours if you let her. She said you might want to swing by Plainview to see your folks?"

"Maybe another time," Dalton hedged. "Amala's bringing the mare later this afternoon. I'd like to be there when they arrive. That okay with you?"

"Peachy."

Dalton drove to the Highway 82 interchange and headed east, retracing their route back to the ranch. This time, he didn't speed. Raney sat quietly beside him, staring out the window. After half an hour of silence, he accepted that she wasn't going to speak to him unless he drove her to it.

"What'd I do?" he finally asked.

She turned her head and looked at him. "About what?"

"Whatever it is you're mad at me about."

"I'm not mad at you."

"Then why won't you talk to me?"

She gave a half smile. "I could ask you the same thing."

He thought back to his conversation with her mother and let out a deep breath. "This is about what you said the night of the fight, isn't it? About us not knowing each other."

"We don't. Not really. What do we ever talk about but Rosco and the ranch?"

"Fine. Then what do you want to talk about?"

"Forget it," she snapped, and turned back to the window.

He probably shouldn't have said it so impatiently, but it pissed him off that she'd shut him down when he was trying to do what she'd asked. "Don't pull that crap, Raney. You wanted to talk, so let's talk. But since I'm just a guy and don't know all the rules, you'll have to spell it out. What do you want to talk about?"

"You. For starters."

Hell. But he gamely said, "What do you want to know?"

"Everything." She spread her hands, palms up, then dropped them back to her lap. "There are big sections of your life you won't discuss, Dalton. Maybe you locked them away. Maybe you have good reason. But they're still there, still part of who you are. And if we're to go any further with whatever we have between us, I need to know that stuff. How you think. How you feel. What makes you happy, or sad, or afraid. I need to know you, Dalton. Only then can I trust you."

Dalton was astounded. "You don't trust me?"

"I trust what I know about you. But I don't know much. That's the problem."

He didn't know what to say. Despite the one incident when he'd felt compelled to be otherwise, he'd always considered himself an up-front person. No hidden agendas. No ulterior motives. A forthright, honest, what-you-see-is-what-you-get type of guy.

Naturally, there were things he didn't want to talk about. Mistakes he wished he hadn't made. Regrets over things he'd said, or done, or didn't do. But most of it was in the past. Different time, different place. What good would it do to drag it all up now?

But if he wanted Raney, and that's what she needed . . . *shit*.

"I'm guessing you only want to hear about the bad stuff, not what I got on my fifth birthday, or which ride I liked best at Six Flags, or what my favorite color is." He grinned over at her, hoping to lighten the mood and maybe distract her a little. "Blue. As long as it matches your eyes."

She smiled but said nothing. Definitely not distracted.

"Okay, then. Let's start with prison." Maybe if he worked backward, she'd forget about the wreck. "It was noisy, grim, impersonal, and overrun with guys choking on rage with no way to expend it except on each other. Just like on TV except a lot more boring. And violent. The food was terrible, the monotony awful, the guards tolerable as long as you toed the line."

He didn't mention the few fights he'd had. Or his trips to the infirmary because of them, and how hard he'd worked to bulk up so he wouldn't have to go there again. Or the endless, soul-crushing loneliness of the nights, and the constant brutal savagery that defined his days.

"I spent most of my time reading and counting the days

and working out in the prison yard." Struggling to stay sane and alive.

"What did you read?"

"Child, DeMille, Crichton. *Lonesome Dove*, twice."

She gave him a teasing smile. "No romances?"

"*Lonesome Dove* is romantic. Sort of."

"Only a man would think so. What about Iraq?"

He slumped back in the bucket seat, as if that might distance him from those bleak memories. After spending the last eight years trying to outdistance that dark time, now she was asking him to go through it again.

But again, if he wanted Raney, and that's what she needed . . .

"Iraq definitely wasn't romantic. Brutal in a whole different way from prison. Even more violent and cruel, but at least I had brothers beside me. Did I kill people? I don't know. I aimed to. Did I see terrible things? Definitely."

Billy's head exploding in a red mist that coated his face, his throat, his mind.

He shook the image away. "It was war. Terrible things happened all the time. The worst was watching my buddies get hurt or die around me."

Faces flashing through his mind. Squandered lives. Hope dying in a scream.

"Mostly I remember blood, chaos, the constant noise of explosions and gunfire. Even now, when I think about that time, all I hear is a roar in my head."

Mangled limbs, headless torsos, agonized faces of men he loved.

He pushed through the horror, needing to say it all so maybe he wouldn't have to speak of it ever again. "I'd go days with almost no sleep, figuring the next mortar round would have my name on it. Then there would be a lull. We'd sit around waiting for orders, talking about home and women and what we were going to do when we got back to the States, all the while pretending death wasn't waiting outside the gate. Then it would start all over again. Mostly, it was ugly and dehumanizing. Pointless."

He didn't know he had clenched his fist against his thigh until she reached over and laid her hand on top of his. Odd, how that simple contact eased the tight band of tension around his chest. He took a deep breath, let it out, and twined his fingers through hers. Maybe this was helping. Maybe after talking about it, he could lock it away forever and she'd be happy again.

They sat in silence until he had to let go of her hand to make the left onto 265, a narrow, dusty ranch road. His time with Raney was almost up, but he wasn't sure they'd accomplished anything with all this talk.

"Why did you sign on for two more years after your enlistment was over?"

Guilt. Redemption.

"Because by then I'd learned to hate," he said, which was true, too. "I wanted payback. A reason why I'd survived and others hadn't. I wanted to get bin Laden."

"But you didn't."

"No, I didn't. And after a while I realized it didn't matter. Nothing would ever change and the killing would never stop. So, I mustered out as soon as I could."

Yet the ghosts of his buddies followed him home. He couldn't seem to outrun them and he was so tired of trying. Even now, on the bad nights, they called out his name. But how could he explain that to someone who'd never seen war?

"Do you still hate?" she asked.

"Not much. It was a necessary tool in combat, but not now. I don't even like thinking about Iraq anymore, much less talking about it."

She brushed a hand along his arm. "I'm sorry. I made you go through that again. But I needed to know."

He slowed for the turn onto 193, which would take them to the Whitcomb Four Star main gate. Time had run out.

Yet he felt farther from her than ever. "Did it help? Hearing all that?" He didn't see how. Now she'd have those pictures in her head, too, and what good could come of that?

"Definitely. Knowing what you went through, how it affected you, and how hard you've worked to get past that horrible time is actually a comfort to me."

A comfort? Was she insane?

"I know now that you're capable of violence," she went on. "But you don't like using it. I know you won't go looking to hurt anyone. But when pushed, like you were at the Roadhouse, you'll stand your ground. And that tells me you'll protect me if need be, but you'll never use your strength against me."

He looked away, humbled and a little disturbed to be analyzed so thoroughly.

A moment later, they turned through the gate, bounced over the cattle guard, and headed down the drive toward the house. "So we're okay?" he asked.

Her smile was as open and honest as any she'd ever given him. "We're okay."

"Good." He pulled into the parking area behind the house, shifted into park, set the brake, and punched the ignition button. Then he sat back and said, "Because now I have a question for you."

CHAPTER 14

"Tell me about Trip," Dalton said. "Joss already told me what he did. Now I want to hear it from you."

He was sitting sideways, his back to the driver's door, one muscular arm resting across the steering wheel, the other on the console between the bucket seats. His gaze had an intensity that made the narrow space between them seem heated. Or maybe it only seemed that way because the air-conditioning was off.

Raney laughed. She couldn't help it. Dalton was such a guy. Forget about her favorite color, which movie was the all-time best, or which authors she loved. Go straight to the men in her past. Guys could be so predictable.

And easily offended, she thought, when she saw his frown.

He'd answered her questions. It was only fair that she answered his. "Trip is a nobody. A total douche. A Texas good ole boy in the worst possible way."

"Yet you loved him."

"I thought I did. But even as I accepted his proposal, I

had doubts." She thought back, tried to capture the moment in her mind. A candlelit dinner at an expensive restaurant. Flowers. A beautiful ring. A handsome, successful man sitting across from her. Any woman would have been delighted with such a proposal. Yet, thinking back, all she could remember was how relieved she'd felt. Not happy, or ecstatic. Just glad it was over.

What was over? The courtship? The pretense?

The pressure.

It seemed that everyone—her family, the grocer, Bertie, and even the old lady at the dry cleaner's—had been anxiously awaiting the big news that Raney Whitcomb was finally getting married.

"You look upset. What are you thinking about?"

She looked over to find him watching her, that frowning brow shadowing his beautiful green eyes. "I'm thinking it's hot as hell in here. And I also just realized again how close I came to making a catastrophic mistake."

"By marrying the douche?"

"Exactly. Maybe we should turn the AC back on."

"But if you didn't love him, why did you accept his proposal?"

"Because I loved the idea of him. The idea of having someone to help me run the ranch. Of not being single anymore. Of not being thought of as unnatural because I wasn't married. Once I was married, I could just be me and go on with my life without all that bullshit weighing me down. Does that make sense?"

"None whatsoever. But I'm glad you didn't marry him. It was disappointing to think that you'd settle for a douche."

"But I didn't, did I? Nor will I. Next time there's any proposing to be done, I'll be the one doing it. When I'm ready, and when I'm convinced it's right." She tried to moderate her tone. It wasn't Dalton's fault that Trip was an asshole. "All Trip cared about was my money and my connections. He was just another narcissistic good ole boy looking for someone to

parade around on his arm and be hostess to his good ole boy
pals and raise his future good ole boy sons." She was starting
to rant, and reminded herself it was Trip she was mad at, not
Dalton. "It was a mistake. I realized that and ended it. Any
more questions? I'm starting to suffocate."

"I'm guessing you don't much like good ole boys."

"They're anachronisms. Holdovers from a time when
men were men and women were sweet lil thangs who only
knew how to look pretty and do what they were told. It's
time we had more good ole gals calling the shots."

"You're scaring me."

"Get used to it." She sounded bitter and angry again.
She was talking too fast, feeling cornered, but didn't know
why. Maybe she really was suffocating.

"And now you're worried you're making another mistake. With me. Is that it?"

She stared at him, unable to answer.

"Raney . . . I'm not Trip."

"I know that."

"But you're still worried. I can see it. Why?"

She could feel the shutters come down. She didn't want
to talk about this anymore. She had to get some air.

But when she reached for the door handle, he put his
hand on her arm. "Don't shut me out, Raney."

Now he was angry, too.

"At least hear what I have to say."

She wanted to. But she had come to care for Dalton so
much. What if she was wrong this time, too? How could
she bear that? And why was it so hard to breathe?

He leaned close, hemming her in, one arm on the dash-
board, the other on the back of her seat. His eyes were
fierce, his lips drawn tight against his teeth. "I don't give a
rat fuck about your money, Raney. I never have and I never
will. Give it away. Burn it. I don't care. It's you I want."

She could see he believed that. She wanted to believe it,
too. But money changed people. Eroded trust and hope.

Maybe not with Dalton. But that last niggling doubt kept eating away. "It's too hot. I need to get out."

He drew back. "Just give us a chance. That's all I ask."

"Okay." She threw open the door and almost fell out of the Expedition, her lungs sucking in hot, dusty air. Immediately that feeling of suffocation passed. What was wrong with her? This was Dalton. The only man she trusted other than Daddy.

When he appeared at her side, a new kind of desperation seized her. Reaching out, she grabbed his hand in both of hers, needing the contact. He was her lifeline. Her anchor.

"I'm sorry, Dalton," she said in a rush. "I know you're nothing like Trip. But seeing him the other night, then talking about him . . . it brought it all up again. The betrayal. The humiliation. It's not your fault. I just . . . I just need . . ."

"Oh, baby." He pulled her close, his big body wrapping around her. Protective. Asking nothing, giving everything. Making her feel safe and cherished and connected in a way she hadn't since Daddy died. After a few moments, his voice rumbled through his chest. "I'm sorry he hurt you."

"He didn't. Not really. It was doubting myself that hurt more."

"Maybe I should go punch him."

"Maybe you shouldn't." She gave a shaky laugh and pulled back. Dalton always knew what to say to make her feel better. "But thanks for the offer."

Hands clasped, they walked through the gate into the backyard. "I hear he's not doing well. After we split, Mama suggested he move to another company. Which he did. Since then, he's been spending more than he makes and living like a rich man. Probably looking for a new cash cow to pay for it all."

"That seems harsh. I sure never thought of you as a cow."

She let go of his hand to poke him in the side. "I was going to fix you lunch, but after that remark, I don't think I will."

"That's okay. Maria will do it. She likes me."

"Don't we all."

When they went up the veranda steps, Raney saw Joss stretched out on a chaise, a half-finished plate of Dalton's favorite cookies perched on her baby bump. "What were y'all doing in the car all this time—as if I can't tell, as sweaty as you are. But never mind. Who likes Dalton?"

"Maria," he said. "Are those my cookies, Buttercup?"

"They're for the baby, Mr. Fancy Pants."

"Then why are you eating them? And why this sudden interest in my pants?"

Joss ignored him and said to Raney, "It seems Mama likes Dalton, too."

Raney didn't trust that sly look. "Why do you say that?"

Plucking a cookie off the plate, Joss took a bite and chewed thoughtfully, dragging it out for all it was worth. She finally swallowed and said, "She thinks we need protection. She's decided he should stay in the house while she's gone. In the downstairs guest room," she added, with a meaningful glance at Dalton.

He grinned back. "Sounds like a plan." He reached for a cookie.

Joss batted his hand away.

"She didn't say anything to me," Raney argued, sensing a trap but not sure who had set it. Having Dalton under the same roof would be troublesome. And tempting. And she didn't think either of them was ready for that next step. Yet.

"She texted me right before her plane took off. She also wants Dalton to promise he won't go upstairs unless he hears gunshots. And there's to be no . . . what were the words she used? Oh, yeah. Hanky-panky. I don't know what *panky* means, do you? Seems hanky-spanky would make more sense."

"I hear gunfire, I'm sure as hell not going up. I've seen your sister shoot."

"Oh, for heaven's sake," Raney burst out. "We've got a

half-dozen guys within shouting distance and I have a Glock next to my bed. Does she think with her gone, there'll be a stampede of rapists breaking down the door?"

Joss shuddered. "Lord, I hope not. I'm pregnant."

"Your mom's right," Dalton said to Raney, his green eyes alight with laughter. "I think it would be best if I stayed here at the house. For protection."

"And in the downstairs bedroom," Joss added.

"Oh, for heaven's sake."

"Great. I'll go get my stuff while Maria fixes lunch."

Later that afternoon, Raney saw Press Amala's truck and horse trailer go past the office window. Anxious to see this new addition to their growing stable of outstanding quarter horses, she set aside her paperwork and hurried to the barn.

By the time she arrived, Dalton was unloading the mare. She was a beauty. A flaxen chestnut with three white stockings and a white blaze that stretched from the middle of her forehead to her pink nose. Her confirmation was as square as it gets, deep in the chest and muscular in the haunches. Her demeanor seemed calm but attentive, her eyes bright with curiosity. She would definitely be an asset to Four Star, whether she could ever be shown again or not.

"She's beautiful, Press." Raney extended her palm for the mare to sniff. "I can't wait to try her out."

"Just be careful the first few times you take her into the pasture," the old man warned. "She had great training back when. She sees a cow, she might zig while you zag. Happened to me a time or two."

"I'll put her in the arena for now," Dalton said. "Let her get used to the place."

Raney watched him lead her away, liking how the horse moved and the way her blond tail swayed side to side with every stride. Dalton moved nice, too—that swagger again.

It was a joy to watch both of them. "I can see why she's named Sassy," she told Press.

"She's a good horse." He secured the trailer door and walked with Raney to the front of the truck. "I'm glad you took her. You'll treat her right."

"You can count on it. You'll stay for supper?"

"Can't. My daughter's helping me pack. The new owners come next week."

"So soon?"

"It's time." He grinned, showing gaps where teeth used to be. "And time I got to know my grandkids better. What a pair of hellions. Reminds me of you and your older sister back in the day."

"I'll miss you."

"Don't. I'll still be around. But you can tell your mama good-bye for me." A faraway look came into his faded gray eyes. "A real *chingona*, your mama. We had us some good times, damned if we didn't. And Charlie, too, of course."

Raney could imagine. Daddy often said Mama was broke to saddle, but had never accepted the bit. Raney didn't understand what he meant until years later, and it was several years more before she stopped getting the heebie-jeebies whenever she thought of it.

Press opened the truck door, then stood beside it for a moment, watching Dalton and the mare. "That's a good man you got there, Raney. Break him in slow and give him his head now and then and he'll never let you down."

Not sure how to respond, Raney just smiled. "You're always welcome at Four Star, Press. Come anytime."

"I'll do that."

But Raney knew he wouldn't. And as she watched him drive away, it was like watching the past fade into dust. There would never be another Press Amala, world-class roping champion and unequaled horse trainer. A real icon in the horse business. And another old friend leaving her behind.

"Ready to try out the new mare?" Dalton asked when Raney walked into the barn a few minutes later.

"Sure."

She leaned against a stall door while he went to the arena to get the mare, thinking about all the changes going on around her: Four Star getting out of the cattle business and into the breeding business, Mama leaving, Joss having a baby, Dalton stampeding into her life, and Press hanging up his spurs. Good changes for the most part. But scary. And she wasn't always comfortable with changes. Especially the scary ones. Like earlier, in the car, when she'd felt so suffocated and afraid. She still wasn't sure what that was about. But Dalton had known what she'd needed and had helped her find her balance again. A remarkable man.

A few minutes later, he returned with the mare, tied her to a ring in the wall, and began to brush her down. He shot her a look. "Why so glum? Not thinking about the douche, I hope."

"Press sold his barn."

"I heard."

"I'll miss him."

"Me, too. But, hey, little lady," he went on in an exaggerated Texas twang as he ran the brush over Sassy's back. "You got me and this here mare. What more do you want?"

She studied him as he bent to brush the mare's legs. He was so beautiful. Inside and out. How could she bear it if things didn't work out between them? "I want you to kiss me."

He straightened, smile fading. A change came over his face. Hunger. Want. Dropping the brush into a bucket, he walked toward her, a predatory gleam in his eyes. "I can do that."

And he did.

Strangely, the heart-pounding, knee-weakening, mind-boggling, nerve-tingling changes he awakened in her body weren't that scary at all. If they hadn't heard footsteps at the back of the barn, she might have dragged him into one of the stalls. As it was, she barely peeled herself off his strong, sturdy, utterly delicious body before Chuey came in with a wheelbarrow of hay for Rosco. Mumbling something about hunting up a saddle for Sassy, she stepped around the be-fuddled man she'd just been dallying with and went down to the tack room.

Ten minutes later, she was putting Sassy through her paces in the arena.

The mare was amazing. Smooth gaited, responsive, sen-sitive to the lightest touch on the reins, and a rocking-chair lope. "Oh, Dalton," Raney said, reining in where he waited by the gate. "She's awesome! An absolute dream!"

He grinned up at her, so tall she could almost bend down and kiss him without shifting in the saddle. "You like her?"

"I adore her!" *And you.* A dangerous thought. *Too soon,* she reminded herself, remembering how Press had said to break him in slow.

"Then she's yours."

Raney laughed. "I know. I wrote the check."

"Then how about I buy her back, then give her to you."

"How about you saddle up and ride with me. I have a hankering for wide-open spaces, a fast horse beneath me, and the wind in my face. Open the gate, cowboy!"

He did and they shot through. Within moments she heard a horse coming up behind her and looked back to see Dalton racing toward her on one of the geldings, riding bareback, his long legs reaching past the horse's belly, his dark hair whipping in the wind. He rode like a warrior. Like he was born to it and the horse beneath him was sim-ply an extension of his will.

She slowed until he came alongside, then pointed to a lone pine a hundred yards away. "Race you!" she cried, and kicked the mare into a gallop. By the time they neared the tree, she was laughing for the pure joy of it. This was what she'd been missing, what she needed. The speed. The wind.

The pounding of the hooves as the ground swept by. Freedom to run, to escape, to fly.

"God, I've missed this!" she said as he pulled in beside her. "I forgot how much fun it is to just ride."

"I can tell." He smiled, watching her, his expression almost tender. "You should do it more often."

"I wish I could."

"What's holding you back?"

They continued on toward a watering hole near the back fence line, keeping the horses at a walk to cool them down. "Paperwork. Sometimes I feel like I'm drowning in it."

"Then hire someone to help you. You don't have to do it all yourself."

She wondered if she could do that, if she could relinquish control so easily. With the right person, maybe. Someone she could trust to care for the ranch the same way she did. She glanced over at Dalton, wondering if he could be that person. Or if it was too soon to ask.

"Do you consider me a workhorse?" she asked when they stopped at the pond to let the horses drink. "Joss said I was."

He thought for a moment, then shook his head. "Not a workhorse. More like a sleek, spirited Thoroughbred who's been penned too long. Or maybe a high-stepping Arabian. Or a—"

Laughing, she raised a hand. "Enough with the horse analogies. Sorry I asked."

They reined the horses away from the water before they drank too much, and rode on through tall grass already turning brown in the summer sun.

Raney took in a deep breath and let it out. She'd hadn't felt so relaxed in a long time. It was a beautiful, cloudless day, not too hot, despite summer knocking on the door. Blue sky above her, a beautiful horse beneath her, and a handsome man at her side. One of those perfect moments she'd treasure forever.

They came across a small herd of yearling bulls. Remembering what Press had said about keeping the mare away from cattle until she knew what the horse would do, Raney studied them from a distance as they rode by, seeing several strong possibilities for the breeding program.

As they neared the barn, she became aware of Dalton studying her, a thoughtful look on his face. "What?" she asked.

"I was just thinking about all you do to keep this place running. I can see it's a lot of work. It wouldn't be a sign of weakness to ask for help, you know."

"You offering?" she asked.

"You asking?" he countered.

She brushed a horsefly off Sassy's mane and thought about what it would mean to let someone else carry a little of the load. Someone like Dalton. He couldn't train horses all the time. He was probably bored as it was. And Glenn was getting old. No doubt he would welcome the help. Plus, he'd be there to keep an eye on things and let her know if Dalton wasn't cutting it. Although, she wasn't truly concerned about that. Dalton was a smart, capable guy. He'd pick it up in no time. Besides, she'd already turned over her prized colt to him. Why not let him take over some of the ranch chores, too?

She looked over at him. "Yes. I guess I'm asking."

His smile told her she'd given him the answer he wanted. "What do you want me to do?"

"For now, help Hicks. He's good at managing the workers and the stock. But he's a bit baffled by the AI program. It's mostly a matter of paperwork. We have technicians who come in weekly to monitor the equipment and handle the semen extractions and the impregnations, and a vet comes once a month to run labs on the bulls. You willing to take that on?"

"Sure." His smile broadened to a full-on grin, which told her a smart-ass quip was on the way. "I've always been interested in breeding."

"I bet you have. I'll give Glenn the good news at supper. He'll be delighted. Tomorrow he can start familiarizing you with how we do things, the equipment, the bull rotation, our client list, and so on. That way, when the vet comes at the end of the month, you'll be trained on all the breeding procedures."

"I already know how to breed."

She gave him a *shut up* look.

"And what equipment is needed," he went on. "In fact, I've been told, I'm—"

"Stop! Just stop!"

He laughed. "Lighten up, babe. We're just talking about cattle, right? Or were you thinking of something else?"

"You're incorrigible." He was such a goofball. The king of innuendo. His quirky sense of humor always lightened her mood and made her laugh.

A sudden thought burst into her mind. *Dalton makes me happy.*

It was true. Dalton Cardwell, ex-con, gifted horse trainer, awesome kisser, and unrepentant smart-ass, made her happy. He gave her hope again. "Thank you," she said, smiling at him through a sheen of tears.

"For what?"

"For earlier. For this. For making a terrible day into one of the best ones I've had in a long time."

That crooked smile. "For you, Raney, I'd do anything. Don't you know that by now?"

Raney was still smiling as she headed to the house, hoping for a quiet moment on the veranda before cleaning up for supper. With the days growing steadily hotter, she'd already had Harvey and Chuey convert the outdoor patio into an air-conditioned room. Woven see-through blinds now hung from the outer roof beam to block heat and sun. Flexible sprinkler lines strung along the eaves pumped out a fine mist that turned hot, dry air into cool, moist air. Evaporative coolers at either end of the long, rectangular space added more cooling, while three overhead fans kept the air circulating. It was Raney's favorite summertime retreat, and she was looking forward to stretching out on a chaise for a few minutes and enjoying a glass of wine.

Until she came up the steps and found Joss hunched over in one of the cushioned chairs, arms pressed to her stomach, sobbing.

CHAPTER 15

"What is it?" Raney cried, rushing to her sister's side. "Is it the baby? Is she coming?" Be just like Joss to go into premature labor while Mama was gone.

"No, silly," her sister said between sniffs. "She's not due for weeks yet. It's that bastard, Grady. Damn him!"

Raney hurried to the kitchen, ripped off a couple of paper towels, wet one, and went back to her sister. "Wipe your face," she said, holding out the wet towel.

She vaguely remembered Joss mentioning someone named Grady during their drive from Waco. Since her sister had refused to elaborate, Raney wasn't sure what he meant to her, but she was beginning to get an idea.

When Joss finished wiping her face, Raney handed her the dry towel. "Now quit crying and tell me who Grady is."

"My baby daddy."

As Raney had suspected. "What did he do that has you so upset?"

"This!" Joss pointed.

Raney saw a wad of hundred-dollar bills and a crumpled

letter on the floor by her chair. "He gave you money?" she asked, confused.

"Like I was a whore! Like he was paying me for sleeping with him! God, I hate that man!" More tears rose.

While Joss wiped her face again, Raney gathered up the bills—a thousand dollars' worth—put them on the side table, then picked up the crumpled letter.

"Is this from him? Can I read it?"

"Like I care."

There wasn't much to it. *The money is for the baby. Our baby. I'll send more soon. I still do and always will love you, Joss, even though you're being irresponsible and hardheaded about this. See you soon, Grady.*

Nothing about whores or services rendered.

Dalton came up the steps, saw Joss was crying, and did an about-face.

"Joss is upset," Raney said.

"I can see that." With reluctance, he turned back around, walked over, gave Joss an awkward *there, there* pat on her shoulder, and said, "What's up, Buttercup?"

Raney rolled her eyes. The guy had been in a war and prison, but a few tears freaked him out? "She got a letter from Grady, her baby's father. Can Dalton read it, Joss?"

"He can post it on the Internet, for all I care."

Dalton read the letter, glanced at the money, then at Raney, his brows raised in question.

Raney shrugged.

"He sent you money," he said to Joss.

"Exactly! The bastard! I can't believe he'd do that to me!"

"Money is bad?"

Seeing that her sister was about to go nuclear, Raney explained that Joss saw the money as Grady's payment for sleeping with him, like she was a prostitute.

Dalton studied the letter again. "It doesn't say that. All it says here is that the money is for the baby. Nothing about you being a prostitute."

"She's not a prostitute!" Raney defended.

"It's implied," Joss muttered.

An implacable expression came over Dalton's face. Raney had seen it twice before—at their run-in on the day she'd tried to fire him, and earlier in the car when he'd told her he didn't want her money. She had hoped never to see it again.

"No, it isn't, Joss," Dalton said with a noticeable lack of sympathy for Raney's distraught sister. "You're putting in words that aren't there. All I see is a guy trying to do the right thing for his baby. And you."

"He said I was being irresponsible and hardheaded."

"Maybe you are."

Raney glared at him.

Joss teared up.

Dalton thrust the letter at her. "Read it again, Joss. He also said he still loved you. Isn't that worth something?"

While she read it again, Dalton hunkered beside her chair and stroked a hand down her back. "Whatever happened between the two of you," he went on in a gentler tone, "at least the guy's trying. Can you give him that, at least?"

Joss smoothed the crinkles out of the letter then carefully folded it. "He doesn't deserve it," she said. But her voice held less anger now and the tears had stopped.

How did he do that? Raney wondered. How did he know exactly what to say?

"Probably not," Dalton agreed, still stroking her back. "But he's just a guy, and we can be pretty dumb sometimes."

Joss gave him a wobbly smile. "Sometimes?"

Raney sank into another cushioned chair, relieved the sobfest was over. Joss's emotional fits always left her rattled. She never knew what to say or do, other than to lose patience. And as happened too often in the past, she had been so desperate to end the shitstorm and do something, even if it was wrong, she hadn't realized what Joss really needed.

But Dalton knew. Like when Raney had panicked and shut down. He hadn't given up. Not then and not now with Joss. With the same soothing approach he used on frightened horses, he had calmed her fears and Joss's hysterics, while giving them both the reassurance they'd needed. He should be canonized.

With a last pat on Joss's back, Dalton rose. "You done crying, Buttercup?"

"For now. Fancy Pants."

"Good. I don't like it." He settled in another chair. "Now tell us about this Grady guy and why you're mad at him, and what you want us to do about it."

Us? We're a family now? The man certainly knew how to take charge.

Raney knew within a few minutes after Joss began that her sister was still in love with the man she claimed to hate. As she talked about him, her expression softened into something wistful, almost sad. Her voice lost that sharp edge of anger, and she trailed her fingers over the letter in her lap almost as if she were touching the man himself.

This could be bad, Raney thought.

His name was Grady Douglas. He was seven years older than Joss and close to Dalton's age. Raney got the impression from things her sister said—and things she didn't say—that Grady was a lot more mature than she was and had taken on the role of protector in the drug-and-alcohol-infused world of touring musicians. Protector, and lover, it seemed.

Grady managed Crystal, the headliner, Joss explained. He booked appearances, arranged transportation, handled security, and kept the aging singer sober enough to go onstage. "Touring with a band isn't as glamorous as I thought it would be," Joss admitted. "I wouldn't have lasted as long as I did if it hadn't been for Grady." She gave a sad smile. "I know I said some mean things about him, but he really did take good care of me."

"In what way?" Raney asked.

"It was his idea to have me open for Crystal. And he's the one who convinced her to sing a couple of my songs at the concert in Houston. They sounded amazing with the band behind them, although between you and me, I might have sung them better. He also showed me how to copyright my songs so no one could record them without paying me. And he even helped me cut a demo and showed me who to send it to. He's smart that way. He told me I would be a star if only I could get my music in front of the right people." She gave a long sigh and slumped back in her chair. "Fat chance that'll happen now."

"Why? What's changed?" Dalton asked.

"I got pregnant, that's what changed. As soon as I told him, he started ragging on me all the time. That's why I got off the bus in Waco. I couldn't take it anymore. Now I'm afraid he'll show up here and start nagging me again."

"He won't," Raney assured her. "Dalton and I won't let him bother you."

Dalton nodded. "Just part of my new job as household security."

"What does he nag you about?" Raney asked.

"Everything. What I eat. How much I sleep. How I feel. Who I spend time with. Will I marry him? Do I need a back rub? He never lets up."

Raney glanced at Dalton. He seemed as baffled as she was. "Grady asked you to marry him? And you said *no*? Why?"

"I already told you. He nags me all the time. Sort of like you and Mama, if you must know. And for the record, I'm not an idiot. I can manage my own life."

And how's that going for you? Raney couldn't say that, of course, or point out that if Joss was so adept at managing her life, why was she living at home again, unemployed, with an unplanned baby on the way and an unplanned future ahead?

"So, you don't intend to marry him," Dalton said as if trying to find a place for that idea in his head.

"Not unless he quits ragging on me and doesn't insist I give up my music."

"He's asked you to do that?"

"He implied it."

Dalton got that look on his face again, but before he said anything, the hall clock chimed the hour.

Raney checked her watch and saw that it was almost time for supper. The mutes would be showing up soon, and she had planned to talk to Glenn about turning over the AI program to Dalton. She stood, figuring this was a good place to stop before Joss and Dalton said things neither would like hearing.

Knowing his manners, Dalton stood, too.

"We'll finish this later, Joss," she said to her sister. "It's almost supper. You have time for a quick shower, if you want." If she came to the table looking as weepy as she did now, the mutes would turn tail.

"I think I'll skip dinner tonight." Joss stuffed the money and letter back into the mailer they'd come in. "I'm not hungry."

"You need to eat something. I can have Maria send up a tray."

"Don't bother. I think I'll take a nap instead."

Seeing her baby sister hurting threw Raney back into the anxious-big-sister role she thought had ended years ago. It was weird, but nice to be needed again. "I'll come up and check on you after the guys leave. We can talk then."

"Dalton's not allowed upstairs."

It was no surprise that Joss would want Dalton there while they talked. He had that effect on people. Calm, reassuring, willing to listen. It made people open up to him, like she had that night here on the veranda, and today, when she'd spewed all that garbage about Trip. Maybe he could help her little sister, too. "All right." She patted Joss's shoulder. "Go take your nap. I'll have Maria set aside a plate."

As she watched her sister walk away, Raney felt Dalton's arm slide across her shoulders. Pulling her against his side in a one-arm hug, he muttered, "You're a fucking saint," and kissed her temple. "And a hell of a good big sister."

She leaned into him, needing the support, the strength of his arm around her. "And you're a good big brother." She certainly hoped that was the way Joss and Dalton felt about each other. "I wish you'd been around in her wilder days. You might have kept her in line better than I did."

"I doubt Joss was as wild as everybody thinks she was. Just . . . flighty."

Raney wondered if that was code for *dumb*. Although she didn't truly think Joss was dumb. She was too creative, too curious and enthusiastic about everything around her. Dumb people were boring. Joss was anything but that. "Then why was her bra hanging over the goalpost upright the morning after homecoming?"

A chuckle. Another kiss on her cheek. "The guys are still doing that?"

"What guys?" She drew away to look at him. "What are you talking about?"

He pulled her against his chest and this time wrapped both arms around her, loose enough that they could still see each other, but close enough that she could feel the heat of him from her waist to her knees. It was nice.

"Buddy Anderson and I threw that bra up there our freshman year."

"You did? Why?"

"To drive the cheerleaders crazy trying to figure out who it belonged to." He kissed the tip of her nose. "You have the cutest nose."

Raney remembered seeing bras on the goalpost crossbar several times. She didn't realize Dalton had started it all. "It wasn't Joss's?"

"Hardly. She would have been a kid at the time. But maybe she got in on the act later. Lots of girls gave bras to their boyfriends to toss up there. Thought it made them cool. Want to go to my room? You could watch me shower. Or something."

"Mama said no hanky-panky. Her house, her rules."

A kiss at the corner of her mouth. "Mama's not here. I'll make it quick. Ten minutes, tops."

"I hope you're not bragging." She turned her head in case he wanted to kiss the other side of her face. Which he did. "Who owned the bra you tossed up there?"

"Mrs. Langers."

Raney's mouth fell open, snapped shut. "Toby's mother? Oh my God."

"Buddy pulled it off their clothesline. Do you know how hard it's been, sleeping in the same house with you and not sneaking up to your room?"

Raney had to laugh, picturing two gawky fourteen-year-old boys boosting a bra. Probably the first one they'd ever touched that hadn't belonged to a family member. At least, she hoped so. "No wonder Toby hates you."

"He never knew." He nibbled a trail down her neck. "Sort of wished now that I'd told him. You smell good."

"Horse manure and alfalfa. It's called Cowboy's Delight."

With a sigh, he lifted his head. "You're not taking this seriously, are you? Here I am doing my best work and you—"

"I'm worried about Joss. She looked so broken. I don't know how to help her."

"You can help her by not worrying so much. She'll be fine."

"You think so?"

"I do. In fact, after considering everything she said about the guy, I'm thinking Grady Douglas might be exactly what your sister needs." He gave her a last quick kiss, then let his arms drop back to his sides. "I've got to shower. You should, too. You've got slobber all over your neck."

*   *   *

The mutes showed up exactly on time, as predictable as sunrise. Dalton came in a few minutes later with wet hair. Raney was glad she had settled for a quick rinse-off and hadn't taken the time to wash and dry her own hair. No use raising eyebrows until she and Dalton had actually done something to warrant it.

Alejandro was in an especially good mood. As he loaded his plate with roasted pork, candied sweet potatoes, and green beans, he told them his ex-wife had decided to leave Uno with him for the summer while she visited her family in Honduras. "I pick him up *mañana*," he said, adding two slices of fresh-baked bread to his plate.

"Bring him to supper," Raney suggested.

Alejandro shook his head. "Uno is a big, sturdy boy. He will work while he is here, and it is best if he eats and sleeps where the other workers do."

Raney was about to argue with him when Alejandro smiled and shook his head again. "*Esta bien*, Jefe. Las esposas plan a big fiesta for him. And he will feel *muy importante* working with Chuey and Harvey."

"I could use help with the horses, too," Dalton said. "Think he'd be interested?"

"*Sí*. He can teach you *mucho*."

"And I can teach him English while we work," Dalton countered.

Alejandro muttered something under his breath.

Dalton grinned. "*No delante de la dama, mi amigo.*" Not in front of the lady.

Raney pretended she hadn't heard and suggested if the weather was nice, they could have a yard party at the house, too. "With games and ice cream and cake and a piñata. What do you think?"

They thought it was a grand idea.

"And since we're breaking Mama's rule about speaking

Spanish at the table," she went on with a meaningful look at both Dalton and Alejandro, "can either of you tell me what *chingona* means?"

They glanced at each other, both fighting smiles. Dalton asked Raney where she'd heard that word. "Did someone call you that?"

"Press called Mama that."

Which amused all three men no end. "*Chingona* means 'bad-ass woman,'" Dalton explained. "We're laughing because the same could apply to you."

"I never said that," Glenn cut in. "Not about you, Miss Raney."

"But it's true, isn't it?" Dalton asked Alejandro.

The Mexican wisely remained silent, although his grin spoke volumes.

Raney gave up. The meal was almost over and she still had two more topics to discuss. "I need you to be serious for a moment," she said in her no-nonsense voice. "Maria," she called. "Could you please come in here?"

Maria came in, a worried look on her face. "The food is okay?"

Raney gave her a reassuring smile. "It's wonderful, as always."

Once she was sure she had everyone's attention, Raney said, "There's a man named Grady Douglas who may come to the ranch to see Joss. She doesn't want to see him. If you or any of the other workers see a stranger hanging around, tell me or Dalton right away. And if we're not here"—she looked at Glenn and Alejandro—"you two see what he wants."

"Do you expect trouble, Jefe?" Alejandro asked.

Raney pushed her plate away, appetite gone. She felt like she was siccing the dogs on an innocent person. No matter what Joss said, Grady didn't sound like he meant any harm to her sister or their baby. But she couldn't take the risk. "No, I don't expect trouble. Just make sure he leaves, and tell him if he wants to come again, he should call first. Maria, will you warn the other wives to be on the look-out, too?"

Maria nodded.

"Who is this man?" Alejandro asked, that protectiveness he'd always shown toward the Whitcomb girls evident in the hard glint in his dark eyes.

"The father of Joss's baby. Joss said they parted on bad terms and now she's worried he'll come here."

"We will not let him near her."

Maria and Glenn nodded in agreement.

Dalton watched in silence, that unyielding expression back on his face.

"Should I lock the main gate?" Hicks asked.

"I don't think that's necessary, Glenn. He may not come. And anyway, we have no reason to think he's a bad guy or that he would cause trouble. All we know right now is that Joss doesn't want to see him. So, no rough stuff. Everybody got that?"

Nods all around.

"Good. Maria, you can bring dessert whenever it's convenient."

"Sí, Miss Raney."

"On a happier note," Raney said after Maria left, "I may have good news for you, Glenn."

He perked up.

"How would you feel about training Dalton on the breeding program?"

Instead of being happy, the old man gave Dalton a skeptical look. "You sure he wants to know all that stuff? It's unnatural, is what it is. Don't know why we'd want to interfere with the way the good Lord intended things to be."

Glenn was no fan of artificial insemination. Despite the advantages of higher impregnation rates, less risk of injury or disease through proper management and genetics, and strengthening the breed by using only the strongest, healthiest bulls to produce stronger, healthier offspring, Glenn had never approved of the program. Probably a guy thing. The cows certainly offered no complaints.

But rather than point all that out yet again, Raney took a gentler approach. "I know it's been a burden, Glenn, managing the AI program with all the other things you do for the ranch. I really appreciate how hard you've worked. But Dalton told me today he had a keen interest in breeding." She didn't look at him when she said that, but could swear she heard him grin. "And he's offered to take over the program. If that's okay with you, of course."

That perked up the old fellow again. "Damn straight, it's okay. Just hope the boy knows what he's getting into. Liable to put him off breeding altogether."

"Oh, I doubt that," Raney said over Dalton's sudden coughing fit.

CHAPTER 16

That night Dalton was especially restless, knowing Raney was in a room nearby and he couldn't go to her. In his mind, they were already committed to each other and this enforced separation felt wrong. He was almost looking forward to Mrs. Whitcomb's return so he could go back to the workers' dorm and avoid all this temptation. After an hour of tossing and turning, he got up, pulled on jeans and a T-shirt in case he ran into anybody, and went into the kitchen for something to eat.

Joss was sitting at the small breakfast table, crying into a peanut butter and jelly sandwich. Before he could escape, she looked up and saw him, so he reluctantly continued into the room.

"Hey," he said, and tried to inject interest into his voice.

In truth, he was weary of Joss's theatrics. At her age he'd traveled halfway around the world to fight a war. But she seemed stuck in high school, and the way her family treated her, she was liable to be trapped there forever. Still, he wasn't unsympathetic. He'd had his low times, too. "What's up, Buttercup?" Seeing she'd left the PBJ makings on the counter, he built one for himself. "Is it Grady?"

She nodded. "Him and the baby. I don't know what to do."

That didn't surprise him. He finished making his sandwich, set his plate across from hers, then went back and hunted up two glasses. "Do you care about him?" he asked, filling them with milk and taking them back to the table.

"I'm pregnant with his baby, aren't I?"

Not much of an answer, but he let it pass. He sat down and started on his sandwich. "Do you think he cares about you?" he mumbled as he chewed.

"He says he does."

"Do you believe him?"

"He's not a liar, just a nag. But yes, I believe him."

"Then what's the problem?"

She gave one of those rolling-eye things women do so well. "It's not that simple."

"Yeah, Joss, it is. You either care about each other enough to try and work it out, or you don't." But these Whitcomb girls sure made that hard.

Another eye roll, accompanied by a long-suffering sigh.

Dalton finished his sandwich, got up, and went to the refrigerator. He rummaged around, found two apples in the vegetable bin, asked if she wanted one—which she didn't—then brought both of them back to the table. They were small apples. "Have you talked to him? Told him what's bothering you?"

"I tried."

He took a bite of apple and studied her. "Try harder."

"He won't listen."

"If you were crying when you talked to him, he probably couldn't. A guy sees tears, it shuts off the listening part of his brain."

Before she made herself dizzy with another eye roll, he said, "Look, Joss. Most men try to do the right thing. Where we get into trouble is not knowing what the right thing is. But not wanting to admit that, we punt, and usually miss the ball. If you want this to work, you need to tell Grady straight out what you want, what you don't want, and what you expect from him. Then he can either take the ball and run with it or fumble and lose the game."

"Neatly put, Coach."

Dalton shrugged and bit into the apple. He'd done his best. If he was going to hold anybody's hand through a crisis, it would be Raney's.

He wondered if she was sleeping. And what she was wearing while she did it.

"I don't know what to do about the baby, either," Joss said, breaking up a really nice picture in his head of her naked sister. "I want to stick with my music, but I want to be a good mother, too. I don't know if I can do both."

Dalton figured that was a dilemma most mothers faced at one time or another. He didn't have any answers, but he suspected Grady Douglas would take his role as father pretty seriously, which might lighten the load for Joss. He finished off the first apple and started on the second. "Which is more important to you?" he asked. "Music or the baby?"

She gave him that glare. "The baby, of course." Then she sighed, and added, "But music is important to me, too. It's not fair that I have to choose one over the other. But I'm afraid if I try to do both, I won't be any good at either and probably end up like Crystal, alone and boozing it up just to get through the night."

Dalton smiled. "You won't do that. Your mama would never allow it."

"Then what do I do?"

"You try. And if it doesn't work, you try a different way. You're smart, Joss. You'll figure it out. Although it would be a damn sight easier if you had someone at your back. And not just your mama."

"Grady?"

"That's for you to decide."

She thought for a moment, then nodded. A resigned nod, but with a hint of enthusiasm, too. "Maybe I should talk to him. Thanks for the advice."

He took a last bite of apple and grinned. "Just part of the service."

She studied him. "Speaking of servicing, what are your plans for my sister?"

Dalton almost choked. He was either the most transparent guy in history, or the Whitcomb women were all psychics. They should start their own psychic hotline.

"Here's my advice." Joss pushed her plate aside, leaned forward, folded her arms on the tabletop, and looked him hard in the eye. Hard enough to make him lean back in his own chair.

"Raney doesn't hold grudges. You lie to her or screw her around, she'll toss you out like a moldy grape and never think of you again. Be like you were never born. She would never think of retaliating. But Mama would. And the last guy who hurt one of her baby girls is now facing bankruptcy and a broken career. And if that's not enough, I can always come up with a dozen creative ways to ruin a man's social life." She sat back, a scary smile on her tearstained face.

Dalton stared. "Who are you? And where is the gentle-hearted, crybaby airhead I've grown so fond of?"

Boom. And there it was. That full, shit-eating grin he had so grossly underestimated. "You're fond of me?"

"I better be."

"Exactly." Joss picked up her dishes and carried them to the sink. "Nice talk." With a backward wave, she headed for the door. "By the way," she called back as she stepped into the hall, "you need bigger T-shirts."

Definitely not gentle-hearted. Or an airhead. And he did need bigger Ts.

That put an end to Dalton's midnight kitchen forays. Between his new tasks in the AI program and stepping up

Rosco's training, he fell into bed each night too exhausted to raid refrigerators. But not too exhausted to visit Raney in his dreams.

June got hotter and time passed faster.

Mama texted that the cruise was amazing, Alaska was beautiful, she'd gained three pounds and had met a lot of fun widowers. Raney could imagine. Now she was visiting friends on an island in Puget Sound before going on her pack trip around Mount Rainier. She was having way too much fun for a woman her age.

Alejandro's son Uno arrived. He was a handsome boy, heading into puberty, solidly built like his father, and twice as talkative, which wasn't saying much. He loved horses as much as Dalton did, and was a big help to him around the barn.

Raney spent her days trapped in the office doing paperwork, and her nights staring at the ceiling and thinking about Dalton. She would lie on her bed, watching the slowly rotating overhead fan, and picture him in the room below hers, stretched out on his bed, his body so long, his feet hung over the end.

Did he snore? Did he sleep in pajamas? Did he think about her, too?

Joss continued to expand. Her monthly forty-mile trips to see the obstetrician in Aspenmont increased to every two weeks. Raney could see her excitement build as her mid-September due date approached. But there was worry, too. Would the baby be healthy? What should she name her? Would she be a good mother?

No amount of reassurance reassured her, but Raney kept trying. And while she did, she often caught herself wondering what kind of mother she might make. And whenever she pictured herself with a baby in her arms, Dalton was standing behind her, grinning that goofy, sideways grin she loved.

More money came from Grady Douglas, and with each letter, Joss's agitation grew. She hated him. She didn't hate him. She wondered what he was doing, if he thought of her, if he would come to see her, and when. They were a pair, Raney and Joss. Neither of them knew what to do about the men in their lives.

By July, the local cutting shows were in full swing. Rosco couldn't compete in any of them, or in any show until his November debut at the annual USCHA Futurity in Fort Worth. But he could watch, and exercise in the loping area, and for a small fee, work cows in one of the smaller pens. But mostly, he was there to grow accustomed to all the noise and fanfare of the show ring.

Assuming he handled all that well, in October and early November, Dalton would take him to several two-day pre-works at some of the private cutting horse training facilities around Weatherford and Parker County. That was where the real work began. And the real scrutiny. And the pressure.

Pre-works were the lead-up to the big dance in Fort Worth. Rosco would participate with other debuting horses on a noncompetitive basis—no judges, no prize money, no scoring—but a whole lot of eyeballing going on between Dalton and the other trainers to see what his horse could do compared to what theirs could do. Sort of a horse-trainer pissing contest. These pre-works weren't open to the public and only the more prominent owners and trainers were invited. Four Star had always been welcome, but since Dalton was new to the circuit, it would be a new experience for both him and Rosco.

Then finally, on November 15th, after months of hard work, Rosco and Dalton would have their make-or-break moment in the arena of the Will Rogers Coliseum and complex in Fort Worth. Just thinking about it made Raney's stomach flutter.

The USCHA Futurity was a three-week-long event that drew close to a thousand horses, both as competitors for the four million–plus in prize money, or as offerings at the high-stakes auctions that went on throughout the competition. If all went well, Rosco would prove himself to be the outstanding colt they thought he was, Dalton would establish himself as an exceptional trainer, and Raney's dream of making Whitcomb Four Star into a preeminent cutting horse training and breeding ranch would start to become a reality.

No pressure. None at all.

That was almost four months away. It sounded like a long time, but there was still a lot of work ahead, and not all of it would be done in the arena. Creating advance interest in the colt was important, too, as well as finding ways to boost Dalton's credibility as a trainer. And nothing could elevate him faster above the other new-to-the-circuit trainers than having a well-respected, successful trainer vouch for him. And Raney knew just whom to call.

Press said he'd be happy to do it, and before Raney could even ask, he offered to attend some of the local pre-works close by his daughter's place in Oklahoma and give his thoughts on how Rosco and Dalton were doing.

"I expect big things from those two," he told her. "They got the talent and the drive. They'll make a great showing in Fort Worth. Probably get offers on Rosco long before you get there, so be prepared. The kid, too. Smart outfit would try to snatch him up soon as they saw how he handled a green horse. Hope you're ready for that, too."

Raney wasn't. The idea of Dalton moving on to a more prestigious position somewhere else was something she didn't want to think about. He was talented. Gifted, even. And if she could see that, others in the business would, too.

Could he be lured away? How far would she go to keep him at Four Star?

Questions she couldn't answer. But that didn't keep them from adding to her conflicted feelings about the man who occupied more of her thoughts as time passed. She had worked hard to keep firm control over whatever was happening between them. But she had never thought he might up and leave her.

It felt like everything was moving too fast, that a crossroads was approaching too soon, and she'd have to face decisions she wasn't ready to make. All she knew for certain was that the idea of losing Dalton was suddenly a lot more frightening than the idea of keeping him.

On the Friday before Rosco's first small show, Harvey and Uno washed the newer of the two ranch trucks and the smaller horse trailer, taking extra care to shine up the Whitcomb Four Star logos on the sides of both the truck and trailer, and the rear loading door. Good advertising, Dalton thought.

Then, after Rosco's daily workout and Dalton went to tend to his new duties at the breeding offices, they cleaned and oiled the tack, loaded it into the trailer with enough feed and hay for two horses, and made sure the gas tank was full.

Rosco got the full treatment, too. Alejandro checked his hooves and made sure the shoes were tight and his legs were sound. Then he gave the colt a trim, a bath, a rubdown, and called it a day.

Meanwhile, Raney was trapped in the office going over the quarterly reports—her least favorite task in running the ranch. The transition from cattle ranch to breeding facility was going well, despite still being in the red. But since the losses were less than those in the first quarter, neither Raney nor the accountants were worried. She was almost through when Maria came in, her face flushed, her eyes round with worry. "Miss Raney, someone comes. In Miss Joss's car."

"Where's my sister?"

"Napping, I think."

"Don't wake her. We'll see who it is first." Raney picked up her cell phone and left the office, Maria on her heels.

"I think he went to the back where the cars park," the housekeeper said.

"It was a man?"

"Sí. I think so."

Raney quickly punched in Dalton's number.

"I see him," he said before she even spoke. "I'm on my way."

Raney ended the call and told Maria to come with her as she hurried through the kitchen toward the veranda.

It had to be Grady Douglas. Who else would drive all the way from Houston to return her sister's car? As she stepped out onto the veranda, she heard men's voices approaching from the parking area. Dalton's, she recognized. The other, she didn't.

When they came around the corner of the house, she studied the newcomer.

Nice-looking. Neat, rather than scruffy like most of the musicians she'd met. Fit. No obvious signs of drug use. Blond, blue eyed, no man bun or weird haircut, no obvious piercings or visible tattoos. Rather mild for Joss's tastes. He was a couple of inches shorter than Dalton, and moved like an athlete. His features weren't as chiseled as Dalton's, his jaw less obstinate, his eyes not as deep set. Sort of a softer version. Younger-looking, too, even though Joss had said he and Dalton were about the same age. But then, he hadn't spent his life outdoors, or gone to war, or spent time in prison. She hoped.

She met them as they came up the veranda steps. "Hello," she said, and extended her hand. "I'm Raney Whitcomb."

"Grady Douglas. Pleased to meet you."

It was true that you could tell a lot about a man by his handshake. Grady's hand wasn't as large as Dalton's, or as callused. But he had a firm grip and took her hand fully into his, rather than just clasping her fingers. She liked that. Not an overly robust grip, like a man trying to show dominance, or as tentative as that of a surgeon or pianist who was protective of his, or her, fingers. Just a normal, regular handshake from a normal, regular-looking guy. Raney was relieved. And a little surprised. Not exactly what she had expected from her semiwild sister.

"This is Maria, our housekeeper." Raney nodded to the woman hovering in the hall doorway. "Can she get you something to drink? Beer, iced tea, fruit—"

"Iced tea would be great," Grady cut in.

"Me, too," Dalton said, then added with a boyishly disarming grin, "And maybe some of your wonderful cookies, Maria, if you have them."

He was such a suck-up.

As Maria left, Raney sat in one of the cushioned chairs by the patio fireplace and motioned for the men to sit in two others. "Thanks, Grady, for bringing Joss's car. That's a long drive from Houston."

"I was motivated."

She raised her brows. "To see my sister?"

"To find out why she won't marry me."

The man certainly didn't waste time on trivialities. Raney liked that, too. But before she could respond, he leaned forward, elbows on armrests, hands clasped in front of him. "I may have overplayed my hand."

"In what way?"

"I'll admit, when she told me she was pregnant, it was a shocker. But only for a minute. Soon as I thought about it, I realized there was nothing more I wanted in this world than to have Joss and our baby in my life."

Score one for Grady Douglas.

"I can take care of them," he went on, his voice and expression earnest. "And I will, whether she marries me or not. But I might have pressured her about marriage more than I should have." He gave a sheepish and utterly charming smile. "I tend to worry about her. She thinks that means

I don't think she can take care of herself, but that's the farthest thing from the truth. Joss may act a little wild, but it's mostly a front. She's smarter than she lets on. Creative. And totally dedicated to her music. I respect that. But the music world isn't always a healthy place. Booze, drugs, wild parties, you name it. Not healthy at all. I tried to shield her from the worst of it. Nagged her a lot. Maybe too much." He sat back, as though exhausted by his long speech and relieved to have gotten it all out. "And I'm sorry for that."

"What about her music?" Dalton asked. "She thinks you want her to give it up after the baby comes."

Grady's shock was evident. "No way. I'd never ask her to do that. Joss is too talented to give it up. And she wouldn't have to if I was there to help out. That's what I keep telling her. She's got a great future. But not the way Crystal does it, moving from one casino to another. That's no way to live. No way to raise a kid. Joss can do better than that, especially with me helping her."

Raney looked at Dalton. *Is this guy for real?*

He gave a slight shrug. *Looks like it.*

Grady didn't seem to notice. "In fact," he continued, "she's already on her way. I heard back from one of the producers I sent her demo to and he said—"

"Stop!" Raney held up a hand like she was directing traffic. "Don't say anything else. Tell Joss first." She rose from her chair. "I'll see if she's awake."

As soon as Raney left, Dalton said, "You'll have your hands full."

"I know." Grady's expression indicated he was looking forward to it.

"And not just with Joss," Dalton warned. "Raney, too. These Whitcomb girls stick up for each other. And then there's Mama."

"I heard."

Dalton had to laugh at the look of mild panic on the

other man's face. "She's not so bad. Get on her good side and treat her daughter right, and you're solid."

"Glad to hear that."

They sat in silence for a moment, then Dalton said, "You serious about Joss making it big?"

"It could happen. People are showing interest. And she's definitely got the talent to be a big success."

"How do you feel about that?"

"About her being a success? I'm all for it. Always have been. But it's a tough business. And it's not always pretty."

Dalton figured the sisters would be coming down soon. If he was going to speak his mind, he'd best get to it. "I know you didn't ask, but here's my advice. Be patient. Don't even try to rein her in. Let her go full gallop. It won't be easy with a kid in tow, but let her find that out for herself. In the long run, she'll do what's right. For herself and her baby. She's already more worried about being a good mother than being a big star."

"I think she can do both."

Footsteps sounded in the hallway from the kitchen. Dalton sat back. "Then I wish you both good luck."

Dalton and Raney excused themselves when they saw there would be no fireworks from Joss. In fact, it was just the opposite. As soon as she came out onto the veranda, Joss went straight to Grady and put her arms around him.

That was good enough for Dalton, especially when she started crying and blubbering into the guy's shirt. "I'm out of here," he said to Raney.

"I'm right behind you," she muttered, shoving him toward the steps to the lawn.

Their reunion must have gone well, since Grady was still there for the evening meal. And judging by the suitcase he carried up to Joss's room earlier, he planned to stay for several more.

The mutes stayed mute, staring from one to the other while the newly reunited couple grinned and sighed at each other throughout the meal. Dalton couldn't look, afraid it would ruin his appetite.

"How come he can stay in Joss's room," he complained to Raney later, when Joss and Grady headed upstairs for the night, "but I can't stay in yours?"

"They've already hanky-pankied. We haven't."

"Yet," he said, and pulled her in for a kiss.

She met him with enthusiasm, which told him he was making progress. But all this tiptoeing around was starting to get on his nerves. This wasn't high school. They were adults. Time they acted like it. "Come to my room tonight," he whispered into her ear. "I'll give you a ride you'll never forget."

She didn't refuse him outright, which he took to mean she was actually considering it. He pulled back to study her face. Saw the wanting in her expressive blue eyes, but he also saw indecision. "What?"

"If this goes bad, I'll lose a trainer. Rosco will lose his chance to make a name for himself, and you'll have to start over somewhere else."

He wouldn't let that happen. "And if it goes good?"

"Then we'll expect more. More time together. More commitment. We'll be a couple then, which brings its own problems and expectations—especially with my family. That would be a huge distraction. We've both worked hard to make a good showing at the Futurity. Do we really want to lose focus this late in the game?"

Dalton didn't know how to respond to that. Women overthought and overcomplicated the simplest things. He'd been hoping for sex. Raney was hoping for a lifelong commitment. He certainly wasn't ruling that out, but they both needed more time. Meanwhile, couldn't they maybe fool around a little?

Her expression said *no*. She still had doubts.

He was disappointed, but not surprised. He knew sex

with Raney wouldn't be a simple hookup. It would change everything. And it would definitely be a distraction. *Hell*.

She must have seen his frustration. She gave him a slow smile that put a spark in her eyes. "But now you can tell me you think you love me, if that'll help."

"Will you say it back?"

"I'll say it first." She slid her palm up his chest, around the back of his neck, and pulled his head down. It was a whole new kind of kiss and revved him up so much he thought his heart would bust out of his chest. When it ended, he was gasping and she just smiled. The little tease.

"I think I'm pretty sure I might love you, Dalton."

"You think you're pretty sure?"

She raked her fingernails along the back of his head in a way that made nerves hum up and down his spine. "I'm definitely pretty sure I might."

That was good enough for Dalton. For now.

CHAPTER 17

Soon after dawn the next morning, Raney and Uno watched Dalton and Alejandro load the colt and the help horse into the trailer.

Bringing along an extra horse for a small show wasn't strictly necessary since Rosco wouldn't be competing and, therefore, wouldn't require a horse and rider to help manage the herd while he worked his cow. But Big Mike was a mellow, show-wise, eleven-year-old gelding, and ever since he and Alejandro had joined Rosco's daily workouts— turning back errant cattle who tried to break free and holding the rest of the herd together—Rosco had grown accustomed to having him around. Mike was a really good turn-back and help horse. He and Alejandro made a great team. And for this first, stressful outing, Dalton felt the colt might be more relaxed if the older, more experienced horse came along.

By the time they were ready to go, neither Joss nor Grady had put in an appearance. Not surprising, since, for now at least, Joss was back in love. Raney left a note on the kitchen counter saying where they'd be and that they'd be back late in the afternoon, then they left, Dalton driving, Raney riding shotgun, Alejandro and Uno in the backseat.

Raney was as nervous as a kid headed to her first 4-H show, which was ridiculous. She'd been to plenty of horse shows. But it was all new to Rosco, and this would be Dalton's first since he'd become a part of Four Star, and she was anxious that they do well. She wondered how soccer moms handled the pressure of watching their kids perform. Booze in their thermoses, probably. She was sorry she hadn't thought to bring along a toddy for herself.

Dalton tried to keep things calm by reminding her it wasn't a big show, maybe a hundred or so horses. "No use overexposing Rosco to too much, too soon," he said, making it sound like this first show was just a tiny step in Rosco's training.

Which it was. A tiny first step. And if the blare of the loudspeaker didn't send him bouncing off the walls, or the chaos of having a hundred strange horses and people milling around didn't frazzle his nerves, he would be fine. Probably.

"I was able to buy a practice session with cattle in one of the smaller pens," she said. "During the break, like you asked."

"I know." He looked over with a condescending smile. "You told me already. Three times."

"Bite me."

Scheduling Rosco's practice during the break would hopefully bring other trainers over to see what the colt could do. If he did well, that would build on the hype, so that when he went to the Futurity, there would already be a lot of interest. The cows used at these shows were usually rerun yearling heifers and wouldn't offer much of a challenge, which was good. Having an easy first run would bolster Rosco's confidence and help settle his nerves. Raney's, too, she hoped.

Dalton reached across the truck console and laced his fingers through hers. "He'll do fine."

The warm, strong fingers gripping hers felt like a lifeline to Raney. On reflex, she put her other hand over both of theirs to anchor him to her. "You're right. I don't know why I'm so nervous. Aren't you nervous?"

"Not when I know what I'm doing and I'm prepared." He gave her that crooked smile. "Think of it as a social outing. You'll know half of the people there. Be fun to catch up."

It suddenly occurred to Raney how awkward this might be for Dalton, seeing people he hadn't heard from since he'd left for prison. And with that thought came the realization that she wasn't nervous about how Dalton and Rosco would do, but about what others might do when they saw the man who had caused the death of the county commissioner's nephew.

An image popped into her mind—Dalton facing those two bullies outside the Roadhouse. He'd looked so alone. So resigned. Like he knew he'd be facing that kind of hostility for the rest of his life.

Anger shot through Raney. *Not this time.* She would make certain of it.

"Relax, sweetheart."

"I am relaxed." Now that she had a plan, she actually was.

"Then why are you squeezing my hand so hard?"

She grinned over at him. "I don't want you to get away. Not before you do what you said you would." She wondered if he remembered he'd promised her a ride she'd never forget.

By the rush of color up his neck, he did.

By the snort from the backseat, Alejandro guessed, too.

Balance happily restored, Raney settled back for the rest of the drive.

Even though they arrived well before the competition began, the stands were already half-filled. They found a parking place near the bleachers and not too far from a tall pole with a speaker on it. Guaranteed to be noisy and busy. Good training for Rosco. After they unloaded the horses and tied them to the trailer, Raney pulled Alejandro aside and reminded him about the fight outside the Roadhouse.

"I don't want it happening again, Alejandro. You watch his back."

"Sí, Jefe."

"And if it looks like trouble, find me. Or better yet, send Uno. ¿Tú comprende?"

He gave a small, knowing smile. "Sí. I will keep *su novio* safe, Jefe."

Raney didn't correct him. After all, he had heard their conversation and had seen them holding hands. "Thank you, my friend. I can always count on you."

"Sí. Always."

Once the horses were saddled, Raney took Uno to the stands, while Dalton and Alejandro rode to the arena to work out the kinks from being trailered.

The arena was divided in two by a portable metal fence. The competition would take place at one end. The other was an open area where horses could be exercised and people might be wandering around. Often, horses just starting out were tied close to the competition area and near the judges' stand. A busy spot with a lot going on—the boom of the loudspeaker, the applause of the onlookers, horses and cattle working on one side of the fence, and exercising horses moving around behind them. It would be interesting to see how Rosco handled it.

While they waited for the competition to start, Raney and Uno hunted up the porta-potties and the concession area. After buying a bag of popcorn and cold drinks, they went to the stands rising on one side of the arena.

Pausing at the front, Raney scanned the rows for a place to sit and for people she knew. The first face she recognized wasn't happy. County Commissioner Adkins, heading her way, fists clenched at his sides.

Before the commissioner had gone into politics, he had been in real estate—mostly dealing with oil and gas leases—and had worked with her father on a few lease projects. Raney had met him years ago and had seen him several times since, but they had never been more than distant acquaintances. She guessed by his expression as he stomped toward her and Uno, that was about to change.

"Was that Dalton Cardwell I saw you come in with?" he demanded.

"Good morning, Commissioner," Raney answered with a polite smile.

"Are you here with Dalton Cardwell?"

"I am. He's training a promising colt for me."

"You know he killed Jim Bob."

"I know he took responsibility for his part in that terrible tragedy and went to jail for it. I'm so sorry for your loss. Jim Bob is sorely missed." She tried to inject sympathy into her tone, although she doubted the commissioner would be mollified.

He wasn't. "His part? Are you saying my nephew had a hand in his own death?"

"Not at all. But since there was never a trial and all the facts weren't made public, we'll never know for certain." Dropping a hand onto Uno's shoulder, she started to steer him around the commissioner. "Now, if you'll excuse us—"

The older man sidestepped to block their way. "Cardwell also put two of Jim Bob's cousins in the hospital. Did you know that?"

"Yes. I was there. I regret that Jim Bob's cousins were hurt, but they did start the fight and take the first swing."

"So say you. Deputy Langers says different."

Raney gave up on the niceties. "So says a dozen videos on the Internet, Commissioner. Look them up. You'll see exactly what happened and what Deputy Langers did about it. Which was nothing. Toby Langers has a long-standing grudge against Cardwell. It led him to make an error in judgment that has put a big kink in his career. I'd hate to see him talk you into making the same mistake."

"Is that a threat, Miss Whitcomb?"

Raney showed her teeth in what she hoped was a smile. "Of course not, Commissioner. But it's obvious you feel Cardwell's time in prison wasn't enough to compensate for your loss. I understand that. Losing a loved one is hard. I still struggle over my father's death. But I'm trying to move on. I suggest you do, too. Enjoy the rest of your day." —

By the time she and Uno found seats near the top of the bleachers, she was shaking with anger. And adrenaline. And the urge to hit something. Instead, she took a deep breath, let it out, and turned to Uno. "I think I've made an enemy."

"*No es importante, Jefe.* Senor Dalton and *mi padre* will protect you."

She fought the urge to ruffle his dark hair. "Of course they will. They're the bravest men I know. But I don't want to bother them about this right now, so let's not mention it to them, *¿tú comprende?*"

He looked uncertain, but nodded.

"Any popcorn left? It really smells good."

While they sat munching popcorn, the stands slowly filled. Raney saw no sign of the commissioner and hoped he'd left. She did see several people she knew, and smiled and waved, but made no effort to join them. She was still too worked up to be pleasant company.

The show started with the usual fanfare—music blasting over the loudspeakers, clapping, a cheerfully exuberant announcer introducing the judges and the names of each horse and rider as they came into the arena to make their two-and-a-half-minute run at the cows.

Raney studied Rosco. Dalton had tied him on the end of the dividing fence close by the judges' stand. He definitely perked up when all the hoopla started, but didn't seem overly agitated. After a while, his head dropped a little, but he still stayed focused on the doings on the other side of the rail fence. As the show progressed, Raney noticed several trainers she recognized talking to Dalton and checking out Rosco. She wasn't sure what to make of that. It was a little early for offers. Or maybe it was just curiosity about a new face in their midst.

Raney chatted with Uno from time to time and occasionally he chatted back. Definitely his father's son. But she could see his interest was down in the exercise area with his father and Dalton, so after a while, she relented and sent him down there, while she continued to monitor Rosco from the stands. And Dalton.

He looked magnificent. The snug jeans emphasizing the long, muscular strength of his legs. The sway of his wide shoulders as Rosco moved into a lope. The tilt of his head and the suppleness of his broad, strong back as he rounded the turns. Dalton was born to the saddle and his athletic grace drew the attention of every woman sitting near Raney.

Rosco seemed to be doing well, too, and loped through his exercise laps without any signs of nervousness, despite the noise and action around him. Slowly, Raney allowed herself to relax and enjoy the show. Several friends dropped by. A few asked about Dalton, but most were more interested in Rosco. Raney downplayed both. She didn't want interest in Rosco to build too fast. And she didn't want interest in her and Dalton to build at all. Not that she was ashamed of him, but after the fiasco with Trip, she'd had her fill of speculation about her personal life.

When the announcer called a break to change out the cows, she saw Dalton wave to get her attention, then point at his wrist, where a watch would be if he wore one. She checked her phone, saw it was nearing time for Rosco's turn to work cows in the small pen, and left the stands. As she went around behind the arena to the practice pens, she noticed several trainers heading that way, too.

Rosco's first cow was easy. Alejandro and Big Mike did their part keeping the cattle bunched together after Dalton cut his choice from the herd. Rosco kept his head down and his mind focused, and after a few feints and a halfhearted attempt to get past him, the cow gave up.

The second heifer was deeper inside the herd, so Rosco had to go into the herd without scattering them, bring out the one Dalton wanted, then keep her away from the others until Dalton put his right hand on his withers to signal him to stop. He did okay, but misread one of the cow's moves and almost had a miss. The third heifer didn't even put up a fight. About what you'd expect from cattle that had done this exercise a dozen times. Still, they made Rosco look good, which made Dalton look good, which made the other trainers take notice, and made Raney so proud it was hard not to jump up and down. A credible first showing.

The rest of the show was anticlimactic. Raney had signed Rosco up for only one practice session, so there was nothing left to do but watch. They stayed to see who made the finals, offered turn-back help but had no takers, then loaded up and headed out before traffic piled up at the exit gate.

Raney was so exhausted she fell asleep halfway home.

That set the pattern for the next two shows, although Raney missed both. With each outing, Rosco improved, and Dalton gained a little more respect from the other trainers.

They were a close-knit group. Horse trainers, first, but businessmen, too, and despite being fierce competitors, they helped one another out when needed. Alejandro and Big Mike drew a lot of attention as a helper team, and several times during the two shows, helped other riders.

Raney heard all about it secondhand. Things were getting too hectic at home for her to attend. Grady had left but promised to return the first week of September. He and Joss seemed to have reached an understanding, although Joss hadn't shared the details with Raney. Mostly, her sister re-organized the baby's room daily, complained about her gi-normous belly after every meal, and wore a pinched look of terror when she thought no one was looking. It didn't help that Mama was still galloping around the mountains in Washington State out of cell range, and no one knew how to reach KD.

On a stifling Monday morning in August, Joss and Raney were in the office, making a list of things they'd need on hand for when Joss brought the baby home, when Raney's cell buzzed. Seeing who it was, she put the phone on speaker.

"About time you called, Mama. We can't locate KD and Joss—"

"Mama," Joss yelled, snatching the phone from Raney's hand. "You better get back here quick! The baby's coming and I—"

"Right now? You're in labor?"

"No, but I'm already dilated two centimeters and the doctor says it'll be soon."

"How soon?"

"Within two weeks. Three, at most. Maybe four."

Mama let out a deep breath that sounded like a hurri-cane gust through the phone. "Stop worrying. I'll be home tomorrow. I'm on the way to Seattle now and will fly out first thing. But I'm in the mountains and may lose coverage, so don't panic if I cut out. Now, who is this Grady person who's been staying at the house? I got your voice mail, but it was all garbled. Is he still there?"

Raney could hear Mama's voice starting to fade in and out. Before she lost her altogether, she grabbed the phone from Joss. "We'll talk about all that later, Mama. You're starting to break up. Are you still coming in on the shuttle from Lubbock to Gunther?"

A muddled answer, but it sounded like *yes*.

"Text me your flight number and arrival time as soon as you can. And how to reach KD. We can't find her."

Mama started to answer when another rush of static drowned her out. All they could make out was "Germany" before the call ended.

Raney looked at Joss. "Germany? Did she say KD is in Germany?"

Joss started to tear up. "I don't care about KD. I just need Mama to get here. I can't have this baby without her."

"You'll have to," Raney said drily. "Mama's too old to do it for you."

"God, I knew this would happen!"

While Joss rummaged through the desk for Kleenex, Raney Googled army bases in Germany and read there were approximately thirty-six of them. Approximately? Shouldn't they know how many they had? "The biggest army installation in Germany is a training base in a place I can't pronounce," she told Joss. "It has six thousand soldiers and trains them in all sorts of stuff. Including tanks."

"KD's too claustrophobic for tanks," Joss said, and blew her nose.

"If she was that claustrophobic, they wouldn't have let her in. Maybe they moved her there because of her size. Or lack of it."

KD was the smallest of the Whitcomb girls and probably the fiercest. The high school basketball coach said she was too short to play defense and would never be able to block a shot. KD showed him she didn't need to block, as long as she was fast enough to steal the ball from under the tall shooters. She made all-state her senior year. When KD set her mind to something, she never quit. She wouldn't have made it through West Point Cadet Basic Training if she gave up easily.

"Forget about KD," Joss said. "She'd never get back in time for the baby, even if they'd let her come."

"You'll be too busy to care anyway. We'll send her lots of pictures. It'll give new meaning to *crotch shots*."

"That's disgusting."

Raney agreed. "Glad it won't be my crotch. But look on the bright side. You'll be trending in an hour."

"No way! You are not putting any pictures of me or my crotch on the Internet!"

"You sure? You'd be an instant sensation."

"Raney! Stop it! You're upsetting the baby!"

"Okay, okay," Raney said with a laugh. She wondered what Joss would do after the baby came and she no longer had her pregnancy to hide behind. Her smile faded. "I hope Len is able to come."

She had concerns about her older sister. Len hadn't returned any of her calls or texts. Not that unusual, since her big sister was always headed somewhere—bridge at the country club, tennis league, PTA, being a docent at the museum, driving her kids around. She was a busy lady. But lately, it felt like her sister was brushing her off. It made Raney wonder if Len and Ryan were having trouble again. It wasn't easy being married to a surgeon as career-focused as Ryan was. And with the kids getting older and becoming more independent, Len probably felt at loose ends.

"We should call her," she said on impulse. "Make her come for a long visit. Maybe when Mama gets back."

"Better call soon, then. You know how Len has to plan every move she takes."

"She's not that bad."

"Have you seen her lists?"

Raney had always been closer to her older sister because their age gap was shortest. Len was only three years older than Raney, while Joss was five years younger, and KD was younger by eight years. Raney had been an attendant in Len's wedding, and being seventeen, had thought it was the most romantic thing she'd ever seen. She had also been in the waiting room when Jake was born two years later, then again when Len's daughter, Kendra, came two years after Jake.

Then Daddy died a few months later, and she and Len both got busy and drifted apart, although their paths still crossed several times a year. But that separation had given Raney a new perspective. Over time, she had been able to see the subtle changes the years had brought to Len and Ryan's marriage. Len had always been the golden girl through school. First in everything she'd tried. But once Ryan finished his surgical residency, she had dropped to second place in his life, behind her husband's budding surgical career.

Since then, Raney had noted the restlessness, the poorly hidden anxiety that had honed her sister down to a thin shadow of the beautiful, vivacious girl she had adored. Raney missed that Len. It made her sad and cynical, reinforcing all her doubts about marriage being the key to her own personal happily-ever-after.

Although, with Dalton . . .

"I'll call her tonight," she decided, and reminded herself to make sure Len's room was ready. "Thank goodness we turned KD's bedroom into the nursery rather than Len's. Lord knows when the army will give KD leave to visit."

Joss sighed and pressed a palm against her back. "I really don't care if either one of them gets here in time. I just want this baby out of me. And soon."

"I don't know why you'd want to rush it," Raney teased. "You carry another person around inside of you for nine months, then go through shrieking agony to get it out, and your reward is to bring it home so it can cry, poop, pee, and puke all over you for the next three years? Seems like a bad deal to me."

Joss planted both fists on her hips and glared at Raney. She looked like a winged whale coming in for a landing. "You're horrible, Raney Marie Whitcomb! You're going to be the worst aunt ever! See if I let you babysit."

"Oh, please. You'll be paying me."

Joss let her hands drop. Her eyes teared up. Again. "Surely that stuff won't last three entire years, will it?"

Raney relented. Joss was no fun to tease since she got pregnant. "Of course not. Your baby will come out with a mop of blond hair and singing 'Amazing Grace' in three-part harmony. She'll be sewing her own clothes in a year."

Joss frowned. "I wouldn't want her to be hairy. But singing would be okay."

Raney had no response to that.

Nor did she have to call Len. Her sister showed up that afternoon. And she looked awful.

CHAPTER 18

It was late afternoon when Dalton pulled the horse trailer through the main gate. The cutting show had been a small one with less than eighty entries, and since none of the other trainers had needed turn-back help, he and Alejandro and Uno had been able to load up and leave early. If they got the horses brushed down and fed quickly enough, Dalton would have time for a shower before supper. Maybe even a chance to tell Raney the news.

When he came around the corner of the house, he heard raised voices behind the screen on the veranda. He stopped and listened. He'd seen an unfamiliar, very expensive car parked out back and had assumed Grady Douglas had returned. But these were female voices. He recognized Raney's and Joss's, but the third was muffled. He couldn't make out words, but it sounded like she was crying. *Shit.*

Dalton had no sisters, and his mother may have shed five or six tears in all the time he'd been aware of such things, so he'd been spared a lot of drama growing up. Yet in the Whitcomb household someone seemed to be crying all the time. Mostly Joss. He had little tolerance for it. Not today. He had other things on his mind.

Turning around, he retraced his steps around to the side door, hoping to make it to his room before being seen and dragged into another family crisis.

When he entered the kitchen, he smelled roast beef and saw Maria standing in the hallway leading to the veranda, fingers twisting in her apron. Crying. And eavesdropping. His hopes of a clean getaway dwindled.

When she heard Dalton close the door, she whipped around and raised a finger to her lips, warning him to keep quiet.

"What's going on?" he whispered as she hurried toward him.

"Oh, Mr. Dalton, *es muy malo.* La senora has been hurt."

Dalton felt a jolt of fear. Then he realized Maria couldn't be talking about Raney or Joss. Neither was a married senora. Must be the third woman.

"Hurt how?" he asked.

"No sé. Los ojos"—she pointed to her eyes—"they are black-and-blue."

So much for escaping drama.

Shouldering past the Mexican woman, Dalton walked down the hall. As he stepped out onto the veranda, three faces turned toward him. Two appeared fine. The third looked like the loser in a bar fight. She also looked familiar. Len. The oldest Whitcomb girl. Dalton remembered her from his high school years. She'd been a year older than him and a real babe.

She wasn't now. Eyes swollen and bruised, nose running, and no makeup to cover the damage. "What happened?"

Raney came toward him. "Dalton, this is my older sister, Len."

"I remember who she is. Hi, Len."

"Good to see you, Dalton." She smiled. It looked gro-

tesque with all the swelling. "Although I wouldn't have recognized you. You've changed."

"War and prison will do that. What's going on?"

Before Len could answer, Raney said, "Jake and Kendra
are in summer camp for the next two weeks, so she's come
for a visit."

Dalton waited. When nothing more was said, he frowned.
"And that's it? We're just going to ignore her two black
eyes?"

"She had them done."

"With what? A fist?"

Joss snickered. Turning to Len, she said, "Mama ap-
pointed Dalton our personal security force. That's why he's
been staying in the guest room. To keep us safe while she's
gone. He's certainly built for the job, don't you think?"

The oldest sister looked at Dalton then at Raney with
speculation in her swollen eyes. At least, Dalton read it as
speculation. Hard to tell.

"Excuse us a minute." Raney took Dalton's arm and led
him into the pass-through into the kitchen. Stopping in the
middle where they couldn't be easily seen from either the
kitchen or the veranda, she said, "Len had blepharoplasty.
Eyelid surgery."

"Why?"

"To make her look younger. Better."

"Better than what? She was already beautiful."

"I heard that," Len called from the veranda. "And I can
see why you're so taken with him, Raney."

Raney gave him a *now look what you've done* look. Like
it was somehow his fault that the sisters had been gossiping
about him.

"Is that true?" He slid an arm around her slender waist
and pulled her close. The feel of her soft body pressed up
against his made him forget how tired he was. "You're
taken with me?" he whispered into her ear.

She put both palms on his chest. But not to push him away. Instead, she leaned up to plant a quick kiss on his jaw, then gave him a pat. "Ask me after you shower. Supper's almost ready."

"Tease." He turned away.

She pulled him back by his shirt. "How'd the show go?"

"Good. Since there weren't many entries, I bought a second practice run. He did so well we got offers."

She let go of his shirt. An odd look crossed her face. Not the happy expression he'd expected. "Offers for you or Rosco?"

"Both. We'll talk later." This time when he turned to go, she let him.

Raney seemed nervous at supper. Dalton didn't know why. But because of the worried crease between her brows whenever she looked at him, which was often, he was pleased to note, he suspected it had to do with him. Could be anything: something he said or didn't say—something he did or didn't do—something he might be, or not be fixing to do. It was never simple with Raney. Eventually, she'd get around to it. Meanwhile, he'd work on a general all-purpose defense.

Everybody else seemed in a good mood, once Alejandro and Hicks got over their shock at Len's appearance. They also seemed as skeptical of the eye surgery explanation as Dalton was. The woman was only thirty-three. And beautiful. Why the hell would she need surgical enhancements?

Women. He'd never figure them out.

He was a little surprised that Raney hadn't asked about the show, or the offers he'd mentioned. Not that either offer was worth considering this early in the cutting show season. Or maybe worth considering ever. Rosco would probably make Four Star more money as a stud than as a cutting horse, assuming he did well over the next two or three years. Still, Dalton had expected her to show interest.

"Mama's coming home tomorrow," Joss announced. "Anybody want to get her in Gunther? She's on the afternoon shuttle from Lubbock. Len's taking me to my obstetrician appointment in Aspenmont, so we can't do it. Raney, can you?"

Raney blinked like she was just tuning in to the conversation. "Pick up Mama? Sure. When's she due in?"

"Around four, give or take. The shuttle's almost never on time."

Dalton wondered if Mama's return meant he'd lose his security job and be sent back to the dorm. He was conflicted about that. It was nice having a snore-free room and a private shower. But if he stayed, how could he put a move on Raney with her mother hanging around? Not that he'd made any headway on that so far. But rather than dwelling on it, he decided to wait and see what Mama wanted.

After Joss's announcement, there was a lull in the conversation, as if everyone was contemplating what it would mean having the head chingona back in the house. They'd probably have to start eating in the dining room again. And dressing up for Sunday dinner. Judging by their sour expressions, Alejandro and Hicks had come to that same realization.

A few minutes later, seeing his opening—which didn't come often with three women at the table—Dalton jumped in. "Got an offer on Rosco at the show today."

"I forgot about the show," Joss said. "He did well?"

"He did."

"Rosco is that pretty little buckskin colt?" Len asked.

Dalton nodded. "He's three now, and not so little anymore."

"A good offer?" Hicks asked, breaking his week-long supper silence.

"Nothing special. But it shows interest. If the colt continues to improve, that interest will probably peak at the Futurity in November."

Joss frowned at Raney, who was staring at Dalton with that pinched look again. "I didn't know you were considering selling Rosco."

Raney gave a weak smile. "I'm not. He's a cornerstone in our quarter horse program. More wine, anyone?"

That was all she had to say? Dalton watched her empty her half-full goblet in two swallows, then pour it full again. She was sure worked up about something.

Another lull. This time, Alejandro jumped in. "Dalton got an offer, as well."

All eyes turned to Dalton. Most showed curiosity. Raney's showed panic.

"From whom?" Len asked.

When Alejandro didn't answer, Dalton said, "An outfit out of Oklahoma looking to build up their training staff."

"A good offer?" Joss asked.

"Middling."

Joss glanced at Raney again, who was staring into her wineglass. She turned back to Dalton, "Are you going to take it?"

"No." He spoke firmly and decisively, then waited for Raney to look up. When she did, he smiled at her and said, "I'm happy where I am."

There was a moment of awkward silence as unspoken messages rounded the table. Then irrepressible Joss laughed. "I think he's hinting for a raise, Raney."

Dalton shook his head. "It's not about money, Joss. It's about building something worthwhile. Rosco is part of that. I'm not looking to move on. But I'll take more of that roast beef, if there's any left."

That broke the tension and the rest of the meal continued without incident.

Dalton was relieved to see the pinched look leave Raney's face. She even smiled at him over her wineglass. Small steps. But at least he was still in the game and she didn't seem upset with him anymore. For whatever reason.

Women. Emotional quagmires. He'd never figure them out.

Alejandro and Hicks left soon after the meal ended.

Dalton headed to his room a few minutes later, leaving the sisters to catch up on all the gossip, trade recipes, fix one another's hair, polish their toes, or whatever it was women did when they got together. He was lights-out and asleep by nine.

At eleven thirty, his phone buzzed. He started to ignore it, then remembered he was the security guy. Muttering under his breath, he fumbled for it on his nightstand, and punched ACCEPT. "What?"

"You awake?"

Raney. He sat up. "I am now."

"Want company?"

"Ah . . . sure." Then, just to needle her, he said, "Who is this?"

"Asshat."

"Asshat who?"

The call ended.

Dalton slumped back. He stared up at the ceiling, wondering what had just happened. Was he still asleep? Awake? Was Raney really coming to his room?

Holy shit. He was off the bed and zipping his jeans when he heard the first tentative knock. He opened the door to find Raney standing there.

In a satiny robe.

And not much else.

"Hey," he said, too befuddled to think of anything snappy to say.

She whipped inside and closed the door with barely a

sound, then leaned against it, arms behind her, palms flat against the wooden panels, breathing hard. "I didn't want them to see me."

"Who?" he asked, appreciating the way the thin cloth of her robe tightened across her breasts with every breath.

"My sisters."

That sounded like she was ashamed of him. But Dalton didn't pursue it just then. He was having more fun concentrating on her breasts. They were really nice breasts. "You're thirty. A little old to be sneaking around, don't you think?"

"Twenty-nine and two-thirds. And you don't know my sisters."

Actually, he did.

But before he could point that out, she said, "Do you have any condoms?"

Condoms? He forced his gaze to her face. She was smiling. Or trying to. It didn't match the anxiousness in her eyes. "Condoms?"

"Rubbers. Prophylactics. Whatever. Do you have any?"

His heart started to race. "Yeah."

"How many?"

"Enough."

"Pretty sure of yourself, aren't you?"

"What?"

"That you just happened to have a bunch of condoms on hand."

"I didn't say I had a bunch of them. And they're old." That didn't sound right.

"How old?"

"From before prison. Look, before we go any further, I need to know the rules."

"What rules?"

"You've been holding me at arm's length for months now, and suddenly you show up at my door in the middle of the night, half-dressed and asking if I have condoms. Not that I'm complaining. You look great, by the way. I really like your robe. But I just need to know why you're here before I do something that might get me in trouble."

She blinked at him like a night bird caught in a beam of light. "I just asked you if you had condoms, for heaven's sake," she said in an exasperated tone. "Why do you think I'm here?"

She was starting to lose that anxious look. Now she looked more irritated. In Dalton's mind, a step in the right direction. Raney was a lot more fun when she was riled up than when she was skittish and fearful.

"For all I know, you're just here to borrow my condoms. But the ones I've got I've been saving for a special occasion."

"Like what?"

"Like you showing up at my door in the middle of the night, half-dressed and asking if—"

"You're such an asshat."

"You keep saying that." But rather than carry it too far, Dalton put on a smile, and with total sincerity, said, "I'm happy you're here, Raney."

"You don't look happy."

"No?" He motioned to the front of his jeans, and the bulge that was starting to get uncomfortable. "Does that look unhappy to you?"

She looked away. But not before she looked down.

"I still need to know why you're here, sweetheart. If this is another string-along—"

"It isn't," she broke in.

"Okay, then. Great. But just for my own edification, what changed your mind?"

She finally, hesitantly, came away from the door and closed the space between them. Anticipation almost made him pant.

"I thought I had all the time in the world." As she spoke, she put her hand on his bare chest, watched the motion of it as she stroked her palm over his lightly furred pectoral and the thundering heart beneath it.

His whole body quivered.

"I already made one mistake. I didn't want to make another." Her fingertips traced the arc of his nipple.

He thought his knees would buckle.

"But then you got the offer," she went on, watching her hand as it moved down, one fingertip following the thin line of dark hair disappearing into his jeans. "And I realized if I didn't do something, you'd leave and I'd never know."

She was killing him, and she didn't even seem to care. "Know what?"

Her hand stopped. She stared at the puckered scar by his waist. "Iraq?"

"Hay baler. As you were saying? You would never know about what?"

Her hand stopped its exploration.

"About us. This." She looked up. Her gaze moved over his face, settled on his mouth. "I don't want you to leave, Dalton."

"This is an inducement to stay?"

"Yes."

"It's working." He decided he'd better move this along before his heart gave out. "Do you want to take off your robe, or should I?"

"You can."

It was like unwrapping every Christmas present of his whole life all at once. Times ten.

Neither of them were virgins, but since there would be only this one first time together, Dalton resolved to go slow and do it right. But as soon as her robe slid in a whisper to the floor, and she reached for the zipper on his jeans, he lost focus and sank into pure sensation.

Nerves jumping under his skin when she slowly pulled down his jeans. The softness of her skin against his palm.

The flowery scent of her hair. The way her breathing changed to match his when he touched her breasts.

Great breasts. Amazing breasts. And a perfect fit for his big hands. Soft and firm at the same time, and so smooth it was like stroking sleek, warm satin.

Which he did. While she stroked him.

Then they went wild. Too long without, too long waiting for this to happen. Mouth open against his, she climbed him like a cat up a pole, her long, strong legs wrapping tight around his waist as he lifted her up and held her against him.

The kiss went on and on. Until his arms started shaking and they were both out of breath. And still, it wasn't enough.

"We have to stop," he whispered against her lips.

He felt her smile. "This isn't working for you?"

"It's working too well. But I'd need a third hand to get on the condom, and soon, or it won't matter. This time."

"I'm on the pill."

He drew his head back and looked at her. "Is that wise?"

"Are you worried about STDs? I'm clean. Are you?"

"I've been in prison."

She nipped his nose. "I know. That's why I asked."

He tried to get his head around that. Couldn't. Took it as evidence of her bizarre sense of humor and played along. "You trying to pick a fight?"

"What do you think?"

"I think you are." And in a single twisting movement he dumped her across the bed, followed her down, and pinned her to the mattress. "I win."

She laughed. He felt the vibration of it all through his body.

Then they got busy. And because it was their first time together, everything was new and a little tentative, until she started snapping out instructions like his old drill sergeant—different instructions, of course—and like any good soldier, he followed orders.

It was the best he'd ever had.

Bar none.

The second time was even better because of the learning curve. By then, he knew just how she liked to be touched, and what she wanted most, and how to keep her on the edge of it until it became too much for both of them.

When it was over, Raney slid off onto her stomach beside him, both of them breathing hard, Dalton sprawled on his back, too drained to move and already thinking about another encore.

"That was amazing," he said between gasps. "Ten best for sure."

She muttered something, but her voice was muffled by the pillow.

He rolled onto his side and ran a finger between her shoulder blades, tracing the knobby bumps of her spine in the dip between the long, rounded muscles of her back, all the way down to the dished dimple at the top of her butt. A rider's back. Strong and supple. Leading to a perfect butt. "Definitely top three. You're a seriously sexy woman."

She lifted her head and stared at him through a tangle of curls. "Top three what?"

"Fantasies."

"Seriously? I didn't even make the finals?" She started to push upright.

He pulled her back down. "Relax, sweetheart. All my fantasies are about you. I have an insatiable, endless imagination where you're concerned. It's like you were created in a lab somewhere just to prance naked through my mind."

She blinked at him. "A lab? That's not very romantic."

"Heaven?"

"Better."

She settled back down and got comfortable again, this time tucked against his side. "And I don't prance."

He thought of her dancing and smiled. "Stomp, then."

He had almost drifted off to sleep when she said, "What are one and two?"

He kissed the top of her head and yawned. "You'll see."

CHAPTER 19

Dalton woke with his heart racing and Raney's voice whispering through his mind. He cracked open an eye. The clock on the nightstand read seven minutes after eight. Which made no sense. He never slept past six. Struggling to bring his mind into focus, he rolled onto his back and saw the empty space beside him.

Had he dreamed it all? He looked around. Saw no evidence of Raney ever being there, in his room, in his bed. How could that be?

He reached for the phone.

She answered on the third buzz, her voice thick with sleep.

"You awake?" he asked.

"No."

"Did it really happen?"

"What?"

"You. Me. The best sex I've ever had."

He heard her draw in air on a yawn, then let it out in a rush. "How quickly they forget."

"I'll never forget."

"We need to talk."

That didn't sound good. But she was right. They did need to talk. What happened last night changed everything. "When?"

"Later. At the barn. G'night."

Dalton did a lot of thinking while he took his shower. He might not understand women all that well, but he was getting better at hearing what they didn't say. And he'd heard Raney loud and clear. If she'd been worried last night about her sisters knowing about them, she'd be doubly cautious with her mama in the house.

Shit. He was back to arm's length.

Not unexpected. Still, it rankled. But rather than wait to be booted out, he dressed, packed up his stuff, and headed back to the workers' dorm.

Throughout the rest of the morning he was so busy he didn't have time to fret over what Raney might say. His tasks with the AI program kept him mired in paperwork until lunch, then he scheduled out a few more local cutting shows before the pre-works started in October. He picked the ones he thought would have the biggest draw and largest crowds, then looked over the list of private training barns that were hosting fall pre-works. He was familiar with the names, but had never attended any of their workouts. The man he'd ridden for before, Roy Kilmer, wasn't on a par with these premier outfits. That Whitcomb Four Star was included had more to do with the family status and reputation than their cutting prospects. Until now. And now, Dalton was determined to have Rosco ready to shine.

After lining up the shows, he decided to give the colt a mental break and take him out into the pasture. Being as smart as he was, Rosco could easily grow sour and bored. To combat that, Dalton had taken him out at least once a week since his training began. Hoping Raney would go with them, he had Uno brush Big Mike down just in case.

It was a little after one when he saw her coming up the drive toward the barn, dressed for work in jeans that hugged those long, strong legs that had held him tight last night. The memory of it was so strong he stopped what he was doing and watched her come toward him, images rolling through his mind like a slow-motion movie. Then he realized what he was doing to himself and went back to work before he flung her down in the straw as soon as she walked through the doors.

"Hey," she said, stopping beside him. When she saw he wasn't using the cutting saddle Rosco usually wore during his workouts, she asked if he was taking the colt for a run in the pasture.

Dalton nodded. "Got time to go with us?"

"I'd love to. But I have to go get Mama." She watched him tighten Rosco's cinch, then said, "Since Mama's coming home, you should probably move back into the dormitory."

"I already have."

If she was surprised, or disappointed, or upset by that, she didn't show it. Which irritated him a little.

"It's probably for the best," she said. "If you stayed in the house, we'd end up sneaking around. And I don't like doing that."

"Then don't." It came out more sharply than he intended, so he softened his tone. "Be open. Tell her about us. You're a grown woman, Raney. You can make that decision for yourself." And he was surprised she hadn't. It seemed out of character for a woman as decisive and strong-minded as Raney was to be so concerned about what her mama might think.

"I made my decision last night when I came to your room."

"But now you have regrets?"

She smiled and shook her head. "No regrets. You're every bit the studmuffin I dreamed you were."

"Studmuffin? Sounds girly."

"Trust me, you're not." Her smile faded. "But I think maybe we should slow down. This is all moving pretty fast."

Dalton almost called foul. Jacking him up with talk like that, then telling him to back off. "If it's making you that uncomfortable, maybe I should just move on."

"No." Her hand shot out to grab his arm, as if that might stop him if he did choose to go. Which he didn't. He'd spoken without thinking, and as soon as the words were out, he'd wanted them back. Through Rosco and the AI program, he already felt invested in the ranch. It seemed that for a long time he'd been spinning his wheels and going nowhere. But here, at Four Star, there was hope. A chance to build something meaningful. Make a new start. But it all hinged on the woman beside him. Who was now pushing him away again.

"I don't want you to leave," she said, taking her hand away. "I just need more time."

"For what?" This had already been going on for months. How much longer did she need to figure out what she wanted?

"To decide if this is real. I can't help but think in terms of commitment, Dalton. That's the way I'm built. I don't sleep around, or try guys out, or have hookups. I go all in or nothing. I already made one mistake. I don't want to make another."

Dalton looked away, not trusting himself to speak. That she would even put him and the douche in the same category was an insult.

"I'm not good with change," she went on. "And a permanent commitment would mean a lot of changes. A lot of risk."

"There aren't any guarantees, Raney. If you don't think what we have is worth the risk, let's end it now."

"But I think it is. I think it might work. It might be wonderful. The best thing ever to come into my life. But it's all happened so fast. I just need a little more time to think it through. Can you give me that?"

If he wanted Raney, what choice did he have? And he definitely wanted Raney. He untied Rosco's lead from the ring in the wall. "Sure. Like I said, I'm not going anywhere." The sooner he got away from her, the less chance he'd say something he might regret.

But she followed him out of the barn and stood while he opened the gate into the pasture. "I know you're upset," she said, after he led Rosco through and secured the gate behind him. "And I understand why. But remember what I said about us getting distracted if we went to the next step?"

"I remember." He swung into the saddle, then sat and waited for her to say all she came to say.

"I was right." She looked up at him, blue eyes narrowed against the glare. "After last night, I'm definitely distracted. All day I've been thinking about how great it was with you, and when we would do it again. Not once did I think about Rosco or the Futurity. Joss even had to remind me to go get Mama in Gunther this afternoon. Aren't you even a little bit distracted, too?"

"Sure. I get a hard-on every time you walk into the barn, or I hear your voice, or see you smile. But since I can't always act on those distractions, I put them aside. I compartmentalize. Soldiers are trained to do that. In combat, everything is in the here and now. We don't think in terms of the future since it might never come."

"That's sad."

He shrugged. "It's the way it has to be."

"I couldn't do that. Planning ahead keeps bad things from happening. At least, that's the plan," she added with a crooked smile.

"I know. You see a moment and stretch it to forever. You look at it from all angles. You analyze. And when you're sure, you commit. That's how you've kept the ranch running so well. You're good at it."

"But?"

"But that's all ledgers and spreadsheets, Raney. Handling emotions is harder for you. That's why you need extra time to think it through. I don't like it, but I get it."

She was silent so long, he wondered if his words had hurt her. He hoped not. In his experience, easy commitments didn't last long. Raney's were etched in steel.

"You'd be okay if we slow it down for now?" she asked, that crease back between her brows.

Poor Raney. Always worrying about something. "Disappointed, but not upset. I think we're great together. I think we have a chance for something special and I'm willing to wait for it. For now. But be careful you don't overanalyze it and talk yourself out of it."

She thought for it a moment, then nodded. "You could be right."

Dalton snorted. "I'm right?"

"I know," she said with a wry smile. "I'm as shocked as you are." Her smile faded. "I do tend to overthink things."

Which she did a moment longer, then nodded as if she'd come to a decision or realization. "You're a sly one, aren't you? By not rushing me or trying to force me to your way of thinking, you've given me no reason to resist. You've taken away the need to put space between us."

Hope clambered to the surface. "What does that mean, exactly?"

"It means you're a wise man, Dalton Cardwell. Heavens! Look at the time. I've got to get going."

Ten minutes later, as Dalton watched the Expedition head out the main gate, he wondered what she meant. Was he back in the saddle again? Or standing at the gate waiting to get in? The damn woman had him tied in knots.

Mama was in great spirits and looked happier than Raney had seen her in a long time. It reminded her again that her mother was still a vital woman. And a very attractive one. She had probably been the darling of the geriatric cruise set.

"The trip was a success?" she asked as they headed back to the ranch.

"It was wonderful. So many interesting people. The weather was perfect and the food scrumptious." She went on for a few more minutes, then seemed to catch herself and added, "Although I missed my girls terribly. How is Joss?"

"Pregnant and anxious. Right now, she's at her weekly checkup in Aspenmont. Shouldn't be long. Len says it looks like the baby has dropped." Raney wasn't sure what that meant, but it sounded painful.

"Len's here?"

"Came in yesterday. The kids are at summer camp and she thought she'd hide out with us until her eyes heal and—"

"Heal? My Lord, what happened?"

"Nothing happened. She had them done, is all. Best prepare yourself, though. She's still pretty swollen and bruised."

"That's not good."

"It'll go down."

"No, I mean it's not good that she had them done."

"Why not?"

"I have a theory."

Mama had a theory about nearly everything, including cosmetic surgery. She wasn't a big fan. She felt women— and men—should age gracefully, and a few wrinkles gave a face character. Easy for her to say since she had led a pampered life and was born with amazing bone structure. Mama had one of those faces that would be beautiful into her seventies and beyond.

"Assuming a woman has no medical issues," Mama began, "and she isn't contemplating a sex change and hasn't suffered a disfigurement, there are only five reasonable reasons why a beautiful thirty-three-year-old in her prime would subject herself to the risks of plastic surgery."

Raney settled in for a long lecture.

Raising her left hand, Mama counted off on her fingers. "One—she's grossly insecure about her physical appearance. Which Len isn't.

"Two—she's having an affair with a younger man and wants to look more his age. Which might be interesting, if true, although I doubt Len's been unfaithful.

"Three—her husband is having an affair with a younger woman and she feels she needs to compete. Which Ryan better not be doing or he'll be in big trouble.

"Four—she and her husband have drifted apart and she wants to remind him why he fell in love with her in the first place. Which I sincerely hope is the case with Len and Ryan since it's fixable.

"Or five—she's newly divorced or widowed and is contemplating going on the marriage market again. Which I doubt is the issue, or we would have heard." She frowned at her hand. "I need a manicure. Remind me to make an appointment."

"You forgot reason number six," Raney pointed out.

Mama turned to look at her.

"If you have the puffy eyes from Daddy's side of the family. Len thinks they make her look tired all the time."

"They're not that bad yet."

"They will be. And the change will be less noticeable if she does it now rather than if she waits until they're like Daddy's."

"You might be right. I'll admit I considered a tuck here and there after your father died."

"You obviously decided against it."

"Obviously?"

"What I meant was—"

Mama chuckled. "I know what you meant. Back then, I had no intention of ever trying to replace your father, so I didn't truly contemplate surgery."

"Are you considering it now?"

"Not yet."

Not yet? "What does that mean?"

"It means there may come a time when I will consider it."

Raney was intrigued. And a little shocked. "You met someone on the cruise."

"I met many people on the cruise, although none stood out in that way. But I did learn one thing. I'm not too old to have fun. And sometimes the most fun of all is having someone to share that fun with. Now, who is this Grady person and why has he been staying at the house?"

Raney spent the next fifteen minutes reassuring Mama that Grady seemed to be a good guy, had been sending money for the baby, had offered to marry Joss, but so far, she'd refused, and promised he'd be back a few days before the baby was due, which was soon.

"He'd better. It's his baby, too. I suppose he expects to stay in the house."

"He did before."

"We'll see. Has she decided on a name?"

"Something musical is all I know."

"Lord help us. Now tell me about Dalton."

Having expected the question, Raney didn't react. "What about him?"

"Did he behave himself?"

"Dalton always behaves himself. He was an excellent—if unnecessary—protector, and put Grady through a full interrogation when he showed up at the house. Plus, he and Rosco have done so well in the local cutting shows, they've both gotten offers."

"That's not what I meant."

Knowing from many previous experiences that her mother could read minds, Raney didn't look at her or respond to that. Slowing down, she turned into the gate and drove toward the parking area behind the house.

"Then tell me about the offers," Mama said, trying a different tack.

"They don't matter. I'm not selling Rosco and Dalton's not leaving Four Star."

"He told you that?"

"Twice."

"That's promising."

"What do you mean?"

Instead of answering, Mama pointed at the crowded parking area. "Is that Grady's car?"

Raney recognized Joss's and Len's cars, but not the boxy BMW parked in the Expedition's usual spot. "I don't know. When he came before, he brought Joss's car back from Houston."

"Park by the gate. It will be easier to unload and we can switch the cars around later. I'll text Glenn to have one of the boys come take the luggage inside." As she opened the car door, Dalton hurried out of the side door by the kitchen.

"Hey," he called, looking more relieved than happy to see them. "Glad you're here. Things are popping. Good to see you, Mrs. Whitcomb."

"Popping? What do you mean?"

Len rushed out behind him. "Thank God you're here. Joss's obstetrician wants us to take her to University Medical in Lubbock." Seeing Mama's look of alarm, she raised her hands in a calming gesture. "It's okay, Mama. Nothing bad. She's fine. The baby's fine. But he thinks she's breech and may be coming early, so he's being cautious. They have a good neonatal center there and lots of doctors on staff. There's no rush. We can take her tonight or in the morning."

As was her custom, Mama immediately took over. "We'll go tonight. If we put the seats down in the Expedition, she'll be able to stretch out. Dalton, please see to it. Len, bring your car, too, in case you have to get home. How long do you think we'll need to be there?"

"At least a week is my guess," Len answered.

"Don't worry about things here, Mrs. Whitcomb," Dalton said. "Hicks and I can run things while you're gone."

"I may need for you to drive us."

"I can drive," a new voice said.

They all turned.

Grady came from the direction of the veranda. While he introduced himself to Mama, Raney cornered her older sister.

"The truth, Len."

Speaking in a voice that wouldn't carry back to Mama, Len said, "The truth is Joss is a little hysterical. This isn't an emergency, but the small clinic in Aspenmont isn't that well equipped if there's a problem. And if the baby is breech, there could be a problem."

Mama left Grady and Dalton to unload her luggage and came over to her daughters. "Len, tell me everything you just said to Raney. No secrets."

The woman had eyes in the back of her head.

"I'm the one who pushed for Joss to go to Lubbock," Len admitted. "The baby might be breech. This is only a precaution, Mama. The Aspenmont doctor has already set up an appointment with an obstetrician at University Medical. If Joss isn't ready to be admitted, we'll go to a hotel nearby until she is. It shouldn't be for long. She's already dilated six centimeters."

"Do we need to go tonight?"

"That's up to Joss. And you, Mama. You must be tired after your flight. Her appointment with the hospital obstetrician isn't until one o'clock tomorrow and the hospital is less than two hours away. We can leave first thing in the morning, and you can get a good night's rest. Like I told Raney, this isn't an emergency. We have plenty of time."

"I'll go talk to Joss," Mama decided. She gave Len a flustered once-over. "Are you sure you're up for this? You look . . . painful."

Len laughed. "You mean awful. But as long as I keep icing and stay upright for another day or so, I'll be fine."

"I hope so. Lord knows, I can't be worrying about two of you at the same time."

As Raney followed them into the house, she decided only her family could turn something as simple as an impending birth into such a clusterfuck. She just hoped her little sister's antics didn't send Grady shrieking into the night before Mama could convince Joss to accept his proposal and the new parents could go live happily ever after somewhere else. Far away.

After much discussion it was decided that they would leave in the morning. Grady would drive Mama and Joss to Lubbock in the Expedition, since the three of them would be staying for the duration. Len and Raney would remain at the ranch until Joss met with the hospital obstetrician, Dr. Jamison, and they had a better idea of Joss's condition and whether she would be admitted right away to University Medical. Len would continue to ice and sleep upright. Raney would continue to manage the ranch, and if she and Len had to leave, Hicks and Dalton would take charge. Meanwhile, Dalton would move back into the house to keep an eye on Mama's precious girls.

Raney didn't dare look at Dalton when that last pronouncement was made. This morning, she'd decided that with Mama back in the house, and Dalton back in the dormitory, she would have a better chance of tamping down her rampaging libido. But now . . . just thinking about Dalton being in the room below hers sent all sorts of weird pulses running through her body.

Dinner on the veranda was a festive occasion. Joss lay stretched out on a chaise like a Roman empress while Grady attended her every need and Mama entertained them in dramatic fashion with every detail of her various adventures. Who knew grizzles could eat so much salmon? Especially with a mob of people only yards away with cameras recording their every mouthful? And who cared, anyway?

Neither Alejandro nor Hicks attended, no doubt terrified

that Joss's water would break in front of them. Raney was a bit concerned, herself. Luckily the veranda floor was tile, rather than carpet.

She spent most of the meal trying not to look at Dalton, or think about running her hands over his amazing body, or having his hands running over hers, and wondering how soon she could show up at his door in the middle of the night, horny and half-dressed again. She hardly recognized herself. She had always thought she had total control of her emotions. But now . . .

Was lust an emotion? Or a character flaw? Either way, she was shocked at how anxious she was for Mama and Joss to leave.

She couldn't tell if Dalton fought the same battle. Throughout dinner, he never once looked up from his plate and stayed only long enough to gobble two helpings of everything before making a hurried escape to the barn. The coward. Which left Raney fretting on her own about all the changes ahead with her all-seeing mama back, Len having needless surgery, a new baby on the way, and Joss and Grady struggling to come to terms with each other and the miracle they had wrought.

That, and how soon could she get to Dalton's room again?

Fun times.

CHAPTER 20

The next morning, Dalton stood in the open doorway of the barn, his gaze fixed on the two figures waving after the Expedition as it left the parking area. When the car turned though the main gate, one figure went back inside. The other stayed.

Raney.

As soon as the door closed behind her sister, she turned and looked at the barn.

At him. He felt it. Like an unseen hand brushing his cheek. A whisper in his ear. Even after she followed her sister inside, he stood staring at the closed door, his blood running hot and thick, his nerves pulsing. Wanting. Remembering.

After a while, distant voices caught his attention. With a last glance at the house, he went back into the barn and tried to remember what he'd been doing.

He was an idiot to think compartmentalizing would work with Raney. As soon as he heard he'd be back in the house after Mama left, his mind had exploded with possibilities. He thought once he'd breached Raney's armor the first time, he'd be able to get his mind—and his obsession with her—under control.

But, hell no. It was even worse. Thoughts of his night with her chased him from dawn to dusk, then invaded his dreams. And he didn't think it was only because he'd gone so long without sex.

It was Raney.

She might not want to hear him say it yet, but he was in love with her. Had been, ever since the evening on the porch when she'd told him about her father. He'd had to force himself to walk away from her that night, and he'd been fighting and losing that battle ever since. Now with Mrs. Whitcomb gone . . .

God help him.

Later that afternoon, Raney and Len were putting finishing touches in the nursery when Mama called. Raney put her cell phone on speaker and asked how Joss was doing and what the Lubbock doctor said.

"Joss is well. Tired and a bit of a backache, but that's to be expected this late in the pregnancy. Dr. Jamison isn't admitting her yet, but feels it won't be long. I really like this doctor. She has a very calm way about her."

"She'll need it with Joss as a patient," Raney muttered to Len.

Len waved her to silence. "Is the baby breech?" she asked. "The obstetrician in Aspenmont thought she might be."

"No, she's head-down, although faced the wrong way, toward Joss's spine. The doctor called it posterior, or back-to-back position. It's not uncommon, and she assured us many babies move into the head-to-front anterior position during labor."

It all sounded ghastly to Raney, having something inside

of you, rolling around and kicking organs. "If she doesn't get turned around, will Joss have to have a c-section?"

"Not necessarily. But labor might take longer and involve a bit of back pain."

Len made a face. "Poor Joss. She must be frantic."

"She was at first. But Dr. Jamison talked her down and gave her some exercises that might help shift the baby into the right position."

"What do you want us to do?" Raney asked.

"Nothing for now. We're to call Dr. Jamison if anything changes. If not, Joss is to go back to see her in two days. How are things there?"

"Hot," Len said.

Mama asked if the smoked salmon she'd shipped from Alaska had arrived—which it had—and said she'd had other things shipped, but they were surprises and not to open them. She gave them the name and number of their hotel, adding they probably wouldn't get much sleep since there was some sort of event at Texas Tech and the noise and traffic were already terrible.

"Mrs. Ledbetter called," Raney said. "She was worried since she hadn't heard from you. How did she get my cell number? Did you block her on yours? She wanted to know if you were hiding out because you were pregnant now, too."

Mama laughed. "That old biddy has the raunchiest sense of humor, God bless her. I gave her your cell number since coverage on the cruise was so spotty. I'll give her a call later before she spreads it around that I'm having twins. By the way, I really like Grady Douglas, even if he is in the music business. We have to convince your sister to marry him. She could do a lot worse. Room service is here, so I better go. Love to you both. I'll check in again tomorrow."

"A reprieve," Raney said, taking the phone off speaker.

Len sighed. "I know. If Joss is this hysterical now, wait until she brings the precious bundle home."

Raney gave her a surprised look. "You didn't like having your babies?"

"Of course I did . . . once they slept more than four hours at a time. They're the most wonderful things in my life. And also, the most exhausting. I don't think I've slept through the night since I brought Jake home. But they're worth it. Don't let Joss's freak-outs turn you off of having kids someday. You'd be a great mother."

"How do you figure that?"

"Because you've been a great sister."

Raney wasn't sure how one impacted the other, but didn't argue about it. The dinner bell had just sounded, and she was more interested in seeing Dalton. Just to look at, of course. She had told him they should slow it down, and she would stick by that. As long as she could.

The mutes showed up on time. Dalton didn't. Glenn said he'd gone to visit his folks but would return either late tonight or early in the morning.

"Is anything wrong?" she asked.

"Didn't say. Didn't look worried, either. Suspect he'll let us know if there's a problem. You ladies be okay on your own tonight, or should I have one of the boys camp out on the veranda?"

Len smiled. "We'll be fine, Mr. Hicks. But thank you for your concern."

And that was about it for conversation.

Which gave Raney plenty of uninterrupted time to wonder what Dalton was up to. She had asked him to slow it down a little—was this his way of giving her the space she'd asked for? *Hell.* Since when did a man ever do what you wanted him to do except when you didn't want him to do it?

The mutes left as soon as supper was over. Raney and Len were stretched on chaises on the veranda, enjoying fresh grapes washed down with fermented grapes, when Mama called. Wondering why she'd called again, Raney put her on speaker.

"How's it going, Mama?"

No change, she told them, although Joss was having a bit more trouble with her back. "The exercises Dr. Jamison gave her aren't helping at all. I doubt the woman ever carried a child, or she'd never suggest to a woman in late pregnancy that she spend ten minutes twice a day on her hands and knees. Joss's back always hurts worse after that. And that birth ball! I never heard of such a thing! Just a fancy name for a kid's beach ball, if you ask me. Although Joss did say that when she leans over it while sitting, it seems to help." A long-suffering sigh. "Things were much easier in my day when they gave you drugs during labor, so you could sleep through the whole thing. How are things at home?"

"Same as they were when you called earlier, although Len's starting to look less like the loser of a bar fight and more like a pink-and-purple raccoon."

"Don't listen to her, Mama. She's just upset that Dalton preferred to go visit his folks rather than having her give him googly eyes all through supper."

Raney rolled her eyes. She couldn't be that transparent.

"I hope his parents and Timmy are well," Mama said.

"I'm sure they are."

"He's staying in the house like I asked him to?"

"Yes, and my Glock is loaded. Stop worrying."

They spoke awhile longer, then Mama finally gave the reason she'd called again. "We need clothes. With Joss dilly-dallying the way she is, we'll be out of underwear in two days. Just throw some stuff into a bag and bring it when you come. Meanwhile, I'll send our things to the hotel laundry, although Lord knows the condition they'll be in when they come back." A promise to call again tomorrow evening after Joss saw Dr. Jamison, then she ended the call.

"She sounds tired," Len said.

"She sounds bored," Raney countered. "Thank heavens we didn't have to go."

"Hopefully, it'll be over soon."

Raney studied her sister. She seemed bored, too. Or maybe depressed would better describe it. "You missing the kids?"

Len nodded. "I haven't heard from them yet, even though I gave them each several self-addressed, stamped envelopes and stationery. Probably should have written the letters, too. That way, all they'd have to do is sign them."

"What about Ryan? Heard from him?"

"No." She gave a wan smile. "Probably doesn't realize any of us are gone."

They hadn't talked about Len's cosmetic surgery. Hadn't really had time. But Raney had thought about it a lot, especially after Mama's five-point theory. "Did it hurt? The surgery?"

Len shrugged. "Certainly not as much as what's about to happen to Joss."

"Why'd you do it? You didn't need to. You're still beautiful."

She was a long time answering. "With my kids growing up and away, I feel like I'm losing my babies. I've already lost Ryan to his work. I didn't want to lose my youth, too. Yet every time I look in the mirror, I seem a decade older."

"And you think surgery will help?"

"It's supposed to. I doubt it will. The kids will keep pulling away and Ryan will keep working until all hours, and I'll continue to age. But, what the hell." She raised her goblet high like she was offering a toast. "It was worth a try, right? Oh, damn. I'm empty again. Do we have another bottle?"

Raney got up and opened another bottle, poured Len's goblet full, and topped off her own. Then before she stretched out again, she turned off all the veranda lights to keep the moths from dive-bombing the screen.

They sat in silence, except for the soft whir of the coolers, the drone of crickets on the other side of the screen, and the lowing of cattle as they watered at the creek. Faint strains of music drifting up from the workers' quarters added to a sense of loneliness as Raney thought about what her sister had said.

Theory number four. The slow slide into indifference, and maybe the saddest of them all. Raney hoped not. She didn't know this Len, this discouraged, defeated shadow of her big sister. She didn't like what was happening to her.

"I'm thinking of going back to school," Len said after a while.

"You are?" Raney looked at her in surprise. "To study what?"

"I don't know yet. Southern Methodist has an excellent business college. Maybe I'll pick up where I left off thirteen years ago."

Raney had been feeling sad for her sister a moment ago. Now she felt envious. She hadn't realized how much she'd regretted not going to college until Dalton had talked about his two years at Texas Tech and Joss had referred to Raney's missed chance when Daddy died. But how could she go to college and still manage the ranch and the AI program and the quarter horse expansion?

She'd have to think about that. And decide if she really wanted to go to college and why. Was she just looking for an escape from all the responsibilities that seemed to grow heavier every year? But college was a big commitment, too, and a drain in time and energy. And what would she study?

Here I go, she thought with a sigh. *Overthinking again.*

Dalton called just after ten o'clock. Raney had already showered and was sitting in bed in her pj's, trying to read when her phone buzzed. She couldn't ignore it. Especially after she saw who it was. But she wasn't sure she wanted to talk to him, either. Not after he'd run off without telling her. She answered anyway.

"Hey," she said.

"You awake?"

Did all of their phone conversations have to start with those words?

"And before you answer," he added before she spoke, "I can see your light is on, so don't lie."

"You're back?" She refrained from jumping up and looking out the window.

"Sitting in my truck, wondering if you stayed up late just to kiss me good night."

"I didn't know you were coming in tonight. Hicks said you might not get back until tomorrow. How are your folks and Timmy?"

"All good. Timmy likes his group home. He's reading better and has just started a handyman job. He's already earned enough to open a bank account. Mom is happy to have a grocery store less than five minutes away and a church she can walk to. And Dad told me all about this newfangled cable TV thing that plays football games all day long, and has fishing shows, and even a program that explains how to make stuff. Did you know polar fleece is made from recycled plastic bottles? What are you doing?"

"Reading."

"How's Joss?"

"Nothing new. She sees the doctor tomorrow. I thought you were avoiding me."

"I was."

"Why?"

"You wanted us to go slow. The only way to keep from chasing you down as soon as your mother left was to go see mine."

"Do you think I should go to college?"

"Not tonight. Tonight, I think you should come get in my truck so we can hook up like we should have back in high school."

"I didn't know you in high school. And your truck has a

console between the front seats and you'd never fit into the back. Besides, I'm not that kind of girl." *Or I wasn't until I met you.*

"What are you wearing?"

"Pj's."

"Something frilly?"

"Something like running shorts and a tank top."

"Want to take them off?"

"In your truck?"

"Wherever. We could go to the creek and skinny-dip."

"Just us and the mosquitoes and the snakes. Sounds fun."

"Then come to my room. You remember where it is, right? You can help me shower."

"I thought we were going to go slow."

"I'll go slow. In fact, I'll let you take all the time you need to scrub me down."

Raney laughed, loving his sense of humor. "I've already had my shower. But I'll meet you in the kitchen with a beer. That should cool you down."

"Maybe you could practice your domestic skills and make a sandwich to go with it. You do know how to make a sandwich, don't you?"

"Bite me."

Ten minutes later, Raney was building a ham and cheese when Dalton walked barefoot into the kitchen, wearing jeans that barely clung to his narrow hips, a still-damp T-shirt plastered across all those muscles she admired, and a devilish grin on his unshaven face.

Without a word, he walked over, pulled her into his arms and kissed her so thoroughly she didn't realize they weren't alone until she caught movement out of the corner of her eye and looked over to see her sister leaning against the doorjamb, arms crossed, watching them.

She jumped back, startled. "Damn, Len. You freaked me out."

Dalton just grinned.

"You knew she was there," Raney accused him.

"I might have heard her coming down the stairs. Hi, Len."

"Hi, Dalton. Hope you didn't loosen any of my sister's fillings with that kiss." Len walked the rest of the way into the kitchen. "Is this a private party or can I have a snack, too?"

"We can share my sandwich," Dalton offered. "I only asked your sister to make me one so I could lure her out of her room to check her fillings."

Len laughed. "Horse trainer, security guard, and dental technician. Who would have guessed? How's your family?"

"Doing great. And loving Plainview. They probably should have made the move years ago."

"I'm glad." When Raney started to get out more bread, Len shook her head. "Just some cheese and a glass of milk. My stomach is still bubbling from all that wine you made me drink."

As they carried their plates to the kitchen table, Raney thought again how seamlessly Dalton had settled into her family. Everyone seemed to accept him, ex-con and all. He was part of them now, and if things didn't work between the two of them, they would all mourn the loss.

While they ate, they chatted about Rosco's progress, Grady, and what they thought Joss should name the baby. They were all worried about her, which dampened the mood until Len asked about the AI program.

That set Dalton off on a hysterical rant about his horror at the application of low-voltage electrical pulses to get the bull primed and the use of an artificial vagina to collect the semen, and his profound relief that they had technicians to do all that as well as handle the impregnation of the cows. "No wonder Hicks didn't want to do it," he finished with a dramatic shudder.

Raney hadn't laughed so hard in a long time.

"I can't believe they used to call you Beanpole in high

school," Len said to him once she'd gotten her own laughter under control. "Look at you now."

"Joss likes me better, too. Can't stop talking about my pants. I never realized the Whitcomb girls would be so interested in my weight."

"It's not the weight or the pants," Len said with a wink. "It's the distribution."

"Want me to flex for you? Raney really likes it when I do that."

Ignoring him, Raney said to Len, "Speaking of high school, remember the first time they found a bra hanging over the goalpost bar the day after homecoming?"

"I do. It caused quite a flap. We were sure it belonged to one of the girls on the cheer squad but no one owned up to it. Then the next year, there were half a dozen bras up there. Drove the coaches crazy. It became a tradition after that."

"Guess who started it."

Len glanced from Raney to Dalton. "Not you? Quiet, studious Beanpole? You didn't even go to our high school."

"Probably why we weren't recognized or caught."

"And guess whose bra it was," Raney went on. "But you can't tell. Dalton's already in enough trouble with our esteemed deputy Langers."

"You don't mean . . ."

"It was his mother's. Isn't that a hoot?"

Len looked at Dalton with an expression of appalled disbelief. "You were what, fourteen? Please tell me you didn't get it directly from her . . . hand."

"God, no!" Dalton gave another shudder. "Buddy Anderson stole it off their clothesline. Then once we had it, we didn't know what to do with it."

And he was off again, sending Raney and Len into renewed laughter as he described in great detail the heist of the four-foot-long, cotton double E–cup bra—"big enough to serve as feed bags for a team of draft horses"—hanging next to a pair of huge cotton drawers they were afraid to touch—"we didn't know they made women that big"—their desperate attempts to get their plunder to stay on the goalpost crossbar without sliding off, and their narrow escape over a back fence when a police cruiser drove by. "We had no idea we'd be starting a tradition."

"Did you ever do it again?" Len asked, still laughing.

"Hell, no. Too scary. For months after, we expected the cops to show up at our doors with handcuffs."

"Was yours ever up there?" Raney asked her sister.

"I'll never tell. But I guess I should keep a closer eye on Jake and my bras, although I doubt the boys in his Catholic school would ever think of such a prank."

"Don't kid yourself, Mom," Dalton warned her. "All boys, no matter the age or school, spend most of their time thinking about bras and what goes into them. Or so I've heard."

"Uh-huh." Len rose and carried her plate and glass to the sink. "Thanks for the snacks and the laughs. It's been fun. But it's almost midnight so I'm heading up."

Raney rose. "I'm right behind you."

Len paused in the doorway, then turned and gave her sister a gentle smile. "Just so you know, Raney, I don't care when, or if, you come upstairs. You're both grown-ups." Her gaze shifted to Dalton. "But if it makes you feel any better, I approve of your choice. Good night, kids."

Raney looked at Dalton, indecision and desire battling within her.

He must have seen it. "That was sweet of Len to give us permission to do what we've already done. But it doesn't change anything."

As he spoke, he rose, carried his plate to the sink, and dropped his empty beer bottle into the recycle bin. Then he leaned back against the counter, elbows bent behind him, his big hands gripping the edge of the granite in a pose that pulled the cloth of his wash-worn, too-small T-shirt tight across his amazing chest.

Raney barely heard him as he added, "You wanted to go slow until the Futurity, so we'll go slow. Think of it as a courtship. A really, really long, totally unnecessary, unbelievably frustrating courtship. Now give me a kiss good night and go to bed. I'll clean up here since you went to all the trouble of smearing mayo on two slices of bread. Next time, maybe you could add mustard, too."

"Bite me," she said, laughing.

"Come over here so I can, pretty lady."

It was probably the longest kiss in history. And the least satisfying. But it pushed Raney another step closer to the magic words that she hadn't yet been able to say to him.

CHAPTER 21

The next morning over breakfast, Raney and Len made shopping lists. Normally, Raney would have waited until the first of the month to replenish the ranch supplies. But not knowing when they'd have to go to Lubbock, or how long they'd be away, she decided to get it done a few days early.

The first list was for groceries and miscellaneous items for both the main house and the workers' quarters. Raney gave the housekeeping and grocery list to Maria. She usually made the bimonthly run to Guthrie, which was bigger than Rough Creek and had a larger selection of stores to fill the order.

The grain and feed list she sent down to Glenn. He would fill it at the co-op out on the highway, or order what wasn't available there.

The last list was for personal supplies for the family, last-minute nursery items for when the baby came home, and a few things Len wanted Raney to get for her, since she didn't want to go to Rough Creek until her eyes looked less clownish. It also included a stop at the dry cleaner's and a haircut for Raney.

A half hour later, Raney closed her notepad and sat back with a sigh. "Done."

Len studied her over the rim of her coffee cup. "I had no idea how much work running this place could be. I see you going over ledgers in the office, working ranch problems with Hicks, talking to the accountants and lawyers, dealing with the house, the workers' quarters, the insemination program, and all the cattle and horses here on the ranch. But I rarely see you take time for yourself or friends. You're amazing."

Raney shrugged, both embarrassed and pleased by the praise. "I like doing it."

"Aren't you lonely?"

An image of Bertie flitted across her mind but Raney pushed it aside. "Sometimes. Mostly I'm too tired to think about it."

"Dalton could help you."

"He is helping me. Both with training and taking over the AI program. He joked about it last night, but he's doing a great job."

"He's in love with you, you know."

Raney looked away. "Maybe."

"How do you feel about him?"

Raney gave a brittle laugh. "Conflicted. After Trip—"

"Dalton is nothing like Trip."

"I know. I'm just not sure I'm ready yet. Especially after what happened."

Len smiled. "You mean you're not ready to trust again."

"That, too." Hoping to end her sister's interrogation, Raney slipped the notepad and pen into her purse, then rose from the table. "If you think of anything else you want me to get in town, text me." She started for the door.

"Raney," her sister said.

With reluctance, she stopped and turned back.

"I like Dalton. I like the way you are when you're with him. You seem happy. Confident. I wish you'd give him a chance."

"I will. I am. It just takes time."

"Don't wait too long. Happiness doesn't always last. Grab it while you can."

Raney sensed her sister might be talking about herself, as much as warning her about her hesitancy with Dalton. Were things that bad between her and Ryan?

"Well, that's my lecture for today," Len said, rising from her chair with a self-conscious laugh. "Call Mama before you go."

"One lecture is all I need."

"I meant call to see if she has anything to add to the list. And to check on Joss."

"Right." Raney pulled her cell phone from her purse, put it on speaker, and punched in Mama's number. "Hi, Mama," she said when her mother answered. "I'm running errands today. You want me to pick up anything?"

"Brochures for another cruise."

"Seriously?"

"No. But I am getting tired of doing nothing."

"How's Joss?"

"I'm a little concerned. She had a few pains overnight. I doubt they were contractions since they were very irregular and widely spaced, but I worry."

"When do you see the doctor again?" Len asked. She looked worried, too.

"At one."

"Call us if she decides to admit Joss, or thinks she's going into labor."

"I will. This is dragging on too long. I'd feel better if she were in the obstetrical unit being monitored."

"She'll be fine, I'm sure." But Len didn't look sure. "Keep us posted."

After the call ended, Len asked if Raney had a bag

packed. "This might happen soon. We should be prepared for an overnight stay. I'll pack stuff for Mama, too."

Raney headed upstairs. She had just finished packing when her phone buzzed.

"Hey," Dalton said. "Hicks told me you were going into town. Mind if I go with you? Timmy's birthday is coming up and I wanted to get him something."

"Sure. But I may have to go directly on to the hospital if Joss is admitted."

"Is she in labor?"

"Maybe. We're not sure."

"What about Len? Is she going to town, too?"

"No. If Joss is admitted, she'll drive her own car to Lubbock."

"Then we'll take my truck," he decided. "Meet me at the back gate."

A few minutes later, Raney tossed her bag into the backseat and climbed into Dalton's dark blue truck.

He glanced at the bag, then at Raney. "We eloping?"

"You know me. I like being prepared."

"If we're eloping, you won't need all those clothes."

Raney gave him a look. One that told him they probably weren't eloping. He loved her looks, whether they were scolding, smirking, or smoldering. He especially loved seeing that banked fire in her blue eyes when he ran his hands over her beautiful body.

"You're not working Rosco today?"

He shifted into gear and headed toward the main gate. "Alejandro noticed a slight stiffness in his right shoulder, so we're giving him the day off."

They drove in silence for a mile or two, then she said, "I'm glad you're going with me. Maybe we could have lunch at the diner after I get my hair cut."

"Like a real date?"

"More like a nice meal while you tell me what I could get for Timmy."

"You don't need to get him anything. You already gave him a cat, remember? Which, incidentally, he named after you. Probably because she's been indiscreet with a big, handsome tomcat who lives in the alley behind the group home."

"That hussy."

"You know cats. When an especially sexy tom comes by, they can't seem to help themselves."

"So I've heard. What are you getting Timmy?"

"A tool belt and some tools for his new handyman job."

"Maybe I could get him his own toolbox. I could get those stick-on letters and put his name on it."

Dalton smiled at her, warmed by her kindness toward his brother. Most folks treated Timmy with kid gloves or pretended they didn't see him. "He'd like that."

Rough Creek was hopping, which meant almost a dozen cars and trucks were parked along Main Street. Dalton wondered how much longer all the mom-and-pop stores could hold out against the big-box warehouses that were slowly spreading along the highways out from Lubbock. He loved the small-town atmosphere of Rough Creek, and the fact that everyone knew most everyone else, and the churches were still the place to be on Sunday. He would hate to see it end.

"Let's go to the hardware store first," Raney suggested. "By the way, when is Timmy's birthday?"

"Today."

She gave him another look. This one was indignant. "That's today? Waiting kind of late, aren't you?"

"I forgot until my mother mentioned it yesterday." Dalton parked in front of Ace Hardware and opened his door. "Let's see what they've got."

The store had exactly what they wanted: a leather tool belt with several pouches and hangers to hold Timmy's new hammer, screwdrivers, pliers, wrenches, etc., and a red toolbox with a lock and removable tray for smaller items. Raney also found silver stick-on letters, but since *Tim Cardwell* was too long to fit, she settled for his initials. After Dalton added a pair of red suspenders to help hold up the belt, they went to the drugstore for gift bags.

Dalton found a card for his brother, then followed Raney around while she filled a basket from a long list. He never realized women needed so much makeup to make it look like they didn't wear any makeup at all. Another stop at the dry cleaner's, then Dalton decided that while Raney had her hair cut, he'd get a fill-up and an oil change in case he had to drive her to Lubbock. He sure as hell wasn't going to sit and wait on her in a beauty salon.

"Give me an hour," she said as they put the packages and dry cleaning in the truck. "Then meet me at the diner. Burger and iced tea."

Marlene was the owner-operator of the town's only beauty parlor and had been doing haircuts and manicures for the Whitcomb women forever. She was also the biggest gossip in Rough Creek, but not in a malicious way. Mostly she kept her patrons informed of the latest news—50 percent of which might actually be true.

"How's Joss doing?" she asked as she shampooed Raney's hair. "Heard she was at the hospital in Lubbock with her baby's daddy. Think they'll get married?"

News sure traveled fast in Rough Creek. "He's asked, but so far, Joss hasn't accepted. We're hoping she will. He's a nice guy."

"Hmmm," said a woman wearing a foil cap and sitting in a nearby chair. A retired teacher named Ruthie and a busybody if there ever was one. Raney reminded herself to watch her words or before the week was over, she'd hear five different versions of everything she'd said.

A few minutes later, Marlene wrapped a towel around Raney's wet head and moved her to a worn barber chair. As she put on the drape and adjusted the height, she studied Raney in the mirror. "Is it true Dalton Cardwell is working at your ranch? I hear he changed a lot in prison. How much do you want trimmed?"

"An inch. No bangs."

In the chair beside Raney and Marlene, Helen Foster, an elderly lady with wads of cotton between her freshly mani-cured toes, said, "Suze Anderson told me he's put on a lot of weight and muscle. Got into a fight out at the Roadhouse and put three men in the hospital. They ought to shut that place down."

"Hmmm," Ruthie said from her chair across the room. "'Roid rage."

"Actually, he only sent the two men who started the fight to the hospital," Raney corrected. "And he doesn't take ste-roids." Was this what Dalton had to face every time he came to town?

"Your mama know you've got an ex-con working out there?" Marlene asked.

"Of course she does. She's the one who hired him."

None of the ladies responded to that. No one questioned Mama or cast doubt on her decisions. Four Star—and by extension, her mother—spent a great deal of money in Rough Creek, and that carried a lot of sway with the towns-folk, especially struggling shop owners like Marlene.

"Heard his family up and moved to Plainview," Helen Foster said. "Was it because of his arrest, do you think?"

"Probably ashamed," Ruthie muttered.

"It had nothing to do with their son," Raney assured them. "They moved to Plainview because they were tired of working their ranch and sold it." Hoping to shift the talk away from Dalton and his family before she really gave Ruthie something to talk about, Raney threw out a tidbit of her own. "Did you hear that Bertie Barton eloped to Las Vegas and is moving to Oklahoma?"

Three shocked faces turned her way.

Marlene recovered first. "Who did she marry?"

"A veterinarian named Phil. They worked at the same clinic in Fort Worth."

"What'd her mama have to say about that?" Ruthie wanted to know.

"I haven't talked to her. I just heard about it."

"I'm sure she's disappointed," Helen said. "Poor thing just had her knee replaced, you know."

"It was her hip," Raney corrected.

Which opened up a long and lively discussion about hips, knees, arthritic hands, and all sorts of postmenopausal female ailments Raney didn't want to know about, so she let her mind drift until Ruthie said, "Speak of the devil."

Raney followed her gaze out the grimy front window and saw Dalton standing on the sidewalk across the street, talking to Karla Jenkins.

"Is that the Cardwell boy?" Helen asked, squinting in Dalton's direction. "Goodness gracious. He certainly has changed. How'd he get so big?"

Ruthie sniffed. "Supplements. They take all kinds of things in prison."

"Dalton Cardwell didn't take supplements," Raney snapped. "Or anything. He just worked out a lot."

"Hmmm."

"Isn't that the Jenkins girl with him?" Helen asked.

Marlene nodded. "Karla. They were an item before he went to prison. Head straight, Raney. I'm almost done."

Raney stared at her reflection in the mirror, her mind eaten up with curiosity, her ears perked to the talk going on around her.

"Looks like they still might be," Ruthie observed. "The

way she's clinging to his arm. She better watch out. I've read about 'roid rage."

He doesn't take steroids! Raney almost shouted.

"Heard she sent him a Dear John letter while he was in prison," Marlene said, turning the chair enough that Raney could see what was going on across the street without moving her head.

"Not surprising," Helen said. "Him being a convict and all."

They didn't look that chummy to Raney. In fact, Dalton seemed to be leaning away from Karla, despite her hold on his arm.

"They do make a handsome couple, though," Helen observed. "Hard to believe they called him Beanpole in school."

Across the street, Dalton and Karla separated, Dalton walking on toward the diner, Karla staring after him for a few moments, then turning and heading in the opposite direction.

Raney didn't know what to make of it and wondered if this angry, unsettled churn in her stomach was what Dalton had felt when he'd seen her talking to Trip at the Roadhouse.

Dalton had just given Suze their orders when Raney walked in. Her hair didn't look much different, but her face sure did. She was upset, and the way her eyes homed in on him, he figured he was the reason she was. What had he done now?

Karla. She must have seen him talking to Karla. *Shit.*

"Hey," he said as she slid into the booth across from him. "Your hair looks great."

No reaction, other than to ask if he'd ordered already.

"Suze just put it in." Then realizing she was going to shut him out if he didn't fess up, he said, "Guess who I just ran into."

"Karla Jenkins. I saw you through the salon window. She has her nerve."

Dalton gave her a questioning look.

"It was a tacky thing to do, writing you a Dear John letter in prison."

Hell. Did everybody in town know about that? "She was moving to Fort Worth anyway."

"How did that work out for her?"

"Apparently, not well."

"So now she's moving back?"

"Appears so."

Suze brought their burgers and drinks. Dalton waited until she left, then said, "You answered my questions about the douche. I guess turnabout is fair play."

Raney studied him in silence as she ate three of his fries.

Dalton couldn't read her expression. That surprised him and made him nervous. He thought he knew all of her "looks." Yet, watching her now, he doubted he would ever fully understand how her mind worked. She was a complicated woman. Which was one of the reasons he loved her. And the most important thing he'd learned about her was that she was as committed to honesty as he was . . . except for that one notable exception that could still send him bolting upright in the middle of the night, choking on fear and regret.

"Go ahead," he prodded, breaking the long silence, "ask your questions."

"There's only one." She took another fry. "Do you still care about her?"

"As a friend. That's all. And I never cared for her the way I care for you."

She ate two more fries, then nodded. "Good enough for me. You done with the ketchup?"

Dalton almost sagged in relief. If they hadn't been in public, he would have leaned over the table and kissed her. The depth of his reaction made him realize how involved he'd become. Which was disconcerting. Over the last few years, he'd kept a large part of himself closed off. In combat and later, in prison, he had pushed emotion, expectation, even hope aside. But now, with Raney, anything was possible. It was like starting all over again.

"Can I tell you now that I love you?" he asked.

"Not yet." She reached over and brushed something from the corner of his mouth. For a moment, her fingers lingered like she wanted to lean in and give him the kiss he'd denied himself a moment ago. Then she took her hand away and stole another fry from his plate. "But soon."

Not the answer he'd hoped for. Pushing down his disappointment, he took a bite of burger, chewed, and swallowed. "You wouldn't have to say it back."

"I know. But when I do, I want to be sure. Those aren't just words to me, Dalton. They're a lifetime commitment."

"No room for doubt?"

"None." She tipped her head to the side and studied him, a tiny smile playing along her beautiful mouth. "Does that scare you?"

"That you won't admit yet that you adore me beyond reason?" He took another bite. "I'll manage."

"Some people fear promises and obligations. I hope you're not one of them."

He wanted to tell her just how far he'd go to keep the promises he'd made, but of course, he couldn't. Instead, he tried to put into words how he felt about her and his hopes of building a future with her by his side.

"The way I see it, Raney," he said between fries, "throughout a lifetime, there's only one thing a person has complete control over. His—or her—word. Plans fail, buddies die, shit happens. But if you make a promise and keep it, you're solid. Nothing else matters. You can do no better."

He finished his burger and what few fries she'd left him, then pushed the plate aside. Crossing his arms on the tabletop, he leaned forward, hoping she could see the truth of what he was about to say in his eyes and hear it in his voice. "My promise to you, Raney Whitcomb—whether or not you want to hear it yet, or whether you ever say the words back to me—is that I love you. I'm committed to you and to making this work, no matter what it takes. Or how long."

He sat back and put on a smile. "Now, finish your burger before it gets cold."

She looked at him, her eyes misty, her lips pressed in a tight smile.

Horrified she might cry, he put on a bigger smile. "Or, I could finish it for you, if you'd like. Since you ate most of my fries."

"Oh, Dalton . . ." She started to say something more, then flinched when her phone buzzed. Blinking hard, she pulled it out of her purse, checked the caller ID, and accepted the call. "What's happening?" she said.

She listened for a few moments, a multitude of emotions flicking across her expressive face. "Thank God." A pause. "To the house? Why not meet us at the hospital?" Another pause, then she said, "Okay," punched out, and put the phone back into her purse.

"You can have my burger," she said. "But eat fast. The planets are aligning. Len is on the way to the hospital, her husband, Ryan, is meeting us there, and Joss just went into labor."

CHAPTER 22

"Why won't they talk?" Coralee complained. "I thought when we moved over here, they might start talking. But they're just sitting there."

"She's fretting," Len said. "Raney always fusses with her nails when she's upset. I wonder what's keeping Ryan?"

"She worries too much."

"You should have seen her last night." Len smiled. "I bet she hasn't laughed that hard in a long time. I sure haven't."

"He's good for her. I wish she'd figure that out." Tipping her head toward her oldest daughter, Coralee put a hand to her mouth and lowered her voice. "I was hoping when I had him move into the house while I was gone it might move things along, if you know what I mean."

"Isn't that called *pimping*?"

"Hush that talk." Coralee thought for a moment, then tipped her head again. "Maybe we should send them somewhere. Nothing's going to happen with us watching."

"It's a hospital waiting room. What do you expect to happen?"

"I expect Joss to get busy and have that baby, that's what I expect. Stopping in the middle of labor! That's just foolish and rude. And it certainly won't keep that baby from being born. If they won't give her drugs, she'll just have to man up and get the job done."

"Man up?" Len shook her head. "Do you ever listen to what you say, Mama?"

"If this drags out much longer, we'll have to do something."

"About Joss?"

"About Raney and Dalton. Try to keep up, dear."

Dalton was so bored he was seeing patterns in the waiting room carpet. If he'd been in Iraq, he could have stretched out against the back wall and gotten some sleep, rather than sitting here, watching Raney trim her nails with her teeth and smooth the rough edges against her jeans.

In chairs against the opposite wall, Mrs. Whitcomb and Len were having an animated conversation. Probably planning Joss's wedding, if she ever decided to have one, and assuming Grady didn't withdraw his proposal. Dalton would have. About nine months ago. He wasn't much for drama. Which was one of the many reasons he deeply appreciated levelheaded Raney. His silent, nail-biting worrier.

With a sigh, he leaned his head back and studied the number and placement of recessed lights in the ceiling. Sixteen on this side of the nurses' station. It irritated him that several were out of alignment, so he didn't bother to count those on the other side of the station.

Now the Whitcomb duo were frowning at Raney and whispering behind their hands. She didn't notice and he didn't warn her. She was nervous enough as it was.

He wished he'd brought something to read. The puzzles in the *Highlights* magazine weren't that challenging and the stack of "Miracle of Birth" pamphlets on the side table had disturbing drawings of lactating breasts and tilted uteruses and other stuff men didn't need to know about. They also reminded him too much of his first sex-ed class, when the boys' PE teacher had taped on the board a huge poster with a cross section of a penis. He didn't remember much about the lecture, but that giant penis had haunted him for weeks and made him feel inadequate for months after. Then he discovered if you pull on it, it will grow.

That was a good day.

"What are you smiling about?" Raney asked.

"I'm not smiling. It's an autonomic muscular response to extreme boredom." He rose. "I'm going for coffee. Want some?"

She shook her head and bit off a hangnail on her right thumb.

He wandered over to the coffee machine on a table beside a water fountain and filled a foam cup—black, no sugar—then almost scalded his hand when he turned and found the two older Whitcombs standing right behind him. With an apologetic look, he stepped aside to give them access to the machine.

They didn't move. Both were staring at him.

"How's it going?" he asked, just for something to say.

"At this rate, she'll never have any babies," Mrs. Whitcomb said.

"Kind of late to worry about that now, don't you think?" Dalton quipped.

Neither smiled.

"I was referring to Raney," Mrs. Whitcomb told him. "You need to do something."

"About what?" he asked warily. Surely, she wasn't asking him to impregnate her daughter. Not that he was opposed. But shouldn't Raney have a say in it, too?

Len edged closer. Her hair smelled like Raney's. They must use the same shampoo. Or maybe it was genetic. "You need to get her out of here, Dalton."

"She's worrying too much," Mama added, hemming him in on his other side. "It'll sour her on babies altogether."

"Isn't there someplace you can take her for a few hours?" Len asked.

He was starting to get a neck ache from all the head swiveling to follow the conversation.

"Didn't your parents move somewhere around here?"

"Plainview?"

"Perfect!" Mama burst out, patting his arm. She lowered her voice again. "Take your time. No rush. Joss may not have that baby for hours yet. Days, even. Go." She gave him a push that almost spilled his coffee. Again.

Dalton went.

"What did Mama and Len want?" Raney asked when he returned to his seat.

"I'm not sure. They were either asking me to get you pregnant or take you to Plainview. Maybe both. I'm not sure why."

"What?"

"I know. Weird. But if we went to Plainview, we could deliver Timmy's presents. Unless you'd rather I get you preg—"

"Great!" Raney bolted from the chair. "Let's go."

"To Plainview?"

"Of course, to Plainview. Hurry. Before Joss starts into labor again."

When they crossed the main lobby, they ran into Len's husband, Ryan, on his way in. Raney hadn't seen him in several months and was surprised at how much he'd aged. Or maybe it was worry that had etched those deep lines in his face.

She introduced him to Dalton, and they chatted for a moment about Joss's condition and Grady, then they sent him on his way up to maternity. Raney wondered if he knew about Len's eye surgery. If not, he was in for a surprise.

As they drove out of the hospital parking lot, Dalton called ahead to let his parents know they were coming. Which worked out perfectly, his mom told him, since Timmy was coming for supper that night, and now they could turn it into a party. "He'll be thrilled. Drive safe."

"Well, that's disappointing," Dalton said as he set his cell phone back in the cradle on the dash. "Guess I won't be impregnating you tonight."

"Bummer."

"Maybe tomorrow. Unless you're already knocked up. How reliable are those pills you've been taking?"

"That's not funny."

An hour later, they pulled up to the curb in front of a neat, but modest, house completely shaded by two big pecan trees and a wide front porch. Apparently, Timmy had been watching for them. As soon as they started up the walk, he banged out the front door, wearing a big grin. "Dalton! You came back!"

Raney watched the brothers hug, and thought again how kind Dalton was, and how gently he treated those he loved. He would make a wonderful father someday. Maybe a father to her own children. Although what they were going through with Joss made her a bit apprehensive about the whole motherhood thing.

Supper was a grand affair with all the trimmings—pork chops, green beans, potatoes, and a fresh fruit salad. Conversation throughout the meal centered around Timmy, who talked almost continually and with great enthusiasm about his job washing windows, cleaning gutters, repairing the wood fence, and anything else that needed doing around the group home. "I am a good worker," he said proudly. "I do repairs at the church, too. And guess what! They pay me lots of money."

"You like staying in the group home?" Dalton asked.

Timmy nodded. "People there are nice to me. And I have a friend. His name is George. He sleeps by me in the boys' room. He never wets the bed, but he snores a lot. And guess what! I can read. Maybe I can read to you sometimes, Dalton, like you used to read to me before you went away."

"I'd like that, buddy. But not tonight. Tonight, we get to open presents."

"Because it's my birthday!" Timmy shouted, so happy he could hardly sit still.

After they cleaned up the dishes, they had cake and ice cream, then Timmy opened his gifts. He was thrilled with the belt and toolbox and spent an hour packing and unpacking each several times. But the most treasured gift was the red suspenders, which he insisted on wearing with his jeans. "I look like Dad now," he announced, hooking his thumbs under the red straps. "I am a hard worker, too. Just like Dalton."

Raney suspected he'd try to wear the suspenders with his pj's that night. She smiled, enjoying Dalton's family more every time she was around them. There was a lot of love in that house. Like Mama said, the Cardwells were good people.

She and Dalton were giving their final good-byes when Mama called, saying Joss had finally gotten busy. "It's going fast. You'll probably have a new niece by the time you get here. Visiting hours are over at eight, so you'd best hurry."

Once they'd cleared town and were heading south on I-27, Raney said, "That was fun. I like your family."

"They like you, too." Dalton grinned at her. "Even though my dad thinks you're too good for me."

Raney looked at him in surprise. She'd thought she and Mr. Cardwell were on great terms. Granted, he wasn't particularly talkative with her, but she'd thought that was a natural reticence. Was he really trying to discourage Dalton from pursuing her? "In what way am I too good?"

"Money, position, probably brains, too. And I know for a fact you're prettier."

Raney didn't agree. With any of it. "That's terrible. Why would he say that? I thought he liked me."

"He does. It's me who's not measuring up. Probably thinks you'll figure that out before long, and he's trying to shield me." He said it with a smile.

Raney wasn't amused. "Shield you from being hurt again? Like with Karla?"

"Hell," he muttered. "Why does everybody think our split-up was a big deal?" There was an edge to his voice that surprised Raney. "We both knew it was coming and were okay with it."

"And yet," Raney said, watching him carefully, "she's back and trying to pick up where she left off."

He laughed. "Can't blame the poor girl for having great taste in men, can you?"

No, Raney couldn't. And she couldn't make light of what his father said, either. "Maybe your dad's afraid the Whitcombs will gobble you up and you'll forget all about him. He's already given up his ranch and one son. Losing you, too, would be a terrible blow."

Dalton looked surprised. "He's not losing me."

"No? How often have you talked to them, or visited them since they moved?" She saw by the downturn in his expression that he thought she was criticizing. She wasn't. But she could empathize with his parents because she knew what it felt like to be left behind while everyone else moved on. She didn't want Dalton to unknowingly make his parents feel that way.

"I've visited them twice this week," he reminded her.

"And look how happy that's made them. Your mother mentioned several times how much she missed her boys. You should try to visit them a couple of times a month, at least. I'll go with you, if you'd like. Your mother's cooking alone would make the trip worthwhile. And maybe you could call more often. Keep them informed about what you're doing. I can see it means a lot to my mother when she hears from Len and KD."

He glanced over again. This time his expression was more pensive than defensive. "No wonder you Whitcombs are so close-knit."

Raney nodded. "Especially since Daddy died. That was a hard lesson about how quickly things could change, and how people could simply disappear from your life without warning. Now speed up. I want to meet my beautiful new niece."

Actually, she wasn't all that beautiful, Raney decided later, when they stood in the corner of Joss's crowded room, watching a nurse show Grady how to change a baby, while another nurse showed Joss how to work a breast pump.

They had only just arrived and wouldn't be able to stay long since visiting hours were almost over. Raney had barely had a chance to hold the baby. So tiny, such precious doll-like hands, and barely enough hair to show she'd be blond like her parents. Raney was terrified she'd break her. But didn't want to let her go.

Then the nurses had come in to show Grady how to swaddle her, and the doctor had breezed through, saying everything had gone well, Joss was doing fine, and the baby's head should assume a normal shape within a few weeks.

Raney's horror must have shown. Even Dalton had been struck mute.

On her way out, the doctor had pulled them aside. "It's nothing to worry about." She'd gone on to explain that since Joss's cervix had dilated days before delivery, when the baby's head dropped into the expanded opening, it caused two small, plum-sized hematomas to form on the back of her head. "It's superficial. In a few weeks you won't even notice. Best say your good-byes soon. It's almost eight."

Superficial, okay. Not that noticeable from the front, maybe. But when the nurse showed Grady how to hold the baby against his shoulder to burp her, and Raney and Dalton saw for the first time how the two rounded lumps sort of squared off the back of her head, it was still shocking. And a little funny-looking.

Dalton dipped his head down and whispered in Raney's ear, "Sorta gives new meaning to the word *blockhead*, doesn't it?"

"Hush," she whispered, fighting a smile now that she knew the baby was okay.

"Look on the bright side. She probably won't roll off the changing table."

Raney choked back a laugh and elbowed him in the ribs. "Stop."

After answering a raft of questions and assuring the new parents that everything was fine, the two nurses made their escape. Before Dalton could get them both into trouble, Raney went to Joss's side. "How are you feeling, Little Mama?"

"Sore. Happy." She yawned. "Grateful."

Raney patted her sister's shoulder. "You're tired. We should go. If we leave now, we can make it back to the ranch by ten. Unless you want us to stay?"

"No," Joss said around another yawn. "They want me to sleep so I can recover faster. Almost sounds like they're trying to get rid of us." She smiled over at Grady, who was beaming down at his precious square-headed daughter. "But before you go, we want to ask you to do something."

"Sure. What do you need?"

"Plan our wedding."

"Are you serious? Dalton, did you hear that? My baby sister's getting married!"

Dalton grinned and thumped the new father's shoulder. "Well done, Grady."

"Nothing elaborate," Joss said. "Just something simple, like Len's."

Len had had two hundred guests at a lawn wedding. It had been a logistical nightmare. "Have you set a date?" Raney asked.

"Not yet. But probably December."

An outdoor wedding in December? That would never happen. But rather than get into it now, Raney leaned over and gave her sister a hug. "I'm so happy for the two of you. Grady's a great guy. We really like him and are delighted to have him in the family." A thought arose. "Where are you two planning to live?"

Not at the ranch . . . please.

"At the ranch," Grady said. "Until I find us a place in Austin."

Raney fought to keep her dismay from showing.

Apparently not well enough to fool Dalton. His arm came around her shoulders in support. Or maybe in a one-armed warning. Trying to sound cheery, she said, "Not L.A. or New York? Maybe Nashville? I thought those were the hot spots of the music industry." Not that she wanted to get rid of her sister. Not really. But the chaos that always surrounded Joss could be exhausting. And with a baby . . .

"Austin has a big music scene. And one of the buyers for my songs lives there."

Raney didn't have to fake her delight at that news. "You sold some of your songs? That's wonderful!"

"I know." Joss beamed at her fiancé. "Grady just told me. He thinks I can make good money writing songs, and we won't have to tour unless we want to."

"And once Lyric gets older," Grady added, "we can all tour together."

"Lyric?"

"Oh, I forgot!" Joss cried. "That's what we named her. Do you like it?"

"It's perfect. She's perfect."

"I know! Right? Except for her head, but that should go down soon."

As the men wandered over to the crib with Lyric, tears flooded Joss's hazel eyes. Reaching out, she took Raney's hand. "Isn't it amazing, sis? Me, wild child and dream chaser, now a mother. Crazy, huh? But I've never been happier."

Raney could see that. She had read somewhere that childbirth was a natural high. Maybe it was true. Her sister certainly looked happier and more radiant than she had six hours ago. A baby and a fiancé and a songwriting career, all in the same day. Yet, somehow, the family had survived.

Raney glanced over to see Grady reluctantly hand over his daughter to Dalton. The look on Dalton's face as he smiled down at the baby brought a catch in Raney's throat. He was such a good, dear man.

"Let's hope Len is as lucky with Ryan," Joss said, yawning again.

Realizing she hadn't seen her older sister and her husband since she and Dalton had returned, Raney asked where they were.

"On their way to the Dallas/Fort Worth Airport."

"Really?" Raney thought they were hardly speaking. "Where are they going?"

"Hawaii. On a long-deserved second honeymoon, Ryan said. He already had the tickets when he arrived. First class. They fly out tonight, that's why they had to rush off. With the four-hour time difference, they'll arrive in time for a fabulous oceanside dinner at their resort—some big, fancy place with so many vowels in its name I can't begin to pronounce it. They don't even have time to pack. Ryan said they can buy whatever they need while they're there. Isn't that romantic? I told them if they waited a bit, Grady and Lyric and I could go with them. Sort of a two-honeymoon deal. But Len said they had to go now while the kids are at camp."

Raney could imagine her older sister's panic at that suggestion. But she was glad Len and Ryan were trying to work things out. "Did Ryan say anything about Len's surgery?"

"Not in front of me. But I think it surprised him. He kept looking at her funny."

Across the room, Grady wore a worried frown and held out his hands, obviously anxious to have his baby back in his possession. Raney thought it amusing that Dalton, who might never have held a newborn before, seemed more relaxed handling an infant than Grady did.

"Where's Mama?" she asked Joss.

"At the hotel, checking out. She's been waiting for you and Dalton to come back so she can go home and sleep in her own bed. Dr. Jamison thinks we can go home day after tomorrow, too."

Joss let out a deep sigh and looked over to where Dalton and Grady were making faces at her daughter. "Oh, Raney, it's all so wonderful. This has been the most wonderful day of my whole life! Other than the actual birth, of course. That was awful. But look what I got for all that hard work. My turn, Daddy," she called, holding out her hands.

Grady came and gently laid the infant in Joss's arms. Seeing the look on her sister's face gave Raney a twinge of envy. Would she ever be so happy and so in love and so fulfilled?

She might.

With Dalton.

So why was she fighting it?

CHAPTER 23

Poor Mama must have been exhausted. She slept most of the way to the ranch. Raney was tired, too. She'd never realized having a baby could be so tiring for those waiting for it to happen. When they finally got home, it was almost midnight. With muttered good-nights to Dalton, she and Mama stumbled upstairs.

The next two days were blessedly quiet. Mama said to enjoy them, as all would change once the new parents arrived with that precious, beautiful little baby—Mama's words, not Raney's. And she was right.

On the afternoon of the third day, Joss and Lyric and Grady descended. And right behind them came a mountain of baby things Mama had ordered—a stroller, car seat, playpen, toys and more toys, a baby bathtub complete with tub pals, monogrammed hooded towels, bibs for every occasion, picture books, mobiles, enough stuffed animals to fill a zoo, and tiny hangers full of hideously expensive but adorable little outfits that Lyric would outgrow in a month.

Seemed like a lot of stuff for a baby who couldn't hold

up her head yet, or focus her eyes well enough to see her new belongings. But such was the power and spending habits of grandmothers.

As Mama had warned, literally overnight, life as they knew it changed forever. Crying at all hours—the baby, too. Puking, peeing, and pails of dirty diapers to cart out. Careful examinations of every small scratch or bump or flake of dry skin—on the baby, too. And general, continual chaos. All because of one tiny, square-headed, seven-pound-eleven-ounce scrap of wailing humanity. And the baby's mother, too, bless her heart.

After two weeks, Grady decamped, giving the paltry excuse that he had to make a living and find a place for his new family to live. Raney wouldn't have been surprised if they never saw him again. Not that she would have blamed him.

Then they all settled in for the siege. The baby ate and grew. The new mother ate and whined. The grandmother struggled to maintain reason. And with Raney trapped in Babyville trying to help, she got a taste of life without Dalton, except for hurried dinners at night. She didn't like it.

September passed in a haze of exhaustion. Raney helped as best she could and escaped to the barn whenever she had the chance, which wasn't often enough. She had heard that all babies came into the world as sociopaths, totally fixated on their own needs and wants, with no concern whatsoever for the people around them. Then over the next twenty years, the parents were supposed to turn them into functioning, productive, independent, and loving human beings.

No wonder the jails were full.

And yet . . .

Whenever Raney held the little darling and looked down into those innocent blue eyes, something shifted inside of her. Her brain would turn to mush and she'd find herself doing the most idiotic things for a smile, a burp, a tiny hand wrapping around her finger. And even more incomprehensible, whenever that happened, she yearned for a square-headed baby sociopath of her very own.

Such was the power of newborns.

It was confusing and exhausting, yet strangely compelling.

And when Raney wasn't dealing with all the changes a baby brought, catering to Joss's every whim, managing the ranch, keeping up with the AI program and Rosco's training, or meeting with the moneymen, she struggled to plan Rough Creek's most anticipated December wedding. Luckily, Mama was a huge help, as was Len once she returned from Hawaii, tanned, reenergized, and back to her vibrant self. Raney hoped it was a lasting improvement, but Len and Ryan had had ups and downs before, so who knew. Len and Mama even got the wedding and reception moved to a church that could accommodate the 150 guests.

Being master planners, the dynamic mother-daughter duo quickly took over—as Raney had hoped they would—thereby allowing her to gracefully back away until the final planning stage after Thanksgiving.

She hardly ever saw Dalton alone. He had moved back into the workers' dorm as soon as they had returned after Lyric's birth, and since then, they had both been too busy to spend much time together. It seemed every time she tried to talk to him, there were a dozen people hovering around. Even at the barn.

It was driving her crazy.

By mid-October, the pre-works began at the top cutting horse ranches in the area. They were important for Rosco because they were intense two-day workouts with fresh cattle and would put the final touches on his months of training. Raney would be able to attend only one of the four she'd scheduled, since she couldn't escape the madhouse very often.

Which was also driving her crazy.

Other than the nightly meal—now back in the dining room with Mama's return and since the veranda was crowded with baby paraphernalia—she hardly saw Dalton except when she was able to sneak off to the barn or ride out with him when he took Rosco into the pasture. A few stolen kisses. A touch here or there. That was it. And the less she saw of him, the more she thought of him.

At odd times, she would laugh about something amusing and think, *Dalton would get a kick out of that.* Or, she would be wrestling with a problem and wonder what Dalton would advise. Or, she'd remember something goofy he'd said and catch herself smiling. And often—too often— memories of the things he'd done with those magical hands would send heat pulsing through her body.

But nights were the worst. Dreams of him would have her tangling in the sheets until she awoke, heart thudding, breathing his name into the still, night air.

And always, night or day, a voice in her head would ask her what she was going to do. About him. Them. This obsession that was consuming her mind.

But now, with Rosco's final pre-work fast approaching, that was about to change. She had a plan. It was decision time. The point of no return. She couldn't continue in this emotional limbo any longer.

Since the pre-works were multiday events, Dalton usually took the big fifth-wheel horse trailer, which, in addition to stalls for Rosco and Big Mike, also contained a tack room, sleeping quarters, a kitchen, a sitting area, and a bathroom with a shower and toilet. Perfect for him and Alejandro and Uno. But this time, she would be going, too, and had already booked rooms for her and Dalton at a nearby lodge where most of the other owners and trainers would be staying.

The scene was set. The seduction of Dalton Cardwell could begin.

She didn't anticipate it would be a long or difficult task.

"Go," Mama said to her the morning they were to leave. "Have some fun. You've been working too hard. Dalton, too."

"This is work, too," Raney pointed out. "At least for him."

"I'm not talking about the horse part of it. I'm talking about socializing. Making time for yourselves. Taking a chance."

"On what?"

"Yourself. Him."

"Back to that again, are we?"

"I'm only thinking of you, dear. You're almost thirty. You don't want to spend the rest of your life alone, do you?"

Raney let out a deep sigh. "Why do you keep trying to foist me on him?"

Mama threw her hands up in exasperation. "I'm trying to get you to foist yourself on him. He's perfect for you, Raney. Surely, you can see that. But you can't expect him to wait on you forever."

Raney couldn't believe they were having this ridiculous conversation. "What are you trying to say, Mama?"

Her mother put on a long-suffering smile—one of her specialties—and cupped Raney's cheek. "Just be happy, dear. That's all I ask. Stop worrying and be happy. Now go."

Dalton would get a kick out of that conversation, too.

Dalton was loading tack into the big horse trailer when Raney walked up with a small suitcase in her hand. "Going somewhere?" he asked.

"To the pre-work. Is that okay?"

"Sure. You're the boss. I'll tell Alejandro and Uno to bring sleeping bags."

"They don't need to. Unless they won't share the bed in the trailer."

"Not sure all four of us could fit."

"That's what I thought. So, you and I will be staying at the Pair-O-Dice Lodge with the other owners and trainers."

"Ah," he said, hope soaring. "One room?"

"Of course not. It would be way too crowded if all the trainers and owners stayed in the same room."

"I meant one room for you and me." She was such a tease.

"I booked two."

Hope nose-dived into the dirt. "Oh."

"But we'll only use one," she added. "The other is just to protect our reputations. I know what a stickler you are for appearances."

And hope shot up again. He could tell by her smirk she knew exactly the roller-coaster ride she had him on. "You're just being mean," he accused.

"You have no idea. You like whips?"

He laughed out loud, exhilaration and anticipation thrumming through his body. "Depends on how you use them." He looked past her to see Alejandro and Uno leading the horses toward the loading ramp. "We'll talk more about that later."

After an easy three-hour drive, Dalton turned under an elaborate, black ironwork arch bearing the sign RENFREW TOP SIX RANCH, one of the finest of Parker County. The Renfrews had been longtime friends of Raney's parents and were highly respected in the horse business. Good people to know. If things went well, Bud Renfrew could be a powerful advocate for Dalton.

When they passed the corrals, she saw Press Amala leaning against the rails, talking to several trainers she had seen at local shows, and a few other men she suspected were owners of other horses here for the pre-work. Press nodded as they drove by. The other men turned to watch, gazes flicking from the Whitcomb Four Star Ranch logos on the sides of the truck and trailer to the buckskin face looking out the stall window.

Dalton smiled and gave a two-fingered wave as they

drove on toward the big-rig parking area behind the arena. "See that?" he said to Alejandro, who was sitting with Uno in the backseat. "Lined up like groupies at the stage door, waiting for the star of the show."

"Kind of cocky, aren't you?" Raney teased.

He feigned innocence. "I was talking about Rosco, not me."

"Una y las mismas," Alejandro said. One and the same. "Both horse's asses."

"Now, boys, play nice," Raney scolded, trying not to smile. Apparently, exchanging verbal insults was the way guys showed affection for each other. Not something she and her sisters did. Women were more into quick jabs of sarcasm, nonverbal smirks, and eye rolls. She was glad Uno didn't take any of it seriously.

Bud Renfrew was in the lot, welcoming newcomers. After directing Dalton to a parking spot, he walked over to meet Raney as she climbed out of the truck. "Welcome to Top Six," he said, extending his hand. "Glad you could make it."

Raney shook his hand. "Glad to be here, Mr. Renfrew. Thanks for asking us."

"You know better than that, Raney. Call me Bud." He chuckled, adding, "And your mama said I'd better include you. She's got high hopes for your trainer and the colt he's been working. Amala, too. Said the two of them were a force to reckon with."

"Let's hope." Raney turned, saw Dalton, Alejandro, and Uno walking up and introduced them to Bud. They chatted for a moment, then at Dalton's nod, Alejandro and Uno went to the back of the trailer to drop the ramp.

Bud watched them unload the horses, motioning to the big barn beside the arena. "You'll find open stalls in the barn," he told them. "Take your pick."

He studied Rosco with a practiced eye as Alejandro led him away. "Nice colt."

"He does all right," Dalton allowed.

Masters at understatement. No smack talk in these elevated circles.

"Well." Bud hitched his sagging jeans and turned back to Raney. "Y'all settle in, then come on up to the house. Marilyn's got drinks and itty-bitty snacks set up on the back porch. You staying in the trailer or up at the lodge?"

"The lodge," Raney answered. "I've already booked our rooms."

"Good girl. I told Cattleman's Steak House to expect a crowd for dinner. Best go early to get a table. See you up at the house." With a backward wave, he walked over to another rig just pulling in.

"Nice guy," Dalton said, watching the bowlegged man walk away. He looked around at the arena, the outsized barn, the ironwork gates. "Nice place, too. I'm in high cotton for an ex-con."

"But not for a premier cutting horse trainer," Raney countered. "What say we get unloaded and go have us some itty-bitty snacks? I'm starved."

Mama was right. The socializing was fun. And Dalton was surprisingly adept at it, considering his rocky return to the social scene at Harley's Roadhouse. Maybe because, for these owners and trainers, this was more than simply mingling with friends. It was business. And a very competitive business, at that.

Dalton handled it with poise, projecting confidence as well as modesty, all with that disarming grin that brought ladies, young and old alike, flocking to his side.

As soon as he finished his dinner at the steak house, Dalton went to check on the horses, and Alejandro and his son. Raney stayed awhile longer—just for appearances. In actuality, she was chomping at the bit to get back to her room at the Pair-O-Dice Lodge. She had plans. And a seduction to perform.

She needn't have been so anxious. Seducing Dalton was

even easier than she had imagined. All she had to do was take off her clothes and get into the shower. Ten minutes later, he arrived, using the extra key she'd given him, and took it from there.

She'd never enjoyed a shower more. But after thirty minutes, fearing if they stayed in too long they would empty the lodge of hot water, they dried off—which was also a lot of fun.

Then between one heartbeat and the next, the mood changed from playful to solemn. Still wet from the shower and wearing nothing but their damp towels, Dalton reached out and framed her face with his big, rough hands. "Raney," he said. "Sweetheart. What are we doing here?"

A dozen snappy answers rattled through her brain. But none left her mouth.

When she didn't answer, he said, "I swore to myself I wouldn't do this until the Futurity, or until you said you were ready."

"And I swore to myself I wouldn't let you until the Futurity or until I was sure I was ready." Raney hated feeling so out of her depth. This was Dalton. They'd seen each other naked. So why was she feeling so awkward?

"Yet here we are," he said, his thumbs gently brushing over her cheekbones. "And the Futurity is still almost two weeks away. What do you want me to do?"

All her fine words and grand plans crumbled at her feet. Doubts rushed in. She was a crappy seductress. "What do you want to do?"

"You planned this party," he reminded her. "You must have given some thought to how you wanted it to go."

She tried for a teasing smile, but the muscles in her face wouldn't behave. "This is as far as I got. I figured the rest would take care of itself. Any ideas?"

"A few." His beautiful green eyes seemed to darken with intent. "What I want to do is lay you down and run my hands over your beautiful body. I want to sweep away all the hurt and doubt in your mind. And I want to hold you and love you and make you want me as much as I want you." He smiled, slow and sweet, his gaze traveling over her face, coming to rest on her mouth. "But mostly, I want to hear you say the words you've been afraid to say. How about we start with that?"

"We could. But . . ."

A hurt look crossed his face. He took his hands from her face. "But what?"

And suddenly, all her confidence returned. She felt beautiful and daring and very much the tease he accused her of being. "I'd rather start here." She unwound her towel and let it drop to her feet. While he was distracted, she pulled his towel loose from around his hips, then took him in her hand. "And with this," she said, stroking gently. "Later, while you rest up, we can talk. It's going to be a long night, I fear."

He didn't argue.

And it was very much a long and incredible night. Until five o'clock the next morning, when the alarm on Dalton's phone went off.

"What the hell?" Raney muttered, bolting upright, thinking it was time for another baby feeding and wondering why it was so cold.

"Rise and shine, sweetheart," a gravelly voice said.

She looked over, saw Dalton sprawled on all of their pillows and under all of their covers, yawning and scratching his head. No wonder she was cold and had a neck ache. They had set the AC on the coldest setting in the middle of the night because they'd gotten sweaty from their exertions and now the room was freezing. With a shiver, she flopped back down beside him and started grabbing blankets. "Why are you up so early?"

He grinned. Something moved under the covers and he did that waggly thing with his eyebrows. Apparently, he thought it was sexy at five in the morning. "I'm up like this every morning. Want to see?"

How could the man joke at this ungodly hour? "Just give me a blanket and go back to sleep," she muttered, snuggling against his side, locking him close with an arm across his chest and her cheek on his chest. The smell of him, his warmth, the strength of the big body against hers gave her a sense of wholeness and comfort and safety she had never felt before. This was where she belonged. Smiling, she burrowed closer and closed her eyes. But couldn't sleep now that her body was fully awake. "I suppose you want to fool around," she said hopefully.

"Course I do. But I can't." His voice rumbled through his chest to vibrate in her ear. "I'm meeting some of the other trainers for breakfast. The lodge better serve regular-sized food, and not that itty-bitty stuff Mrs. Renfrew set out."

Raney yawned. "I'm not going."

"You weren't invited." She felt him kiss the top of her head. "But you could give me a proper send-off, if you wanted."

"Can't. I have a headache. Someone stole my pillow." She gave a long, contented sigh. "I just want to snuggle a while longer. These last weeks, I've missed you so much. It felt like my day wasn't compete without a smile or a kiss from you."

"I felt the same. A hundred and twenty-eight."

She tilted her head back and looked at him.

"Days since I told you I loved you."

"At the Roadhouse? If I remember correctly, you only thought you loved me."

"Fifty-one, then. That's when I promised I did. As I recall, you still weren't ready to hear it." He watched her. Still waiting. Even after all this time.

"Oh, Dalton." Ashamed that she had been so fearful, she scooched up his chest and put her hand along his jaw. His whiskers felt like sandpaper against her palm. "You dear, sweet, patient man." Leaning closer, she pressed her lips to his. Not in a teasing kiss like those in the shower the previous night. Or openmouthed and demanding like the ones that had come later.

A solemn kiss. Gentle. So full of emotion her heart felt too small to hold it all. Then she drew back so she could look into his beautiful green eyes through the tears forming in her own. "I'm sorry it's taken me so long to say it, dear heart. I wanted to be sure. No doubts or hesitation. And I am." She let out a deep breath and gave him a wobbly smile. "I love you, Dalton Cardwell. I love your honesty. Your strength of character. Your kindness. And especially your patience while I fought my way to this moment."

"Not my brains?" The man couldn't help himself. Even now, he had to made a joke.

She laughed, adoring his goofy, irreverent, wry sense of humor, loving that he found joy in everything and didn't take himself or her foolishness too seriously. "Of course, your brains, too. And your incredible green eyes."

"What about my muscles? Your sisters seemed to like my big muscles."

"Well, naturally, I admire your big muscles. Almost as much as your modesty." She tipped her head to the side and pretended to give it some thought. "But there's one muscle I'm not quite sure about."

He lifted the covers. "This one?"

She peeked. "I think so. Although it seemed bigger last night. Maybe I should try it out again, just to be certain."

He chuckled softly and swooped in for a quick kiss. "As you can probably tell, I'm up for that. The guys can wait another five minutes."

"Five? You're spoiling me."

"Okay. Six. But only if we start now."

Since the horses at the pre-works were all three-year-olds that weren't allowed to compete until the Futurity, there were no judges or points given at the Renfrew Top Six

Ranch workout. But if there had been, the consensus was that Rosco would have won. Or so Press Amala told Raney the following afternoon when they were loading up to go home to the ranch.

"The colt handled himself well, as I knew he would," he told her. "And it was smart of Cardwell to lend a hand when called on. Big Mike is as fine a helper horse as I've ever seen. With him along to keep things calm, your colt and his trainer have earned themselves a high regard among the other trainers. They'll do well at the Futurity."

"I hope so."

"Count on it. And count on me being there to see it. Tell your mama hidey."

As Raney watched him drive away, she was filled with gratitude for all that the wise old trainer had done to get Dalton and Rosco ready for the trial ahead. In less than two weeks, Dalton would either make his name, Rosco would prove himself a winner, and Whitcomb Four Star would join the ranks of the top breeders of prize-winning cutting horses.

Or they'd fail.

No pressure. None at all.

CHAPTER 24

The three-week-long, annual fall United States Cutting Horse Association Futurity in Fort Worth was a world-class event. Raney had been to it once, a decade ago with Daddy, but remembered little except the gigantic exhibition hall. It was like Fantasyland for horse lovers, and she was excited to take Uno to see it after they checked in with the USCHA office.

And that wasn't all there was to see and do.

In addition to the various horse competitions and the exhibits, there was also a multimillion-dollar auction during the last ten days of the Futurity, where bids for outstanding mares and studs with impeccable bloodlines ran into the hundreds of thousands of dollars or more. Promising yearlings and two-year-olds, debuting three-year-olds, as well as previous Futurity winners, finalists, and their offspring, all brought top dollar. In the cutting horse industry, breeding always tells, and well-bred horses were constantly in demand. It was serious business, the USCHA Futurity, and through it flowed millions and millions of dollars, all centered around the best quarter horses and cutting horses in the world.

Raney had planned long in advance for their attendance. Following the same setup as with the pre-works, they took the big horse trailer, although this time, she brought her truck as well, should they need transportation while the rig was parked. She also booked two rooms at a nearby hotel—one for her and Dalton, and the other for Mama should she escape her baby duties and join them. As before, Alejandro and Uno would stay in the trailer to keep an eye on Rosco and Big Mike.

They arrived late morning on the day the competition began. They already knew that for Rosco's first go-round, he had drawn number 111, which meant he would compete early on the second day. That gave them plenty of time to unload and ready the stalls that Raney had reserved. After feeding and watering the horses, they all headed out to a popular nearby Tex-Mex restaurant.

Raney was too excited to eat much. She also thought Dalton and Alejandro were too relaxed, but she supposed that was better than being as anxious as she was. After they ate, Dalton and Alejandro took the horses to one of the exercise areas for a lope and brief post-trailering workout, while Raney and Uno went to the USCHA offices to ensure that all their paperwork was in order and to get instructions about competition procedures. And there were a lot of procedures.

Each team would consist of the competing rider and horse, and the helper and his horse, whose job would be to help manage the herd while the cutter worked the cows. Each competitor would have two and a half minutes to separate a cow from the herd, hold it, then release it back to the herd before selecting the next cow. They were expected to work two cows and make an attempt on a third during the time allotted. After twelve horses had completed their runs, the cows would be exchanged for fresh stock and the arena would be raked. It was a well-choreographed process, yet it would still take six days to get through all six hundred–plus entrants scheduled in Round One.

Raney was glad Rosco wouldn't start until the second day. That would allow him time to settle before his first go, and give him a four-day break before Round Two began— assuming he made it into Round Two, since the competition was single elimination. Easy on the horse, hard on those waiting. During that four-day wait, to minimize stress and give the horses a chance to relax between rounds, Press Amala had graciously arranged for both horses to stay at the Running Bar Ranch just outside of town, unless Mike was needed to help out other riders. He and Alejandro were so good at their job requests were already coming in.

But today, Raney and Uno had come to explore. Once Raney had finished registering, USCHA officials verified her membership was current and that the three thousand– plus entry fee had been paid, as well as the fees for stalls and time in the practice arena, then she and Uno were finally able to check out the huge exhibition hall.

It was an amazing place. She got a kick out of watching Uno's look of awe as they walked past the dozens of exhibits and booths where vendors sold everything from custom saddles, boots, hats, chaps, jewelry, bridles, monogrammed blankets, or anything else having to do with horses. There were also food stalls and an endless supply of event memorabilia, mugs, jackets, caps, shirts, sweatshirts, all with the USCHA Futurity logo. When Raney saw the boy eyeing USCHA baseball caps, she told him to pick one. "And one you think your father would like. I'll get one each for me and Dalton."

From there, they moved on to the belt-maker's booth, where she fitted Uno for a leather belt and had his name put on the back in silver letters. The boy was so proud he almost strutted.

Then they continued past booths of training films and

videos of studs available for bookings. If Rosco did well enough, he might have his own video before long. But Raney didn't dwell on it, afraid to jinx his chances.

"What are those for?" Uno asked, pointing to the darkened monitors posted throughout the hall.

"Once the competition is in full swing, those TV monitors will live-stream the events going on in the main arena. There are over six hundred horses competing in the Futurity and it will take days to whittle them down to a single champion. Those screens will be on all day and into the night."

"Mr. Dalton and Rosco will be TV stars?"

Raney laughed. "Your father and Big Mike, too. Because neither Dalton nor Rosco can do their job without their help."

"Someday maybe I can help."

"You already do. You've been a huge help to Dalton. And he appreciates it."

The boy grinned and pointed to a mechanical horse and cow. "What is that?"

"That's a machine for people to ride if they want to know what it's like to be on a cutting horse. And no," she added, anticipating his next question. "You can't ride it unless your father is with you. You hungry?"

Foolish question. They'd eaten lunch less than two hours ago. But she'd ceased to be surprised at how much the adolescent boy could eat, so they grabbed a bag of caramel popcorn, then headed back to the stalls.

That night, Dalton stayed out late, networking with other trainers and talking horses. Raney thought she was too nervous to sleep, but she never heard Dalton come in, and didn't wake up until after he left the next morning. But she did find a note on the bathroom counter that read, *Celebration tonight. Bring whips.*

The second day of Round One dawned clear and cool, but sitting in the indoor arena with Uno, Raney was aware of nothing but the buckskin horse and the handsome, broad-shouldered man riding him through the in gate into the arena. Less than three minutes later it was over and they were riding out the exit gate. It reminded Raney of Thanksgiving dinner—hours to prepare, minutes to devour.

Nonetheless, she thought they both did well, and the score flashing on the overhead leaderboard was a respectable one. But when she went back to the stall, Dalton seemed to think the colt could do better once he'd settled down. After they'd brushed him and hosed him off, they loaded him into the trailer and took him to Running Bar Ranch for the long, four-day wait until they found out if he'd made it into Round Two. Big Mike would remain behind to help other riders, so Dalton brought the trailer back for Alejandro and Uno to use.

Then, he and Raney looked over the horses arriving for the auction that would begin later next week. Raney hadn't brought stock to sell, but she hoped to buy another proven brood mare with solid bloodlines to help build her stable. It wouldn't be easy. There were hundreds to choose from.

On the sixth evening after the Futurity began, Dalton and Raney joined the other trainers and owners haunting the hallway outside of the USCHA offices where the final scores for Round One were to be posted.

"Don't worry," she murmured to Dalton, even though she was so nervous she was about to throw up. "You've got this."

Several minutes later, the official finally came out of the office with the list of those moving on to Round Two. Dalton waited until he'd pinned it to the board, then left Raney's side and stepped forward.

A moment later, he walked back, took Raney's hand, and led her away from the crowd and down the hall. "He made it."

Raney almost squealed with joy, but tamped it down to a single, "Holy shit!"

Heads turned.

Trying to regain dignity and act casual, she said, "You're surprised?"

"Grateful." Dropping his head so others couldn't hear, he whispered, "Now I get to sleep with you again, instead of driving back to the ranch."

"Will all the trainers who made the cut get to sleep with me, too?"

"Be nice. Or I won't let you play with the whips."

As soon as they told Alejandro and Uno the news, they rushed back to their hotel room and had a big celebration that lasted well into the night. No whips were involved, but there was a lot of laughing and thrashing around. And a long shower.

Early the following morning, an exhausted Raney drove Dalton out to the Running Bar Ranch to load up the rig and bring the colt back for a scheduled workout with cattle later that afternoon. Round Two would take three days, and only sixty horses would move up to the semifinal round. This time, Rosco drew 162, which meant he would again ride on the second day.

Over the next twenty-four hours pressure built. Interest in Dalton and the colt did, too. But they all tried to ignore it and stay focused, knowing it would only get worse if Rosco made it into the next round. Afraid her nervousness would be contagious, Raney stayed away from the stables and Dalton, and spent the afternoon doing laps around the complex grounds.

That night, she hardly slept and was up with Dalton and heading to the stables before dawn. While Raney did more laps, he spent the morning with Rosco, or scouting cows with Alejandro from the observation deck above the arena, or talking with other trainers. He seemed confident and at ease. Which amazed Raney.

By noon, the horses were saddled and ready. An hour later, number 162 was called, and Dalton and Alejandro moved into position at the in gate. Raney sat beside Uno in the stands, her hands clasped so tightly her fingers turned white. She heard Rosco's name announced, then Dalton's as the rider, hers as the owner, and finally, the name of the ranch. Then the gate opened.

It seemed surreal—the noise, the smells, the thundering of her heart as she watched the man she loved pour his heart and soul into a two-and-a-half-minute ride on the horse he'd brought from a gangly colt to a superb cutting horse. He looked magnificent. Unstoppable. Each move fluid and relaxed. Totally in control.

Then suddenly, it was over. The next rider was announced, and Rosco's score flashed on the overhead screen. 216. Raney blinked. Looked again. Even with the highest and lowest scores from the five judges thrown out, Rosco still scored 216!

She cried.

Dalton laughed.

Uno did an intricate dance across the stable floor.

Too nervous to sit around and wait for the other scores of the day to come in, Raney walked back to their hotel and called Press.

When he didn't answer, she left a voice mail, telling him Rosco's score for the first two rounds and thanking him for setting up the break at the ranch. Then she texted Mama the score, afraid if she called, she'd be stuck on the phone for hours, then took a long, hot soak.

"He's going to make it!" Dalton told Raney when he barged into the room after waiting for the day's scores. "There are still horses left to compete tomorrow, but after the first two days, he's in the top ten!" Laughing, he swept Raney up in his arms, swung her around, then tossed her onto the bed and began unbuckling his belt. "He's going to the semis, sweetheart! And if he does, he'll earn back triple the entry fee in his first competition—" He froze, shirt half-off, staring at her sprawled across the bed where he'd thrown her. "You're naked."

"I am."

"You didn't start without me, did you?"

"Do I need to?"

"Hell, no." And laughing, he fell on top of her, horse-stink, boots, and all.

"Mama would be scandalized," she said later, drawing circles in the sweaty hair on his chest while he struggled to catch his breath. "I've never done that before."

"We did it in the shower yesterday."

"Not with your boots on."

"Boots?" He looked down, shocked to see his jeans around his ankles and the toes of his boots showing. "Damn. No wonder the bed feels gritty."

"Maybe next time you can wear chaps, too. For modesty's sake." She drew a circle with dots. It felt like a happy face, but Dalton didn't look.

"How many will Rosco be competing against if he makes the semis?"

"Sixty. That tickles."

"How many of those go to the finals?"

"Twenty. I need a shower. You do, too. This bed smells like horse."

"I wonder why."

The next evening, while the rankings for Round Two were being tabulated to see who would move on to the semifinals, the crowd outside of the USCHA office grew. Raney was too nervous to wait and had gone back to the hotel. But Dalton was there, trying to pretend to the other trainers this was just another day. Being on the list of the sixty top three-year-old cutting horses in the country was a huge accomplishment. And Dalton felt sure Rosco had a chance. But when they posted the list and he saw Rosco's name in the upper half, Dalton's heart felt like it would kick its way out of his chest. They'd done it! *Semifinals, here we come!*

As soon as he ended the call after giving Raney the news, he headed over to the stables. Even though it was late, Alejandro and Uno were still up, leaning against Rosco's stall door, waiting. As soon as they saw Dalton's face, Alejandro started grinning and Uno did a hopping shuffle across the hay-strewn aisleway.

"What is his draw?" Alejandro asked when Dalton stopped before him.

"Number 26."

"*¿Es bueno?*" Uno asked, pausing in his dance.

"It's *muy bueno*." Dalton clapped the boy's shoulder. "It means we have time to give the horses a morning practice run in the exercise arena before his go."

They decided on a time to have the horses fed, brushed, saddled, skid boots and rear boots on, ready for the workout, leaving no more than an hour's wait time before they had to line up at the gate into the arena. This round, all sixty horses would compete on the same day. Tomorrow, in fact. So, Dalton urged Alejandro and Uno to get some sleep, then headed back to the hotel and Raney.

And another celebration.

"Text me when you get to the hotel," Raney was saying into her cell phone when Dalton walked into the hotel room. "Tell Joss hi and give Lyric kisses."

"Mama?" he asked, settling on the edge of the bed to pull off his boots.

"Assuming she can get out by seven, she should be here by noon tomorrow."

"We won't know if he made the finals until tomorrow evening."

"She'll come anyway. She's desperate to get away from Babyville."

Fifteen minutes later, after a thorough scrubbing—apparently, from his careful attention to every inch of her skin, Dalton thought she needed help with that—they stepped out of the shower just as his phone buzzed in the bedroom.

He ignored it and continued to dry her off. A moment later, Raney's cell buzzed. "It might be important," she said. "We should answer."

She got to her phone just before it went to voice mail. The caller ID said it was Clovis Cardwell. "Hello, Mrs. Cardwell," she said, giving Dalton a puzzled glance.

He had pulled on his jeans and was now frowning as he checked his calls.

"Is Dalton there?" his mother asked Raney. "I need to talk to him."

"Of course." Raney handed her phone to Dalton, dread circling in her mind.

It was a short conversation: "When? How bad? Are you there now? I'll talk to Raney and call you back." He tossed her cell on the bed and pulled on a T-shirt. "Timmy's had an accident. They're at University Medical in Lubbock."

Raney clapped a hand to her throat. "How bad?"

"A bump on the head. Maybe some cracked ribs and a broken arm. They're waiting on X-rays now. Damn!" He sat on the bed again and began pulling on the socks he'd taken off thirty minutes earlier.

Raney sat beside him, her hand on his back. "What happened?"

"He fell off a ladder while he was cleaning the church gutters. I can't believe they let him do that. He has terrible balance." He pulled on one boot, reached for the other. "I was afraid something like this would happen when he told us he was washing windows. But I didn't think they'd put him on a fucking ladder!"

"What are you going to do?"

"Go to Lubbock."

"That's a five-hour drive. You won't get there before midnight. Then you have to be back here first thing to be ready for the semis."

"Timmy needs me. Alejandro can ride Rosco."

But they both knew that wouldn't work, even though a change of riders was allowed. Alejandro was good, but not as good as Dalton. "How about I go to Lubbock," Raney offered. "I can check on Timmy, talk to the doctor, then report back to you." Raney hated to push him, but they'd worked too hard to get here, and they'd never have a chance like this again. "It sounds like Timmy is mostly banged up, not seriously hurt. Your parents will understand, Dalton. They know how much you have riding on this."

"Damn! Fuck! Shit!"

She saw defeat in the slump of his shoulders. "Stay here and do what you came to do. Let me take care of this. Please, Dalton."

Five minutes later, she was heading out the door with her duffel while Dalton explained to his mother that Raney was on her way and he'd be there as soon as he could.

At that time of the evening, the drive only took four and a half hours. Visiting hours were long over, but the Cardwells had left word at the nurses' station to send her on to Timmy's room as soon as she arrived.

Timmy was asleep. So was Mr. Cardwell, stretched out on the padded bench beneath the window, snoring softly. Mrs. Cardwell was awake, but looked exhausted. When Raney tiptoed in, Clovis gave a worn smile, rose, and waved her back into the hall. "We can talk in the waiting room. How was the drive?"

"Fine. How are you?" Raney asked her. "Have you had any rest, or gotten anything to eat?"

"Coffee, mostly. But I have a muffin in my purse if you're hungry."

Raney shook her head and waited for the older woman to settle in a chair before sitting down beside her. "How badly is Timmy hurt?"

"He'll live, but I doubt he'll ever climb a ladder again." In a thin, weary voice, she listed her younger son's injuries. A slight concussion, a cracked radius in his left arm, three bruised ribs, and a few cuts and scrapes. "Because of the ribs, he'll be sore for a while, but his arm should heal fast. He only has a splint, rather than a full cast. They'll probably send him home in a couple of days unless the concussion acts up. How's Dalton doing in the horse show?"

"Very well." Raney explained about the semifinal ride tomorrow and the finals the day after. "We won't know if he made the finals until tomorrow evening when they post the rankings, but he has a good chance. He and Rosco are doing an amazing job. They're both getting a lot of attention." Raney hesitated, then added, "Dalton was all set to have someone else ride for him tomorrow so he could come to Lubbock. I talked him out of it. He's building a great career as a trainer, Mrs. Cardwell, and these next two days could make or break him. I hope I didn't overstep, coming in his place."

Mrs. Cardwell reached over and laid a wrinkled, blue-veined hand over Raney's. "You didn't. I'm glad you came in his stead. Dalton has given up too much for his family, as it is. He deserves his chance after what he's been through."

Raney felt a swell of gratitude. "I'll tell him you said that."

Blinking hard, the older woman took her hand away and smoothed the faded cotton of her shirtwaist dress with arthritic fingers, obviously embarrassed by her spontaneous show of emotion. Raney wondered how such a reserved woman could raise a son as openhearted as Dalton. But then, Dalton had his hidden places, too.

"I hope you won't try to drive back tonight, Raney," Mrs. Cardwell said.

"I had planned on staying until Timmy is discharged, in case you need help getting him home."

"What about Dalton's ride tomorrow? Don't you want to be there for that?"

"The semifinals? I doubt I'd make it back in time even if I left first thing tomorrow. But if he gets into the finals, I'd definitely like to make that."

Mrs. Cardwell studied her for several moments, a thoughtful look in eyes that might once have been as bright a green as her oldest son's. "He's in love with you, you know," she said. "You mind me asking if you have feelings for him, too?"

"I do, ma'am. I think he's a remarkable man."

"Probably more so than you know."

Raney thought that was an odd thing to say, but simply smiled in response. This conversation was becoming uncomfortable enough as it was.

"Do you have somewhere to stay tonight?" Mrs. Cardwell asked.

"I thought I would go by the hotel where we stayed when my sister was here having her baby. Will you share it with me? Or could I get a room for you and Mr. Cardwell?"

"No need. It's my turn on the couch, and Dad has spent many a night dozing in a chair. Especially since the new TV plays football all night long. We'll be fine. But you run on. Get some rest. Come see Timmy in the morning. He'd like that."

Luckily the hotel had a vacancy, probably because the Texas Tech Red Raiders football team was playing away this week. As soon as she reached her room, Raney called Dalton, assured him Timmy was doing well and would probably be discharged the day after tomorrow.

"Stay until then," Dalton suggested. "If we make it, the finals won't start until afternoon day after tomorrow. If you leave early, you can make it. We can both use the rest, but I'll miss you."

She would miss him, too. She loved having him beside her at night and knowing he was just an arm's length away.

"Let me know your draw for the finals as soon as you get it," she said.

He chuckled. "Now who's being cocky?"

"I have total faith in you and Rosco. You've got this."

"I hope. But even if we don't make the finals, be ready for offers. I'm already being stalked."

"Offers for both of you?"

"I've made it pretty clear I'm not going anywhere, so don't worry about me."

Raney was trying not to. But the lure of being the big dog at a top-tier ranch had to look better to Dalton than what she could offer.

"Your mother's here," he said. "Hope the maid got to your room before she checked in."

"My room?"

"That's the one they put her in. Seems we've been using the room under Whitcomb, rather than the one for Cardwell. Think she'll believe it if you told her you've started wearing boxers and using men's deodorant? Although, I'd bet she already knows we're knocking boots."

"Oh, Lord."

He laughed. "You're not still worried about her knowing, are you?"

"Of course I am. As soon as it's out, she'll be pushing for a double December wedding."

"Would that be so bad?"

"Seriously? Can you imagine the circus it would be? Joss, a crying baby, everybody looking at my waist and wondering if I'm having a baby, too? If I were Grady, I might not even show up."

"I'm surprised you care that much about what others think."

She thought about it, then sighed. "Actually, I don't. Not

really. I just want my wedding to be mine. Not Mama's or Joss's."

"And mine, too, I hope."

"Mercy, Mr. Cardwell, are you proposing to me?"

"Hell, no. You said when the time came, you would do the proposing."

"Did I? Well, let's see how you do in the finals before we do anything drastic. Good night, Muffin."

"Muffin?"

"Sorry. Studmuffin."

Laughter rumbled through the phone. "Good night, sweetheart. And don't wear anything to bed tonight. It makes my dreams more fun."

CHAPTER 25

The semifinals didn't start until afternoon. Rosco had drawn 26, which meant he was the second rider in the third herd. A good spot. Since they changed cows after every twelve rides, his herd would still be fresh and lively, which allowed for a higher score. Dalton gave the colt an early-morning workout, hosed him off, then spent a long time with him in the stall, giving him a rubdown, brushing him, and telling him what an outstanding job he was doing.

Rosco responded by dozing, which was what Dalton had hoped for.

By noon, Alejandro and Uno were off cruising the auction pens, so Dalton ate lunch alone in a restaurant in the exhibition hall. He was finishing a piece of pie when two men stopped at his table and asked if they could join him.

Max Rayburn and Sid Falk.

Rayburn owned a well-respected cutting horse outfit in Oklahoma, and Sid was an experienced, successful trainer who had been with him for years. Maybe too many years. The guy must be over sixty and moved with the stiff-backed gait of a man who'd spent most of those years in a saddle. Maybe he was retiring or stepping back from active training. Maybe Rayburn was looking for a replacement. Dalton doubted they were after Rosco—he'd already told Sid the colt wasn't for sale. Dalton waved to the empty chairs at the table. "Have a seat."

"Congratulations on making the semifinals," Rayburn said after he sat down. "Sid, here, thinks your colt has a chance to go even higher."

"That'd be nice." Dalton didn't expound on it, aware that neither of the Rayburn entries had made it past Round Two. Any horse can have an off day.

They chatted for a while, then Rayburn said, "Sid, here, is looking to retire."

"Is that right? Sorry to hear that, Sid. You've got a hell of a track record."

The older man shrugged. "Had some outstanding horses to work with."

"He'll be a hard man to replace." Having dispensed with the prelims, Rayburn got down to business. "You're definitely on our short list, Cardwell. You interested in making a change?"

Dalton started to answer, but Rayburn cut him off. "I'll top whatever you're making now. House included. If you're on contract, I can take care of that, too."

Dalton put on a regretful smile and sat back. "That's mighty generous, sir. And I appreciate the offer. But I'm not looking to make a move right now."

"You sure?"

"Yes, sir. I am."

With a sigh, Rayburn rose. "If you change your mind, let me know."

"I will. And thanks for considering me."

"Good luck this afternoon," Sid said, and followed his boss out of the restaurant.

Dalton watched them leave, hoping he'd done the right

thing. Although he felt fairly confident things were working out with Raney, he wasn't sure he wanted to be her employee forever. But he didn't want to move on, either. Maybe he should keep his options open for a while.

Alejandro and Uno were saddling the horses when he got back to the stalls.

"We should leave now," Alejandro suggested. "I am helping in the first go. When I am done, Uno can stay with the horses while we check out the cows in your herd."

After Alejandro finished helping another rider in the first herd, he came back to the holding area where Uno stood with Rosco, loosened Mike's cinch to let him breathe, and told the boy to hand walk him until he was cool before giving him any water. Then he and Dalton watched the remaining entrants in the first go and the scores flashing on the leaderboard.

All the horses did well, although, so far, none scored higher than Rosco's 216 of the previous day. Not that that signified anything, since this was another day and a fresh scoresheet. But it told Dalton that if Rosco could score that high once, he might be able to do it again.

The second herd was a little tougher, with three horses out of twelve scoring over 210, although none higher than 216. But there were still thirty-six horses left and a lot could happen, including Rosco making a miss or having a poor ride.

While arena tenders drove out the cows in the second herd and brought in the ones for the third go-round, Dalton and Alejandro went up to the observation area above and behind the arena wall where the cows were being bunched, and studied them carefully.

They were a good group, and it took the handlers a while to settle them down and get them grouped against the wall. There were several standouts—cows that would offer a challenge rather than an easy ride.

"Ahí." Alejandro pointed to a heifer with a pink nose and a white ring around her left eye. "There is the money cow."

Dalton studied her for a moment and nodded. The man trying to settle the herd was having the most trouble keeping her bunched with the rest.

"I like that Angus with the white-tipped tail, too," Dalton said. "And that smaller Hereford. She likes hiding in the middle of the herd. She'll be harder to bring out."

It was important to find stock that would be the least cooperative. A risk, but if successful, it might bring a higher score. After selecting several alternative prospects, in case the first rider picked the cows Dalton wanted, he and Alejandro returned to the holding area just as the tenders finished raking the arena. A few minutes later, the announcer listed the "up next, on deck, and in-the-hole" riders for the third go. It was now or never. Dalton and Alejandro mounted up and moved their horses into second position at the in gate.

Showtime.

Knowing she would be staying in Lubbock until tomorrow, Raney slept late the morning after her drive and went by a nearby bookstore before going to the hospital. Timmy was awake and eating an early lunch when she stepped into his room.

"Hi, Raney!" he called when he saw her. "Did Dalton come, too?"

"Maybe next time. How are you feeling?"

"Okay. My arm broke. See?" He held up his bandaged arm. "And my side hurts. And my head hurts. The doctor said I was brave. He said I could go back to my group home tomorrow. But I have to eat my lunch now."

"Why don't you do that while I talk to your mother?"

"Yeah. Okay. I have applesauce. See?"

Mrs. Cardwell looked a little better than she had the previous night, but it was clear sleeping on a bench, even if it was padded, was hard on her. "Did you get any rest?" Raney asked her.

"As much as I usually do. Dad's gone to the cafeteria downstairs. It's not bad, if you're hungry."

Raney wasn't and suggested Mrs. Cardwell go have lunch with her husband while she stayed with Timmy. "How is he today?"

"Better. Had a bit of a rough night, but they've given him something for the sore ribs. Are you sure I can't get you anything while I'm downstairs?"

"No thanks. Take your time."

Raney and Timmy chatted about the group home and his friend George until Timmy finished his meal, then Raney gave him the flash cards she'd bought that showed how to make change. He did well but tired easily and was ready for a nap when his parents came back from lunch.

At about the same time Dalton was heading to the arena for his semifinal go, the doctor came in and told them Timmy could go home the following day.

After the Cardwells assured Raney that she didn't need to accompany them to Plainview, Raney told them that after Timmy was discharged in the morning, she would head back to Fort Worth, in case Dalton and Rosco made it into the finals.

Raney was glad she wasn't at the arena. The waiting was taking its toll on her, and with every passing hour, the knot in her stomach grew tighter.

Her phone buzzed fifteen minutes after four. Raney saw it was Dalton and stepped out of Timmy's room into the hall. She took a deep breath, let it out, and punched ACCEPT.

"214.5."

His voice sounded tense, but not depressed. Or maybe that was wishful thinking on her part. "That's wonderful!"

"Not wonderful, but maybe good enough. He had a

slight misstep on the second cow, but corrected and finished strong."

"How are the other horses doing?"

"Pretty good. We're about halfway through, but Rosco's score is holding in the top third."

"You'll make it. I'm sure of it."

He let go a deep breath that rustled through the phone. "This waiting is killing me. I wish you were here. I always feel better when you're around."

"Me, too. It's like I'm missing a foot or something."

"A foot? That's the best you can do?"

Smiling, she added, "Okay, I miss your muscles, too. I would elaborate but I'm in the hall at the hospital and wouldn't want to rile up the patients."

He chuckled and some of the tension faded.

"When do you think the finals' list will be posted?" she asked.

"Nine tonight. If we're in, I'll get my draw then, too. I'll call as soon as I know." There was a pause, the muffled sound of other voices, then Dalton said, "Better go. Press just walked up. Later, babe."

"Fingers crossed. And tell Press 'hi' for me."

Nine? How was she going to fill five more hours without losing her mind?

With Raney there to keep an eye on Timmy, the elder Cardwell left to run errands, fill prescriptions, and get gas for the car.

Meanwhile, Raney kept Timmy entertained. They read to each other, went over the flash cards again, watched cartoons on the ceiling-mounted TV. Later, she went downstairs, got a dinner plate, and came back up and ate with him while his parents ate in the cafeteria.

Nine o'clock came. Nine thirty. Still, no call. Raney was thinking of pacing in the hall, when her cell buzzed again.

"We made it!" Dalton almost shouted. "We're in the Futurity finals, baby! Can you believe it?"

"That's wonderful!" She could hardly hear him because of all the background noise, but she got the gist of it. She slumped against the wall, her heart thudding and her mind spinning. She wanted to do a happy dance, cry, raise a fist in triumph. Instead, she closed her eyes and whispered, "Thank you, God."

"Gotta go. Some of the trainers are heading to a later supper. Oh, and our draw is 8, so we're in the first go. We have to be ready by five P.M. Can you make it?"

"Absolutely! I'm so proud of you and Rosco. Have you called Mama?"

"You do it. Love you. Later."

Once Raney settled down, she called Mama and gave her the news. It still didn't seem real. For a debuting trainer to make the Futurity finals was almost too good to be true. But Dalton had done it.

Mama was excited, too. She didn't say anything about boxer underwear or men's deodorant being in her room, and Raney certainly didn't bring it up. They talked for a minute about the baby, the new parents, and how well Len and Ryan were doing. "And did I tell you I heard from KD?" Mama said. "She sent the cutest little glockenspiel for Lyric, although it'll be months before she can start banging on it, thank the Lord."

"What's a glockenspiel?"

"Some sort of keyboard percussion instrument. Sounds like bells. You hear them in Christmas music." Mama went on to say that KD was still in Germany, but would be getting new orders any day. "Probably Middle East or Africa. She can't say where, but the whole area is a war zone, so I'm already starting to worry."

"Don't," Raney said. "KD can take care of herself." Raney hoped that was true.

"You're right," Mama said. "Instead I'll worry about what you're going to do with all Dalton's winnings. It's a sizable amount for those who make the finals. Have you decided how you're going to handle that?"

Raney wasn't sure why her mother was interested. "I believe it all goes to the owners, and they share it with the trainer if they so choose."

"Just don't give him all of it. He might misunderstand."

"Misunderstand what?"

"You know how men are. How is Timmy?"

Grateful for the change in subject, Raney said he was doing well enough to go home tomorrow. "I'll head back to Fort Worth then. Dalton and Rosco are riding in the first group, so I need to be there no later than four. I'll go directly to the trailer. If you can, take the hotel shuttle to the arena early, so you can get us good seats. Look for Press. He might be there, too. The finals! I still can't believe it!"

Hours later, she was still in disbelief, but eventually fell into an exhausted sleep with Dalton's name whispering through her mind.

She awoke early, showered, dressed, and was on her way to the hospital by eight thirty. If she was to make it back to the arena by four, she'd have to leave no later than eleven, and she wanted to tell the Cardwells good-bye before she left.

As she came through the hospital doors, she saw Dalton's parents exiting the elevator. Mr. Cardwell waved and hurried on down the hall, while Mrs. Cardwell waited for Raney. "Glad you came early," she said as Raney walked up. "Looks like they'll be discharging Timmy fairly soon."

"Great! He had a good night?"

"Yes, praise the Lord. Dad's going to the accounting office to take care of the paperwork, and I thought I'd grab something from the cafeteria for the trip home. Timmy was worried he wouldn't see you before we left. Why don't you go on up and give him your good-byes? We'll be along directly."

As soon as Raney walked into his room, Timmy gave her a big smile and asked the same question he had asked her every time she'd arrived, even if she'd been gone only a few minutes.

"Where's Dalton? Did Dalton come, too?"

He seemed fixated on where his brother might be. It had seemed amusing and touching at first, but now Raney was beginning to wonder if there was more to it than that. And now, when Raney said Dalton didn't come, tears filled Timmy's eyes.

"Timmy, what's wrong?"

"He's mad at me. He's going away again."

"No, he's not mad at you, Timmy. Why would you think he's mad at you?"

"It's not my fault my arm broke." More tears rolled down his cheeks.

"Of course it isn't." Raney moved over to sit on the edge of the bed. She took Timmy's good hand in hers. "What's wrong, Timmy?"

"I don't like it when Dalton goes away."

"He's not going away. He's at the horse show, remember?"

"I didn't mean to fall."

Raney patted the big hand in hers. "He knows, Timmy. He's not mad at you."

He looked up with tear-filled eyes. "He's not going to the bad place?"

"What bad place?"

"I'm not supposed to tell."

His gaze moved past Raney and she turned to see the Cardwells in the doorway. They looked distressed, too. "Timmy's upset," she told them. "He's afraid Dalton's going away again. Do you know what he's talking about?"

The Cardwells exchanged a glance. Mr. Cardwell gave

a slight nod and stepped around his wife into the room. "Let's get you ready to go home, Timmy."

Mrs. Cardwell remained in the doorway. She motioned to Raney. "Best come with me, Raney. We can talk in the waiting area by the nurses' station."

Raney rose from the bed and followed her out, a sense of foreboding jangling along her nerves. "Talk about what, Mrs. Cardwell?" she asked when they reached the waiting area.

The older woman motioned to two chairs beside a big window along the back wall. "We can talk privately here."

Once they were both seated, Mrs. Cardwell rubbed her palms along the skirt draped over her knees several times, then finally said, "If you're serious about my son, there's something you need to know."

And at that moment, as if something that had been hidden in her mind all along suddenly shifted into view, Raney knew. She had sensed it from the beginning. Had questioned the incongruities, wondered at Dalton's unwillingness to talk about it and his surprising lack of remorse that had troubled her so much. Yet, even knowing, Raney still tried to block it. The worst had already happened. Dalton had been convicted and sent to prison. What more could Mrs. Cardwell tell her?

"Is this about the wreck that killed the county commissioner's nephew?"

"Yes." Mrs. Cardwell took a deep breath, and in a weary, defeated voice said, "First of all, you have to understand how deeply Dalton's emotions run. As soon as his brother was born, he took it upon himself to be Timmy's guardian and watchdog. Even more so when we realized Timmy was special. If his little brother fell, or skinned a knee, or broke a plate, Dalton assumed that if he had been watching better, he could have prevented it from happening."

Raney understood that. She'd felt the same way about

Joss when they were younger. Even into high school, she was still covering for her little sister.

"There's no one in the world as loyal as Dalton is," the older woman went on with a brief smile. "And no one more intent on keeping his word or doing what he said he would do."

"I know." Raney thought of what Dalton had said in the diner about promises being the only thing in this world a person had any control over. "What are you trying to tell me, ma'am?"

"It wasn't Dalton who caused the wreck. It was Timmy."

Raney had expected it. Even so, hearing the words spoken aloud was like a blow to her heart. And beneath the shock and dismay and confusion, fury bubbled. "Why?" A part of her was surprised at how calm her voice sounded. "Why did he take the blame for it?"

"Because that's what Dalton always did for Timmy, what he thought his job was. And because that night he was tired and it was late, and when Timmy asked if he could drive the tractor across the road to the other pasture, he said *yes*."

The anger burst forth. "That's no reason to allow yourself to be branded a felon and give up almost two years of your life."

Surprisingly, Mrs. Cardwell agreed. "No, it's not. But we couldn't talk him out of it. In Dalton's mind, because he'd allowed it to happen—because he hadn't been vigilant enough—it truly was his fault."

"And he never spoke up about what really happened."

"No. He made us promise we wouldn't, either. But I thought you should know."

Raney sat for a moment, staring out the picture window, trying to bring her anger under control. It was a stupid sacrifice. Considering his disability, nothing would have happened to Timmy had he admitted he was at fault. They don't put the mentally challenged in jail. But even if Dalton insisted on taking the blame, if he had taken it to trial, he might have gotten off. She couldn't get her mind past that. And even harder to accept was that Dalton hadn't told her the truth of what had happened. How could they go on if there were secrets like that between them?

"I can see you're angry," Mrs. Cardwell said, breaking into Raney's thoughts. "Dad and I felt the same way. But nothing we did or said would sway him. Dalton loves Timmy. And that means he will do everything in his power to protect and defend his little brother. It's part of his nature."

Raney knew that. She had seen it in action. Had felt it directed at her. It probably even accounted for his special bond with horses. But she still thought it was wrong. If he was so driven to honesty, why had he lied about the wreck? And why had he lied to her about it? And what else might he be lying about?

She would ask him.

Raney stood. "Thank you for telling me all this, Mrs. Cardwell. I know it was difficult. But I should leave now if I'm to make it back in time for the finals."

"What are you going to do?"

"Talk to him. He owes me an explanation himself. If he won't allow himself to give it, then I guess we're done." The thought of that opened a dark, empty place in her chest. But she couldn't spend the rest of her life wondering what secrets might lurk between them. "Please tell Timmy and Mr. Cardwell good-bye."

Five minutes later, Raney was on the road to Fort Worth.

CHAPTER 26

Dalton didn't hear from Raney that morning, and she didn't answer her cell when he called. He thought that odd, but figured she had gotten out early and was on the road.

He and Alejandro gave the horses a morning workout, then cleaned them up and let them rest. Dalton tried to rest, too. He'd been out late the night before, celebrating with other finalists, and had downed more than his usual two-beer limit. As a result, he had a low-grade headache and rumbly stomach. At lunch, rather than risk being accosted again by Rayburn or another owner, he grabbed something from a booth in the exhibition hall and ate it back at the trailer, then stretched out on the couch for a short nap.

It seemed he had just closed his eyes when he heard the trailer door open. Still half-asleep, he looked over to see Raney coming through the doorway. She didn't look happy.

"You made it," he said, sitting up.

She closed the door, then stood there, a guarded expression on her face.

"What's wrong?" he asked.

"I know what happened the night of the wreck."

It was so out of context he couldn't process it. "What?"

"Your brother let it slip and your mother filled in the rest. Why couldn't you tell me, yourself, Dalton? Why did you let me think you were the one who caused Jim Bob's death? Didn't you trust me with the truth?"

He was still so groggy he was having trouble making sense of what she was saying. Or why she was talking about the wreck now. Or why his mother had even told her about it in the first place. "Hey, slow down." He raked a hand through his hair and waved her toward the armchair beside the couch. "Give me a minute to wake up. Then we'll talk."

"I'd rather stand. I've been sitting for the last five hours."

And stewing, he guessed. "Sit down anyway. Please."

Wide awake now, he sat back, watched her settle into the chair, legs and arms crossed, her face stiff with anger. Shutting him out.

He should have known this would happen. He should have told her. Raney wasn't one to settle for half answers. *Hell*. If she was that determined to hear it, he'd give her the whole truth, ugly as it was. "I didn't tell you because I promised my folks I'd never discuss it."

"And a promise given is a promise kept, right?"

He'd never heard that tone before. It awakened his own anger. "Yeah."

"Well, not to worry. They released you from that promise, so now you can explain it to me. Why didn't you tell anyone your brother caused the wreck? People like Timmy don't go to prison."

"Maybe not. More likely he would have been warehoused in some state institution. Which would have been as bad as prison for Timmy."

"He might have gotten off with probation."

"I doubt it. Commissioner Adkins wouldn't have settled for that. If he'd known Timmy was driving the tractor, he would have filed a wrongful death suit and taken everything my parents had. Since I had nothing, he didn't bother to sue me and took his pound of flesh by sending me to prison, instead."

She studied him, leg swinging, arms crossed. "So you took the blame."

He spread his hands in frustration. "Because I was to blame, Raney. I let him take the tractor to the other pasture. And I forgot to tell him to stop and look both ways before he crossed the road. Such a simple thing you forget to mention it, you assume a person would know." He sighed and shook his head, the burden of guilt no lighter now than it had been two years ago. "But I didn't remind him like I should have and Timmy didn't look and because of it, a man died. In balance"—he lifted a hand, then let it drop back to his knee—"a year and a half in prison for me, compared to the horrors that might await Timmy in prison, or being sent to an institution. I couldn't do that to my brother."

They sat in silence. Then she said, "But if you hadn't confessed, if you'd gone to trial—"

He cut her off. "I don't play what-if games, Raney. Not with the lives of people I love, and not after the fact. I did what I thought was right. Period." Couldn't she understand that? Couldn't she see what she was doing to the fragile trust between them?

In the distance, the announcer's voice sounded. Dalton saw on his watch that it was after four o'clock. The lead-up to the finals had begun. "Are we done here?"

"Not quite."

"What else do you need to know?" He tried to keep impatience out of his voice, but it was hard. *Why now?* All this was past history and rehashing wouldn't change it.

"Were you ever going to tell me?"

"It was over and done with. I saw no reason to." He rubbed a hand over his face, as if he could wipe the whole conversation away. How could this be happening? How could she see only the bad and ignore what they meant to each other?

"So, you lied to me instead."

His head shot up. "I never lied to you, Raney. Not once."

"You let me think you'd caused Jim Bob's death. Isn't that a lie?"

He felt half-sick. He didn't know what to say or do, or how to make her see it didn't matter anymore. All that was important was that they loved each other. He'd do anything in his power to make this right, but he couldn't change the past.

"I understand why you did what you did," she admitted. "I might even have made the same decision. But what I don't understand, Dalton," she added, her voice starting to wobble, "is why you didn't trust me enough to tell me the truth. That's what I can't get past."

"You're right. I should have told you. I'm sorry." What more could he say?

"I'm not sure that's good enough."

The loudspeaker blared out the opening music. He shut his mind to it. "Then what do you want, Raney? What can I do to fix this? Tell me, and I'll do it."

She just looked at him, tears filling her eyes.

He saw defeat. An uncrossable distance spreading between them. And the realization came—as unexpected and unimaginable as an incoming mortar round—that he was losing her.

Panic paralyzed him. He couldn't breathe or think. "Don't do this, Raney. Don't let this be the end of us."

Before she could respond, the trailer door opened and Alejandro stuck his head inside. "It is time. The horses are saddled and ready. We must hurry."

"You do it," Dalton told him. "You ride for me."

"No!" Raney bolted from the chair. "You can't do that to Rosco. Or to me. Do what you came to do. Go on," she said to Alejandro. "He's coming."

Alejandro left.

Dalton rose. He started for the door, stopped, and turned back, watched the tears roll down her face, and felt like puking.

"This isn't over, Raney. Nothing's changed for me. I still love you. But you need to figure out how you feel, and where we go from here. Whatever you decide, this conversation is done. Accept it or don't. I'm not talking about it again." Then, while he still could, he left.

As soon as the door closed behind him, emptiness engulfed Raney. She doubled over, arms pressed against her stomach, sobs tearing through her throat.

How had it come to this? How had they let it come to this?

Dimly, she heard the loudspeaker calling out the opening order for first go. Heard Rosco's name, his sire and dam, Dalton's name, then hers, as the owner. It was starting. Without her.

Left behind again.

A moment later, she was racing toward the arena.

Mama met her halfway. "Where have you been? They're starting! Oh, Lord, Raney, you're crying! What have you done?"

"Hurry!" Raney shouted as she ran on.

They made it into the arena just as the first rider's name was called. "We have time to reach the observation deck," she said to her mother as she raced up the stairs.

They made it. Raney ducked through the other owners and trainers gathered on the deck and looked down, saw Dalton standing beside Rosco, and something seemed to rip apart inside.

So strong. So sure. So willing to sacrifice everything for a promise he shouldn't have made in the first place.

"Well, this is apropos," Mama muttered, panting as she pushed in beside Raney.

"What do you mean?"

"Looking down on Dalton. Isn't that what you've done all along?"

Raney stared at her, too shocked to deny it.

"He is, after all, a convicted criminal," her mother added in a low voice. "Isn't that what you said? Several times?"

"He didn't do it!" Raney hissed, hoping the other watchers couldn't hear them over the noise of the crowd. "His mother told me he didn't and he confirmed it."

"Then what are you so upset about?"

"He deceived me! That's what. How can I ever trust him again?"

"Oh, darling, don't be naive. Life is filled with little lies and omissions and disappointments. If you expect perfection, you're doomed to a lifetime of loneliness. Dalton is an honorable man. I'm sad you can't see that. Now hush. They're starting."

Alejandro led Big Mike over to where Dalton and Rosco stood second in line at the in gate. He looked angry. Hell, everybody was pissed off with him today.

Keeping his voice low, Alejandro said, "Since you did not come to look over the cows, how will you tell me which ones you want without the judges noticing?" Once the ride started, communicating with your helper was frowned upon.

"You'll know. Watch my eyes. And if we miss, we miss."

Muttering under his breath, Alejandro gathered Big Mike's reins and swung into the saddle.

Dalton tightened Rosco's cinch, checked his front and rear skid boots, then stood there, his mind retracing every word of the fight with Raney and wondering what he could have said differently. Was this really the end for them? He couldn't accept that. But he didn't regret any of his decisions, either. She was putting hidden meanings on every move he'd made, and she thought he didn't trust her?

Alejandro leaned down and said, "You better get your head straight, pendejo, or we will lose this thing."

Overhead, the loudspeaker blared as the first rider went through the gate. Dalton heard his and Rosco's names listed as "on deck," and nodded to Alejandro. "You're right," he said, and mounted up.

Doing what he'd done in Iraq and later in Huntsville, Dalton shut his mind to the noise around him and concentrated on breathing. In and out, slow and steady. Pushing all the pain and fear and fury deep inside so he could focus only on the here and now. If this was to be the end of him and Raney, so be it. But he'd go out on the ride of his life.

Bending down, he stroked Rosco's neck. "We've got this, boy. We can do it." Then the in gate opened, and Dalton sent him into the arena.

He felt a shiver of excitement run through the colt as they crossed the time line and walked into the back of the herd, flushing half of the cows out into the working area. Spotting the heifer he wanted, Dalton kept his eyes fixed on her as the other cows started to regroup. Alejandro got the message. He and Mike cleared the working area by sending the stragglers back to the handlers keeping the herd bunched along the back wall.

Dalton pointed the colt at the chosen heifer, dropped his rein hand to Rosco's neck, and gripped the horn with his right hand as the horse jumped into action, mirroring the cow's movements to keep her from getting back to the herd.

She didn't put up much of a fight and within twenty seconds had almost slowed to a standstill. Dalton immediately lifted the reins, put his right hand on Rosco's neck to signal him to quit, then turned to find the next cow. He spotted her hiding deep inside the herd.

Hoping she would offer a better challenge, he sent Rosco

forward, moving slowly so they didn't spook the other cows. After he reached the heifer he wanted, he had Rosco drive her toward the outside until she broke from the herd. Then he dropped his rein hand to the colt's neck again, grabbed the horn, and let Rosco do his magic.

This one was livelier and had Rosco scrambling. Dalton kept a tight grip on the horn as the colt darted and lunged to keep the cow from slipping past him and back to the herd. After almost thirty seconds, the heifer finally tired. Dalton signaled Rosco to let her go and went after the third cow. He got her into the working area and held her until the buzzer sounded and the ride was over.

Dalton thanked the other handlers, shook Alejandro's hand, then reined Rosco toward the exit gate. "Good boy," he murmured, stroking the colt's sweat-slick neck. "You did good. I'm proud of you."

Alejandro stopped beside them. "We were lucky. That was his best go. But that first heifer will cost you."

"I know. My fault, not Rosco's. I made a bad pick."

"They don't seem to think so." Alejandro nodded toward several men leaning against the fence, watching them. Two gave Dalton a thumbs-up, another nodded.

Dalton looked up at the leaderboard, saw that the previous rider had scored 220. Definitely a winning score. Then it flashed Rosco's score: 218.5. Dalton felt a shock, looked again, then a surge of relief that made his eyes sting.

Better than he expected. He couldn't have asked for more.

By the time he'd dismounted and loosened Rosco's cinch, the vultures were descending.

Raney was about to cry again. 218.5! They'd done it! And she could see by the crowd gathering around Rosco and Dalton that she wasn't the only one who thought so.

"Let's hope he isn't receptive," Mama murmured.

Raney glanced at her. "What are you talking about?"

"Those men aren't giving Dalton congratulations. They're making offers."

"Rosco's not for sale."

"I'm not talking about the horse."

Raney looked again. She recognized Max Rayburn and Tom Hadley, both owners. The others she didn't know. "Dalton said he wasn't looking to move."

"Unless you run him off."

"That's a terrible thing to say!" Furious, Raney left the observation deck and headed down the stairs, so upset with her mother she couldn't get away from her fast enough. But once at the bottom, she slowed, wondering if Mama might be right. After the things she'd said, would Dalton actually consider leaving Four Star? The thought made her chest so tight she couldn't take a full breath.

"Raney!" Her mother came up beside her, breathing hard and looking worried. "I'm sorry I said that. But you've got to do something. Things can't continue the way they are. You either accept a man, warts and all, or you let him go. And I don't think you're truly ready to let him go, are you?"

"No. But what do I do?"

"Put in your own offer."

Dalton felt cornered. Men were bidding on him like he was a piece of horseflesh they wanted for their stable. In some ways it was flattering. In others, it was demeaning. But another part of him saw it as a way out. If Raney decided they were done, at least he'd have someplace to go. And judging by the offers, someplace a lot more lucrative.

"I'm flattered, fellas, but I—"

"Are you gentlemen trying to poach my trainer?"

He turned, saw Raney walking toward him, a determined look in her eye. Not smiling. Face flushed. Still upset. Seeing that closed expression broke something inside of him. "What are you doing?" he asked her.

Before she could answer, Tom Hadley turned to her. "Is he on contract? If so, I'll buy it out. Name your price."

Other men came forward.

Heart drumming, Raney stopped before them, hands on hips. Her gaze swung over the men crowding around, then stopped on Dalton. "I have no hold on him. He can go wherever he wants." She watched disappointment tighten Dalton's face and had to look away. "But I want him to stay," she went on to the men gathered around. "Whitcomb Four Star needs him. Our program needs him. I need him."

Putting on a smile, she glanced from one man to the other. "Gentlemen, I know I can't compete with your prestigious outfits. Not yet. And certainly not financially. But I can offer him something better." She finally looked directly at Dalton and said, "A lifetime commitment."

His dark brows came down in a frown. His eyes narrowed. But he didn't look away.

Beside her, Tom Hadley chuckled. "You can't promise that. What if he gets injured? You going to keep him on forever?"

"Or if your program fails?" another man cut in. "Will you still guarantee his salary for the rest of his life?"

"I can and I will," Raney said, still looking at Dalton.

"That's ridiculous."

"No, that's a promise. From me to him."

Dalton's wary look eased. Mischief danced in his beautiful green eyes and the smile lurking at the corners of his mouth gave her hope that there was still hope.

"Makes no sense," a man said.

Another nodded. "Why would you make a promise like that?"

"Because I'm in love with the guy."

"Ah, hell," a voice muttered.

Mumblings all around. Raney ignored them and continued to watch Dalton. Waiting. Hoping.

It seemed forever before he spoke. "Is that a proposal, Miss Whitcomb?"

Her throat was so tight she had to clear it before she could say, "It is."

"Because I won't let you have your way with me unless I get a ring."

"I'll get one tomorrow."

Several onlookers wandered away in disgust.

Max Rayburn stayed, a big grin splitting his face as he patted her crying mother's shoulder.

Dalton got out his phone and held it up. He stepped toward her. "Could you repeat that, ma'am? And with the proper words this time. Just for legal purposes, of course."

"You're such an asshat."

"Seriously? That's your proposal?"

Raney didn't know whether to cry or laugh. So she did both. "Dalton Cardwell, will you marry me?"

Another step. Then another. Until he was looking down at her, his own eyes suspiciously bright. "I'd be honored to, Raney Whitcomb. Sorry, fellows," he said, without looking their way. "I'm staying with her." Then, slipping his phone back into his pocket, he swept her up in his arms. "Sweetheart, you're killing me." He planted a big, long, hard kiss on her mouth, then whispered in her ear, "Now stop crying. I'm fixing to get embarrassed."

"I will if you will."

"Done."

EPILOGUE

The next day, both on the society page and in the sporting section of the *Fort Worth Beacon*, there were similar articles:

As announced at the Will Rogers Memorial Center in Fort Worth, Dalton Cardwell, on Rosco Rides High, out of Follow Me Boys, sired by Hidey Ho, and owned by Raney Whitcomb of Whitcomb Four Star Ranch, tied for third place in the Open Division of the 2017 United States Cutting Horse Association Futurity, taking home prize money of well over one hundred thousand dollars. After the winners were announced, Mrs. Coralee Lennox Whitcomb hosted an impromptu and well-attended gathering at a local Tex-Mex restaurant in Fort Worth to celebrate the Futurity results as well as the engagement of her daughter Raney Whitcomb to Dalton Cardwell, both of Rough Creek. The happy couple will be managing partners of Whitcomb Four Star Ranch near Rough Creek, where they intend to build on their recent success as a leading cutting horse training and breeding facility.

Don't miss

Home to Texas

Coming Summer 2021 from Berkley!

Landstuhl Regional Medical Center
Landstuhl, Germany
March 2018

Determined to try to interview Army Second Lieutenant KD
Whitcomb again, CID Warrant Officer Richard Murdock
adopted a cheery expression as he walked into her hospital
room. "Afternoon, Lieutenant. You're looking better."

Actually, she looked like shit. Yet despite the weary
droop of her eyes—brown or black, he couldn't tell—and
the pinched tightness of her mouth—pain, probably—and
the rat's nest in her brown hair, her beauty was still there.
With her looks and delicate frame, she should never have
been in the army. Yet she had overcome the odds, graduating with a top rank from West Point, then suffering through
boot camp and officer training to earn her right to be a
soldier. From what he'd read in her file, she was determined
and committed, headed for the top. Richard hated that he
might be the tool used to bring her down.

He'd done a lot of thinking over the last few days—
about this case, his future, how far he'd go to cover the army's ass, and whether or not he'd be willing to ruin this

career as a soldier to keep his job. Which is what would happen if he turned in the report his next-in-command wanted and bent the facts to avoid another Afghanistan scandal. A no-win situation for everybody but the army. And another reason for him to get out of the military before he lost all respect for the army and himself.

Pushing that thought away, Richard put on a smile. "Ready for a few questions, Lieutenant?"

"Ready as I'll ever be."

And totally lacking in enthusiasm, it seemed. But Richard was accustomed to that. No one liked being interrogated by the Criminal Investigation Division.

He got out his notepad and pen and took a chair beside the bed. Hoping to put her more at ease, he said, "Again, I'm sorry about Captain Mouton. From everything I've heard, she was a fine officer."

"And friend," Whitcomb added, blinking hard.

To give her a chance to pull herself together—he hated when they cried—Richard shuffled through the pages a bit. When he figured she'd had enough time, he started with, "When did Captain Mouton decide to go to Farid's quarters?"

"We were at mess. COM radioed two women were at the gate asking for her."

"That would be your Afghan interpreter, Samira, and a local woman?"

"Yes. Azyan. I don't know her last name."

Richard jotted that down. "And what did they say to the Captain?"

"That Farid had taken Azyan's eight-year-old son, and she wanted him back."

"And Mouton agreed to go get him?"

"Not at first. Especially after she learned Farid was the ANP commanding officer. We have enough problems with the Afghan National Police without stirring up more. Mouton explained that we couldn't interfere in local matters, and asked why Azyan couldn't go get her son herself. Samira told us she'd tried, but Farid had hit her. Azyan showed us cuts and bruises on her face and arms."

"And that's when your captain decided to go to Farid's?"

"Not until Azyan told us why Farid had taken her son." A look of disgust crossed her face. "For sex. Captain Mouton made it clear that she could only ask Farid to return the boy. If he refused, there was nothing more we could do."

Richard started a new page, wishing he'd brought new batteries for his recorder. "Did she order you to go with her?"

"No."

"But you went anyway. Despite the noninterference policy in local matters."

A hard look came over the lieutenant's face, making her look older, less vulnerable. And definitely not broken. "She was my captain. I had her back. That was part of my mission."

Instead of responding, Richard sat quietly and waited. After two years with the 8th Psychological Operations Group and six with CID, he'd found that silence often worked better than questions to keep a conversation going.

This time was no exception. "Actually, she didn't want me going," Whitcomb finally said. "She knew the risks, and didn't want me to damage my career. I told her she wasn't going alone."

"So both of you knowingly disobeyed the Department of Defense policy of ignoring Afghan cultural matters?"

Emotion flashed in her eyes. Brown eyes, he saw now, showing flecks of yellow when she was mad. She studied him for a long time, her mouth set, her hands fisted against the sheets. She gave off an unbreachable aura of strength, as if showing weakness was the same as accepting defeat. She might be small, but she was tough. He couldn't help but admire that.

"I think I see where this is going, Warrant Officer Murdock." She spoke calmly. Precisely. Every word carefully enunciated. "The army is worried about an international shitstorm, so they've sent you to find a way to spin it so Captain Mouton takes the blame." She smiled. It wasn't a pleasant smile and did nothing to bank the fire in those amazing eyes. "You'll get no help from me. Captain Mouton was an excellent soldier. Honest, fair, courageous. And I will *never* let anyone paint her differently."

"I wasn't trying to. I only want the truth."

"Oh, really? Then here's the truth. We went to Farid's as a courtesy to a desperate mother. That's why female soldiers are in Afghanistan. To offer help to the Afghan women wherever and however we can. Captain Mouton had no intention of doing anything in violation of noninterference policy, and she didn't order me to go with her. The only thing she asked of me was that we both wear headscarves to show respect."

Richard wrote furiously, intent on getting down every word. The woman should have been in JAG. She would have made a hell of a lawyer. When he finally finished, he absently shook a cramp out of his hand and looked up.

The hard-faced resolve was gone, replaced by one of those looks women did so well—a cross between a smirk and bored impatience—one of those *why do I have to do all the thinking* looks. "Do you have a cell phone, Officer Murdock?"

He blinked, caught off guard by the question. "Yes."

"Most of them have an app for that."

"For what?"

"Notes, dictation, recording conversations. Or in your case, interviews. You don't have to write it all down. Your phone can probably do it for you."

He pulled out his cell, looked at it, then looked back at her. "Really?"

And there was the eye roll he'd half expected. "I'm tired,

Murdock. I don't want to talk any more. If you need verification of why we went to Farid's, talk to Samira."

A pause, then, "Samira's dead. Her body was found last night."

She made a sound—part cry, part moan. Then she did that vomiting thing again, and one of her machines started beeping, and nurses rushed into the room.

Which ended the interview.

KD didn't want it, but they gave her a sedative and another dose of the pain meds. Once they kicked in, she was able to stop vomiting and finally drifted into a deep, dreamless sleep. Five hours later, she awoke to see another liquid dinner on the rolling table thing by her bed, and Warrant Officer Murdock dozing in the chair.

His head was thrown back, his mouth sagging open. Long legs stretched past the end of the bed. His elbows rested on the armrests, hands clasped over his belt, and he was snoring. The picture of relaxation. She wanted to hit him. Wake him up and ask him why he'd told her about Samira in such an abrupt way.

But she had known, even before he had said the words. The regret had been in his face, the way his eyes had slid to the side just before he spoke. He didn't like telling her any more than she liked hearing it.

Another death, another loss. Soldiers were supposed to accept losing friends and brothers. Casualties of war. Maybe she wasn't such a good soldier after all. Maybe she should have stayed home in Texas, where her biggest problem would have been staying off Mama's radar and figuring out what to do with her life that didn't involve horses or cattle.

Had her family even been notified that she'd been shot? Were they wondering why she'd missed their weekly Face-Time call?

With a weary sigh, she studied the man in the chair.

Murdock wasn't as old as she had originally thought. Early thirties, maybe. But she guessed in his job, he had heard enough lies and witnessed enough terrible things to prematurely age him and put that weary, cynical look in his eyes. She hadn't seen him smile, and wondered if he found anything worth the effort. He might be a handsome man if he ever did. Another casualty of war—the capacity for joy. That's what she had admired most about Nataleah—her ability to bring a smile to those around her, to make them feel a little less alone.

Irritated at where her thoughts were headed, KD reached out to pull the rolling table with her dinner tray closer and accidentally knocked the pink barf bowl off the nightstand. Luckily, it was clean. But it landed with a clatter that brought Murdock bolting upright in his chair.

"What?" he almost shouted, blinking and looking around. When he saw her leaning over the side of the bed and the bowl upended on the floor, he immediately rose. "Are you sick again? Should I call the nurse? I'll call the nurse."

"Don't," she blurted out before he'd gone two steps. "I'm okay. I accidentally knocked it off when I reached for my dinner tray." And even that simple effort had been exhausting. Fearing another bout of lightheadedness, KD slumped back against the pillows. "I'm okay."

He picked up the bowl and set it back on the nightstand, then positioned her rolling table closer so that it crossed her lap. He studied the items on the tray. "That's all you get?"

Unwilling to go into an explanation of postsurgical bowel function, she simply said "For now," and punched the button on her bed to raise the back so she could sit up. Which didn't work as well as she'd hoped, since she'd slid down in her sleep so that the bend hit just below her shoulder blades. She tried to scoot up, then inhaled sharply when a jolt of pain ran through her.

"Here. Let me help." And before she could stop him,

Murdock grabbed her under the arms and bodily lifted her higher. His hands were so big, his thumbs reached past her collarbones. It hurt so much it stole her breath away, or she might have started shouting at him.

Once he'd pulled the covers up, he pushed the edge of the table into her chest and stood back, a pleased look on his stubbled face. "Better?"

"Much," she gasped, terrified he might do something else to accidentally hurt her.

He started to open her various little juice and tea containers, but seeing he had a hard time with the tiny tabs on the seals and fearing those big hands would make a mess of it, she waved him away. "I can do that. Thanks anyway."

"Okay." He looked around for something else to do, spotted the pink plastic water pitcher on the nightstand, grabbed a cup, and started pouring. "Anything else?" he asked, only spilling a little of it as he put it on her tray.

"You've done more than enough."

"Well. Okay, then. Feel up to a few more questions? I'd like to get this over with as soon as possible."

KD took a sip of lukewarm broth. "Get what over with? My career?" She said it as a joke.

He didn't smile. Probably used to being snarked at.

He let out a deep breath and rested one of those farmer's hands on the butt of the pistol holstered at his hip. She wondered how he got his index finger through the trigger guard. "I'm not trying to jam you up, Lieutenant. I see no fault in what you did. But you were right in thinking CENTCOM is looking for a way to make this go away as soon as possible."

She moved on to the cranberry juice. "And they figure to use me?"

"I already told them you killed Farid in self-defense."

"Then what's the problem?"

"Some might see your going to Farid's as a violation of DOD policy."

She set the cup down so hard juice sloshed over the side. "But I explained that. We went as a courtesy to a distraught mother."

"Whose idea was it to go? Yours, or the Captain's?"

"Mouton's. But I backed her." KD wiped the spilled juice from her fingers, then slapped the napkin back onto the tray. "This is ridiculous! You know what Farid had planned for the kid, don't you? An eight-year-old boy. It's disgusting."

"I agree. If Mouton hadn't already decided on going, would you have suggested it?"

KD was the one who had made the biggest mistakes—not checking Farid for a gun, not going back to the front room when the argument escalated to shouts. Why did he keep asking about Nataleah? "Maybe not. I'll admit, I was worried about the policy of looking the other way in such matters. But I'd like to think I'd have done the moral thing. Farid was an animal. He needed to be stopped."

"I agree with that, too. I just question your captain's reasoning."

"She was a good soldier!"

"I'm not disputing that."

"Then why are you trying to drag her reputation through the mud?" KD was shaking now. Furious that her captain and friend wasn't here to defend herself. "I will never say anything against Captain Mouton," she said in a voice that shook with fury. "No matter what you throw at me!"

"I can't believe this!" He stomped away, then whirled and came back. Frustration poured off of him like sweat. KD could almost smell it. "Captain Mouton doesn't need you to defend her," he said in clipped tones. "She did what she felt she had to do. I respect that. But now it's time for you to do the right thing and tell the truth."

"I *am* telling the truth!"

"Then try telling it with fewer words and less emotion!"

Sexist pig. KD pressed a hand against the throbbing in her side and reminded herself to stop shouting. A nurse came up to the window, a questioning look on her face. KD waved her away.

Obviously trying to tamp down his irritation, Murdock said with tight lips, "If you're ever called for an Article 32 hearing, Lieutenant, I advise you to get some coaching. A lot of coaching."

"Go to hell. I'm done talking to—"

"Then try listening for a change! I'm trying to help you, here. You go ballistic like this before a judge or an Article 32 panel, you not only risk a big blot on your record, but you could be dismissed from service altogether. Is that what you want?"

The words hit KD like a blow. Was he serious? A dismissal was the commissioned officer's equivalent of an enlisted soldier's dishonorable discharge. Would the army really do that to her?

Murdock took a long deep breath and let it out. Some of the anger seemed to go with it. "Look. I'm not trying to throw blame on you or your captain," he told her. "But you're the only surviving witness to what happened that night. It's important that you understand the kind of scrutiny you'll face. I'm only suggesting that when you're questioned—and you will be, I'm afraid—you don't give out more information than necessary. Stay on point and give simple answers. Don't try to sidestep anything, and don't get defensive. Just tell the truth."

The fight went out of her. He was right. If she didn't get ahold of herself, she could ruin everything. "You really think they'll convene an Article 32 hearing?"

He shrugged and looked away. "I doubt they'll like my version of the facts. They'll probably want to ask you the pertinent questions themselves."

"But we did nothing wrong. We just went there to talk to him."

"I know."

"If you report everything I've told you, and they still

convene a hearing, does that mean they've already decided I've done something wrong?"

He shook his head. "An Article 32 isn't a court-martial. It's an inquiry into the facts to decide if any charges should be brought. Like what a civilian grand jury does, except in this case, you have a lawyer with you and you can question witnesses. If you don't lose your temper, and answer the panel's questions calmly with short, truthful responses, they'll probably decide not to charge you."

"Questions like what? And how do I stay calm when I'm being accused of something I didn't do?"

"Not accused. Questioned. For instance: *Whose idea was it to go to Farid's?*—Answer: Captain Mouton's.

"*Did the Captain order you to go?*—No.

"*Then why did you?*—Female soldiers are not supposed to leave the inner forward operating base alone at night.

"*Did you knowingly disregard the DOD noninterference policy?*—No. We're the cultural support team. Our primary mission is to offer help and support to Afghan women in hopes they will aid us in identifying local insurgents and insurgent activity. It's a fine line. We work hard not to cross it.

"*Then why did you confront Captain Farid?*—A local woman told us Farid had taken her son. We agreed to talk to the captain in hopes he would release the boy. We didn't anticipate Farid would be combative and high on cocaine.

"*Who fired the first shot?*—Captain Farid. After he shot and killed Captain Mouton, he shot me in the back. I was forced to return fire in self-defense. Period."

It sounded so reasonable the way Murdock said it. But how could she shove all the anger and fear and grief aside and answer so calmly? It was her life, her future that hung in the balance.

"You're not at fault here, Lieutenant," he said in a gentler tone. "You need to believe that so they can believe it, too."

She nodded. It was a lot to take in. Especially when she'd

made mistakes that had cost Nataleah her life. That was the hardest thing to get past. She looked at Murdock and saw that his anger had dissipated, too. He seemed as troubled by all this as she was. "Why are you trying to help me?"

He shrugged. "Because you're probably a good soldier. Because I don't want the army to use you as a scapegoat for their mistake. But mostly, because I might have done the same thing."

She gave a weary smile. "Thank you for that. And for telling me what I'm up against. I appreciate your honesty."

He shrugged again and looked away. Not comfortable with compliments, she guessed. Probably didn't get many in his job.

"So how long until I find out what they're going to do?" she asked.

"Once I present my findings, CenCom will probably request an Article 32 panel to cover their butts. They'll have a hundred and twenty days to decide whether to bring charges or not."

Four months. July. Would she even be well enough by then to withstand such an ordeal? "If they do bring charges, will you testify on my behalf?"

"Be glad to." He bent to retrieve his notepad and pen from the nightstand.

"Thank you. But clean up first," she added.

He straightened, dark brows raised in question. "Pardon?"

"You could use a shave, Warrant Officer Murdock."

For a moment, he looked surprised. Then a laugh burst out of him. A real laugh, one that showed a flash of white teeth, and crinkled the corners of his blue eyes, and changed a grim face into one that had a lot of appeal. "And you could use a hairbrush, Second Lieutenant Whitcomb."

"I'll try to rustle one up."

"See that you do. Just remember what I said, and you'll

do fine." He turned toward the door, calling over his shoulder as he stepped into the hall, "Probably see you stateside before this is over." Then, with a backhand wave, he was gone.

The room seemed bigger without him. And quieter. But that laugh echoed through KD's mind for a long time.

Ready to find
your next great read?

Let us help.

Visit prh.com/nextread